The Perfect Nanny

KAREN CLARKE &
AMANDA BRITTANY

ONE PLACE. MANY STORIES

HQ
An imprint of HarperCollins*Publishers* Ltd
1 London Bridge Street
London SE1 9GF

www.harpercollins.co.uk

HarperCollins*Publishers*
1st Floor, Watermarque Building, Ringsend Road
Dublin 4, Ireland

This paperback edition 2021

1

First published in Great Britain by
HQ, an imprint of HarperCollins*Publishers* Ltd 2021

A catalogue record for this book is
available from the British Library.

ISBN: 9780008378523

MIX
Paper from
responsible sources
FSC™ C007454

This book is produced from independently certified FSC™ paper
to ensure responsible forest management.

For more information visit: www.harpercollins.co.uk/green

Printed and bound in Great Britain by
CPI Group (UK) Ltd, Melksham, SN12 6TR

To my wonderful husband Tim love from Karen
To my amazing husband Kev love from Amanda

Prologue

*"When you've seen him smile, you know that
the world's not bad ..."*
Unknown

I think of that quote whenever I remember his smile, his shining eyes, the way they looked at me, so big and trusting. Even after all this time, I can recall how it felt to put someone else first; to want to be a better person.

When I think about how he never got to achieve his potential, snatched away too soon, how he'll never see the world, get married, have children ... it still has the power to bring me to my knees. I couldn't save him and I'll never forgive myself for that.

That quote is wrong. The world *is* bad. But maybe, now, I can do something good. It might mean someone gets hurt, but as another quote goes: *That's life.*

Chapter 1

Liv

I scrolled through the photographs of Ben on my phone. Mum had uploaded them onto Facebook the night before, and now, as I lost myself in my brother's bright, cheeky smile, tears burned. I paused on an image of the two of us. Ben aged eleven in our garden in Chells Way, me looking up at him from the swing: his adoring, grubby-kneed, tomboy sister.

'Why, Mum?' I whispered, a puff of mist leaving my mouth and disappearing into the chilly morning. But I knew why. It was the anniversary of his death.

Ben left us sixteen years ago, a lifetime ago, yet sometimes I imagined him turning up on Mum's doorstep. Imagined him taking my hand and dragging me back to a time when we were happy. Because we were so happy back then, *weren't we*?

'Mum, Mum,' Evie chirped from her pushchair beside me, her blue eyes staring up at me, as mine had looked up at my brother's all those years ago.

'No, sweetie, I'm Liv, remember?' I leant forward from the bench on The Avenue, where I was waiting for 'Mums Meet Up' to start, and stroked the child's white-blonde hair. She was eighteen months old and picking up a few words – an easy-going little girl, as long as she had her favourite teddy, despite having ogres for parents.

I shoved my phone into my bag, and took a swig from the mug of tea I'd picked up en route, feeling immediately revived. Today was bright, but cold. One of those days between autumn and winter, which fooled everyone with its pastel blue sky, and blinding, watery sun. I finished my tea, rose, steeling myself to face the middle-class parents with their precious children dressed in designer gear, before bending to push Evie's cold hands into the ridiculous fluffy pink muff dangling around her neck. Her mother made her wear it. It was about as useful to a toddler as a bidet. She needed gloves. Old-fashioned. Warm. Gloves. The kind on a string my mother made me wear as a child.

I straightened up. 'Well don't blame me if you get cold, missy,' I said, as Evie pulled free her hands. I took off the pushchair brake, and headed up the hill towards Petra Rose's house. Petra held 'Mums Meet Up' – a mother and baby group – in her annexe, which was almost the size of my mum's house in Stevenage where I grew up. She charges a fortune for affluent mothers to join, and is fussy who she lets in. You have to fit her criteria. I don't. But Clare was one of Petra's elite.

'Olivia!'

I glanced across the road to see Kim, one arm raised in a wave. I quite liked Kim. She seemed more down-to-earth than some of the other mothers.

'Olivia,' she called again.

It says Liv on my birth certificate, but when I applied to be Evie's nanny two months ago, the name Olivia fell out of my mouth, along with a fake posh accent I was now struggling to keep up. Maybe a part of me wanted to be like *them*. Maybe I would have given anything to have what they all had: big houses, handsome husbands who surprised them with roses and took them to grotesquely priced restaurants. Maybe I envied them.

4

After all, my life had been a train wreck up until that point. But if I dug deeper, I knew this wasn't about any of that. This was about Sophy.

'Hi, Kim,' I called, crossing the quiet tree-lined road. She was heaving Dougie from the back of her car, his chubby legs kicking with excitement. He was large for nine months, and had inherited Kim's ruddy cheeks, fair hair, and small eyes. But he was a cute enough kid, with his constant smiles – much like his mum's.

Kim squeezed Dougie into his padded sling. 'He refuses to go in his pram,' she told me once. 'Screams the place down if I even try. I should probably try a pushchair, but he does so love being close to me.' I'd wondered how hard she'd tried, as from what I could see, it seemed it was more that *she* wanted him close to *her*.

'We've got a new member joining today.' Kim nodded towards number seven, one of the grander houses on The Avenue, and I knew exactly whose house it was. My pulse thumped in my neck. This was my moment. 'Sophy Pemberton,' she continued.

This was my doorway. My opening. I would finally get my chance to meet the woman who destroyed my family.

'I've chatted with her mother-in-law a few times, at the park,' Kim went on, and, dropping her voice to a whisper, she said, 'She told me Sophy isn't coping too well – that she has to spend a lot of time at the house helping out.'

Perfect.

'Apparently Sophy's husband called Petra last week to ask if his wife could join. Have you seen him?' Kim's eyes shone.

'Who?'

'The husband: Dom Pemberton.' Her cheeks flushed as though the thought of him excited her. She locked her car, and adjusted Dougie.

I had seen him before. The first time was on the front cover of *Pony and Rider* magazine. I was wandering around Tesco – looking at the paperbacks – when my eyes fell, not on Dom's face, but on Sophy – her face so solemn. I would have known her anywhere.

She was on the edge of the photo next to a tall, dark-haired Dom, and her mother-in-law, Elizabeth Pemberton. Elizabeth's hand rested on a beautiful chestnut-brown horse, who had won some kind of championship. There were other family members in the photo – Elizabeth's daughter and son-in-law, according to the feature inside, and, of course, Sophy's baby boy Finn.

'I'm not normally one for judging people on appearance alone, but he is rather gorgeous,' Kim went on.

The second time I saw Dom was in the street, chatting with Clare and Gary, Evie's parents. They didn't see me, but I listened to Clare saying she needed extra help with Evie. And when I saw Clare and Gary go round Dom and Sophy's with a bottle of wine one evening, I felt sure they were close friends. That it was my way in.

It was Gary who took me on to care for Evie. I'd followed him to the park and we got chatting. I told him I was out of work, that I was a qualified nanny. I reeled him in like trout.

I put up with Gary and Clare for one reason only: to get close to Sophy Edwards. Though things hadn't quite gone to plan. I'd thought the couple were friends of Sophy and Dom's. That I would get close to Sophy that way. But I'd learnt from watching her, on the rare times she ventured out, or those moments I glimpsed her standing alone in her bedroom window, that Sophy had no friends, a fact that suited me. My moment would come. I would bide my time. After all, I'd been waiting sixteen years for this.

Now the door of number seven stood open, and Dom was shrugging on a black coat as he stepped out.

'Oh my word, there he is.' Kim's already rosy cheeks flushed, and she breathed deeply, as though he was a celebrity. 'Dom Pemberton.'

He turned, and lifted a small; expensive-looking pushchair down the three white steps, as a woman appeared behind him, snuggled in a knee-length green coat, her red hair tumbling to her shoulders. She was beautiful, but pale, and even from a distance

6

I could see dark rings around her eyes. Sophy Edwards. I would never think of her as Sophy Pemberton.

As she moved across the drive, it was as though the world slowed. My heart thudded against my ribs, as I was transported back to the night when Ben's best friend Ryan told me about her. To that moment when he showed me the photo of her standing out amongst a group of twenty of so university students, laughing, beautiful.

She'd moved to London after university – that's all Ryan could find out about her at the time. She was impossible to find – until now.

'Sophy Edwards,' I whispered, my voice cracking.

'Pemberton,' Kim corrected. 'Sophy Pemberton.' I could feel Kim's eyes boring into me, but couldn't tear my gaze from Sophy and her husband, despite feeling foolish for muttering her maiden name aloud. 'We should go,' Kim said, snapping me back to the moment. 'You know what Petra's like if we're late.'

We headed away, but I glanced back once more. Dom was pushing the buggy, Sophy's arm linked through his as though he was holding her up. I was aware Kim was talking. 'Sorry?' I said.

'I was just saying we've bought a villa in Spain as a holiday retreat. My sister's there at the moment trying to save her marriage.' She was rambling as usual. 'If she can't, she's going move in with me at Indigo Cottage.'

Truth was, although Kim was OK in many ways, she still had everything and more, and I despised her for taking it all for granted.

'Well here we are,' she said, keying the code into the gate that led to the annexe, which was set apart from the main house with its own entrance. Dougie grinned my way, and I poked out my tongue.

'Please don't do that, Olivia,' Kim said, as though I was six. 'It's not something I want to encourage.'

As I stepped through the gate, I took a long deep breath. I

hated my life. I hated everything about it – but I knew, once I'd introduced myself to Sophy, everything would change. Revenge is everything.

Chapter 2

Sophy

I looked around the noisy group, already wondering how soon I could leave.

On my lap, Finn squirmed, his chubby hands reaching for my hair. I should have tied it back but it had felt like too much effort, like most things did these days.

Even so, an involuntary smile tugged at my mouth at the sight of my nine-month-old son in his corduroy trousers and checked shirt – like a tiny farmer – his feather-soft hair a crown of russet curls. His blue eyes almost disappeared as his cheeks bunched in a smile and love swelled in my chest. It was good to see him smiling instead of crying, even as my own eyes watered. His grip on my hair had tightened.

'They're surprisingly strong at that age, aren't they?'

The voice belonged to a ruddy-cheeked woman who'd introduced herself as Kim when we arrived, the avid gleam in her deep-set eyes suggesting her interest extended beyond the mere presence of a new member at the gathering of mothers and babies – and a couple of toddlers – in a very grand annexe in what my mother would call 'grounds' as opposed to a garden.

It was bigger and better landscaped than the one at the back of the house a few doors down, where Dom and I had lived for the past three months.

'He's just started doing this.' I tried to release Finn's fingers while keeping a smile in place. My face muscles already ached with the effort of being sociable after barely leaving the house in weeks. Finn began to grizzle and I stooped awkwardly to pull his blue dummy from his changing bag.

'Oh, he doesn't need that.' Before I could insert the dummy into Finn's mouth, the woman leant across, her strong perfume reminding me I'd forgotten to apply deodorant after my hasty shower that morning. 'They're horrible things,' she said, causing a flush to sweep across my face. I hadn't expected to be in favour of using a dummy to pacify my baby either, but sometimes, when all else failed, it was the only way to stop Finn crying and seemed to comfort him. 'I'm Kim Harrison, by the way. I live round the corner, down the end of the lane, at Indigo Cottage.' She beamed at Finn. 'I've met you before, haven't I, little fellow?' she cooed as she deftly unlocked Finn's grip and held him aloft like a trophy. 'His grandmother's Elizabeth, right?'

I nodded dumbly, wondering what my mother-in-law had told her. Elizabeth hadn't been able to hide her displeasure at Finn having a dummy either, though she hadn't said anything to me.

'We've met at the park a few times,' Kim said, before laying Finn on his front on a play mat, opposite a giant baby that looked like her mini-me. 'Say hello to Dougie,' she instructed Finn. To my surprise, he smiled and gurgled, pushing himself up on his hands and knees, eyes alight with interest as Dougie dangled a set of plastic keys in front of his face.

Maybe Dom had been right to insist I come along; to get us both out of the house where Finn seemed to cry all day and, sometimes, I did too. I loved Finn so much it hurt, but I missed my old life. *Myself.*

'Don't worry, you'll soon get used to us.' Kim settled her broad frame back on the small wicker-backed sofa – one of several in the spacious room, which had underfloor heating to combat the chill of the autumn day – and fluttered her fingers at Dougie.

Through a wall of glass, I watched a flurry of dead leaves blowing across the neatly cut grass and imagined our host, Petra, instructing a gardener to round them up.

Petra Rose was one of those women the others probably aspired to be: a successful jewellery designer (so Kim had informed me) sleekly attractive with fine bone structure and a winning smile that revealed expensive dentistry. Her angelic daughter was inter- acting happily with a solemn-faced toddler I was certain had filled his nappy.

When Petra had graciously introduced us – *Hey, everyone, say hi to Sophy Pemberton and Finn from number seven* – there'd been a cacophony of hellos accompanied by friendly waves, but I'd instantly forgotten everyone's name. Things were foggy at the moment and my head felt stuffed with cotton wool. I was permanently exhausted because Finn wouldn't settle – though sometimes it felt like more than normal exhaustion. A tiredness I couldn't seem to fight, even after sleeping for hours.

'How are you enjoying living on The Avenue?' Although one of Kim's big freckled hands stroked her son's blond hair as he chewed the plastic keys, she fixed her rather piggy dark eyes on me.

'Oh, it's lovely, thank you.' I watched Finn as I eased off the coat Dom had bought for my birthday, which no longer buttoned up. The baby weight around my middle refused to shift, even though some days I forgot to eat. 'Dom, my husband, wanted us to get out of London and thought it would be an excellent place to raise a family,' I added, aware Kim was waiting for more, certain Elizabeth had already told her all this. I folded my hands in my lap to hide a slight tremor. 'His grandparents were born around here and his parents live nearby.' I didn't mention that The Avenue had struck me like a street from a film set – not quite real, too perfect – knowing since having Finn, my reactions were off and my instincts not to be trusted.

'He's very handsome.' Kim gave what I supposed she thought was a cheeky smile that made her look slightly unhinged. 'We saw him walking you down.'

Walking you down. Making sure we went in, more like. That I didn't run back to the sanctuary of my bed, as I often did once he'd left for work and my mother-in-law had taken charge of Finn.

As Kim said *we*, a woman standing by the sofa, balancing a little blonde-haired girl on one hip, caught my eye. For a second, I felt panicky at the thought of meeting another mother. Heat pricked down my back and I felt a spinning sensation. The room was too warm, too noisy, Kim's perfume too strong.

I stood up and looked around. Petra had asked us to remove our footwear at the door and I felt exposed, too short without my heeled black boots, but before I could move, the woman stuck out one arm.

'Hey, I'm Liv … Olivia Granger,' she said. 'Nice to meet you, Sophy.'

My palms felt clammy. I wiped them on my too-tight jeans before taking her hand. 'You too.'

Her fingers were cold and gripped too tightly. She was a few inches taller than me and closer to my age – thirty-two – than most of the other mums. Strikingly pretty, with wavy dark hair cut just below her jaw. Her wide-apart grey eyes studied me with unusual intensity; she was probably wondering what someone like me had in common with the rest of them.

'This is Evie.' Letting go of my fingers at last, she jiggled her little girl and smoothed a strand of hair off her forehead. 'Say hello, Evie.'

Her voice sounded stilted and I realised that she felt as out of place as I did in the overheated room. As I opened my mouth to respond, Kim broke in once more.

'So, what does your husband do?'

Not *what do you do?* Maybe it was obvious I could barely look after my baby, let alone hold down a job.

'Dom? He works for Apex TV, where I worked too.' I bent to scoop Finn up. When I straightened, Olivia had turned and was showing a beaming Evie something through the window. 'As an account executive,' I clarified, seeing Kim's eyebrows shoot up. People got excited when I mentioned working in television. Though she must know this already if she'd been talking to Elizabeth. 'He generates revenue, develops business contacts, assists company growth – that sort of thing.'

Kim rearranged her expression. 'It must pay well.' It was a crass thing to say, even if it was true. And we lived in St Albans, in an area where houses were eye-wateringly expensive, so it was pointless denying it. 'He doesn't mind commuting every day?'

'No,' I said shortly. I didn't add, *He's happy to get out of the house.*

I wished I could too. Not here, though. If only Dom hadn't paid the extortionate 'term' fee. Ridiculous, really. And elitist. Petra clearly didn't need the money.

It's worth it, Dom had said, even though he'd looked shocked by the charge. *It'll be good for you to meet other mothers and good for Finn. If you click, we can invite people round for dinner.*

The first and last time we'd had guests hadn't been a roaring success. Dom invited a couple from Lavender Drive to eat with us, not long after we moved in, after bumping into the husband at the station. I'd been too tired to cook and when I confessed we'd ordered the food in, the wife – Clare – had looked at me with disdain, even as her husband, Gary, shovelled it in.

'I worked there too,' I heard myself say to Kim. 'At the TV station, I mean. I was a researcher on *Back in the Day*, the history series?' I hated myself for wanting to impress her. 'It won an award for best factual programme two years ago.'

Kim's eyes widened. 'Really?' I wasn't sure whether I felt flattered or offended by her obvious surprise. 'Not really my thing,' she said with a wince. 'I prefer house makeover shows, or nature documentaries.'

I felt myself deflate and simply nodded.

After another interminable half hour, listening to Kim talk about her holiday home, followed by a boisterous sing-song that made Finn cry, I noticed Olivia manoeuvring Evie into a push-chair by the door, something pink and fluffy thrown over the shoulder of her thin coat.

As she pushed her feet into a pair of sneakers, I pressed Finn to my shoulder and grabbed our things, nodding vaguely when Kim suggested a playdate for Finn and Dougie, as I joined Olivia at the door.

'Are you doing anything, now?' I said, when all I'd intended was to get away.

Olivia looked startled. Close up, she seemed younger. There was something vulnerable in her face before a shutter came down. 'Now?' she echoed, straightening, one hand in the small of her back as though it ached.

'I wondered whether you'd like to have lunch with us?' I hadn't tidied the house, but somehow knew Olivia wouldn't mind. 'If you're not busy,' I added, my cheeks exploding with heat. I was badly out of practice at making friends.

Olivia's face was blank but I sensed her mind was working. In the pushchair, Evie wriggled and Olivia handed her a curly-eared teddy bear. Finn twisted in my arms and looked at Evie. She caught his eye and grew still, hugging her bear.

'She loves her teddy,' I said, to break the awkward silence. 'Finn has a cat he loves at the moment, though it doesn't—'

'About lunch,' Olivia cut in. Her eyes met mine so I felt pinned down. 'Maybe another time.'

Chapter 3

Liv

Sophy certainly didn't fit in with the rest of the mums, and seemed to see me as some kind of ally, a possible friend. I wanted to laugh. She'd picked the wrong person. We could never be friends. But I was so glad she'd approached me – she'd saved me no end of work.

'In fact,' I said, throwing her my best smile. 'How about Friday? Say one o'clock at The Busy Bean.' It was a café on the High Street.

'I'd like that,' she said, far too grateful – but there was something else. Fear? Doubt? Anxiety? 'Or maybe you could come to mine for lunch?'

She didn't like going out. Kim had said she wasn't coping. This was even more perfect.

'I live at number seven.' She nodded down the road.

I know. 'Sounds great,' I said – *a chance to get inside your house.*

'Lovely,' she called, as I headed away.

As the other mums started to come out of Petra's gate, clustering together, gossiping, I melted into a crop of trees nearby and watched Sophy make her way down The Avenue. Eventually, I moved out and followed.

She didn't see me behind her, seemed keen to get home. Taking quick strides; her boots clipping the pavement. I'd always found The Avenue claustrophobic, with its trees uniform in size and shape, equally spaced, its houses tall and oppressive, most half-hidden from view behind walls and immaculate hedges.

By the time I reached Sophy's house, she was slamming the heavy oak door. My eyes skittered across the bay-fronted window, the ivy climbing the walls. *You don't deserve this, Sophy Edwards. I will take it all from you, like you took my brother from me.*

By the time I reached Lavender Drive with its six double-fronted detached houses, Evie was sleeping.

Gary's white BMW saloon was parked on the drive next to my Mini, but there was no sign of Clare's Audi TT. I hated it when Gary was home alone. He may have been Evie's father, but he was a total creep. Only last week he brushed his hand against my thigh. It was no accident. He even called me a tease, when I shoved him away. Said I'd led him on in the park. It was true that I may have flirted a tiny bit to get the position, but I was broke, and needed a job as much as I needed to get close to Sophy.

I pushed the buggy around the curve in the pavement and onto the path. Gary was standing in the window, as though waiting for me. He raised his hand in a wave, but I ignored him and picked up speed, heading towards the front door.

Once inside, I took off my jacket and trainers, and bent to wrestle a waking Evie from the pushchair.

'How's my little angel?' Gary said, coming up behind me. He was shorter than me, with cropped white-blond hair, and a round, pale face; piercing blue eyes his only attractive feature. 'Here, let me take her.' He held out his arms.

'Go to your daddy, sweetie,' I said, handing her to him.

'This thing is hardly suitable,' he said, shuffling her from the coat I'd put on her that morning. 'Her pink duffel would have been better.'

'I hadn't realised it would turn chilly. It looked bright first thing.' I went to move past him, and he leant forward and touched my cheek. I startled.

'It's OK, Liv. I don't bite.' I hated that he called me Liv, when I'd introduced myself as Olivia. It was as though he could see right through me. Knew who I really was. He adjusted Evie in his arms. I couldn't believe he would make a pass in front of his daughter. 'Your cheeks look pink, that's all.'

I felt a familiar surge of panic as I wondered what was going through his mind. 'I hadn't realised you were working from home today.'

He smiled. 'Any chance I can get these days.' He'd started a social media company ten years ago, which was bought out by one of the giants five years later for a stupid amount of money. Now he owned IT companies in London and Italy, and spent much of his time travelling between both, unless he was working from home. I hated that he was there.

I moved past him and into the kitchen. And trying to keep things civil, said, 'Coffee?'

'Sounds good.' He followed me and slipped his daughter into her highchair. We both reached for the kettle, and he pressed his body against mine.

'Where's Clare?' I said, wiggling free.

'Shopping.' He moved closer. 'She's always shopping. You know that, Liv.'

'You have to stop this, Gary. I will tell her.' I hated the tremble in my voice.

He laughed. 'You need the money, Liv. Even I can see that.' He eyed me up and down, focused on the hole in my sock. 'And you're a crap nanny – you'd never get a job anywhere else.'

Anger bubbled. I was a good nanny. Evie loved me.

Gary stared, as though waiting for me to respond. His breath reeked of coffee and cigarettes. Though he never smoked in the house – Clare wouldn't allow it.

The front door opened, and the tension in my shoulders lifted. Clare. Thank God. She bustled into the kitchen with three expensive-looking carrier bags, dropping them on the kitchen table. She hurried to Evie, planted a lipstick kiss on her cheek. 'So how was Mums Meet Up?' she said, aiming the question at me, as she took off her tartan coat.

'Fine.'

'Fine?'

'Yes.' I grabbed the kettle and began filling it. 'Would you like some coffee? I was about to make some.'

'Please. So did you see Petra?'

'Mmm.' I flicked on the kettle, and pulled out three mugs, and Gary took two steps back and leant against the worktop.

'How is she?' Clare flicked her hair behind her ears. 'I really must catch up with her soon.'

'She seemed OK.' Truth was I hadn't spoken to the woman. 'Sophy Ed ... Pemberton was there.'

'Well that's a turn-up.' Clare widened her hazel eyes. 'Did you speak to her?'

'Yes, I'm going to meet up with her on Friday.'

'Well good luck with that. She's a bit of a strange one, isn't she, Gary?' She didn't wait for a reply, simply turned her attention once again to Evie. 'So did you enjoy it, my little cutie-pie?' Evie's chin crinkled and she burst into tears. Clare turned back to me. 'Whatever's the matter with her, Olivia?'

I looked around, spotted her teddy bear. 'Here you go, sweetie,' I said, picking it up and handing it to the child, who, at the sight of her favourite bear stopped crying.

I spooned coffee into the mugs. 'Listen, I'll make these, and take her up to the nursery. Read her a story. She might be tired after a busy morning.'

I filled Evie's cup with juice. 'Here you go, little one,' I said, and she took the mug and guzzled back the juice, her bear snuggled against her ear. I stood between Gary and Clare, waiting for the water in the kettle to reach a crescendo, while they conducted a terse conversation over my head about their plans that evening.

Once I'd made the drinks, I tugged Evie from the highchair and made my way upstairs. I would be OK now Clare was home. Gary kept his distance when she was around.

Once in the nursery – a stunning room with three lemon-painted walls, and a mural of an enchanted forest on the far wall – I set Evie's musical box going, changed her nappy, and lowered myself into the white rocking chair, with Evie in my arms. As I began reading *The Very Hungry Caterpillar*, her eyelids grew heavy. Once she'd dropped off to sleep, I placed her gently in her cot, and covered her with a blanket.

From the window, I took in the long, rambling garden, eyes falling on my nanny pad tucked away at the bottom, almost out of sight, as though Gary and Clare didn't want a reminder that someone else cared for their daughter. The sky had clouded over, and light rain speckled the window, and my thoughts drifted to my mother. Should I tell her I was going out to lunch with Ben's ex-girlfriend? Should I tell her I was about to get revenge for all of us?

Chapter 4

Sophy

As I settled Finn into his highchair ready for lunch, I allowed myself a glimmer of positivity. I'd got out of the house, spoken to people – listened, at least – and even extended an invitation to lunch without so much as a yawn. It was more than I'd managed in ages. I imagined telling Dom about it later, over dinner. Maybe I'd cook this evening.

I recalled the look on Olivia's face when she accepted my invitation. An initial moment of doubt had been banished by a friendly smile that lifted her face, transforming her into someone beautiful. But as I imagined her in the house, flatness descended, as if my batteries had drained. It was often like this: a surge of optimism, before reality hit and I realised I wasn't quite ready to change my life.

Finn smacked his pudgy fists on the tray of his highchair, his eyebrows raised as if curious about why I was standing in the middle of our high-ceilinged living room, staring unseeingly in the gilt-framed mirror above the stone fireplace where the log burner squatted. I should get the fire going but the central heating was on and the house felt warm and cosy. Our dream house, with Farrow and Ball paint on the walls and contemporary, co-ordinating furnishings. Dom's sister Natasha was an interior designer who'd relished the opportunity to turn our four-bedroomed Victorian house into a stylish home, though it didn't look particularly stylish with Finn's toys scattered around and a heap of laundry in the armchair by the window. At least the laundry was clean.

I turned away from a framed picture hanging by the window – a professional family portrait taken at Dom's parents' home at Elizabeth's insistence when Finn was twelve weeks old, and I was still sleep-deprived and weepy – and I looked at my wedding photo instead. My red hair had been pulled back in a chignon, revealing my narrow nose, freckled cheeks and pale green eyes. I looked solemn, as I tended to in photos, but relaxed, certain of my place in the world. Beside me, Dom was tall and handsome, a softness to his smile, a summer tan emphasising his blue eyes and long, dark lashes.

We'd been set up by a friend of his who used to work in production at Apex TV and thought I'd be a good match for Dom – the sort of person he'd described wanting to settle down with, but never seemed to meet – and after a dry spell, where I'd focused on work instead of men, Dom had seemed perfect. I'd seen him around at work, and my heart flipped when he waited for me to leave the building one day and suggested a drink. He was attractive but unassuming, unaware of the effect he was having, and I'd liked that. I also liked that, despite his family background, he wasn't too interested in material things, happy living in the same exposed-brick-and-beam warehouse apartment he'd rented for years, overlooking the Tower of London and close to his favourite pub, The Dickens Inn, though he told me his mother disapproved and thought he should 'upgrade'.

That was four years ago. He'd certainly upgraded now. Shame he wasn't happier, but that was my fault. He loved his son with all his heart, but I wasn't the same person I'd been before having Finn. *Maybe I never would be.*

21

Another bash of the highchair tray, followed by a sound that might be *Mumma*, brought me back to the moment. 'What do you fancy for lunch today, sir?' I adopted a cheery tone because my biggest fear was infecting Finn with whatever had me in its grip. Not depression exactly – not anymore – but a bone-deep exhaustion and occasional forgetfulness that I couldn't seem to shake. 'Maybe a nice lamb casserole?' I felt guilty Finn's lunch would be out of a jar, albeit organic, and resolved yet again to start cooking from scratch, like my mother-in-law had for her children when they were babies. She'd offered to help but I knew if I let her, I'd never get around to doing it myself. 'Macaroni cheese?'

As Finn's face split into a grin that showed his dimples, I experienced a familiar burst of love mingled with fear. *What if I wasn't good enough for him?* 'Play with Jiggles while I heat it up.' I plucked his favourite toy off the sofa, a faded and matted blue and white cat that used to belong to Dom, and presented it to Finn.

'Dadda,' he chortled, grabbing the cat and clutching it under his chin.

'Dadda will be home soon.'

I moved through the hallway on autopilot and into the country-style kitchen I'd hoped would inspire me to start baking. I took a jar from one of the glossy white cupboards and decanted it into a bowl before placing it in the microwave, eyeing the half-empty bottle of red wine on the worktop. Dom had urged me to have a glass the evening before to relax me. It had knocked me out. I couldn't even remember climbing the stairs to bed. That happened sometimes; losing time. It was as though I'd gone somewhere in my head, coming to a while later with no recollection of what I'd been doing. I hadn't told Dom. He was worried enough about me as it was and he had a lot on at work, the details of which eluded me – something about a merger, and an ex-employee suing for unfair dismissal. I often zoned out when he was talking, though I'd once loved sharing details of our days, working in different areas of the same company.

I opened the dishwasher. There were two glasses inside, along with our clean dinner plates, a pair of mugs and gleaming crockery. Dom must have loaded it and set it going before he left for work. Guilt curled through me, imagining him with his shirt sleeves rolled up while I slept on as though I'd completed a marathon, or a full week's work plus overtime.

I jumped when the microwave pinged, and again when the landline started ringing in the living room. Dom had taken to calling me on it during the day, as I often forgot to switch on my mobile or charge it up. He'd worry if I didn't answer, but I let it ring out while I checked the temperature in Finn's Peter Rabbit bowl before hurrying through, worried that I'd left him alone, even though I could hear him babbling to himself.

'Here we are!' He was keen to hold his little plastic spoon and dug it into his bowl while smacking his lips together. 'Good boy!'

I'd thought mothering would come easily, but I tiptoed around my son like he was a priceless object I was terrified of breaking.

'Let Mummy help.'

Finn waved the spoon, splattering yellow blobs everywhere. Thank God we didn't have carpet, the wide oak floorboards forgiving of crumbs and stains.

Why not put his highchair in the kitchen? Dom had asked, but I liked it where it was, by the patio doors, overlooking the garden where a swing left by the previous owners hung from the branches of the apple tree.

A jaunty piano tune erupted from my bag on the floor. I dipped my hand in and pulled my phone out, keeping my eyes on Finn as he scooped a fistful of food out of his bowl and mashed it around his face.

'Hi,' I said brightly.

'Sophy, I called the landline, you didn't pick up.' Dom's voice was full of apprehension. 'How did it go at the baby group?' he said, as if deciding to skate over why I hadn't answered.

'Fine.' I perched on the edge of a dining chair, reaching to take the spoon from Finn, so I could feed him what was left in his bowl.

'Did you meet anyone nice?'

The question reminded me of Mum, before Dom and I got together, desperate to pair me off so she'd feel less guilty about having a boyfriend.

'Yes,' I said, with sudden conviction. 'Actually, I did. A woman called Olivia.' A movement caught my eye through the window, to the side of the garden. There was a gap in the flint and stone wall where a gate had once been, leading to an access lane at the side of the house. For a split second, I thought I glimpsed a pale face peering round, a whisk of pink. Hadn't Olivia been wearing something that colour?

'Sophy, that's great.' The relief in Dom's voice was hard to bear. 'You should invite her round.'

'I already did.' I glanced again at the window, but there was no one there, just a flutter of gold as the apple tree shed the last of its leaves. 'She's coming for lunch on Friday.'

Chapter 5

Liv

I put Evie to bed around six-thirty, and made my way to my nanny pad, away from Gary's roaming eyes and grabbing hands, and Clare's shrill excitement about what she'd bought in town. I was relieved to turn the key in the door, and be alone with my thoughts.

I stepped inside, closing the door behind me, taking deep breaths.

It had a small shower room, and a lounge area with a bright yellow sofa, a coffee table, and TV. My double bed, suspended above a row of cupboards with a stepladder to reach it, made perfect use of the limited space – though sometimes I would wake in the middle of the night feeling panicked by how close the ceiling was. Feeling as though I was trapped in a coffin.

I flopped on the sofa. Not feeling myself. Seeing Sophy had messed with my head, and I couldn't get her out of my mind.

I thought about how Mum had closed herself off from Dad and me when Ben died. She went from a bright fun-loving person, to a woman who barely spoke. Dad had tried to bring her out of it, but he was grieving too, and five years after Ben's death he'd left – moved to New Zealand.

It was a year after that Mum crashed her car. She was on her way to the supermarket, when she thought she saw Ben sitting on a bench in the park, a place he'd taken to going alone in the weeks before he died. It wasn't him of course; Ben had been gone six years by then. But she lost concentration, skidded off the road, her injuries making her permanently paralysed from the waist down.

If it wasn't for Sophy Mum wouldn't be in a wheelchair, Ben would be here now, Dad wouldn't have left us, and Ryan wouldn't be a complete mess.

I picked up my phone, deciding to FaceTime Mum. Tell her I'd seen *her*. I clicked on her details.

A lump rose in my throat, as it always did when I saw Mum's face appear on the screen, and heard her say, 'Hello, love.' She always smiled, though I was never quite sure how genuine it was.

She'd blamed herself for so many years, saying she should have seen the signs, claiming she was a terrible mother. Spending hours analysing the way she'd brought Ben up – *Had she been overprotective? Pushed him too hard with his studies? Given him too much attention? Not enough attention? Should she have listened more?*

But when Freya became her carer nine years ago, her spirits lifted gradually. Somehow Freya managed to do what Dad and I never could. She got Mum interested in life again. Perhaps because she was separate from the family, allowing Mum to reflect without getting upset herself. She knew the right things to say.

Mum fumbled for her glasses, and slipped them on.

'Loving the new haircut,' I said. It was shorter than usual, neat, grey layers close to her head. She was seventy-three, but looked older. She'd met my dad in her mid-thirties, had Ben a few years later and me in her early forties.

'Nice, isn't it?' She touched it gently. 'Freya trimmed it earlier. Have you had a good day?'

She always asked that when I called her, most evenings. I worried about her, feared the past would creep up on her again,

26

and take her back to the dark place that had swallowed her for so long after Ben's death. I tried to get to see her as much as I could too. In fact I was going over at the weekend.

'Not bad,' I said. 'I took Evie to a baby group this morning.'

'Oh that's nice,' she said, her voice brightening at the mention of Evie. 'Did you enjoy it?'

'Well that's why I'm calling.' Mum suddenly bobbed out of sight, and all I could see was the lounge where I'd spent a lot of happy years as a child. 'Mum?'

She appeared again with Sparky, her Yorkshire terrier, in her arms. 'Say hello to Livy,' she said to the dog, who looked content in her arms.

'Hello, Sparky,' I said, with a quirky wave.

Mum sniffed the dog's head. 'He keeps rolling in bird droppings,' she said. 'I'll have to ask Freya to give him a bath.'

I smiled. 'Mum, I've got something to tell you.'

'OK,' she said, still sniffing the dog. 'I'm listening.'

'Are you? Because this is really important.'

'Yes, of course.' She stared at the screen, as if to prove she was concentrating.

'The thing is, I've found Sophy Edwards.'

'Oh, Liv. Not this again.' Mum's smile disappeared. 'I thought you'd let that go. Moved on.'

'Only because I couldn't find her.' I took a deep breath. Mum knew how Sophy Edwards had played on my mind for years. 'Her life's perfect, Mum.' I could hear the tears in my voice, anger surging. 'She's married to this bloke who looks like he's jumped out of a magazine, and they live in a massive house in St Albans.'

'None of that means she's happy.'

'She's got a little boy. A perfect little boy.'

Mum was crying suddenly.

'Oh, Mum, I'm so sorry, I didn't mean to upset you.'

She blotted her cheek with a tissue. 'It just brings back memories, that's all.' Her eyes met mine through the screen. 'I've told you before, Liv. Ben wouldn't have wanted you to be so full of hate.'

I bit down hard on my lip. It was OK for her. She'd managed to accept things now.

'I'm sorry, Mum. But Ben would still be here if it wasn't for Sophy.'

'Oh, Liv, please let it go.'

'I can't.' Bitterness surged through my veins, and my eyes stung with tears. I hadn't realised just how angry I was.

She stroked the dog's head, the screwed-up tissue in her fist. 'We all miss him, love—'

'But she's the reason Dad left, the reason you're in that wheelchair.'

'Sweetheart, please.'

I thought back to Ben's friend Ryan searching for Sophy just after my brother's death, unable to track her down. How devastated Mum had been when he couldn't find her. At that time Mum was as angry as I was, to the point she'd stopped eating, couldn't sleep. She even started drinking for a while and stopped seeing friends.

'Sophy never came to Ben's funeral, Mum. She didn't care about him enough to call us when he died. That's why I can't let this go.' I gulped. This was sixteen years of pent-up rage prickling my skin.

A dark shadow appeared behind Mum, and a face bobbed into view. 'Hello, Liv.'

'Oh, Freya.' I dashed my hand across my cheeks and sniffed. 'You freaked me out for a minute. I hadn't realised you were there.'

'I was in the kitchen, making a cuppa.'

I tried to get my act together, calm down. 'I love Mum's hair; you've done a great job. Is there nothing you can't turn your hand to?'

'Missed my vocation, clearly,' she said with a smile, as she leant onto Mum's wheelchair, her small pale grey eyes studying me. Freya was around fifty. Her fair hair was a mass of frizzy curls, and her skin was pale, and almost line-free. 'It was only a little trim,' she continued, her voice soft and musical. 'Just to keep it neat and tidy, aye, Martha?'

'Oh it is that,' Mum said, stroking her hair. 'Nice and tidy, just how I like it.'

'Thanks,' I said, knowing how good Freya was to Mum. Always popping round to see her even when she wasn't getting paid. Taking Mum shopping, or for a coffee at the nearby café. She was a good friend to her.

'My pleasure,' she said, bobbing out of view. 'We have great fun together, don't we, Martha?'

'We do indeed,' Mum said, looking up. 'Freya knows how to cheer me up.'

I felt a pang of guilt. I wasn't good at cheering Mum up, and had just managed to make her cry. 'Mum,' I said, wanting to say sorry.

'You're breaking up, love. I can't—'

And then she was gone, and I realised my fists were clenched into hard balls, my nails embedded into my flesh.

Why couldn't Mum understand that Sophy had to pay for what she did?

Chapter 6

Sophy

By the time Friday came around, I'd been veering between anticipation and dread to the point where I'd developed an even worse headache than usual. One minute, I was looking forward to having a lunch guest and the opportunity to make a new friend, the next I was wishing I had Olivia's number so I could ring and call it off.

It had been my turn to get up in the night to Finn, despite the gargantuan effort to wake myself up, but after taking a quick shower, my tiredness eased and my mood took an upward swing.

'You look nice,' Dom said, as I entered the bedroom swathed in a towel I'd snatched from the laundry basket.

'This old thing?' I patted the smaller towel turbaned around my head, surprised to find I was attempting a joke. 'I've had it for ages.'

Smiling, he came towards me, buttoning his shirt. His hair was damp from the steamy bathroom, drying into waves, which he would spend half the day pushing back from his forehead. I used to love pushing my fingers through it too.

As though reading my mind, Dom held out a hand and drew me to him, a look in his eyes I hadn't seen for a while. On cue, Finn emitted a series of half-hearted wails in the nursery next door and Dom let me go with a rueful smile. 'It's almost as if he knew,' he said, tucking his shirt into his dark blue suit trousers.

Guiltily relieved at the interruption, knowing I'd have pushed Dom away, I summoned a smile. 'You have to get to work anyway.' It wasn't just that I feared falling pregnant again; I couldn't quite locate my feelings for Dom these days. It was as if they were concealed behind thick glass coated with repellent.

'Looking forward to your lunch date?' he said a few minutes later, as I joined him in the kitchen wearing my fleecy dressing gown, hair damp around my shoulders, carrying Finn. He'd just bashed my nose with his head so my eyes were swimming with tears.

'Yes, I am.' I tried to recapture my earlier enthusiasm. 'It'll be good to find out more about her.'

'If she's got a husband or partner, maybe we could get Mum to babysit one Saturday night and go out for dinner?'

Looking at me over his mug of freshly filtered coffee – he couldn't stand the instant brand I loved – Dom's eyes held a glint of something: hope, or maybe it was a challenge. He must be sick of being cooped up here every weekend evening, if he wasn't working, because his wife no longer felt like socialising – especially after the awkward meal with the couple from Lavender Drive.

'You didn't make me a coffee?' I hadn't meant it to sound like an accusation. 'I suppose I'm invisible now I'm just a mum.'

To his credit, Dom didn't respond. He'd heard it all before, had gone to great lengths to reassure me that he loved me and 'saw' me more clearly than ever since I'd given birth to our son – that I'd never be invisible to him.

Instead, he turned and picked up my favourite sunshine-patterned mug, which I hadn't spotted on the counter behind him, and placed it on the breakfast bar in front of me.

'Have a good day,' he said quietly, bending to kiss Finn's hair as he passed, grabbing his bag, jacket and keys on his way to the door. He paused and turned once more, his face harshly lit by a strip of sunlight pouring into the kitchen. 'Maybe you should make an appointment to see the doctor.' His tone was kind, but firm. 'You might need to take something again, just for a while, to get you back on your feet.'

'I'm fine.' I swallowed more tears, aware of Finn in my arms solemnly watching our exchange. I hated myself for not being the sunny, smiling, happy mum he deserved.

'You are taking the vitamins Natasha recommended?'

I nodded, keen to reassure him. His sister had struggled with exhaustion after her son Toby was born and swore that a particular brand of multivitamins, recommended by a nutritionist, had got her back on her feet. She'd sent me several jars but I hadn't been taking them long enough yet to feel the effects. 'I'll have one with my breakfast.'

He hesitated, as if there were lots of things he wanted to say but didn't know where to start and settled for, 'I love you, Sophy. Have a good day.'

'You have a good day too.' *With your wonderful colleagues, who don't have miserable wives at home.*

Less than two minutes later there was a rap at the front door, followed by a cheerful, 'Yoo-hoo! It's only me!' It was almost as if she'd been waiting for Dom's car to turn out of the street, towards the station.

My mother-in-law materialised in all her flowery-perfumed, expensive-skirted, smiling glory, a thick, iron-grey bob framing her aristocratic face.

Dom gave her a spare key just after we moved in, insisting she wanted to help so I could get some rest, and she'd taken to dropping in most days, usually after Dom left as though guessing that once alone, I felt out of my depth, still not moulded into motherhood the way I longed to be.

'How's my little prince?' she cooed. Flashing me a smile, she put down her tan leather handbag, shrugged off her tweedy jacket and plucked Finn from my arms.

'Hi, Elizabeth,' I said dully. I'd stopped asking her to let me know before dropping in. She was only trying to help because we were family and she was in love with her grandson. I'd only broached the subject once, when I began to wonder whether her almost constant presence might be doing more harm than good, creating a safety barrier that meant I didn't have to try to be a better mother, but Dom pointed out how helpful she'd been when Finn was born, when my mother couldn't leave the guesthouse in Portugal she ran with her boyfriend Tomas, and how much Finn adored her.

It was true. Our son went to his grandmother with almost insulting haste, his little face lighting up whenever he saw her. He'd even started saying *Nana*, with Elizabeth's coaching, despite her initial assertion that she'd rather he called her Lizzie. The trouble was, she wasn't how I'd imagine a typical Lizzie, warm and cuddly-looking. She was tall and broad-shouldered, for a start, and could be an intimidating presence. She was on the board of several charitable foundations, an ex-riding instructor with a stable of horses at their home. An ex-pupil had gone on to win a prestigious horse show, and a horse she'd bred recently won the Irish Derby, leading to a spread about her in a magazine, featuring the whole family – including a washed-out version of me – on the cover. And then there was the thing I found impossible to argue against.

'Finn means so much to Mum, because of losing Christopher.'

Christopher. Dom's older brother, who'd only lived nine months. He'd been born with a heart defect that couldn't be fixed. From the moment she'd cradled Finn at the hospital, I'd known it was her baby boy that Elizabeth was seeing. My heart had gone out to her, and though I couldn't help wishing now that she'd visit less often, I tried my best not to show it.

'Has he had breakfast yet?' She gave me a sweeping glance as she cuddled her grandson, taking in my bedraggled state of undress. Her blue eyes – paler than Dom's – narrowed a fraction. As usual, she was elegantly made-up, her features softened with pricey cosmetics, her 'barely there' lipstick matching the shade of the cashmere, polo-necked sweater, worn to disguise the loose skin around her throat that gave away her age.

'I was about to give him some porridge,' I said, heat flushing my face.

Elizabeth looked at Finn, who was gazing at her with such an expression of wonder, a shot of jealousy ran through me. 'Why don't I do that, while you get yourself dressed?' She didn't wait for a reply as she moved effortlessly around the kitchen, gently bouncing Finn in one arm. She was strong, from years of training and restraining horses.

'OK.'

Neither of them gave me a second look as I backed away and trudged upstairs. I stayed up there a while, taking extra care with my appearance for once, while Elizabeth fed my son and sang a lullaby I couldn't quite hear the words to. I wondered whether Olivia had a mother-in-law. Maybe we could compare notes. Did she live on The Avenue? She had to have money, if so. Perhaps her husband was a hedge-fund manager, or she was an entrepreneur selling handmade baby clothes, or artisan cakes from her kitchen, or maybe she was a mummy-vlogger, reaching out to millions of subscribers with her parenting tips.

Somehow, I doubted it, though I couldn't have said why.

I chose a navy, long-sleeved dress I hadn't worn for at least a year, and pulled out one of the scarves Elizabeth had bought me – leaping ponies on a background of cream silk – and looped it round my neck. By her own admission she wasn't good at 'gifting'. Natasha and I got scarves and expensive perfume for birthdays and Christmas, while Dom and his father received sweaters and luxury ties.

Back downstairs, my hair pinned in a topknot and my eyelashes weighted with mascara, I was shocked to see an hour had passed.

'You don't need to do that,' I said, seeing Elizabeth taking the vacuum cleaner from the cupboard under the stairs, her sweater sleeves rolled up to reveal the slim gold watch Dom had bought for her sixtieth birthday, two years ago.

'Well, if you won't get a cleaner …'

She let the words hang, her thin eyebrows arched. She'd offered to loan us her cleaner a couple of mornings a week, but I'd refused.

'I can manage, thank you.' Finn looked up from his bouncy chair, positioned within Elizabeth's eyeline, as if alerted by my unusually authoritative tone. 'I've a guest coming for lunch, so—'

'All the more reason to let me help.'

My words seemed to bounce off Elizabeth like ping-pong balls. 'I just heated your coffee in the microwave,' she said, looking around for the plug socket. 'Why not sit down and relax for five minutes.'

It wasn't a question. I found myself obeying, sitting on one of the cream leather stools at the breakfast bar, while Elizabeth pushed the vacuum around, keeping up a running commentary to Finn, who gurgled happily.

I sipped my coffee, grateful she'd bothered to reheat it, a practical gesture typical of how she treated the rest of her family, when she wasn't distracted by her horses.

'I sometimes expect a bale of hay for dinner,' Dom's father Robert occasionally joked, used to Elizabeth's passion for all things equine. He was less driven than his wife, retired from his civil engineering job and happy to potter in the garden and tend his roses.

I spotted the bottle of multivitamins on the worktop, an expensive brand with an artfully drawn label. Dom must have left them out, knowing I'd probably forget to take one if they were in the cupboard and I swallowed one with the last of my coffee.

I should check the fridge, see what I could offer Olivia for lunch. I had no idea what she liked to eat. A salad would be safe if she was vegetarian. I could always add ham or smoked salmon if not. And there should be fresh bread in the cupboard. We'd had a food delivery a couple of days ago.

'I'll take him out, shall I, while you have lunch with your friend?'

Elizabeth was back, slipping her arms into her jacket.

I blinked at her, overcome with a wave of tiredness so strong I wanted to lay my head on my arms and sleep. 'Sure,' I murmured, looking round with an effort for Finn. He was in his buggy by the door, dressed in his outdoor clothes, his chunky, pastel striped blanket tucked around him. *When had she got him dressed?* 'Don't be too long.'

'We'll be fine.' She gave me a concerned look as she picked up her bag. 'Are you OK?'

'I wish everyone would stop asking me that.'

I regretted my tone when she drew her head back, as though I'd tried to slap her, a line cutting between her eyebrows. 'I was only asking,' she said, her well-bred vowels more pronounced than usual. 'We do care about you, Sophy.'

'I know,' I said. 'I'm sorry.'

'Maybe you should have a nap.'

I wanted to say something; tell her to leave Finn with me, that I could be a good mother if only she'd let me try, but she opened the door, letting in a blast of cold air, and seconds later it slammed behind them.

Pressure built at my temples. I glanced at the clock on the wall and saw with a shock it was almost one o'clock. The room felt unsteady – or maybe it was me. I couldn't face any lunch. I wasn't up to making conversation with a stranger. I wanted to rip off my dress and go back to bed.

36

Should I hide?

I only had a second to register the ridiculousness of the thought when the doorbell pealed through the house, sending a jolt of adrenaline through me.

It was too late. Olivia had arrived.

Chapter 7

Liv

I recognised Sophy's mother-in-law from the cover of the magazine where I first saw Sophy. Elizabeth Pemberton was in her early sixties, tall, and had an air of a scary head teacher. She lifted the pushchair down the steps from the front door, chirping sweetly to the little boy who I knew was Finn – though I recognised the expensive pushchair rather than the baby. Elizabeth turned and furrowed her forehead at Evie and me. 'Are you here to have lunch with Sophy?'

I nodded, and she touched my arm. 'It's good to see Sophy finally find a friend. Treat her gently though; she's fragile.' She slipped on her sunglasses, and hurried away down the road.

I climbed the three steps and blasted the doorbell and waited. And waited. Despite the sun being out, there was a cutting wind that whipped across the porch, and I shivered.

I bent down and opened the letterbox. 'Hey, Sophy, it's me, Olivia. It's bloody freezing out here. Are you going to let me in or not?'

The door opened slightly, and I rose to see Sophy, pale and heavy-eyed, peering through the gap.

'I'm not feeling too well,' she said. 'I'm sorry I've wasted your time. I would have let you know, but I didn't have your number.' She looked down at Evie jabbering happily in her buggy. 'Sorry,' she said again. *Was that a slur in her voice?*

I swallowed a surge of anger. This was meant to be my way in, a way to find out more about her. If I couldn't get close, how could I make her pay? 'No worries,' I said. 'Let's do it another time, shall we?'

'Thanks for understanding.'

She went to close the door, and I pushed my hand against it. 'I couldn't trouble you for a drop of juice for Evie, could I?' I hurried down the steps, and prised Evie's mug from her sticky fingers. 'Sorry, sweetie,' I said, pushing back her hair from her forehead. I held out the mug towards Sophy as I ran up the steps, giving her no choice.

'OK.' She dashed her hand across her eyes. She was crying. 'Oh, God, are you OK?' I said, attempting to sound sincere. 'I mean, I know you don't feel well but if you need someone to talk to … a friend.' The word stuck in my throat. She would never be a friend of mine.

She opened the door further, as though glad I'd noticed. 'Come in,' she said, her head down.

I lifted Evie from her pushchair, and we followed Sophy in, and through to the kitchen. I didn't want to listen to this woman's troubles. I wanted to grab her by the neck, pin her against the wall, and demand an apology for what she'd done to my family. I needed her atonement. Whatever was wrong with her couldn't be as painful as losing a brother when he had his whole life ahead of him. I shook away the voice of my mother telling me to stop what I was doing, reminding me, as she'd done so many times, that when someone takes their own life, nobody is to blame.

In the kitchen, Sophy turned, and held out her hand. 'Let me fill that for you,' she said, her voice dull and lifeless, and I gave her Evie's mug. While she filled it with orange juice from the fridge, she took several deep breaths. And was she swaying slightly?

I tore my eyes away from her, and glanced about me. *Wow!* I'd thought Gary and Clare's house was amazing, but this was on another level of class. It wasn't any bigger than Gary and Clare's kitchen, but it was brighter, thanks to the bay window overlooking a patio and garden, the windowsill teeming with herbs. There was a wide range oven, a butler sink and real-wood surfaces that looked as though they'd never seen the bottom of a pan.

'There you go, sweetheart, some juice for you,' Sophy said, handing over the mug, which Evie grabbed and began gulping from.

'This place is bloody amazing,' I said. I couldn't keep my eyes still, as they flitted around the room.

Sophy's cheeks flushed. 'It's no big deal, honestly.'

Realising I'd been a bit over the top, I added, 'I've never been inside a house on The Avenue before.'

'Really? Where do you live now?' she said.

'Actually, I could murder a cup of tea.' I rubbed my hands together. 'Sorry if I'm being a bit cheeky, but it's so cold out there today.'

'Oh. OK.' Her voice was heavy, slow, as though it was taking all her energy to speak.

'We live on Lavender Drive, don't we, Evie?' I said. 'The last house on the corner, but I'm originally from Stevenage.'

'Really? I'm from Stevenage too.' She seemed to revive a little, her eyes less glassy. 'I grew up in the old town, on Haycroft Road.'

'Nice.'

'Not especially.' She gave a small frown. 'It was cramped, the house, really old. It was all my parents could afford at the time and they never got round to doing it up. My dad died when I was two and Mum had to work a lot, so …' Her words trailed off as she turned to fill the kettle.

40

I don't know why, but I'd thought her childhood would have been different and opened my mouth to say sorry about her dad, but she was talking again. 'We were happy though, don't get me wrong. I was best friends with the girl next door. We went to Almond Hill School. I loved it there.'

I didn't bother to tell her whereabouts I'd lived as a child – where my mother still lives – and she didn't ask. It was doubtful our paths would ever have crossed as children. In fact, they wouldn't have crossed now, if Ben hadn't had the misfortune to attend the same university as her.

'Liv, Liv, Liv,' Evie said, coming up for air between gulps of her drink and tilting her head.

Sophy narrowed her eyes. 'She calls you Liv?'

'Yes.' I took a deep breath. I suddenly was worried Sophy would reject me if I told her I wasn't Evie's mother, but I had to come clean. She would find out somehow – she knew Clare and Gary. 'I'm Evie's nanny, not her mum,' I said. 'And my friends, and Evie, call me Liv.'

'Oh, I see.' Sophy's eyes widened. 'I hadn't realised.' She dropped a teabag into one mug, a spoonful of instant coffee in another, before adding boiling water.

'I'll drink my tea and leave you in peace,' I said.

'You can stay, if you like. I've got salad for lunch. I wasn't sure if you were vegetarian.'

I shook my head, relieved she didn't seem concerned that I was 'the nanny'. 'No, I'm a meat eater, for my sins.'

She handed me my tea, a slight shake in her hand. 'Shall we drink this and then I'll make us something to eat?'

'Sounds perfect,' I said. 'But first,' I added, pulling out my phone. 'Let's exchange mobile numbers just in case.'

*

41

The lounge was comfortable, and just as classy as the kitchen: sofas, bookshelves, wool rugs and matt-blue walls, a TV fixed to one. I placed Evie on a thick, wool rug, where she played happily with Finn's toys, and Sophy and I sat on one of the sofas.

'So was Finn going out with his gran?' I said, and she nodded. 'Shame as they could have played together.' Truth was, Evie wasn't much of a team player, inclined to like things her own way, a bit like her dad. Plus, she was nine months older than Finn and would have probably dominated him.

'She's Dom's mum. She takes care of Finn a fair bit,' Sophy said.

Was that why she'd had tears in her eyes? 'She's the mother-in-law from hell kind?'

Sophy half-smiled. 'No, not at all, she only wants to help, I think. I'm a bit of a rubbish mum, if I'm honest. Glad she's around.' Sophy was all over the place, barely concentrating. 'I miss my job,' she went on, randomly. 'I used to work in London. Had a great job.'

I placed my hand on her arm. 'Tell me to mind my own business if you like, but when did you last sleep? You look exhausted.'

'I sleep a lot, but I'm still tired all the time.' She flopped her head back against the sofa and closed her eyes. 'Sorry. I'm a pathetic hostess.'

I shuffled to the edge of the sofa, and put down my mug, and when I turned, her eyelids had dropped over her eyes. Was she falling asleep? 'Sophy?'

She jolted forward, splashing coffee on her dress. 'God, I'm so sorry. Shall we have some lunch?' She rose, and headed into the kitchen.

I caught up, carrying the highchair, Evie trotting by my side. I slipped her into the chair and handed her a couple of wooden spoons from a pottery utensil holder.

'I don't mean to pry,' I said, as Evie drummed the spoons on the highchair tray, and squealed with delight, 'but are you on some kind of medication?'

42

Sophy widened her eyes, and I thought for a moment she was going to tell me to mind my own business. I wouldn't have blamed her. But she shook her head. 'I took anti-depressants for a while after Finn was born. They didn't help. I felt numb and lifeless all the time, so stopped taking them. Now I don't feel low exactly, just exhausted and odd all the time.' She shook her head. 'I can't explain it.'

'But your mother-in-law comes to your rescue.' I wasn't happy about Elizabeth being so good to Sophy, always being there for her. I couldn't get close if she was hanging about. I would need to do something about that.

Sophy nodded. 'She spends a lot of time here.'

My mind flashed to the magazine I'd seen, the picture of the perfect family. Didn't the woman own horses? Well she needed to bugger off and look after them.

'And what about Dom?' I adjusted my expression into one of concern, pushing down anger that this woman was so pathetic, despite having help on tap. 'I'm sure he's there for you too.'

She nodded. 'He said this morning I might need to see the doctor again, but I don't want to. I'm not depressed, just ...' She waved the knife she was holding. 'I don't know, I'm just exhausted.'

I watched her prepare a salad, leaving her to it even though she struggled to co-ordinate.

'So are you married?' she asked me, running a handful of cherry tomatoes under the cold tap for too long, before returning to shred the lettuce, the sharp knife missing her flesh by milli-metres. She looked up, her dull eyes, smudged with mascara, meeting mine. 'God, sorry, what were we saying?' she said. 'I get so forgetful lately.'

'Oh, I forget things all the time, can hardly remember what I had for breakfast.' It wasn't true. I never ate breakfast, and had a brilliant memory. I could remember every moment of that day sixteen years ago. 'You asked if I'm married.'

'Yes, that's right. Are you?'

I shook my head. 'I've never met anyone worthy of me,' I said with a laugh.

She furrowed her forehead as though my attempt at a joke had slipped under her radar. She was a mess, and I realised at that moment just how easy taking my revenge was going to be.

Chapter 8

Sophy

Why had I told Liv I was forgetful? I seemed to be saying whatever came into my head, which was throbbing in time with my heartbeat.

It was true, though. Just the day before, I'd gone up to the bedroom, determined not to sink onto the sofa and doze while Finn had his afternoon nap, but to read a book – something I hadn't done for ages – only to find the paperback that had been on my bedside table for weeks wasn't there. Assuming I must have returned it to the bookshelf, I went to check, but couldn't locate it alongside the biographies and crime books Dom had enjoyed reading before we had Finn and work took over. These days, he had his head stuck in accounting figures most of the time.

It struck me too that my sunshine mug hadn't been in the cupboard the last time I'd looked and I wondered where Dom had found it that morning.

'Oh, I forget things all the time, can hardly remember what I had for breakfast,' Olivia – Liv – said, but even in my tired state it seemed she was saying it in a token way, attempting to empathise while her eyes darted around, drinking everything in, almost as though she'd never seen nice things before. A prickle of curiosity stirred. Hadn't she said she was originally from Stevenage – an odd coincidence – and now lived on Lavender Drive? I vaguely recalled walking down it once, trying to get Finn to sleep in his pushchair, past five or six double-fronted homes set in landscaped gardens.

I wondered which one was Liv's. Or rather, the house where she worked. Funny that I hadn't guessed she was Evie's nanny, though it made sense now she'd told me. I'd assumed the child must take after her father as she looked nothing like Liv. I wondered how she'd become a nanny, but couldn't muster the energy to ask. It had taken enough effort to find my phone, so we could exchange numbers.

'So, you don't work?' she was saying now.

'Used to.' I deposited the food I'd prepared onto plates, slightly nauseated by the sight of the pink, glistening ham with its white edging of fat. 'TV company, London. Research for a long-running history programme.' I didn't ask whether she'd heard of it. Only a twitch of her dark eyebrows betrayed she'd heard me at all. 'It's where I met Dom, my husband.' I put some ham and chopped tomato in one of Finn's bowls and, without a word, Liv picked it up and passed it to Evie.

I was revising my idea of her becoming a friend when she said again, 'You can talk to me, you know. Properly, I mean. If you want to. About whatever's getting you down.'

Her wide grey eyes were avid now, as if trying to see inside my head. I glanced uneasily to where Evie was poking her finger in Finn's bowl and wished Elizabeth would bring him back. I imagined briefly telling Liv everything; about the difficult pregnancy that made me so sick throughout that I struggled to do my job; the emergency caesarean that ended with Finn being handed straight to Dom while I was given several pints of blood to save my life. About the flashbacks that still plagued me sometimes, and how I'd struggled to bond with Finn for the first few weeks

46

of his life. How I hadn't wanted to move to St Albans – hadn't wanted to do anything much. To tell her my mum had sold my childhood home and moved to Portugal, just when I needed her, that Dom worked longer hours than ever and—

'Sophy?'

I started. Liv was looking at me strangely. My mind stretched and snapped back and I blinked. 'I ... thank you.' I moved the plates around with an effort, a flustered warmth rising up my neck. 'Shall we eat at the breakfast bar?'

'Might as well.'

Evie was pushing a piece of tomato into her mouth with one hand and holding a wooden spoon in the other, her hair a spot of brightness in the kitchen. Liv stopped stroking her hand along the breakfast bar and hoisted herself onto a stool.

'I'll give you a tour when we've eaten, if you like,' I said, sitting opposite, awkwardly tugging my dress over my knees and adjusting the scarf, which had slipped from its loop.

'Sure, why not?' Liv pushed one side of her hair behind her ear and picked up her fork. She was wearing a similar pair of jeans and top to the ones she'd worn at the baby group and her face was make-up free. I felt overdone in my outfit and worried I'd rubbed my mascara onto my face. 'You've not lived here long.'

It wasn't a question, but I shook my head as I pushed food around my plate, gripping my fork like a lifeline. 'A few months.' I stifled an urge to yawn. 'Did you say you live on Lavender Drive?'

Liv nodded, swallowing a mouthful of rocket and ham. 'I live in a nanny pad at the foot of Gary and Clare's garden, so I'm close by for Evie.' She looked at me as though expecting a reaction. 'Have you met them?'

I recalled the disastrous night they came round and felt my neck flush. 'They had dinner here, just after we moved in.'

'What did you think of them?'

What was I supposed to say to that? If I told the truth – that

47

I hadn't warmed to them at all – she might pass it on. 'They seemed nice,' I said blandly. 'How's the salad?'

Evie started giggling as though I'd said something funny. The sound was infectious and plucked at my insides, but Liv appeared not to notice, ignoring my question.

'Where did you go to university?'

How did she know I'd gone to university? Colour crept into her cheeks, as if realising she'd been too forward. She was obviously trying too hard.

'I studied history at the University of Hertfordshire,' I said, suddenly wanting to make this work, if only so I could tell Dom and Elizabeth I'd made a friend.

Liv's nose wrinkled. Maybe she couldn't understand my interest in things that had happened centuries ago. *You take after your dad*, Mum had said, smiling, the day I came home raving about a school trip to the Roman Theatre in St Albans when I was ten. *He always had his head in a history book, couldn't get enough of the past.* I loved having that link to him, hoped he would have been proud of my chosen career.

'What about you?' I ate a sliver of ham while I waited for a reply, but it was as if she hadn't heard. She put down her fork and got off the stool.

'Do you mind if I use your bathroom?'

I stared, not registering her words.

She lifted one eyebrow. 'The room where the toilet is?'

'Top of the stairs, first on the right.' I watched with vague surprise as she left the kitchen and walked up the curving staircase without a backward glance, as if she wanted to get away from me. I gave my head a shake. I was being silly. She probably just needed the loo. Maybe she felt ill. I hadn't checked the ham was in date. Or the salad, come to that. What if I'd given her food poisoning? Pushing my plate aside, I stood up, my head foggy and my eyelids droopy. 'Hey, you.' I lifted Evie from the highchair and took her through to the living room where I deposited her on the rug. Sitting beside her, I stretched my legs out and leant my back against the sofa. It was odd, seeing a little girl in the house instead of Finn, who seemed more robust than Evie despite being nine months younger.

Evie picked up a cloth book then lifted her head and studied me with her huge, blue eyes. To my surprise, she clambered into my lap and, resting against me, put her thumb in her mouth. Feeling the weight of her – surprisingly heavy – brought unexpected tears to my eyes. It was such a trusting gesture; as if Evie didn't understand how inept I was and thought I'd take care of her. My arms automatically folded around her and we sat quietly, the only sound her gentle breathing and the tick of the old-fashioned gold clock on the mantelpiece that had been a wedding gift from Elizabeth and Robert.

A feeling of peace stole over me and my eyelids drifted shut, mind wandering to my wedding day; a simple ceremony in the grounds of a hotel that used to be a church – the one where my parents had married – on a perfect, windless summer's day that was only slightly tinged with sadness because my father wasn't there.

'Evie!'

My eyes snapped open. I was back in the living room, Liv towering over us. Bending down, she almost snatched Evie from me. 'Sorry about that,' she said.

'No, no, it's fine.' I struggled to get to my feet, feeling clumsy and slow. 'She's lovely; we were having a cuddle.'

'We should get going.' Her voice was curt and Evie tried to lean away from her, tears springing to her eyes. 'It's time for her sleep.'

'What about the tour of the house?' I said stupidly. 'Evie could nap in the nursery.'

But Liv had hurried into the hall and was stuffing her feet in a pair of loosely laced trainers. 'Thanks for lunch.'

I followed her on legs that felt like rubber. 'You're not ill, are you?'

'What?' Turning, she gave me an unreadable look. 'No, I'm not ill.' She seemed to wrestle with some emotion I couldn't decipher. 'I'll see you soon, OK?'

'I don't think I'll go to the baby group again.' It came out almost before I knew I was going to say it. 'It's not for me.'

Liv became still. 'It's not for me either, to be honest.'

It sounded unguarded and, for the first time, I felt like I'd glimpsed a proper person behind the mask. 'We could go somewhere else,' I said. 'If you like.'

'Maybe.' As she leant back awkwardly to grab Evie's buggy, her coat hanging over the handle, she nodded at the door. 'Could you ...?'

As she settled Evie in the pushchair, I reached past and turned the latch, shivering as a breeze crept around my ankles. The sky had darkened and fat raindrops pattered on the gravel driveway. 'Monday?' I asked as Liv moved past, one arm in her coat, the other bumping the pushchair down the steps before I could offer to help. 'Half eleven?'

I thought she nodded, but couldn't bring myself to call after her. *Why was I even bothering?* She didn't seem to like me that much, yet even through the layer of padding in my brain, I sensed she needed a friend as much as I did.

As I shut the door and sagged against it, a more pressing question occurred.

Where was Elizabeth?

Chapter 9

Liv

I pulled up the hood on the pushchair against the rain, guilt surging through me. Head down, I pounded up The Avenue, one hand pushing Evie, the other in the pocket of my jeans, feeling the necklace I'd taken from Sophy's bedroom. It had looked special somehow, and I felt sure she would miss it. But once I was downstairs, I had to get out of her house, afraid she would see the shape of it in my pocket. Afraid I would give myself away. I'd never taken anything in my life before. Even when the kids in my youth club pinched sweets from the local shop, I'd raced outside onto the street, scared of being caught.

'Sorry!' I bumped into a woman hovering behind the hedge and swerved around her, not looking up. I needed to get back to Lavender Drive.

As I wheeled a sleeping Evie into the kitchen, Clare was propping her bulging suitcase near the door.

'Hey, Olivia,' she said, fluttering her fingers, she'd obviously been at the nail salon, judging by her blood-red talons. 'You look a bit wet and harassed. Is it raining?'

No, I've just taken a shower in my clothes. I removed my jacket, not bothering to answer her question. 'Going away?'

'Sorrento,' she said.

'Sorrento?' I grabbed my forehead. I'd completely forgotten. 'Is that this weekend?'

She nodded, tears filling her eyes. She could turn on the waterworks at the flick of a switch. 'Please don't say you've forgotten, Olivia. It's our wedding anniversary, and Gary's booked the honeymoon suite at a six-star hotel.'

Is there such a thing? 'Of course I haven't forgotten,' I said, knowing if she kept crying Evie would join in, and I'd need to build a bloody dam out of Duplo. The fact was, Clare's parents had spoiled her, Gary spoiled her, and her friends, who she tended to pick with care, only recruiting those who rallied round her, also spoiled her. She struggled with the words 'you can't have' – they weren't allowed in her vocabulary.

'Thank God,' she said. 'I thought for a minute—'

'It's fine.' It wasn't. It would have been Ben's birthday on Sunday, and I'd promised Mum I would go and stay for the weekend; that we would visit his grave together. I'd honestly thought Clare and Gary's anniversary was the following weekend. I didn't want to drag Evie to Mum's, but it looked as though I would have to. I opened the fridge and grabbed a bottle of water. 'When do you leave?' I said, unscrewing the lid and taking a gulp.

'Well it's all gone a bit pear-shaped, if I'm honest.' She caught sight of herself in the mirror – the house was full of mirrors, which I particularly hated – and she touched her cheek, admiring her reflection. She was pretty, and hadn't had fillers like a couple of her friends.

'Why? What's happened?'

She turned to meet my eye. 'Gary's getting a later flight. He can't get out of work until nine. So it's just little old me taking off at six. I could wait for him, I suppose, but the thought of flying during the night would totally mess up my sleep pattern, and I know I'd be a total grumpy-pants, and look pasty and unattractive on our first day.' She glanced at the oversized clock on the wall. 'My taxi will be here shortly.' She looked down at Evie. 'I'm guessing she's not going to wake up so I can give her a big goodbye hug.'

Normally when they went away, I stayed in the main house with Evie, but the thought of being here when Gary returned filled me with dread. I would take Evie to my pad. Clare didn't have to know.

A toot of a horn, and Clare slipped on her lilac leather jacket, and grabbed her matching case. 'I'll see you on Monday evening,' she said, and was gone before I could say goodbye.

The inconsiderate slam of the front door woke Evie and she began to cry. 'Oh, little one,' I said, lifting her from the pushchair, and jiggling her on my hip. Once she'd stopped crying, I made my way into the lounge and sat Evie on the floor with her toys. While she was playing, I pulled Sophy's necklace from my pocket and dangled it in front of my eyes. It was a filigree butterfly on a delicate silver chain. I smiled, now over my guilt at being a thief. I wanted her to miss it. Worry that she'd lost it. Doubt herself.

There was a noise behind me, and I spun round, my heart thudding against my chest. The local newspaper had landed on the doormat.

I looked back at the necklace.

I would meet Sophy on Monday, and take more than her necklace. I would take her already frayed sanity.

It was almost ten o'clock when three fist-thumps landed on the nanny-pad window.

I had got Evie off to sleep about an hour before, and was reading when the sound disturbed me.

I got up, and turned out the light, so I could look through the gap in the curtains. The security light was on, and the sight of him so close to the glass, staring in, startled me. *Gary.*

He raised his hand as I pulled back the curtain, and pointed towards the front door. 'Open up, Liv,' he ordered. 'I want to say goodbye to Evie.'

'She's asleep,' I called back. I didn't want to let him in. I didn't trust him. God only knew what Gary was capable of with Clare in Italy.

'I don't care,' he said. 'She's my daughter, and I want to see her.' He headed towards the door and banged on it. 'Let me in.'

It took a moment for me to realise he'd got a key, and was turning it in the lock. I could hardly stop him. He owned the place.

The door opened and he stepped in, his height almost filling the doorway.

'Da da da da.' I turned to the sound of Evie; relieved she was awake and smiling. I felt sure he wouldn't try anything with his daughter awake, would he?

'Hello there, little one,' he said, crouching down where I'd laid her on the sofa, and covered her with a blanket.

After a moment, he was straightened up, stepped towards me. 'You led me on, Liv. You're a tease. A flirt.'

'What?' I moved backwards.

Another step forward. 'That's why I gave you this job, Liv. Now you need to fulfil your side of the bargain.'

'Now wait a minute, Gary,' I said, cross with myself for trembling, as I moved into the kitchen area. 'You've got it wrong. I was just being friendly that day in the park.'

'Bullshit.' He gripped my upper arms, and pushed me hard against the worktop, his face moving closer to mine.

'Get off me, you fucking bastard,' I yelled, bringing my knee up between his legs. He cowered in pain, before rising up and slapping my face.

There was a thud and sudden scream behind us. Evie had fallen from the sofa onto the floor. Gary turned, and ran towards his daughter, lifted her into his arms. I stared for a moment, wanting to be sure Evie was OK before running towards the door. 'Text me when you're about to leave for Sorrento and I'll come back and look after Evie,' I said as I left. He didn't deserve it, but it wasn't the kid's fault her dad was an arsehole.

As I ran up the garden, not sure what I would do until he was gone, my thoughts slammed back to Sophy; I would tell her about Gary. Persuade her she needed a nanny to look after Finn.

Chapter 10

Sophy

'You don't look very well.'

'Thanks a lot, Mum.' It was our regular Saturday morning call.

'Are you sleeping OK?'

'I've a teething nine-month-old, what do you think?' I felt a stab of guilt, remembering how Dom did more than his fair share of nights with Finn, despite having to get up early for work every morning.

'Maybe you need some vitamin D,' she said. 'You don't get enough sunshine over there, especially at this time of year.'

'Actually, I'm taking a course of vitamins.' I brightened my tone. 'Dom's sister recommended them.'

'Well, that's good.' Mum's freckled face loomed at the screen. 'How's my grandson?' she said, as though trying to spot him in the background. She looked tanned and healthy, and at least five years younger than when she moved to Portugal. It was easy to see why Tomas, ten years her junior, who she'd met on a wine-tasting trip to Arrábida with a friend, worshipped the ground she walked on.

'He's having a nap; he's tired.' I glanced at myself in the corner of the screen and winced. I looked pasty, shadows beneath my eyes despite doing my best with some concealer before our weekly call. My hair was lank, while my mother's fell in auburn waves to her shoulders, and her blue-green eyes held a sparkle that was missing from mine.

'That's a shame.' She sounded disappointed. 'I wanted to give Finny a wave.'

'I tried to keep him awake, but he didn't have a brilliant night.'

'You must come and stay, as soon as you can,' she said, as though it was that simple.

My last proper holiday had been two years ago – my honeymoon to Italy. I had a flashback to sun-drenched hills, to walking hand in hand through ancient, cobbled streets and drinking coffee in the shade of the town square, Dom's eyes on mine.

'I'd love to, Mum, but it's not possible right now.'

She gave a soft sigh, then sipped from a floral teacup I recognised as one that used to belong to my grandmother. As she dipped her head, I spotted a slice of luminous blue sky through the window behind her and wished I was there.

'How's Dom?'

'Fine. He's at work.'

Her pale eyebrows drew together. 'On a Saturday?'

'He's dealing with a new account, but there's a problem with it.'

At first, I thought Dom had gone for a run, but when he hadn't returned by the time I dragged myself downstairs to get Finn his breakfast, I saw he'd left a note saying he had to go to the office for a couple of hours and hoped I was OK.

I knew he was worried after my reaction to Elizabeth keeping Finn out the day before and not answering her phone or any of my frantic messages. I'd been on the verge of calling the police when she finally returned, smiling with mild bemusement when I demanded to know where she'd been.

'I told you I was taking him to the stables to see the horses,' she'd said, bending to scoop Finn out of his buggy before I could get to him. I couldn't recall her mentioning it, and ended up snatching Finn from her grasp, making him cry. Not my finest moment. Elizabeth had looked dumbstruck by my reaction, her hands flying out as though to take Finn back, but I turned away, murmuring I was sorry while hoping she wouldn't tell Dom. I knew she often called him after a visit, to give him an update on how I was, and he'd return from work with worried eyes. Yesterday had been no exception, and I realised it was a look I'd come to dread.

'I overreacted, I know,' I said, as soon as he walked through the door. 'I forgot your mum said they would be out for a while and when I couldn't get hold of her, I panicked.'

'It's fine. She's sorry – she didn't mean to worry you.' He'd taken me in his arms and kissed my hair. He smelt of his favourite aftershave – the same one he'd worn on our first date – and I wept weakly on his shoulder, my mind lumpy with fatigue. Finn had cried on and off for most of the afternoon, once Elizabeth left.

'I sometimes wish she wouldn't tell you everything.'

'You know it's only because she loves Finn and wants to help you too.'

Loves him too much I'd wanted to say, but he moved away to pick up Finn from his playpen and I dried my face and heated up a lasagne I'd found in the freezer. While we ate, he'd asked about my lunch date with Liv and I exaggerated how well we'd got on, because I couldn't bear to see any more anxiety and disappointment in his eyes.

'We're meeting again on Monday,' I told him, relieved when his face had relaxed into a smile, reminding me of the cheerful, laid-back man I married. 'Hopefully, Finn will get to play with Evie, the little girl she looks after.' I decided not to mention Clare and Gary. He didn't need to be reminded of them.

'That would be great,' he'd said, reaching over to squeeze my hand.

Tuning back in to my mother now, I sat forward on the sofa with the mug of coffee I'd made, angling myself to cast my face in a more flattering light. It was tiring, keeping up the pretence that everything was fine for her benefit. She was a hard act to live up to, having single-handedly raised me after my dad died of a brain aneurysm when I was two. She'd worked hard throughout my childhood to pay the rent and bills on our little house in Stevenage, and to make sure I didn't go without, and had been a loving and supportive parent. If she'd struggled, she never showed it, but while I didn't for a second begrudge her the happiness she'd found with Tomas and her new life abroad, I couldn't help feeling like a failure in comparison.

'Where's your necklace?' she said suddenly, eyes dipping to my throat. My fingers automatically went there, feeling its absence.

'I took it off when I had a shower and forgot to put it back on.' I didn't mention it had happened yesterday morning. My grandmother bought me the silver butterfly for my twenty-first birthday and although it wasn't expensive, it meant a lot to me. When I realised it was missing at bedtime, after settling Finn, I'd gone to retrieve it from the bathroom, but it wasn't there. It wasn't in the bedroom either, though the paperback I hadn't been able to find the day before was back on my bedside table.

I hadn't mentioned the missing necklace to Dom, either. I didn't want to give him another reason to suggest I visit the doctor.

'So, what have you been up to?' Changing the subject, my mother's tone was hopeful. I knew, despite my efforts, she wasn't convinced I was coping. I suspected she'd been in touch with Dom but couldn't bring myself to ask.

'Actually, I'm thinking of getting back to work,' I said, impulsively. 'Maybe retrain to teach history, or see if there's somewhere local where I can put my skills to use.'

'Sophy, that's great.' Her tone was careful, as though I'd suggested taking up ice hockey. 'But Finn needs you right now, so don't feel you have to rush into anything.'

Stung by her lack of enthusiasm, I continued, 'Oh, and I've made a new friend. She's called Liv and lives a couple of streets away.' I sounded like an eight-year-old schoolgirl, eager for her teacher's approval.

'That's wonderful!' Mum instantly brightened. 'Does she have a child too?'

'She's nanny to a little girl, nine months older than Finn.'

'Lovely.' Mum's smile was warm. 'Talking of nannies, how's Finn's other grandma?' She hadn't exactly warmed to Elizabeth at the wedding, intimidated by my mother-in-law's social standing, worried that a widow with a much younger, Portuguese boyfriend wasn't in the same class as the Pemberton clan who, Elizabeth had confided, were descended from royalty on her father's side.

'She's fine,' I said, not wanting to mention just how hands-on Elizabeth was in case it hurt Mum's feelings. 'Keeping her hand in.'

'I'm glad you have some help.' Mum paused, as if there was more she wanted to say on the topic, before changing her mind. 'So, this friend of yours ...'

'Liv.' I glanced at the time on my phone. 'I'm going round to see her for coffee when Finn wakes up.' I'd made up my mind when I saw Dom wasn't there that I wanted to see where she lived. It would be good to get out of the house, especially now the rain had stopped, and I knew Dom would be pleased that I'd taken Finn out. If Liv wasn't in, or was busy, maybe I'd carry on to the park.

'Well, I'll let you get ready.' Mum sounded pleased for me. 'Tomas sends his love, by the way. He's on a tour with some last-minute guests this morning.'

'Say hi, and love from us all.'

'Give Finny a big kiss from his gran and send us some more pictures.'

Smiling, I rang off. Feeling unusually galvanised, I tipped my lukewarm coffee down the sink, rinsed the mug, then loaded Finn's baby bag into the bottom of his pram. Once he'd stopped arching his back in protest after I woke him up, I wrangled him into his coat and shoes, strapped him in the buggy and set off for Lavender Drive. I breathed deeply, filling my lungs with fresh, cold air, more alert than normal. It felt good.

Squashing a flare of anxiety as I left The Avenue, I turned the corner onto Willow Grove, neatly lined with trees and immaculate, detached houses, before crossing onto Lavender Drive, my boots clicking the pavement in time with my heartbeat.

The houses were bigger here, spaced further apart and set behind stone walls or well-tended hedges, hidden from view. I was sure Liv had said it was the last house on the street. I paused outside the wrought-iron gate for a moment and took some deep, steadying breaths. My neck prickled. Some sixth sense made me spin round, certain someone was approaching, but apart from a shiny car pulling out of a driveway, the street was deserted.

'Get a grip,' I murmured. Finn gave me a quizzical look from his pushchair and I bent to ruffle his hair. 'It's OK, little bear.'

Making my way up the path to the house, I noticed there were no cars parked on the drive and the blinds were drawn inside the windows.

Despite sensing the house was empty, I pressed the bell, hearing a chime reverberate inside. Finn kicked his heels and strained his arms, hands grasping as if to get out.

'Not yet,' I murmured, stepping back from the door, not sure whether I felt relieved or disappointed there was no one home. Maybe Liv had taken Evie to the park.

Finn was red-faced now, his toy cat Jiggles lying on the neatly trimmed grass at the side of the path where he'd thrown it. 'Nana!' he shouted.

Nerves prickled through me. I picked up Jiggles, dusted it off and handed it back. He immediately tossed it out again. I stuffed it in my pocket and rummaged a rice cake from his baby bag, handing it over like a peace offering. Mollified, he settled back and pushed it into his mouth.

On a whim, I headed round the side of the house on the off-chance Liv might be in the garden, which turned out to be a sweeping stretch of perfect lawn with a swing-and-slide set beside a drooping willow tree at one end. Behind it was a much smaller building made of bricks with a steep, tiled roof and two windows, like a child's drawing. This must be the nanny pad Liv had mentioned, where she lived. Like a dog in a kennel. The thought was oddly upsetting.

As I hurried away with the feeling I'd glimpsed something I shouldn't have, I felt a chill sweep over the back of my neck. Turning, I scanned the street. Had someone just darted out of sight, a darker shadow against the trunk of a tree? My heart began to race. Despite the cold, my forehead was clammy. Finn started crying, the rice cake crushed to crumbs down his front. Rain fell in a sudden deluge and the wind picked up, pushing my hair around. No point going to the park now. I pointed the pushchair towards home and ran all the way back.

Chapter 11

Liv

'She's a little beauty, Liv; you'll miss her terribly, I know you will,' Freya said as I made my way across the lounge with a tray of mugs. She was sitting on the brown Dralon fabric sofa Mum had had since Ben and I were children, her legs curled under her slim body, Evie asleep in her arms, cuddling her teddy bear. It wasn't the first time I'd brought Evie to Mum's – a modern terraced house on Chells Way in Stevenage – and there was no doubting Mum and Freya adored her. Truth was, I'd grown pretty attached to the little one myself over the last two months.

'I will miss her,' I said, putting the tray on the low table. *But I won't miss Gary's wandering hands.*

'She loves this old thing, doesn't she?' Freya stroked the pink ears of Evie's well-loved teddy bear.

'God, yes – if I ever forget it, she sobs her little heart out.'

It was just gone eleven, and I'd been at Mum's for almost an hour, but I'd only just announced I was giving up my job looking after Evie, though I hadn't mentioned Gary was the main reason. It would only upset her.

'So have you got another job lined up, Liv?' Mum said, as she tickled Sparky's fluffy ears. She hadn't mentioned Sophy since I arrived, and neither had I. But now, it was time. I handed her one of the mugs of tea, and remained standing, feeling more confident that way.

'I'm going to kill two birds with one stone.' It was an awful cliché. I had no intention of killing Sophy. I would make her suffer, yes – and if that drove her to do something stupid, then I liked to think that that would be Karma.

'I'm hoping to get a job looking after Sophy Edwards's little boy.' I couldn't think of her as Sophy Pemberton; didn't want to.

'Oh, Liv, why would you do that?' Mum wheeled her chair closer, and I plonked myself down in the armchair.

'I want to …' There was no point trying to explain. In fact I hadn't planned what I would do exactly. All I knew was I had to get close to Sophy and play with her head. Punish her.

'Be careful, Liv.' Freya picked up a mug and blew on it. 'You don't want to do anything silly. Revenge is never sweet.'

My blood pumped around my veins. 'I'm not being funny, Freya, but it's not really any of your business.' I regretted the words instantly. I liked her. Appreciated how good she was with Mum. She was quietly spoken, kind, had qualifications and experience that way surpassed what was needed to care for Mum.

'So Sophy has a son,' Mum said with a sigh. 'She took my boy, and now she has one of her own.'

'Don't go there, Martha, please.' Freya leant over and covered Mum's hand with her own.

'His name's Finn,' I said. 'And the irony is I think Sophy needs help with the boy. She says she's not on medication, but there's something not right with her. She looks terrible, like she hasn't slept for months, and she slurs her words.'

'Do you think she drinks?' Mum asked, a prickle of concern entering her voice.

'Maybe.' I shrugged, and picked up my mug. 'She used to work at Apex TV with her husband Dom Pemberton. I'm pretty sure being a mother doesn't agree with her.' It was hard to imagine Sophy working too, being with colleagues, researching history, or whatever it was she used to do.

'Postnatal depression, perhaps?' Freya stroked Evie's hair, rocking gently.

I sighed, and rose. 'Actually, I think I'll go to my room. Are you OK there with Evie for a bit, Freya?'

'Of course.' She beamed with pleasure. 'She's beautiful.'

As I climbed the stairs, passing the family photos in mismatched frames on the 1970s orange and brown floral wallpaper, I focused on a school photo of Ben. I was only thirteen when he left home, and never met any of his university friends until after his death. He never graduated in the end. Came home before his final exams. There was no doubt, looking back, that he was behaving oddly at the time. Locking himself in his room, not eating, or wandering the streets alone. He'd only been back home six weeks when he took his own life.

My eyes caught on a photo of Mum and Dad smiling on a holiday in Yarmouth, long before Ben died. If Dad had stayed, would Mum be in a wheelchair now?

Tears filled my eyes as I passed Ben's room. The door was closed, as always. A Sabbath sign saying *Do not enter* hung on the peeling paintwork. Mum had never had the heart to remove it, or change anything about his room.

Thoughts of the night before he died drifted in. I'd been on my way out, heading to meet up with mates. We would hang around the fountain in Stevenage town centre. At sixteen, we had no idea what to do with ourselves.

'Hey, cheer up, bro, it may never happen,' I'd said, meeting him on the landing. His eyes were dark and heavy, his hair greasy and too long.

'It already has,' he said, and smiled. 'You haven't got a minute, have you?'

'No can do, I'm afraid.' I pulled on my hoodie. 'I'm late already. Let's talk when I get back, yeah.'

'OK.' He'd turned and headed into his room, closing the door behind him. It was the last time I saw him, alive.

I hadn't seen his desperation. I'd shoved the headphones of my MP3 player into my ears, and raced down the stairs two at a time, not looking back, eager to hang out with my mates.

Now, I entered my bedroom. It looked much the same as it had when I was a child. I sat down at the small desk by the window, and looked out over the sprawling estate, a heavy grey sky lying over the rooftops. I'd been so happy here as a kid.

I pulled out a sheet of paper and pen, staring up at the ceiling for inspiration. *Watch Elizabeth*, I wrote. I folded the note and shoved it in the envelope, and addressed it to Sophy. I would drop it through her door after dark. It would unnerve her, put doubts in her already fragile mind about her ever-present mother-in-law.

Next I picked up my phone and called Ryan.

Ryan sat at the bar drinking a pint of lager, when I walked into the pub in Hatfield, where we'd agreed to meet. It wasn't even noon. He was wearing a red-checked shirt and scruffy jeans.

I wheeled Evie in her pushchair across the patterned carpet towards him, the smell of beer and pub food mingling in the air. Imagining how horrified Clare would be if she knew her precious daughter was in a run-down bar.

Ryan turned, seeming to sense my approach. 'Hey, Liv,' he said, and smiled, a lovely smile that refused to light up his blue eyes. They were shadowed, bloodshot – he looked a bloody wreck. He dragged his hand through his dark, greasy hair. 'Drink?'

'Lemonade,' I said, and handed Evie's cup to him. 'Some tap water in there too. Cheers.' I moved to the corner by the window, and sat down. Waited.

He approached with the drinks, and sat down opposite me.

The first time I met Ryan was at Ben's funeral, when he

introduced himself as Ben's best friend. He got pissed at the wake, and cried. Being younger, I hadn't really absorbed how desperate he was, too focused on the damage done to my own family. But over time we became good friends. Leant on each other a fair bit. But that's all we ever were – friends. In fact, he almost became my replacement brother for a while.

'It's good to see you, Liv,' he said, and turned to Evie, who was chewing a cloth book that she'd been playing with at Sophy's, that I'd forgotten to give back. 'And who's this little one?' He looked into my eyes. 'Have I missed something?'

I laughed. 'God. No. This is Evie. I'm her nanny.' He knew I'd trained in childcare, I'd told him before, but he didn't seem focused back then.

'Ah. OK.' He took a swig of his lager. Rubbed his hand across his stubble. 'She's a cutie.'

'She is.'

'So what have you been up to, Liv? I haven't seen you in ages.'

'Well, I got my qualifications about a year ago, and got a job in a nursery. But you know me, I'm not good with taking orders, and the boss-lady was a right cow.'

He laughed, the sound a welcome reminder of the person he used to be.

'Then I got a job in St Albans.' I was there to tell him about Sophy, but suddenly I was worried that if I did it would stir him up. Make things so much worse for him. 'What about you? How you doing?' I said it like Joey from *Friends*, recalling the back-to-back episodes we'd watched together. Comfort-watching we'd called it.

'Same ol' stuff.' He shook his head, as though disappointed in himself. 'A bit of labouring, and bar work.'

Oh, Ryan.

'You said you wanted to see me.'

I stared into his face, wanted to take him in my arms and hold him close. 'I just wanted to see how you are, that's all.'

The door of the pub opened, and Freya appeared, red-cheeked and out of breath, her curly hair flyaway, her smoke-grey anorak zipped to the neck, over straight-legged jeans. She had Evie's pink teddy in her hand.

'Freya,' I called, as her eyes darted around the empty bar.

'Liv,' she said, spotting me. 'Your mum said you'd be here. You forgot her teddy.' She dashed over and thrust it into Evie's waiting arms.

'Thank you,' I said, bewildered that she would come all the way to Hatfield just to bring the bear.

'You said Evie gets upset without it.' She smiled at the child, and I had the feeling she longed to snatch her up and cuddle her.

'Yes, well that's true, but ... well thank you.'

'No problem at all. We wouldn't want her to be sad, now would we?' She pulled her eyes away from Evie and they landed on Ryan. 'Who's this?' she said, with a friendly smile.

'Oh. This is Ryan. He was Ben's closest friend.'

'Oh, yes, Martha talks about you sometimes, Ryan.' Her voice dipped with concern. 'I'm so sorry about Ben.'

'It was a long time ago,' Ryan said, but I knew; to him – to all of us – it felt like yesterday.

'I agree,' she said. 'And it should be left in the past.' Her eyes moved from Ryan to me. 'That's what I tried to tell Liv. It was in the past, and revenge is never sweet.'

Ryan screwed up his face, and turned to look at me. 'Revenge?'

'It's nothing,' I said, shaking my head, and trying to catch Freya's eye.

'Just because she's found Sophy,' Freya went on, clearly not reading my tone. 'It doesn't mean any good will come of digging it all up.'

'You've found Sophy?' His eyes widened. 'Sophy Edwards?'

'Anyway.' Freya plonked a kiss on Evie's head. 'I'd better get back to your mum.' She dashed across the bar, and out through the door, as though she'd twigged she'd spoken out of turn.

'Sophy?' Ryan said when she'd gone. He took a gulp of his lager. 'You know where she is?'

I nodded, anger stirring inside me once more. 'She lives in St Albans. She's living this great life, Ryan.'

'It doesn't surprise me.' His voice was flat, and he was staring at the table, refusing to look at me. 'She was smart, destined for great things.'

'But she doesn't deserve it, Ryan. Can't you see that? Ben would still be here—'

'We don't know that for sure, Liv.' He flashed me a look. 'And what's all this about revenge, for God's sake?'

My heart raced. I thought out of anyone, Ryan would understand. 'Sophy's a crap mum. She neglects her son. And I intend to become part of her life, so I can make her pay for what she did to Ben. To all of us.'

'That's not a good idea, Liv.' His eyed narrowed. 'Freya's right. Leave well alone.'

I grabbed my head, fingertips digging into my skull as I held in a scream. 'I'm not about to knife her, Ryan, or drug her or anything like that; I just want to mess with her head a bit, that's all. Why can't you see that?' I shook my head. 'I wish I hadn't come.'

He fiddled with his beer glass. Clearly refusing to see the damage Sophy did was far-reaching. That he'd come out of university with an honours degree in chemistry, but had ended up alcohol-dependent and working in bars, thanks to her.

I pulled my phone from my bag and looked at the time. Rested it on the table.

'I need to change Evie,' I said, rising, desperate to get away from him, before I lost it. I lifted her from her buggy, grabbed her changing bag, and headed to the ladies'.

'I should go,' I said, on my return. 'Evie will need her lunch soon.' I leant over to kiss Ryan's cheek, a lump rising in my throat. He was such a mess, but it seemed he couldn't see that Sophy had done that to him. 'I'll call you,' I added, strapping Evie into her pushchair, and picking up my phone. I turned and wheeled her across the bar towards the door, determined he wouldn't let me veer from my goal.

Chapter 12

Sophy

'We didn't want to wake you,' Dom said as we drove home from his parents' on Sunday evening, his face knotting with concern when I asked why he'd left me sleeping on their deep-cushioned leather sofa after a heavy lunch of roast lamb.

Our weekly lunch with his parents at Greenacres, their Grade II listed barn conversion in Harpenden – a routine established as soon as we moved to St Albans – had been the usual affair, for me at least, until I'd woken with a start to find I'd drooled on the tapestry cushion where my head had lolled, and the house empty.

'Mum suggested taking Finn for some fresh air to look at the horses in the paddock,' Dom continued, and I flashed back to the note I'd found in an envelope on the doormat that morning, after Dom had gone to work, addressed to me. *Watch Elizabeth*, had been scrawled in pencil on a small sheet of lined paper and my breathing had quickened, some instinct warning me not to mention it to Dom. When he asked what it was, I said quickly, 'Just a note from Petra about Mums Meet Up,' and stuffed it in my dressing gown pocket. Now, I found myself wondering again, who would have put the note through my door and why? Did

Elizabeth have an enemy I didn't know about? Someone with a grudge? An ex-pupil from her riding school days? By all accounts, she'd had a reputation for being difficult to please, but it was her strict, uncompromising style that had made her – and her pupils – succeed.

'We decided to let you rest, as you looked so peaceful,' Dom said, flashing his warm smile. 'Like Sleeping Beauty.'

I let out an undignified snort, which provoked Finn's first real belly laugh – a deep, gurgling sound. Dom asked me to do it again, revelling in the sound of our son's joyful response, but the feeling of goodwill only lasted until we arrived home, when I headed straight to bed, reeling with a bone-deep tiredness that made me feel as if my blood had been drained and replaced with sand. I felt incapable of sitting in front of the TV, or playing with Finn, or even talking to my husband, let alone wonder who had it in for my mother-in-law and thought I should be watching her.

Dom didn't bother waking me for Finn's bath time, or when he came to bed and I wondered whether I'd dreamt that I turned over in the night to see his face, glowing in the light of his phone.

The following morning, I still hadn't shown him the note and knew I wouldn't. It would only worry him, and he had enough on his mind. It had been a warning to me, not him; that much was certain from my name on the envelope.

Once he'd left for London after leaving a mug of cooling coffee by the bed with a vitamin tablet, I forced myself up and into the shower, determined not to let the day slip away from me. I steeled myself against the sting of cold water, letting it sharpen my senses. I had no idea whether Liv would turn up, but wanted to be ready if she did; not just dressed, hair blow-dried, skin moisturised, but in control instead of the shambolic mess I'd been last time.

Finn was sitting up in his cot, rhythmically banging Jiggles against the bars, making *bah, bah* sounds, and the sight of him in his stripy sleep suit made my heart swell with love.

Ignoring my usual pang of apprehension, I crossed to the

window and opened his panda-patterned curtains. The morning was bright, sunlight spreading across the room, over the Winnie-the-Pooh prints on the wall and the comfy chair I'd brought from the apartment, where I used to sit to breastfeed Finn in a sleepy haze, before it became apparent that I didn't have enough milk and had to switch to formula, much to Elizabeth's dismay.

'If you'd persevered, he wouldn't be so colicky,' she'd chided carefully on one of her frequent visits to London, laying on pressure for us to move to St Albans by bringing brochures for houses for sale. I'd suspected she was secretly delighted to have an excuse to take Finn from me and give him a bottle, always 'dropping in' when Dom was working.

'Come on, little man,' I said brightly, padding to Finn's cot. 'Time for breakfast.'

I tried not to mind when he resisted my attempts to pick him up, throwing himself back with a shriek when I finally got him out so he almost toppled from my arms.

'Steady, steady,' I cautioned tearfully, as much to myself as Finn, positivity seeping away as he kicked and bucked through his nappy change, protesting with wails and clenched hands when I tried to dress him. Downstairs, he upended his porridge bowl on the floor. When I gave him some chopped-up banana, he only ate one piece before mashing the rest into the tray of his highchair, finally rejecting his bottle of milk by swiping it out of my hand.

By the time the doorbell rang at eleven-thirty sharp, my nerves were shredded. I hadn't had time to eat breakfast or even drink my coffee, and an aspirin for a thumping headache hadn't helped. Neither had a voicemail from Elizabeth, saying she'd call round after lunch to drop off a homemade casserole for our dinner as, 'I know you don't like cooking.' It was kind of her, but made me feel useless.

I'd already decided to go out, without or without Liv, and had managed to settle Finn with the help of his dummy and wrangle him into his pushchair. I jumped when the doorbell sounded again and hurriedly looked for my keys. They were normally in the front pocket of Finn's baby bag, but a search yielded only a crumpled tissue. They weren't on the hall table – polished to a sheen by Elizabeth – or in the kitchen.

Impatient knuckles rapped the front door and I flew back to the hall and pulled it open to see Liv, backing down the steps.

'You said eleven-thirty.' There was a challenge in her voice and her gaze was frosty.

'Yes, I'm ... I'm sorry for keeping you waiting.' I thrust a strand of hair back, feeling wrong-footed. 'I was looking for something.'

Her gaze dropped and she jammed her hands in her coat pockets, then lifted her head. 'Where would you like to go?'

'Maybe the park?'

Her nose wrinkled. 'How about The Busy Bean café?' She seemed to be making an effort to talk evenly and managed a thin-lipped smile. 'It's a bit cold for the park.'

I wouldn't have minded, especially as the sun was out, but I nodded, smiling at Evie as she waved at me from her buggy. She looked cute in her pink hooded jacket, thick tights and fur-lined boots. 'Sounds good.' I'd leave the door on the latch, I decided. I couldn't face turning the house upside down for my keys, or phoning Dom to ask whether we had a spare one hidden somewhere. I'd only be an hour or so, at the most. 'Let me get my coat.'

It was a ten-minute walk to The Busy Bean. On the way, Finn sleepily sucked his dummy, hands reaching from under his blanket as though trying to catch the clouds scudding across the sky, while Evie peered round the hood of her coat, eyes drinking everything in.

Liv walked fast, keeping up a stream of observations about our surroundings that didn't require much response from me, which was just as well as being outdoors was making me feel light-headed. Everything was brighter and louder than seemed normal. The beep of a horn from a passing van as we reached the high street sent my heart rate rocketing.

'You OK?' As if sensing my tension, Liv paused midway through a comparison of house prices in the area to Scotland and Wales, which I'd only been half-listening to. 'Sorry if I'm babbling,' she said with a shrug. 'It's not been a great morning, to be honest.'

I smiled at her admission, my heartbeat slowing. 'I know what you mean.'

'You too?'

When I nodded, she flashed a quick smile, almost as if she'd guessed. Maybe her stream of chatter had been intended to put me at ease.

We crossed the road to the café, which was sandwiched between a bakery and a shop that seemed to exclusively sell candles, judging by the window display.

'This café's a bit full of itself,' Liv said, bumping the buggy up the kerb, causing Evie to clap her hands and dimple into a smile. 'They do a good hot chocolate though. I've only been a couple of times, when I managed to escape—' She cut herself off, flicking a glance at my face. 'When I managed to get a couple of hours off.'

'Aren't you entitled to a couple of days off a week?'

'You'd think,' was all she said as we entered the steamy warmth of the busy café. The noise of clattering crockery, a hissing coffee machine and chattering voices was deafening after the quiet I was used to at home, where only the muted TV and Finn's cries broke the silence, unless Elizabeth was there.

'My first time,' I said, raising my voice above the cacophony, relieved to see other mothers there with pushchairs. I recognised a couple of mums from the baby group: Petra, who gave me a sugary smile that didn't reach her eyes, and Kim, with Dougie strapped across her chest in a complicated-looking sling. Her smile shrank when she saw Finn waving his dummy. 'He's a bit of a grumpy bear this morning.' I hated that I was making excuses to someone I barely knew. 'Nice to see you.'

I hurried after Liv, who'd parked Evie's buggy at a table in the corner and shrugged her coat off.

'Hot chocolate or coffee?' she said.

'Hot chocolate.' I wasn't keen on café coffee, which was either too strong or too milky for my taste.

'Sit down, I'll get them.' Liv headed for the counter before I could protest or get my purse out, waving hello to Kim on the way.

I removed my coat and sat down. Finn arched his back, indicating he wanted out of his pushchair. Keen to keep him happy, I undid his straps and lifted him onto my lap, prompting Evie to stretch her arms in our direction.

'Me out.'

Panic zipped through me as I looked round. What if she ran off? 'Liv will be back in a moment,' I said brightly. She was almost at the front of the queue, so I bounced Finn on my knees in front of Evie to distract her. As she reached for his wiggling fingers, I looked through the window, catching sight of a familiar figure on the opposite side of the road, hurrying along, dark coat flapping around his knees. *Dom?* I blinked and looked again, but whoever it was had turned the corner. It couldn't have been Dom. He was in London, working.

My heart had started racing again. On impulse, I fished one hand in my bag for my phone, then stopped myself. Surely calling to check my husband was where he was supposed to be would only fuel his belief that I needed to see the doctor? There had to be hundreds of men who, from a distance, might bear a passing resemblance to Dom.

As I straightened, another figure snagged my attention, hurrying in the same direction; tall, with long blonde hair poking from under a red, woolly hat. For a second, I was reminded of Alicia Bainbridge, who used to work with Dom before being

76

head-hunted by another company. I'd met her at a works party once, and thought how coldly beautiful she was, her gaze washing over me as though I wasn't worth bothering with.

'She's got a thing for me,' Dom had said when I commented afterwards, wincing as though it pained him to admit it. 'Don't worry, she'll get over it.' He'd never mentioned her again.

'Here we are.' Liv was back with two big mugs of creamy hot chocolate, a swirl of cinnamon on top. 'I wasn't sure whether you wanted something to eat.'

'I'm fine, thank you.' I was actually starving, but couldn't face a trek to the counter, aware of Kim's judgemental gaze sweeping in my direction, probably noting things to report back to Elizabeth the next time they met in the park.

Liv delved into a canvas bag in the bottom of Evie's buggy and pulled out a sippy cup, along with a little pot of carrot sticks.

When Evie solemnly handed Finn a carrot stick, he gave it an uncertain look before pushing the end between his gums, eyes round as he tried to chew.

'He's so sweet,' Liv said, crossing her legs and leaning forward, more animated around him than she'd been on Friday. She was dressed smartly today, her blue sweater flattering her creamy skin. 'Does he take after you or his dad?'

'A bit of both, according to my mother, though she's only seen him on-screen since he was about six weeks old.'

'She doesn't live locally?'

'Portugal.' I was sure I'd told her before, but her visit to the house was a bit of an embarrassing blur. 'She runs a guesthouse there with her boyfriend.'

When Liv's eyebrows rose, I found myself telling her about Mum relocating to the wine region of Arrábida four years ago, how happy she was with Tomas and how well their business was doing. 'We went there a couple of years ago, and were on our way to visit in the New Year when I went into early labour.' I suppressed a shudder at the flash of memory those words conjured up; the diversion from the airport to the hospital, the escalating pain, Dom's erratic driving through a blizzard, and the certainty that I was going to lose my baby.

'Sounds great.' Liv took a long swallow of hot chocolate, glancing to check that Evie was OK. 'Having a place in Portugal, I mean.' I thought I detected a trace of bitterness in her voice but told myself I'd imagined it. 'Are you an only child?'

I blinked at the change of topic. 'Yes,' I said. 'My dad died young.' I felt the usual pang, my only memories of my father the photos Mum had, of a smiling man with the same unruly red hair I'd inherited and a cheeky smile; one of him looking at her adoringly on their wedding day, another of him gazing at me in his arms just after I was born, his expression dazed but happy, and one where he was pushing me on a little swing in our back garden. Sometimes, I thought I could remember the feel of his woolly sweater against my cheek, the smell of the soap he used, the sound of his gravelly voice, singing me nursery rhymes, and I hoped the memories were real. 'My mum and I get on well, but now she's living abroad, it's ... well, I miss her. I always thought it would be nice to have a brother or sister.'

A pulse ticked in Liv's jaw, her mug poised close to her lips, eyes intent on mine. I felt a ripple of unease.

'I have a sister-in-law called Natasha,' I hurried on, not sure why I felt compelled to fill the weighty silence that had fallen. 'She's the one who decorated our house, or should I say "styled" it.' I made quote marks with my voice, jiggling Finn on my lap. 'She's an interior designer, very successful, but she's moved north, to Cumbria, to be closer to her husband Rory's family and doesn't visit often. I think my mother-in-law misses her and Toby. That's her son, he's five.' *Shut up, Sophy.* 'Natasha and Dom were very close growing up. He misses her too.'

Liv's expression was blank. Perhaps I was boring her as much as I was annoying myself.

'What about you?' I picked up my mug and took a few quick

sips, feeling the milky foam cling to my upper lip. 'Do you have any siblings?'

It was a moment before she spoke. 'I had a brother,' she said at last. 'Ben.'

Had. I felt a roll of nausea. 'Is he …?'

'Dead,' she said flatly.

'Oh, God. Liv, I'm so sorry.'

Before I could gather my thoughts and speak again, she began playing peekaboo with Finn from behind her fingers until he chortled happily. Evie joined in, pressing her fingers over her eyes and shouting, 'Boo!'

Liv seemed to have recovered herself, reaching for Finn to place him on her knees and clap his hands together. As I picked his dummy off the wooden floor where he'd dropped it, I felt a tightness at the back of my throat at how happily he went to her. 'You're good with children.' I forced the words through a smile that felt unnatural. 'Evie really loves you.'

I was relieved to see Liv relax, as though my praise had pleased her. 'I do like kids,' she said, making wide eyes at Finn. 'I'll miss Evie when I leave.'

I couldn't disguise my surprise. 'You're leaving?'

She made a face. 'I haven't got much choice,' she said. 'Gary, Evie's dad, has made it clear he wants more than babysitting duties from me. I'm sick of fighting him off, and his wife doesn't do much but spend his money and criticise everything I do.'

'That's awful.' I was appalled, trying to think whether Gary had seemed like a creep when he and Clare came for dinner. I recalled Clare talking about her hair colourist – I'd felt sure she was having a dig at my 'ginger' tresses – but I'd barely registered Gary, other than thinking he wasn't Dom's kind of person – too full of himself. 'I had no idea.'

'Why would you?'

Seeing Kim look over, I thrust Finn's dummy in my coat pocket. 'Can't you talk to Clare about what's happening with Gary?'

'I doubt she'd believe me and even if she did, she'd probably blame me and kick me out.'

It was a horrible thought, but hard to argue with Liv's logic. 'So, what will you do?'

She puffed out a breath, her shoulders drooping. 'Look for another job,' she said, holding Finn high then plopping him down so his hands shot out with delight. 'I don't suppose you need any help with this one, do you?'

Her wide grey eyes were beseeching as they looked at me over Finn's head, and for a second, I felt as if I was looking over a bridge at swirling water below.

'I could ask Dom,' I heard myself say. 'I know he'd like his mum to do more, but she's there so much already and has her own life, her horses. I'd feel guilty.' *And even more inadequate*, I didn't add, but Liv smiled as though understanding. I thought about the note again. *Watch Elizabeth.*

'She won't need to come round so often if there's someone else there.' Liv's smile grew, her eyes taking on a shine that made me smile back. Maybe she was onto something. Not that I couldn't trust my mother-in-law, despite what the note would have me believe, but Liv didn't really know me and had no expectations. Maybe I would be different with her help. I could learn how to be better with Finn; take her lead. I'd be happier, less concerned about failing in front of Elizabeth, get back to work—

'So?' Liv prompted, her gaze intent.

My mind was whirling like a merry-go-round at this unexpected turn of events. 'I'll have a word with Dom,' I said. 'I expect you'll have to give notice anyway.'

'Only a week, and I'm not even sure I'll work that.'

I felt a spasm of pity for Evie, who was obviously attached to Liv. 'Where will you stay?' I thought of our spare room, cluttered with unpacked boxes from the apartment that I still hadn't got round to dealing with. 'It wouldn't be a live-in position, I'm afraid.'

'Not a problem. I can move back to my mum's in Chells Way.'

My phone began to ring. 'Sorry,' I said, taking it out of my bag, not entirely surprised to see Dom's number. He'd probably tried calling the house and wondered why I hadn't picked up.

'Sophy, where are you?' He sounded frantic.

'I'm at The Busy Bean with Liv,' I said. 'Sorry, I thought you knew I was seeing her.'

'Are you OK?'

'What?' I sensed Liv listening, her arms loosely draped round Finn. His mouth was stained orange with carrot juice. 'I'm fine,' I said, pulse leaping. 'Just having a hot chocolate.'

'Can you go home? It's important.'

'What?'

'Please, Sophy, just do as I ask.' He rang off.

I stared at my phone for a moment, goose bumps rippling across my shoulders.

'Everything OK?'

I started at the sound of Liv's voice. 'I have to go.' I reached to take Finn and his face immediately crumpled. 'I'll be in touch,' I said, feeling her eyes on me as I fumbled Finn into his pushchair, blood roaring in my ears. 'Thanks for the drink.'

'You're welcome.'

As I hurried away, Finn's piercing cries drawing stares from everyone in the café – especially Kim – I wondered what had prompted Dom to order me home.

It wasn't until I reached our house and saw the front door standing open, that I remembered I'd left it unlocked.

Chapter 13

Liv

I took a detour to the park on my way back to Lavender Drive, hoping to push Evie on the swing for ten minutes – share some me and her time – but, by the time I'd wheeled the buggy onto the brightly coloured play area, she was asleep, her teddy bear snuggled to her nose.

I sat down on my usual bench, and stroked her soft cheek with my finger. 'I'm so sorry, sweetheart,' I said. And as I watched her chest rise and fall, tears were close. I hadn't bargained on getting so attached, so quickly. I would miss her terribly.

I lifted my gaze and scanned the area. It was warmer than earlier, but there was barely anyone about. Only a woman with a dog in the distance, and two young women sitting on the grass deep in conversation, their little ones racing around, squealing and giggling.

I closed my eyes, and, almost like turning on a TV, her face appeared in my mind's eye: *Sophy Edwards.*

She looked just like the beautiful young woman in the photograph Ryan had shown Mum, Dad and me just after Ben's death, but she was different to how I thought she would be. I suppose

I'd conjured up a mental image of a monster when I thought of the woman who caused the death of my brother. But Sophy was no monster. In fact, she was more like a rather sad dormouse.

I thought back to her at The Busy Bean earlier. I'd half expected her to mention the note I'd put through the letterbox, but I supposed it was too much to expect her to confide in me that someone had warned her to watch her mother-in-law. She didn't see me as a 'friend' yet. I hadn't intended to mention Ben, but when she asked about siblings I had no choice, his name burning a path to my heart as it left my lips. She had shown pity, felt sorry for me that I'd lost my brother, but there had been no real reaction. Surely the name Ben in itself should have stirred emotions, forced a flicker of remorse.

My eyes snapped open, stinging with tears, my fists clenched, nails buried in my flesh once more. Anger had brewed in me for so long, corroding my insides, but life would be better soon, once I was inside the walls of Sophy's perfect home – getting even – balancing the scales.

The sound of female chatter carried on the air, as women headed across the park towards the play area – towards me. Amongst them I spotted Kim with Dougie in his sling, and a couple of other mums pushing buggies. I jumped to my feet and hurried away, unable to face them and their small talk.

Gary and Clare weren't back from Italy when I returned to Lavender Drive, but they wouldn't be long. Clare had texted me to say they'd landed and would be home around two. I had already packed my holdall.

I spent the next hour giving Evie her lunch, before disappearing upstairs to the nursery, where I read Evie a story. It's unusual for her to sleep in the day, but the trip must have made her more sleepy than usual, as she dropped off in my arms.

I was putting her into her cot, when I heard the front door open. 'Olivia!' It was Gary – using my full name as he always did in front of Clare. They were back, and I was tempted to keep quiet, pretend I was out with Evie for as long as I could.

'Olivia!' It was Clare, and I softened. She would want to see her daughter.

I left the nursery, and made my way downstairs, past photos of Evie that dotted the silver-embossed wallpaper, and into the hallway. Gary and Clare's cases stood next to the front door, and the sound of water streaming into a kettle came from the kitchen. I made my way across the hall and stood in the doorway to see only Gary.

'Where's Clare?' I said.

He turned to face me, the kettle in his hand. 'Those tight jeans suit you,' he said, his tone low and even.

My heartbeat quickened. *Thank God I don't have to be around the creep much longer.*

He shoved the kettle onto its base, and flicked it on. 'In answer to your question, Clare's gone shopping.'

'But I heard her. She called out. She hasn't even seen Evie yet.'

'What can I say? She's a shopaholic. Makes me wonder how I put up with her.' He stepped towards me, and although he was some distance away, I moved backwards, out into the hallway. 'Are you afraid of me, Liv?'

'No. You're an idiot. And I'm out of here now you're back.'

He stared, not moving. I wanted to run. I *was* afraid of him. He was the kind of man who thought he could take what he wanted from a woman, without consequence. I looked towards the back door. I needed to get my holdall. But he grabbed my arm.

'You're hurting me.' I attempted to wriggle free from his grip.

'Can't you feel the chemistry between us, Liv?' He thrust his lips against mine, his body pressing against me. How the hell had I ended up alone with him again? I bit down hard on his lip, and he moved away. 'Bitch!' he said, blood coating his hand, as he covered his mouth. 'Fucking bitch.'

I ran past him, across the kitchen. 'Clare needs to know about you,' I cried, as I dived through the back door, and sprinted down the garden, looking behind me at every step. But he didn't follow me.

Once inside the nanny pad, I grabbed my holdall. I would leave now – go to my mum's.

It was as I went to leave, that Clare barged in. 'Olivia!'

I grabbed my jacket and slipped it on. 'I'm leaving.' There was so much else I wanted to say – but decided to just get out of there.

'Yes you are,' she said, folding her arms.

I went to push past her, but she stood firm in the doorway. 'Gary said you tried it on with him.'

'What? Gary's a total dick, Clare.' Christ I was angry. 'He's a letch, always groping me or trying to kiss me.' My heart thudded. 'If you've got any sense you'll kick him out. Now for God's sake get out of my way.' I went to push past her, but she wouldn't budge. She was stronger than she looked, all her gym sessions paying off.

'If you ever go near my husband again, Olivia, I promise you, you'll wish you hadn't.'

'Jeez,' I yelled. 'Are you bloody blind?'

She turned and left, heading back to the house with long strides.

Fighting back tears, I ran up the garden towards the side gate. From the kitchen window, Gary smiled.

I pulled up outside Mum's house, killed the engine, and pulled on the handbrake. It was almost four o'clock, and the school kids, like a sea of red in their uniforms, were making their way home to the modern terraces lining the street, some in groups, messing around, others alone.

My eyes fell on Mum's house, the yellowing nets, the window frames that needed replacing. I knew she wouldn't mind me moving in until I had enough money to rent a flat, but the truth was, I struggled whenever I walked through the door.

I was about to get out of the car, when Freya came out through the front door, closing it behind her. She'd done her bit for Mum today.

I watched her scurry up the road, taking quick steps as she made her way to the bus stop. She owned a Volvo Estate, but would often take the bus to and from Little Wymondley – the village where she lived, just outside Stevenage – in an effort to protect the environment. I realised at that moment, as I watched her disappear around the corner, that I knew very little about her personal life. But then her life story had never been of interest to me. She did a good job for Mum, and that was all that mattered.

'Can I stay a while?' I said to Mum once I'd let myself into the house. I still had my own key. In fact, it still had a *Harry Potter* key ring attached to it, from when I was obsessed as a teenager.

'Of course you can,' she said, as Sparky jumped up at me, and I tickled his ears. 'Selfishly, I love you being here.' She smiled. 'So I'm guessing you've left your job looking after Evie.'

I nodded, and we chatted for a few moments. She seemed to deliberately avoid any talk of Sophy, before saying, 'You look tired, Liv.'

'Mmm.' I realised I was. I hadn't slept properly since first seeing Sophy, mind spinning into the small hours, memories rising and turning to thoughts of payback. 'I know I've only just arrived, but would you mind if I went to my room?'

'Of course not, love.'

I lugged my holdall up the stairs, and into my room, and after a few moments of staring from my window in a daze, I bent down and pulled my memory box from under my bed. I settled, cross-legged on the floor, to look through it. There were photos of Dad and me fishing or going to the football, pictures of friends through the years, greeting cards – mainly birthday cards from Dad. But I wasn't looking for any of those, however distracting they were, I was looking for the picture of Sophy with Ben.

I found it at the bottom of the box. It was of twenty or so university students ready to set off on a skiing trip to France. I recalled how Ben had desperately wanted to go on the trip, how Mum and Dad struggled to help him with the cost. I'd been jealous at the time – had never been abroad, because our parents couldn't afford to. Dad had been a delivery driver, and Mum only ever worked a few hours in the supermarket, always wanting to be there when I came home from school, so their wages couldn't stretch to many extras. A surge of guilt that I was such a pain-in-the-arse teenager pulsed through me. I'd moaned that we never went abroad, that my parents couldn't afford the latest trainers. I couldn't see that I had everything I could possibly need right there.

I narrowed my eyes, taking in Sophy – so beautiful with her red tumbling hair – standing next to Ben, slightly taller than him. I smiled at Ryan's playful pose, as he stood the other side of Ben; his arm flopped over my brother's shoulder. He looked so handsome and carefree back then – laughing into the camera.

It was as I put the photograph back into the box, that I saw Ben's suicide note. I don't know why I'd kept it – perhaps I thought one day it would lead me to Sophy. Before I could stop myself, I picked it up, tears rising in my chest – a pain in my heart.

It was folded – just as he'd left it the day he cut his wrists – here in this house, in his bedroom. I liked to think he hadn't expected his sixteen-year-old sister would be the one to find him. I'd come back from being out with my mates with a pounding headache, after trying tequila for the first time. Mum and Dad were at the cinema, and would have been home before me, normally. My parents should have found him. *No* – nobody should have found him – because he shouldn't have died.

I read the note for the millionth time, bashing away tears that flowed down my cheeks. Sixteen years later the pain wasn't any less.

'Life's not worth living if I can't share it with the one I love.'

Chapter 14

Sophy

'I can't keep saying it, Dom. My keys weren't there. I looked twice.'

'I know you think you did, but how do you explain them turning up exactly where they were supposed to be?'

I slumped against the pillow, worn out from going over it again and again, stomach vaulting as I recalled my shock when I'd run into the house the day before to find Elizabeth on the sofa, fresh from the stables in her quilted jacket and shiny brown boots, an orange casserole dish on the coffee table in front of her.

'I came to drop this off and the door was open,' she'd said, rising and moving past me with small, neat steps to the hallway, where she bent to remove Finn from his pushchair as though releasing a helpless animal from a cage.

'You should have called me, instead of bothering Dom at work.' I'd clutched my chest, a wave of helplessness washing over me as I watched her ease Finn from his outdoor clothes and carry him into the living room, patting his back and making soothing sounds. I felt as guilty as if I'd gone out and left him home alone.

'I did call, but you weren't picking up.' Elizabeth's voice was sharp, though her expression was soft as she sat down and bounced Finn on her corduroy-trousered lap. Recalling the note, I'd looked at her more closely than normal, realising with a jolt that I didn't know her that well. There was something self-contained about her, a barrier that was hard to break through, despite the friendly façade. I remembered Dom saying that having Finn was the first time he could remember his mother being fully engaged with him, as though he'd finally achieved something she could relate to. I knew he and Natasha had grown up in Christopher's shadow, the tragic death of the brother they'd never known always at the forefront of their mother's mind. *My little angel*, was how she used to refer to him. Forever perfect; the embodiment of hopes and dreams that would never be realised. I hadn't fully absorbed Dom's comment at the time, but not long after that, she'd upped her campaign for us to move out of London so we'd be closer and she could help with Finn.

'I was worried, which is why I called Dom.' Elizabeth's voice had pulled me out of my scrutiny. 'He wanted to come home but I managed to persuade him there was no need, once he'd got hold of you.'

I was certain Elizabeth hadn't called me, that I'd have heard the ringtone even though the café was noisy, yet when I pulled my phone from my pocket, I could see I'd had a missed call from her.

Dom had been torn between relief, and bewilderment that I'd left the door on the latch before going out, having forgotten his mother had planned to drop off our dinner. 'It's a good job she did,' he'd said, voice strained. 'Anyone could have let themselves in.'

After Elizabeth had gone – I insisted Finn needed an afternoon nap – I'd searched once more for my keys, finally locating them in the front pocket of Finn's baby bag at exactly the same moment Dom walked through the front door after leaving work early.

'I couldn't concentrate,' he said, which I interpreted as an accusation, though he swore it wasn't. 'I'm worried about you, Sophy.'

I recalled how I thought I'd spotted him from the café window, but it hadn't seemed a good time to bring it up, or tell him about my conversation with Liv and her offer to be Finn's nanny.

Now, Dom brought our son through from the nursery and laid him next to me on the bed, checking my face as if trying to read my mood. I had a feeling he was going to ask me again to make an appointment to see the doctor, so I sat up straight and made myself smile at him. 'I've found someone to help.' I lifted Finn to nestle against my shoulder. He immediately went rigid, twisting his head to look for his dad.

'Help?' Dom paused in the act of pulling a tie from the wardrobe.

'A nanny,' I said, laying Finn across my legs. I tried to clap his hands together, but he resisted. 'It's Liv.'

'Your lunch date?'

I wondered how many Livs he thought I knew. 'She's desperate to leave her current job.' I smiled as Finn finally relaxed, curling his fingers around my thumbs. 'Evie's dad has been coming on to her.' Dom made a face. 'It's Gary, actually.'

He spun around, eyes widening. 'Our neighbour, Gary?'

'The one who came for dinner with his wife.'

Dom's mouth turned down. 'I must admit, I didn't like him that much.'

I felt a burst of relief that he was on Liv's side.

'They never invited us back to theirs.'

'Would you have wanted to go if they had?'

'No, not really.'

'Me neither,' he admitted with a grimace.

Encouraged, I said, 'I felt sorry for Liv. And she's great with Evie and Finn. She'll be a good nanny.'

'We could ask my mum to help out more and it won't cost anything.' He fastened his tie and swept a hand round his jaw as he settled his gaze on me. 'You know she'd love to be more involved. You only have to say the word.'

'She has her own life, Dom, and does so much already. It'll be good for Finn to see someone new and I think Liv and I could be friends.'

That seemed to clinch it for Dom. To no longer have the spectre of his lonely, friendless, listless wife hanging over him at work must seem like a gift. He nodded and said, 'In that case, let's give it a try.'

'She wouldn't live in,' I rushed on, in case he changed his mind. 'She's moving back to her mum's in Stevenage.' I suddenly remembered her telling me about her brother Ben's death and the way she'd looked at me for a reaction. My emotions were blunted with tiredness sometimes and I hoped I hadn't come across as heartless. To have lost her brother so young … it was hard to imagine the devastation. I wondered how old she'd been when it happened and made a mental note to ask her.

'Did you discuss payment?' Dom said, aiming the words at his reflection.

'Sorry?'

'How much does a nanny cost?'

'I said I'd talk to you before we went any further.'

He nodded, smiling at me in the mirror. 'Do whatever you think is best for you and Finn.'

'I'll call her today.'

Having finished dressing, he pressed his fingertips to his lips and placed them on Finn's forehead, just as his phone vibrated on the dressing table. He snatched it up and looked at the screen. The groove between his eyebrows deepened.

'Work?'

For a second, it was as if he hadn't heard me. He kept staring at the screen, before switching his phone off and shoving it in his trouser pocket. 'I've got to go,' he said absently, as if he'd already left, and only when he'd run downstairs and the front door had shut did I realise that, for the first time I could remember, he hadn't kissed me goodbye.

Once Finn was fed – with minimal fuss – and safe in his

playpen, I called the number Liv had stored in my phone. I was about to hang up when she finally answered, sounding out of breath.

'Sorry, I've been for a run.'

'That's OK.' I remembered with a pang when I used to go running, enjoying the empty streets first thing in the morning, the way putting one foot in front of the other seemed to free my mind. I'd invariably arrive at work feeling energised, while my colleagues were still rubbing sleep from their eyes. I hadn't needed to drink so much coffee to stay awake back then, unless I was on a work deadline. 'I've spoken to Dom,' I said. 'He's happy for you to come and help out with Finn.' It sounded better than using the word *nanny*. As if we were on a more equal footing; less like employer and employee.

'That's great, Sophy, you won't regret it.' The words came in a rush, as though she'd been holding her breath. 'I've left Lavender Drive.'

I felt a pinch of alarm. 'Already?'

'Gary tried to grab me when I got back yesterday, then told his wife I'd been coming on to *him*.'

'Liv, that's terrible,' I said, horrified. 'Do you think you should report him?'

'No doubt they'll get what's coming to them. Bad people always do. I believe in Karma.' Her voice was airy, as if they were the least of her problems. 'They're welcome to each other.'

'What about Evie?'

'I do feel bad and I'll really miss her, but maybe instead of going shopping and spending hours in the gym, Clare will spend some time with her little girl.'

'I hope so.' *As if I was qualified to comment on someone else's mothering.*

'Was everything OK yesterday?' Liv said. 'You left the café in such a hurry.'

I hesitated, not wanting to put her off by admitting I hadn't locked the house before going out. 'Just a mother-in-law

emergency.' I tried out a wry laugh. 'Nothing I couldn't handle.'
There was a long pause at the other end. I wondered whether I'd
said the wrong thing. 'So … you can start right away?'

'Whenever you like.'

A surge of something blossomed in my chest – excitement, or
hope maybe. It was the idea of having someone new on my side.
'Tomorrow morning?' I reached for my jar of coffee. I'd been so
busy with Finn I hadn't had one yet. 'We should probably discuss
payment and hours first.' I didn't want her to feel as if I was
somehow superior. At Apex TV, everyone had worked as a team
and that's what Liv and I would be. *Team Finn.*

'Let's play it by ear to start with,' she said, something in her
tone matching my own. It must feel good to not have to worry
about finding another job. 'What sort of time?'

'Nine-thirty?' That would give me time to get up and dressed,
get Finn ready. I tried not to think about Elizabeth's reaction to
me hiring a nanny.

'I'll be there,' Liv said. 'Maybe you could have some time for
yourself while I get to know Finn better. Meet your husband for
lunch. I bet you haven't done that for ages.'

It seemed an alien idea, like flying to France for the day. 'Maybe.'

When she'd rung off, I curled up on the sofa, still in my dressing
gown and sipped my mug of coffee. Watching Finn pull himself
onto his hands and knees, I murmured words of encouragement.
When he beamed, tears filled my eyes. 'Beautiful boy.'

A yawn took hold of me; the morning lethargy setting in.
Determined not to succumb, I unlocked my phone and sent Dom
a message. He kept his mobile close and always replied. Not that
I messaged him often. *How about lunch tomorrow?*

I imagined his look of surprise and wondered how he would
explain it if anyone was looking. *Just my wife. You've probably
forgotten what she looks like.*

Love to, but got meetings all day. He added a sad face and a red
heart emoji. *Talk later. Love you. Kisses to Finn xx*

Disappointment flooded through me. I opened my emails and read the last one from my friend and ex-colleague Isaac, sent a month ago. *Come into London and have lunch, I miss you x*

I'd been avoiding responding, unable to raise the enthusiasm for a trip into the city, not wanting him to see me in such a state. Not stopping to think, I typed, *Still on for lunch? How about tomorrow, 1 p.m?*

He replied straight away: *Who is this?*

Smiling, I typed back, *Your favourite historian.*

In that case, yes, I am. The usual place?

Please x

For a second, I felt lighter, that small contact bringing me back to myself, but tiredness dragged at my edges, pulling me down and I felt powerless to resist.

'It'll be fine,' I said to Finn, through another wide yawn. 'You'll have a nice time with Liv. You might even like her better than Nana.' I gave a sleepy chuckle, even as I acknowledged that Elizabeth wouldn't like that. *Watch Elizabeth.* I wished I hadn't seen that stupid note. I would throw it away later, I decided. Pretend it hadn't happened.

I settled against the cushions, a warmth in my belly that had nothing to do with the coffee I'd drunk. 'Things are going to get better,' I murmured. 'I promise, Finny-baby.'

I'd have a look at some job sites online, once I'd done a bit of housework and put some washing on – see what was out there for someone with my skill set. I'd been stuck in a rut for long enough. It was time to make some changes.

But first, I needed a little doze.

Chapter 15

Liv

A smile crossed my lips as I recalled telling Sophy yesterday that I was on a run. Truth was, I'd simply rushed up the stairs to answer my phone. I don't know why I lied. Maybe I wanted her to think I had a life. But it boded well how easily lies tripped off my tongue.

I pulled my dressing gown tightly around me, and stared out at the jungle of a garden that had once been a haven for Ben and me. Dad had kept it nice back then, a neat lawn with flowering borders. It was small, but enough space for a swing, and a paddling pool in the summer. I wiped away a tear with my fingers. Crying wouldn't help. I needed to stay strong and resolved. I would be inside Sophy's house by half-nine, caring for her child. My plan may not bring Ben or Dad back, it may not make Mum walk again, or even stop Ryan drinking his life away, but it would sure as hell make me feel a whole lot better.

It was almost nine when Freya arrived. She had her own key, and I found her in the hall, hanging up her grey anorak, when I headed downstairs dressed in jeans and a blue sweatshirt, ready to descend on Sophy's world.

'You're here early.' Freya pushed her wayward curls from her face, and smiled as she bent down to slip off her boots.

'I'm going to be living here for a bit.' I grabbed my jacket and shrugged it on. 'Mum's in the conservatory on her laptop.' I decided not to tell her where I was heading. She'd seemed keen that I left Sophy alone. I opened the front door. 'Bye, Mum,' I called. And before Freya could say another word, I dived into the cool air, and closed the door behind me.

'I'm here,' I said, giving a jazz wave when Sophy answered the door, my overly bright behaviour feeling unnatural. Finn was in her arms crying, and she was still in her dressing gown, her eyes red, although from tears, or a restless night, I wasn't sure.

'Hey, little fella,' I said, stepping in and holding my arms out to Finn. He came to me instantly, and Sophy sighed with what sounded like relief. 'Now go have a shower, and get ready to meet your gorgeous husband for lunch,' I said to Sophy. 'I'm guessing he can't wait.'

'Actually—'

'Just go.' I flicked my hand towards her, and laughed, hoping the sound wasn't as false to her ears as it was to mine.

'Are you sure?' she said, as I closed the front door behind me.

'Of course, that's why I'm here, silly.'

She smiled, and I felt a tiny pang of guilt. She did seem helpless. No, pathetic. She had everything, and was still absolutely pathetic.

'I'll make some tea, shall I?' I said.

'I drink coffee – the instant kind, but yes please.'

'Anything for you, your majesty.' I said it lightly, but it was not how I meant it.

'Thanks,' she said, clearly missing my tiny snipe. I needed to be more careful. 'I'll get ready. I'm heading into London.' She sounded excited suddenly, her face brightening.

'That's brilliant.' I jiggled Finn on my hip, as he tugged at my hair. He was a dear little chap, who only seemed to cry when Sophy was holding him. 'We'll go to the park, won't we, Finn?' He beamed up at me, and I wondered for a moment what would happen to him once I'd ruined his mother's life. But then he had Dom, and Sophy hadn't cared about my family when she broke my brother's heart.

Sophy appeared half an hour later dressed in a shapeless green dress that did nothing for her figure, but matched her eyes and made her red hair stand out.

'You look great,' I said. She did. Make-up and a shower had revived her skin, and her eyes looked brighter. I suddenly cursed my poor judgement. Giving her the chance to meet Dom for a romantic lunch maybe wasn't such a good idea.

I deliberately made two mugs of tea out of spite, knowing Sophy would be too polite to decline it or insist it should have been coffee, and I was right.

She took one sip, before looking at her watch, and placing the mug on the breakfast bar. 'Let me show you where everything is. I've jotted down Finn's routine, which Elizabeth insists I stick to.' Something crossed her face, a flicker of doubt, and I wondered if she was thinking about the note. Had she shown it to Dom? I felt sure he wouldn't like it if Sophy started doubting his mother. 'Though he's pretty flexible,' Sophy continued. 'He has to be as I'm not very organised.'

Once she'd showed me round, and we were standing in the lounge, she took a deep breath. 'Right, I'd better go, I'm catching the 10.45 to St Pancras, and it's a good twenty-minute walk to the station.' She grabbed her bag, and shoved her phone inside.

'OK, well have fun then.' I looked at Finn straddled on my hip. 'We will won't we, sweetie?'

She kissed Finn's head. 'I feel so guilty leaving him,' she said, touching his cheek. 'Are you really sure this is OK?'

'Just go,' I said, with a laugh that sounded more natural this time. *For God's sake, just go.*

'Thanks, Liv.' Her smile reappeared. 'I so appreciate it.'

'Don't be silly. I'm working for you, don't forget.' I followed her into the hall, where she slipped on her coat. 'Whereabouts are you heading?'

She furrowed her forehead. 'A little Italian restaurant on Prebend Street in Islington.'

'Lovely,' I said, as she left.

As the door closed, I looked down at Finn in my arms, and back up towards the staircase. I couldn't wait to explore the house.

I made my way into the lounge and put Finn in his playpen. And, after a moment, he stopped staring up at me with wide eyes, and picked up one of his exploration blocks and shook it in his little fist, making gurgling noises. I looked about me. This house was so quiet, too big, so I picked up the remote controls and turned on the TV, and quickly searched for kid's programmes, finding *Octonauts*, which grabbed Finn's attention.

Photographs of Finn, and one of Sophy and Dom's wedding day, lined the high mantelpiece, and a professional picture of them all when Finn looked to be about three months old, hung on the wall near the door. I headed towards it, placed my index finger on Dom's face, and moved it slowly down his cheek. He reminded me of an actor in *Grey's Anatomy*, though I knew it wasn't just about looks for Sophy. He seemed the caring type – the opposite of Gary. 'She doesn't deserve you,' I whispered.

Finn was so engrossed in the bright colours on the TV, I left the room, and headed into the kitchen, where I made myself another cup of tea, before climbing the stairs. I knew which room was Sophy and Dom's, from when I took her necklace.

The curtains were pulled back, and the brightness of the day lightened the room. The door of the en suite stood open. I made my way towards the dressing table, and put down my mug. Sophy didn't seem to have a lot of make-up, unless she'd got it tucked away somewhere, but there was a bottle of Coco Chanel, that looked barely used. I sprayed it on my wrists and neck, before opening a drawer, looking for some sign of Ben and Sophy's relationship, wondering if there might be an old photograph, at least, tucked away somewhere – or had Sophy been so heartless she'd scrubbed everything about him from her life and memory, not wanting any reminder of her part in his death?

Inside was an array of fancy scarves in various colours. *Who the hell needed so many?* I closed a drawer, and made my way to what was clearly Sophy's side of the bed. A framed photo of her with Finn was on the cabinet, along with a paperback and a glass of water. I opened the drawer to find a diary with no entries, and a couple of photos that seemed to be of Sophy when she was much younger with her mother, and an older woman, a grandmother, perhaps. I closed the drawer and rose once more.

A cream cashmere jumper hung on the front of the wardrobe. I picked up the sleeve and rubbed it against my face. I couldn't recall ever owning something so soft. I picked up my mug, and dipped my fingers in it, and with a wicked smile, splashed tea over the front of it. 'Oh dear, Sophy, how did you manage to get tea all over your best jumper? What will Dom think?'

Sophy's dressing gown was draped across the foot of the bed. I picked it up and rummaged in the pockets, and smiled as my hand touched a crumpled piece of paper. I pulled it out, and flattened the note. *Watch Elizabeth.* I shoved it in my pocket, and was about to carry on snooping, when the landline phone rang. I dashed downstairs and picked it up. 'Hello?' I smiled down at Finn, who was now sucking a rattle.

'Who's that?'

'It's Liv.'

'Oh. Right. It's Dom. Can I have a word with Sophy?'

'She's not here right now. I thought she was with you. She's just left for London.'

'Did she seem OK?' He sounded anxious.

'Fine.'

'And she's left Finn with you?'

'Yes. Hang on.' I placed the phone next to Finn. 'Say hello to Daddy.' Finn smiled, gurgled, and turned his head away. 'Sorry,

Dom.' I pinned the phone to my ear once more. 'That's all you're going to get, I'm afraid.'

'He's not much of a talker. Is he behaving himself?'

'He's as good as gold.'

'That's what my mum always says.' He paused. 'Anyway, I'd better go. I've got meetings all day, and need to make a call.'

The line went dead, and as I hung up the receiver, I knew exactly what I needed to do. 'Right,' I said to Finn. 'We're going to take a trip to London, my little friend, to see what your mummy's up to.'

I headed through Islington, checking in the windows of every Italian restaurant, pushing a sleeping Finn in his buggy, finally spotting Sophy at the back of a pretty place, with hanging baskets outside, and a red and white chequered awning. She was sitting opposite a man wearing glasses and a burgundy polo shirt, with curly, dark hair. It was clear she liked him. Her smile was so natural. I stood outside for some time, staring in, mesmerised by the couple, before pulling out my phone.

I brought up my camera, knowing I'd found, quite by chance, the perfect way to ruin Sophy's life.

Chapter 16

Sophy

'I miss you.' Isaac filled my glass from a bottle of sparkling water before digging into an enormous plate of pasta. Behind his thick-rimmed glasses, his dark eyes were sincere and I realised how much I'd missed him too. 'I still can't believe you're not coming back to Apex.'

'I might have, if I hadn't been replaced,' I said, raising my voice above a burst of laughter from a nearby table. Our favourite lunch spot, Luigi's, was even busier than I remembered. Colours, scents and sounds seemed heightened, as though I'd been living underground for months. 'How's Harriet working out?'

'She's fine, but it's not the same.'

I knew he was just being kind; that my successor was lovely and good at her job – we'd worked together briefly – but Isaac and I had made a good team. We clicked from the moment we started working together on *Back in Time*, bonding in a brother-and-sister way that made going into work every day a pleasure. He was tall and solid with dark, curly hair and a love of plaid shirts that gave him the air of a lumberjack. He was also utterly obsessed with history. When he introduced his girlfriend, she joked he'd only asked her out because her name was Anne, like his favourite monarch.

'I'm thinking of looking for a new job,' I said, pushing my salad around my plate, butterflies in my stomach making it hard to eat. I kept thinking how upset Elizabeth would be that I hadn't left Finn with her, knowing she'd have loved the opportunity to have him to herself for a few hours. 'Something closer to home,' I added. *Home.* It used to be the little house in Stevenage with Mum, then a flat-share in London when I was offered the job with Apex after a work placement there, and then the apartment with Dom. I still didn't think of The Avenue as my home, despite spending every day there for the past three months.

'What sort of job?'

'Maybe retrain as a history teacher.'

Isaac screwed up his nose, his mouth turned down.

'What?'

'The history part's fine, but there'll be pupils involved, probably bored and more interested in their phones?'

'It would be my job to make them interested.' He had a point, though. It was the research element I loved, not so much dealing with other people, particularly young, impressionable people from a position of authority. The idea was suddenly ridiculous. 'Maybe not,' I said.

'If you really want a job, I could put some work your way.' Isaac expertly twirled linguine round his fork. 'We're working on a new programme for next year, a quiz show for history buffs. We need someone to write and research the questions.'

'Isaac, that would be great.' Suddenly, it felt as if a window had opened in my mind, letting in fresh air. 'Would you have mentioned this if I hadn't replied to your email?'

His gaze dipped to his plate. 'I mentioned it to Dom, but he said he thought it was too soon, that you were still struggling a bit since ... you know.'

Flushing, I recalled Isaac and Anne coming to visit me in hospital before I was discharged – their thinly veiled shock that rather than a tired but glowing new mum, cradling her newborn, they were greeted by a vision of white-faced, lank-haired apathy with painful stitches, too exhausted to sit up and greet them properly while Dom paced with the baby, who we hadn't yet named as I'd been sure I was having a girl.

'I think he was worried it would be too much pressure right now.'

My flush deepened. I'd known in an abstract way that as Dom still went to work every day, he was bound to see my ex colleagues and that they would ask about me, perhaps talk about me, but it hadn't really made an impact. Now, I wondered what on earth he'd been saying. Dom liked Isaac and I knew he was looking out for me, but I wanted to make my own decisions. Maybe having something besides Finn to focus on would make me feel better and more alert. 'I think I can cope,' I said, keeping my tone light. 'I'd love to give it a go.'

'Sure?' Isaac gave me a frank look. 'Dom said you're exhausted all the time and to be honest, you do look tired.'

'Thanks for that.' I'd looked a bit clownish in make-up so had swiped it off and made do with mascara and lip gloss, before pulling on an olive-green dress that skimmed my stomach, but I clearly looked different to the version of me Isaac was used to. Namely, someone who didn't think much about what she wore, but was better put together and generally smiling. 'This is me on a good day,' I said.

I'd been on a high, leaving the house after showing Liv around, making sure she knew Finn's routine and where everything was with a promise to call if anything cropped up, but now my spirits were drooping. Maybe I shouldn't have come. Dom didn't even know where I was. *What had I been thinking?* I'd left our son with a virtual stranger to have lunch in London after barely setting foot outside for months.

'You've probably got the new-mum blues,' Isaac said, eliciting a puff of laughter from me.

'I took some tablets for that. If anything, they made me feel worse.'

'Maybe you should go back to your doctor.'

'That's what Dom says.' I took a sip of water. 'I'm taking a course of vitamins, which are starting to kick in.' It was true that I felt less tired than I had in a while, though that might have been due to me dozing on the train, lulled by the rhythmic rocking of the carriage.

'Thirty per cent of new mothers can have postnatal depression for up to a year after giving birth.'

Pushing aside my misgivings, I grinned and grabbed my napkin. Reaching over, I dabbed spaghetti sauce off his chin before scooping a forkful of his lunch into my mouth. 'Have you been reading parenting websites?'

He gave a bashful smile, nudging his glasses further up on his nose. 'Maybe,' he said. 'I got worried when you didn't reply to any of my texts.'

Momentarily distracted by a figure hurrying past the restaurant, shoulders hunched inside a black coat, it took a second for his words to sink in. 'Texts?' I pulled my head back. 'I haven't had any texts from you, just that email,' I said. 'I'm sorry I didn't reply.' I ate some more of my salad, suddenly starving. 'I'm a terrible friend.'

Putting his fork down, Isaac leant back and rootled his phone out of his jeans pocket and jabbed the screen. 'See?' He twisted his wrist so I could see a list of sent messages on the screen – to me. 'Nothing major.' He put his phone on the table with a little shrug. 'Just checking how you were doing because you weren't answering calls and I didn't want to disturb you.'

'You made one call since we moved, which I answered,' I said, still puzzling over the texts. 'You rang the landline and asked how I was enjoying life in suburbia.'

'I rang another time, but your mother-in-law said you wanted to be left alone.'

I stared. 'She never even told me you'd called.' Or had she and I'd forgotten? Those early days at The Avenue had blurred into each other – I'd spent a lot of time in our bedroom and the newly decorated nursery, which Natasha had worked on before we moved in – not that they'd got much better. 'She must have forgotten.' The note bobbed into my mind and I pushed it down. I wasn't going to start doubting Elizabeth's intentions because someone had an axe to grind.

'At least she's got your back,' said Isaac, echoing my thoughts. I remembered he'd met my mother-in-law at our wedding, where she'd gone out of her way to be charming to everyone, and I hated that the note was putting ridiculous thoughts into my head. 'I decided texting would be better and when you didn't reply resorted to emailing.'

'I thought it was a bit odd,' I admitted. 'But I definitely didn't get any texts.' Unless I'd deleted them without reading in one of my befuddled states. I hadn't replied to a couple of WhatsApp messages from Mum, now I thought about it, but when she called me I'd looked to check and they were there – I'd just forgotten about them.

'Anyway, I'm here now, so tell me what's been going on since I left.'

For the next fifteen minutes, I felt almost normal as Isaac filled me in on the comings and goings at the TV station: who'd been promoted, who'd left, a proposed strike as a protest against pay cuts. Dom must surely be involved in that. He hadn't told me about it. Or perhaps he had and I wasn't listening properly.

I was finishing my lunch when my phone rang.

'Sorry,' I said to Isaac, interrupting him midway through telling me about the latest *Back in Time* episode he was working on, featuring Thomas Cromwell who was 'one of the most corrupt ministers to ever hold power in England'.

'Sophy, where are you?'

I felt an odd sense of déjà vu at the sound of Dom's voice, asking the exact same question he had when I was with Liv at The Busy Bean.

'In Luigi's with Isaac,' I said. 'Come and join us if you like.'

'Why didn't you tell me you were going out?'

'I ... I forgot.' My smile faded. 'When you said you weren't free, I asked Isaac to meet me instead.'

There was a moment's pause as he absorbed this information. 'Have you heard from Liv?'

'Liv?' My heart turned over. 'No, why?'

'She's not at home.'

I let out my breath, aware of Isaac's concerned gaze. 'She was taking Finn to the park.' A thought struck. 'How do you know she's not at home?'

I knew what the answer would be before he said it. 'Mum popped round to the house to see if everything was OK.'

Something tightened inside my chest. 'Did you ask her to check up on me?'

'They're not at the park,' he said, ignoring my question. 'Mum said she saw them heading to the station.'

'She *followed* them?'

'Why would Liv be going to the station?'

His words cut through my flare of anxiety. Why *was* Liv going to the station? 'I don't know,' I admitted, my pulse beginning to race. 'I'll call her.'

'Ring me straight back.'

'What's going on?' Isaac's face was creased with alarm.

'It's the nanny I told you about.' I pressed in Liv's number and jammed my phone to my ear.

'Sophy, hi—'

'Where are you?' I said sharply.

'What do you mean?'

'My ... someone saw you going to the station.'

'Oh, right.' She exhaled a small laugh. 'Well, Finn wouldn't stop crying and I remembered that if Evie was upset, she always settled down if we went on the train. Not very far, just a stop or two. I thought it might work for Finn.'

Relief mingled with something else. 'Did it?'

'Sorry?'

'Did it work?'

'It did.' Her tone became jolly. 'You loved it, didn't you, Finny?' I imagined her bouncing my baby, beaming down at him, his eyes shining up at her. 'He went very quiet and we looked out of the window for a while and then he became sleepy so I put him back in his pushchair. He's been as quiet as a mouse ever since.'

Envy coursed through my veins at the thought of my baby having a new experience without me, even though getting on a train with him would never have occurred to me. 'That's great, Liv.' My tone was cool. 'I just wish you'd asked me first if it was OK.'

There was a brief silence at the other end of the line. 'I'm sorry.' Her voice was subdued. 'I suppose it was second nature. I wanted to make him feel better and ...' She sounded close to crying. 'I'm so sorry, Sophy.'

I immediately felt bad. 'No, no, it's fine. I'm sorry.' I caught a frown from Isaac and tried to smile. 'I'm glad Finn's OK. It's hard when he cries all the time.'

'He really is happy. I'll send you a picture.'

'That would be lovely,' I said, feeling silly.

'He phoned to see where you were.'

'Sorry?'

'Dom,' Liv said carefully. 'It sounded as if he didn't know you were going out.'

I swallowed, feeling my face heat up. 'It was a misunderstanding, that's all.' *What must she think of me?* 'Listen, Liv, I'd like you to meet him. You don't have to rush off later, do you?'

'Of course not,' she said without hesitating. 'I was going to suggest it anyway. It'll be good to meet Finn's daddy.'

'I'll see you soon.'

'No rush.'

I ended the call and stared at my phone for a few seconds, jumping when it alerted me to a message. Liv had snapped a photo of Finn in his woolly hat with the teddy-bear ears, his head cocked to one side. His cheeks were pink, his eyes bright, mouth curved into a smile. *He was smiling for her.* Tears rose. All of a sudden, everything felt wrong. I wanted to be with my baby. Liv had said she wanted to get to know Finn. Well, *I* wanted to get to know him. I could hardly do that when I wasn't even there.

'Everything all right?' Isaac asked, putting down his empty glass once I'd called Dom to tell him Finn and Liv were fine and that I was about to head home.

'I shouldn't have come.' I picked up my bag, fighting the tears back. 'I've never left Finn before. I'm a terrible mother.'

'Of course you're not.' Isaac looked shocked at my outburst. 'It's been nine months, Sophy. You're allowed to have a couple of hours to yourself.'

'But even when I'm there, I'm not really *there*.' I thrust my hair back with a shaking hand. I was too hot, the restaurant too loud, the smell of food overwhelming. 'I have to do better. I *was* getting better before we moved out of London, but now I'm worse.' I thought again of the note about Elizabeth, shoved in my dressing gown pocket at home, and nearly told him just how bad things had been, but Isaac was pulling his credit card out and waving the waiter over.

'Don't be so hard on yourself,' he said. 'Look, I'll get this and then walk you to the station.'

'No, I'll be fine. You should get back to work.' I pushed my arms into my coat and stood, sick and dizzy with the need to escape. 'It was good to see you.'

'I'll be in touch,' he called after me as I weaved between tables on rubbery legs towards the exit, not caring that several diners were staring, probably thinking Isaac was my boyfriend and we'd had an argument.

All I cared about was getting home to my son.

Chapter 17

Liv

I'd been caught out. Chastised like a naughty child, by Sophy. And even forty-five minutes later, as I sat in the park, under a grey sky, a bitter wind blasting my cheeks, trying to calm down, I couldn't pop the anger bubbles rising inside me.

Finn had fallen asleep in my arms on the train back from London. And even when I'd moved him to his buggy at St Albans' Station, he'd barely stirred. He was such a good little boy. Sophy didn't deserve him.

Now, I opened my phone and stared at the photo I'd taken of Sophy and her *friend* laughing as they'd enjoyed their meal. Though I wasn't totally convinced she was having an affair. It didn't fit with someone who could barely keep awake. Where would she find the energy for a start? But even if they weren't having an affair, surely this photo would cast doubts in Dom's mind. I would print a copy at Mum's later. Post it through the door with another note. No smoke without fire, as they say.

'Hello, Olivia.' It was Kim. I hadn't seen her approach, or I'd have scarpered. But she was already sitting beside me, lifting Dougie from his sling. She stood him on her ample knee, and

111

gripped his hands. I had to hand it to the little fella, he was the happiest baby I'd ever seen, and Kim clearly adored him – I could see the love in her eyes. 'No Evie today?'

I shook my head, deciding not to fill her in on the gory details of how I'd left Clare and Gary's. 'This is Finn.'

'I know exactly who this little cutie is,' she said, releasing one of Dougie's hands, and leaning forward to tickle Finn's cheek. 'I saw him with Sophy at the mums' group, and Elizabeth brings him to the park regularly. Talk about a doting grandmother – she's amazing with him, and a lovely woman too.' She grabbed Dougie's free hand and bounced her knees, singing a song I didn't recognise about a farmer heading to market. 'I have a lot in common with Elizabeth, actually,' she said, coming to the end of a verse. 'We've both lost babies.' Her eyes glazed over quite suddenly. 'Her son Christopher died of a heart defect, and my little one died of the same thing.'

'Oh, Kim.' Shocked out of my impatience to get away, I touched her arm. 'I'm so sorry.'

'Thank you.' She stared ahead for a moment, before swallowing hard and fumbling a tissue from her bag. 'It was five years ago, but you never get over something like that.'

'No, time is pretty crap at healing, isn't it?'

She dabbed her eyes, looked my way, and smiled, the tip of her nose bright red. 'But I have Dougie.' She tickled his chubby middle, and blew a raspberry on his neck. He shrieked with laughter. 'I don't know what I'd do without him.'

'He's such a sweetie,' I said, and I meant it. 'He's always so happy. So lively.'

She nodded. 'I know. Would you believe he hasn't slept during the day since he was six months old? I mustn't complain though. It's more time I can spend with him. And he sleeps like a baby at night …' She laughed. 'Oh my word, did you hear what I said then?' She blew another raspberry on his neck then bounced him up and down.

A break in the grey clouds lightened the sky, as my phone rumbled in my pocket. I pulled it out. It was a message from Sophy. *Where are you?*

She was back. Time had got away from me.

'I should go.' As I rose, I noticed Clare approaching, pushing a sleeping Evie in her pushchair. I'd never seen the woman without her heels and make-up. She looked different, natural. I looked at Evie asleep, and felt a surge of guilt and sadness that I'd abandoned her.

'So you've found yourself another baby to look after.' Clare's face was red, her eyes blazing. 'Another husband to come on to?'

Kim and Dougie stared at me. She was obviously waiting for me to explain, but I couldn't face it.

'Bye, Kim,' I said, deciding not to get into a row with Clare. I had enough on my mind right now.

'Oh that's right,' Clare yelled after me. 'Just run away. Evie's definitely better off without you. You're a bloody useless nanny.'

I clenched my hands around the handles of the buggy, biting back the words I wanted to say, finally turning the corner. Relieved her nasty words were fading into the distance.

'Where have you been?' Sophy cried, grabbing Finn from his pushchair and squeezing him to her. He yelled, and held out his arms to me.

'Just to the park,' I said. 'I came back as soon as I got your message. I didn't know you would return so soon. You didn't say.'

'No. No, sorry. I'm just so … I'm sorry. Here take him.' She shoved the screaming child at me. 'I'll make some coffee. Do you want one?'

I shook my head, as I followed her into the kitchen, and she handed Finn back to me.

'So did you have a nice time in London with Dom?' I asked.

'No, I mean yes.' She began banging around the kitchen like an angry TV chef, grabbing a mug and spoon, red-faced, and close to tears. 'I didn't meet Dom in the end; he had meetings all day, so couldn't make it. I arranged to catch up with a friend I used to work with.'

Finn stopped crying, and I put him into his highchair and handed him his toy cat. 'Was it a good catch-up?'

'What?' She looked at the giant clock on the wall. It was five o'clock. 'Dom will be home soon,' she said. 'Can you hang on? I want you to meet him. I did mention that didn't I?' She was nowhere near close to making a drink. Hadn't even filled the kettle.

'I'm looking forward to it.'

The front door opened, and within moments Dom was standing in the doorway, loosening his tie, and unbuttoning the top button of his white shirt. 'God the train was packed,' he said. He smiled at me as he bent to kiss Finn's hair, then headed towards the fridge, opened the door and grabbed a bottle of white wine. 'You must be Liv,' he said, staring at me as he poured a glass – not offering one to Sophy, or to me, come to that.

'I am indeed.' I returned the smile, and held his gaze just for a moment.

He turned to his wife. 'So was London OK?' he said. 'Sorry for earlier, I just worry about you and Finn. You know that.'

She nodded, but didn't offer any more, and an awkward silence fell.

'Shall we sit down?' Dom said, after taking a couple of gulps of his wine.

The three of us made our way to the kitchen table, and sat down. 'It's good to finally meet you, Liv,' Dom said. 'Sophy told me what happened with Gary.'

I swallowed, feeling exposed.

'Have you been working as a nanny long?' he went on, when I didn't say anything.

'Not long, but I have qualifications, and I've had a DBS check, plus I'm up to date with my first aid. I can let you see all the documents.'

114

'That's great,' he said. 'Sophy's told me you're good with children.' He took another swallow of wine, his gaze not leaving my face. 'Where were you before you ended up at the Wilsons?'

It took me a moment to realise he meant Gary and Clare.

'Evie was my first nanny position in a home.'

'So what other jobs have you had?'

'I worked for a time in a nursery.'

'Could we get a reference?'

I couldn't tell them my boss hated me. It wouldn't go down well. 'They went out of business,' I lied. 'Before I studied to be a nanny, I had lots of different jobs. I've worked in Sainsbury's in Stevenage, a couple of waitress jobs – Prezzos and The Copper Kettle in Stevenage Old Town. I'm sure I can get some sort of reference.'

'Dom, she's brilliant with him.' Sophy placed her hand on his, and their eyes met. 'He never cries when he's with her.'

'He never cries when he's with my mum either.' He gave a small smile, as if to take the sting out of his words. 'Nothing personal,' he added, returning his gaze to me, but I sensed a rising tension between them.

'Listen, shall we give it a trial?' I said. 'See how it goes. Maybe for the first month or so I can just be here in the house with Sophy, and she can get on with what she wants to do – maybe even get a job working from home, while I care for Finn.' That would give me time to prove to them that I was the perfect nanny.

'I like the sound of that,' Sophy said, her eyes on her husband. 'Dom?'

'OK, a month's trial it is,' he said, and knocked back his wine in one.

It was gone six by the time I got back to Mum's, and as I opened the front door to my old childhood home I heard laughter trickling from inside, the TV blaring out. For a moment I was a kid again, when everything was perfect: my parents watching *Inspector*

Morse, Ben playing on his PlayStation, the rich smell of baking from the kitchen, and our old dog, Molly, chasing her tail and barking at nothing.

In the lounge Mum and Freya sat one each end of the sofa, Sparky curled up between them, as they watched *Mrs Brown's Boys*.

Mum looked up as I entered, her cheeks red from laughing. 'It's *Mrs Brown's Boys*, Liv,' she said. 'Your favourite.'

I shook my head. It wasn't my favourite, but I decided to keep quiet as I flopped down in the armchair, exhausted, just as the programme ended. Mum pointed the remote at the TV, and muted the sound. 'So how was your first day?'

'Good.' I glanced at Freya, knowing she would ask questions. And I was right.

'You've changed jobs then?'

'Yep.'

'So you're not with little Evie anymore?'

'Liv is working for Sophy Edwards,' Mum said.

Freya narrowed her eyes. 'Please tell me you're not still planning some sort of revenge.'

I shrugged. 'Pretty sure Sophy and Dom will destroy themselves without any help from me,' I said. 'He's a bit too wrapped up in his job, and as I said before, Sophy is always falling asleep and is pretty useless with Finn – that's the little boy. He cries at the bloody sight of her.'

'Why is that do you think?' Freya tilted her head like a counsellor.

I shrugged again. 'Kids get a vibe don't they? Can sense when someone isn't coping.'

'Well Ben used to cry a lot when he was a baby,' Mum chirped in. 'And I was a brilliant mum.'

'You still are.' I smiled. 'Listen, is the printer working?' I remembered the photo on my phone, and wanted to get away from the conversation.

'Yes, fresh ink yesterday.' Mum pointed the remote at the

TV, and turned it up as another episode of *Mrs Brown's Boys* started.

I got up, and headed into the conservatory where Mum's computer was, and sent the photo of Sophy and her *friend* to the hard drive.

'Who's that?' It was Freya coming up behind me, as the photo printed.

I picked up the photo. 'Sophy Edwards.'

'She's very pretty. I can see why Ben fell in love with her.'

Her words stung. 'She had lunch with this man today, while I looked after Finn. I think she could be having an affair.' I folded the page. 'How's Mum been today?' I said before she could comment.

Freya's face brightened. 'We've had a lovely day. We went down to the river and fed the ducks.' She turned, then spun back round. 'Oh, I've just remembered, you had a visitor earlier.'

'Who?'

'Ryan, the man you were with the other lunchtime.'

'Really?' For some reason, my heart leapt.

She nodded. 'He was looking for you. Said he wouldn't come in and disturb your mum, but could I pass on a message – something about needing to tell you something about Sophy. Said he'd got no money on his phone, so could you call him.' She paused. 'He seemed a bit drunk, to be honest. Staggered as he left.'

My shoulders slumped. 'He's got a bit of a drink problem. It breaks my heart.'

'I thought so.' Freya shook her head.

I shut down Mum's computer and turned to leave. 'I'll give him a call now.'

'Yes, and I should make a move.' Freya made her way towards the door. 'There's a small casserole in the oven, enough for you and your mum. It should be ready to eat in about ten minutes.'

'That's very kind,' I said following. 'But please don't think you have to look after me too. I can always grab a burger.'

'It's no trouble at all – I like looking after you.'

Freya disappeared into the lounge to say goodbye to Mum, and I took the stairs two at time, pulling out my phone.

'Ryan,' I said, when he picked up. I entered my bedroom and closed the door behind me.

'Liv?'

'You wanted to talk to me?' I flopped onto the bed.

'I did.' Silence.

'Ryan? Are you OK?'

'I may have had a drink. Or two.' Silence.

'You told Freya that you wanted to tell me something about Sophy?'

'Sophy. Sophy Edwards. She's not who she seems.' His voice was a slur. 'There are things you don't know about Sophy, Liv. Things I need to tell you ...'

'What sort of things, Ryan?'

'Not right now. I'm so tired. So, so tired.'

'Ryan? Ryan are you OK?'

But the line had gone dead.

Chapter 18

Sophy

'How long have you been feeling this exhaustion?'

'A few weeks, I suppose.' I tried to hold the doctor's gaze, the instinct to downplay my symptoms overriding the urge to confide in her.

'And do you feel it's more than the tiredness of having a baby to look after?' She flashed a glance at her computer screen but I knew there wasn't much to see, other than what she'd just typed in. I'd joined the surgery soon after moving to The Avenue at Dom's insistence, but this was my first visit. While checking my blood pressure, Dr Crawford had explained they hadn't yet got access to my medical records. Not that they made very interesting reading. Before having Finn, I'd rarely needed to see a doctor once I'd left childhood behind and even then – apart from a badly sprained ankle and a bout of tonsillitis – I'd been healthy.

'I don't really know, never having been a mum before.' I attempted a smile that made my cheeks ache. 'I'm sure that's all it is. Too many sleepless nights, baby teething, that sort of thing.'

Dr Crawford winced in sympathy. There was a gold-framed photo on her desk of two little girls in school uniform with matching smiles and the same, thick dark hair and olive skin as the doctor. 'I can relate to that,' she said. 'You said your husband is concerned?'

I nodded, wishing it didn't sound so serious. By telling her, I'd hoped to convey I was there just to put his mind at rest, not because there was something to be concerned about. 'He thought I should get checked out.'

I recalled the way he'd looked at me yesterday, after Liv had gone home, her eyes lowered so I couldn't read her expression. I'd unexpectedly burst into tears, upset that Finn had rebuffed me after I rushed home, worried Dom was secretly annoyed that I'd chosen to employ a stranger instead of asking Elizabeth to help out, and cross that I'd taken off to London to have lunch with Isaac.

He'd looked at me, a nerve twitching under his eye; a sign of tiredness. 'You have to go to the doctor's,' he'd said, putting down his wine glass. 'I'm worried about you.'

'So you keep saying.'

'You're not ready to be going out, never mind having lunch with friends in London.'

I'd rounded on him. 'By friends, you mean, Isaac.' It was a low blow. Dom had struggled initially with how well I got on with Isaac, certain he felt more for me than friendship, until Anne came on the scene, but he'd done his best to hide it – to not be the sort of man who was suspicious that his wife's best friend was a man. To his credit, he hadn't responded to my barb, just rubbed the space between his eyebrows with his fingertips. 'Fine, I'll go to the doctor's tomorrow,' I said, wiping my face with the back of my hand.

His expression had softened. 'Tell her everything.' He came round the kitchen counter and rested his hands on my shoulders, eyes probing mine as if looking for the real me – the one he married. 'I'll come with you if you like?'

In his highchair, Finn had made a noise that sounded like

agreement, but I shook my head. 'I'll be fine. Liv can come and watch Finn.'

She was in the waiting room now, entertaining Finn, whose face had lit up earlier at the sight of her. Dom had just left for work, clutching a white envelope he'd picked up from the doormat, pulling the car onto the road with a screech of tyres seconds before Liv arrived.

She was clearly curious about why I was going to the doctor's, but hadn't probed when I told her it was a routine check-up.

'... in touch with your health visitor,' the doctor was saying as I tuned back in. 'Was everything fine at your last postnatal check-up?'

I nodded, recalling the woman who turned up at the flat for a fortnight after Finn was born and how I'd felt compelled to pretend I was coping, in case she reported me, despite her assertion that it was normal to feel 'a bit shell-shocked' after my emergency C-section, blood loss and transfusion. *You had a terrible ordeal, Sophy. Don't be afraid to ask for help.*

Not that I was going to tell Dr Crawford about that, or that I'd been prescribed a course of anti-depressants. It was ridiculous to hold back, because she'd find out once she had my medical records, but for now, I wanted to be someone without all that history.

'We'll do some blood tests,' she said. 'You could be anaemic, or have an underactive thyroid, which is common after giving birth, and your blood pressure's a bit low.' She paused. 'Anything else?' Her eyes were kind and tears blocked my throat. 'Plenty of help at home?'

I nodded, forcing my jaw to relax and my fingers to stop plucking at the cuff of my jumper. 'I've just taken on a nanny and my mother-in-law's not far away.'

'Well, that's good.' As if sensing she wasn't going to get anything else out of me, the doctor made a call to the practice nurse and gave me a form. 'She'll do your bloods now.' Her eyes lingered on my face as I stood up, knocking my bag on the floor. 'We should have the results in a week, but if there's anything else in the meantime don't hesitate to come in.'

The blood test was over quickly and Liv suggested we cut through the park on the way back. I was grateful she didn't ask any questions after giving me an inquisitive look when I came out of the consulting room. 'We can get a hot drink at the stall there,' she said.

She seemed on edge, walking too fast. I longed to take the pushchair handle but couldn't think how to do it without seeming rude, so I trotted alongside, hands swinging uselessly by my sides. As the sun dipped behind heavy clouds, I had the crawling sensation I'd had before, on the odd occasion I'd ventured out, of being followed. Glancing over my shoulder, I saw a man some distance behind on the path, shoulders hunched, hands dug deep in his coat pockets. He slowed his pace and bolted his gaze to the trees at the edge of the park. A small dog bounded towards him, and when he bent to pat its head, I let out a breath. My mind was all over the place. Having a baby really had clouded my senses if I thought I was being stalked, as well as seeing people in the street I thought I knew.

Maybe you do need help. The voice in my head sounded a lot like my mum's and I suddenly wanted to see her so much, I felt an ache in my chest.

'What's wrong?' Liv had stopped.

I realised I was motionless, staring into the distance. 'Nothing, just—'

'Oh, isn't he a sweetheart?' An elderly woman with a bird's nest of white hair had paused to peer at Finn, nostalgia written all over her weathered face. 'He's the spit of my William at that age.' She gave Liv a gap-toothed smile. 'You're a lucky woman,' she said, before moving on with dainty steps, pulling a tartan shopping trolley behind her.

'Thank you!' Liv called after her, smiling as though Finn was actually hers.

My mouth had fallen open, ready to form a protest, but nothing came out except my breath, misting the air in front of me. I shivered, huddling deeper into my coat, something close to hysteria threatening to bubble over. 'I'd like to go home.' I sounded hostile.

Liv turned, as if startled at my tone. 'Sure, let's go.' She turned the pushchair, bumping over the grass verging the narrow path. 'Come on, I'll race you!'

'What?' Confused, I watched as she took off, hair swinging, heels kicking up as she headed through the park gates, steering the pushchair like a dodgem car.

'Wait!'

I hurried after her, weaving through a throng of schoolchildren clutching clipboards and pens, being assembled by a couple of harassed-looking teachers.

'I'm not the runner I used to be,' I said, panting as I caught up with Liv on the pavement, trying to make a joke of her sudden dash while I bent to check on Finn. He was fast asleep, eyelids fluttering with dreams, his lips slightly parted. 'Shall I take over?'

'It's OK, we're almost there now.'

Tightening her grip on the buggy, Liv fixed her eyes on the street ahead with an almost defiant tilt to her jaw. I hoped I hadn't upset her. Coming from a difficult situation with Evie's parents, the last thing I wanted was for her to think we were just as bad.

'We'll have a drink at home,' I said, lengthening my stride. 'Hot chocolate if you like, and I'll tell you about the time I bumped into Jude Law at the television centre.'

She threw me a half-hearted smile. *Maybe she wasn't a fan.*

'Sounds good,' she said, looking over her shoulder as we crossed the road leading to The Avenue. 'Was ... was Dom OK this morning?'

I suddenly thought I understood why she was jumpy. She was worried that after meeting Dom yesterday, we might have changed our minds about letting her help with Finn.

'Oh, he was fine.' I recalled how he'd thrown himself into the car earlier; how he hadn't said goodbye before driving off, or made me coffee. Was he fine? He'd said he was happy for me to do what I thought was best, but something felt off. 'Honestly, Liv, don't worry about him,' I said, with a confidence I didn't feel. Liv didn't look reassured. A nerve jumped in her temple, and she looked like she was grinding her teeth, but before I could say something convincing, I noticed a car parked outside our house. For a second, I thought it was Elizabeth's black Range Rover, but as we drew closer, a woman who clearly wasn't my mother-in-law stepped out of the driving seat.

'Sophy Pemberton?' She slammed the car door and adjusted the leather bag thrown across her body. Despite her duffel coat and hand-knitted Dr Who style scarf, she had an officious air that sent a sick swipe through my stomach.

'I'm Sophy Pemberton,' I said, realising she'd looked automatically at Liv. 'Who are you?'

She fished out an identification tag and handed it over. *Tess Bowman.* The photo was clearly the round-faced woman in front of me, though her greying curls were covered by a crimson beret. There was a number on the tag that I didn't take in as my breathing grew shallow, my vision blurring on the words written above. I was aware of Liv frozen beside me, her knuckles white around the handle of the pushchair, and the sense that behind all the windows of the houses on the street, eyes were peering at me.

'As you can see, Mrs Pemberton, I'm from social services.' Tess's eyes were pale and inquiring, her cheeks crimson with broken veins. 'Can we talk inside?' She nodded towards the house. 'We've had a report about a child being neglected at this property.'

Chapter 19

Sophy

Once inside the house, Tess turned in the doorway to watch Liv's departure. 'Friend?'

'Nanny, actually.' I lifted Finn from his pushchair, hoping Tess couldn't see my hands shaking.

'You have a nanny?' She sounded surprised. The news clearly hadn't fitted with whatever she'd expected to find: a baby at home alone, surrounded by squalor while the parents were out drinking, perhaps. 'She doesn't live in?'

'No.' I strived to keep my tone even. It was important to give the illusion I was calm and in control. Or would that look suspicious – as if I was trying too hard? 'She has family nearby, she lives there.' No need to tell Tess that Liv had only just started. 'Can I ask who reported us?'

'I'm afraid I'm not allowed to discuss that.' Tess's thin lips stretched into a smile as I wrestled Finn out of his outdoor clothes. At least he seemed content to be in my arms for once. Freed of his padded all-in-one, he beamed. I pressed my lips to his cheek, which was surprisingly warm.

'It's a bit chilly in here,' I said with a shiver, as though Tess was a friend, popped round for a chat. 'I thought I'd left the heating up.' I fiddled with the thermostat on the wall, my hand not quite steady. 'Can I make you a cup of coffee?'

'No, thank you.' Tess held out her arms. 'I'll hold baby shall I, while you take your coat off, then we can talk.'

It didn't feel like a question. I handed Finn to her, aware she was probably checking him over, looking for evidence of neglect. I felt sick to my stomach at the thought.

'I should ring my husband,' I said, missing the hook so my coat pooled on the floor, blood rushing to my head when I bent to pick it up. 'I'd like him to be here.'

'No need.' Tess bounced Finn in a comfortable way that spoke of years of experience. 'If I have any concerns, I might need to speak to him, but for now, I'd like to talk to you.'

'Is this … is it specifically about me?'

The split-second hesitation before she inclined her head towards the living room door told me the answer was *yes*. The nauseous feeling intensified as I led her to the sofa. She settled easily before handing Finn back, her pale eyes taking everything in as she unwound her scarf and undid the toggles on her coat.

I could have sworn the room had been reasonably tidy before I left the house and was horrified to see it was a tip. The laundry basket was on the dining table, trailing clothes, cushions were scattered everywhere, and hadn't I pulled the curtains back earlier? Finn's toy box was tipped on its side, the contents spread over the floor, and several books had been inexplicably pulled off the shelf and piled by the armchair. I noticed with a shock that my wedding photo was face down on the mantelpiece, and the family portrait on the wall by the window was hanging at an angle. I couldn't recall putting the TV on either, but it was glowing with a daytime quiz show, the volume muted.

'I'm so sorry about the mess,' I stammered, placing Finn in his bouncer before opening the curtains and switching the TV off, stumbling as my foot caught on a wooden train lying on its side on the rug. 'It's not normally this bad.'

'Don't worry, I've seen worse.' Tess's eyes scanned the surfaces, her expression neutral. 'Now, sit down and let's chat.'

It was all straightforward enough, though I couldn't contain a tremor in my voice as I answered her careful questions. Thankfully, she seemed reassured that Finn was being looked after properly, relaxing enough to pull a series of comical faces to make him smile as I held him on my lap, but throughout, all I could think was, *Who?* Who had done this? One of the mums from the baby group? A neighbour, but why? What had led someone to make the assumption I wasn't looking after my baby? I knew I stood out among the glossy residents of The Avenue and adjoining streets, that I was hardly a Stepford wife, but surely I hadn't given anyone a reason to go this far. Yet underneath my thoughts was an oily seam of guilt, because I hadn't exactly been doing a great job with Finn, had I?

Once Tess had left, apparently satisfied – even apologising for the intrusion – I called Dom in tears and he came home early, threatening to ring social services and demand to know who'd reported me.

'Please don't, they won't tell you,' I pleaded. 'And it might make everything worse.'

The following morning, we faced each other across the breakfast bar, the air between us thick with tension. I knew he'd wanted to talk more the night before, but I'd gone to bed early and crashed into a deep sleep that hadn't done much to revive me.

'Dom, I—' He turned away with a weary sigh, as if fed up with the drama our lives had become. I watched him hesitate in the kitchen doorway, one hand on the frame. 'What is it?'

He looked at me with bloodshot eyes that spoke of a sleepless night. 'Liv's coming?'

I nodded, surprised. 'She should be here at nine.'

'And you're going to the baby group this morning?'

I drank the rest of my coffee, playing for time. 'I don't think it was any of the mums there who reported me, if that's what you're thinking.' Even as I said it, I realised I wasn't sure at all. Something about the way Kim had assessed me during our first meeting, as if she knew something I didn't. *Watch Elizabeth.* Someone had put that note through the door. Had it been the same person who reported me? Clare? It was obvious she hadn't liked me much when she came round for dinner, and now I'd employed Liv. Maybe she'd found out and done it out of spite. 'Look, I'm not sure I can face them today.'

'You should go, behave normally,' Dom said. I wondered what his definition of normal was these days. 'If it *was* one of them, something will give them away.'

'And then what?'

He pushed a hand through his hair, jaw tensed. 'I don't know, Sophy.'

Happy burbles crackled through the baby monitor. Finn was awake. 'I'll see how I feel a bit later,' I said.

Dom nodded, seeming distracted, as though something else had occurred to him. 'When will you get the results of your blood test?'

'I told you, sometime next week.' Was he weighing up whether I was safe to be left with Finn? Maybe the social worker's visit had put doubts in his head. 'You do trust me, don't you?' I said. 'What is it, Dom?'

He briefly closed his eyes. With a small shake of his head, he pulled a crumpled piece of paper from his coat pocket. 'Someone put this through the door yesterday morning.'

A shiver travelled up my spine, in spite of the heating. I belted my dressing gown tightly, aware the note about Elizabeth was still in the pocket. 'What is it?'

He shook out the sheet of paper and held it in front of me. As I strained forward for a better look, something tripped in my chest. It was a picture of Isaac and me at the restaurant, blown-up and grainy, but unmistakably us. I was laughing, reaching to dab spaghetti sauce off his chin, his head close to mine. It looked intimate – as though we were more than friends.

'Dom, I … it isn't what it looks like.' I slid off the stool, reaching to take the sheet from him, but he scrunched it up and shoved it back in his pocket. 'Why would …?' My mouth was dry, my voice too high. 'I've no idea why anyone would take a picture. You know Isaac and I are just friends.'

Dom's face looked clenched. I wanted to go to him, smooth out the lines around his eyes, but what had once felt natural now seemed awkward and my arms stayed by my sides.

'I know,' he said, looking at the keys in his hand. 'But clearly someone doesn't.'

'What?' My hand went to my throat, groping for my butterfly necklace, feeling its loss once more. 'You make it sound as if someone's got it in for us.' I paused. 'For *me*.'

Something crossed Dom's face, gone before I could decipher what it was. 'Look don't worry, I'll deal with it,' he said, in a strained attempt at a reassuring tone. 'Just take care OK? I'll see you later.'

'Dom, wait …' I reached in my pocket. 'I got something in the post too. A note about your mum,' I confessed. 'It said, "Watch Elizabeth".'

'What?' His gaze tightened. 'When?'

'Yesterday.'

'Why didn't you tell me?'

'I don't know,' I said, flushing at his sceptical expression. 'I didn't want to worry you.'

He held out his hand. 'Show me.'

My fingers were raking my pocket, but the note wasn't there. I checked the other, but found only a crumpled tissue. 'I … it was here,' I said, turning my pockets inside out. I looked on the

129

floor, in case it had fallen out. 'I definitely had it.' Confusion ripped through me. Could I have thrown it away and forgotten?

'This isn't funny, Sophy.' There was a clipped precision to Dom's voice I'd only ever heard him use on work calls. 'If you got a note, where is it?'

'Well, I'm not making it up.' Panic made me snappy as I ransacked the kitchen drawers, knowing I wouldn't find it. 'Maybe not everyone thinks your mum is as perfect as you do.'

'What's *that* supposed to mean?' Dom was looking at me as though I'd finally lost my senses. 'Mum has done nothing but look out for you since Finn was born.'

'Only because it suits her.' I was surprised by my bitter tone. 'It's Finn she's interested in, not me. You don't see it because you're never here.'

'That's not fair.' Dom shook his head, grim-faced. 'Mum's doing her best but you can't see it because you're not well.'

'Maybe I'd do better if she wasn't always hanging around, waiting for me to mess up so she can step in.'

'If she wasn't always *hanging around* as you put it, I wouldn't dare leave the house.'

'*What?*' I spun to face him, hopeless tears welling. 'You don't trust me with Finn?'

He exhaled heavily, pressing a finger to the bridge of his nose. 'That's not what I meant.'

'You're taking her side.'

'Sophy, it's not about taking sides, it's about doing what's best.'

'What if I don't think your mother being here all the time *is* best?'

'Well, she won't be now you've decided a nanny can do a better job than Finn's own grandmother can.'

I stared at him, dampness on my cheeks. 'You always take her side.'

'I don't have time for this.' There was a sense of forbearance in his tone, as if he was barely tolerating me. 'I have to go.'

'So, you *are* on her side?'

He didn't respond, just turned and left.

'I'll take that as a *yes*,' I yelled when the front door slammed. I ran to the window and watched him pull out of the drive and onto the road with a squeal of rubber. A car appeared out of nowhere and slowed behind him, low and sporty. It was the type Alicia Bainbridge used to drive, and her face flashed through my mind, cold and haughty, when Dom introduced me. *She has a thing for me. Don't worry, she'll get over it.* Maybe she'd have made a better wife and mother.

Upstairs, Finn whimpered and I tried to push off the weight of helplessness that had descended. I hadn't even asked Dom what he was going to do about the photo of Isaac and me. Not that it seemed to matter anymore.

'Hang on, little bear, I'm coming.' I headed upstairs, the shadow of Tess Bowman trailing behind me, watching my every move. What would she have made of my exchange with Dom? 'Let's get you some porridge.'

By the time Liv arrived at nine o'clock, I'd fed Finn and managed to shower, pulling on clean jeans and a jumper, but hadn't got as far as drying my hair as my argument with Dom played on a loop in my head, prompting a fresh torrent of tears. We'd never spoken to each other like that before.

'It's freezing out there,' Liv said, shaking warmth into her hands. 'Everything OK?' She looked from my blotchy face to my top. 'Looks like you've spilt something.'

I glanced down and, stretching my jumper, saw what looked like a coffee-stain on the front. 'I didn't even notice.' I blinked away the heaviness in my eyes. 'It was a gift from my mum. I've never even worn it before. It's been hanging on my wardrobe door for weeks.'

'What happened yesterday?' Liv said, coming inside. 'I felt bad leaving you alone to deal with that woman on your own.'

'It was nothing, a misunderstanding.' I felt slow and treacly as she moved around quickly, slipping her coat off, waving at Finn in his highchair and tucking her hair behind her ears, seemingly all at once. I'd almost forgotten how it felt to be refreshed and alert, my trip to London already a distant memory, the heated exchange with Dom taking on a surreal quality. Tiredness seeped in, dragging at my limbs, slowing everything down. 'She didn't stay very long and won't be taking it any further.'

'Who do you think reported you?' Liv's eyes dipped to my throat and I realised I was feeling for my necklace again.

'I've no idea.' I headed into the kitchen and moved my mug into the sink. I should check the tumble dryer, see if I had a clean top I could put on, but it felt like too much of a slog. 'Maybe it was someone's idea of a joke.' I wanted to change the subject, but before I could speak again there was the rattle of a key in the front door. Turning, I watched a frown cross Liv's brow and realised who was letting herself in.

'Only me!' Elizabeth's voice reverberated through the hallway. I sometimes forgot how strident her tone was.

'It's my mother-in-law.' I felt a pulse of apprehension. 'Look, I'd rather she didn't know about … about yesterday.'

'Mum's the word.' Liv mimed zipping her mouth shut, a flush rising to her cheeks. 'Did you know she was coming this morning?'

I shook my head, which was starting to swim. 'She doesn't phone ahead, she just turns up,' I murmured, gripping the edge of the worktop. *If she wasn't always* hanging around, *I wouldn't dare leave the house.* My skin felt suddenly cold where the ends of my damp hair had soaked through my coffee-stained jumper. 'Best let her get on with it.'

Liv didn't look convinced. 'You should tell her if you don't want her here … Oh hello, I'm Liv Granger,' she said as Elizabeth strode in, bringing a smell of outdoors and a tang of manure. She must have come from the stables. 'I think we met briefly before.'

Elizabeth had stopped in her tracks, eyeing Liv warily, as though I'd invited a homeless person inside. 'Yes, you're Sophy's friend.'

She pulled off her leather gloves as she crossed to Finn and dropped a kiss on his curls. She was clearly making an effort to be amiable, despite her obvious surprise at seeing someone else in the house before her.

'Nanny, actually,' Liv said, before I could offer an explanation. 'Started this week.'

Elizabeth's whole body froze. 'Sophy knows I'm always on hand to help out,' she said, a frown ruffling her brow. 'I'm sure she doesn't want a stranger taking care of her son.'

Seeing anger cloud Liv's face, I held up a hand. 'Elizabeth, you know how much I appreciate everything you do, but Liv's giving me a hand at the moment so you don't need to break up your day.' My attempt to be conciliatory was spoilt by a jaw-splitting yawn. Elizabeth's glance took in my dirty sweater and damp hair and my stomach tightened.

'But you don't know anything about her,' she said as if Liv wasn't there. I realised afresh how cut-glass her accent was, accentuated by an undercurrent of genuine anger. 'It's ridiculous to employ someone when I've made it clear I'm at your disposal.' Seeming to sense the disintegrating atmosphere, Finn began to cry. 'Now look what you've done.' Elizabeth put down her bag, but Liv had already moved to lift Finn from his chair, holding him high then dropping him down, so his cries stopped and he gave a whoop of delight.

'He's fine,' she said, handing Finn to me. 'You don't have to stay, Elizabeth.'

Ignoring the way Finn stiffened, I pressed him against my shoulder. I was holding my breath, forcing my eyes to stay open as I watched a succession of emotions chase across Elizabeth's carefully made-up face.

'I'll get on with some cleaning then.' Patches of red seeped through her foundation. 'This place is a bit of a mess.'

'I didn't get round to tidying up yesterday.' I recalled my shock at the state of the place when I came home.

'Oh, don't worry about that,' Liv said. 'A house is supposed to look lived in.'

'Honestly, Elizabeth, you should go,' I repeated. 'I'm sure you've got lots to do.'

Her gaze fell on Finn and I felt bad when I saw the longing in her eyes. 'You can't stop me seeing my grandson.'

'Of *course* not …' I began, but she picked up her gloves and bag and stalked out, closing the front door quietly behind her.

'Whoops,' Liv said, taking Finn as he struggled to break free of my arms. 'Looks like you're in trouble.'

'She'll probably phone Dom.' *Would he mention the note?* He probably thought I was making it up, that *I* was the one who had it in for his mother. A crushing weariness bore down, and before I'd thought it through, I said, 'Sometimes, I think the only thing she really likes about me, is Finn.'

'You don't think she did that, do you?'

'What?' Liv was looking at the stain on my jumper. 'Why?'

'Just … you said it was brand new and hanging on your wardrobe door. How did the stain get on there unless it was deliberate?' Liv shook her head. 'She seems pretty possessive, that's all. Like she's really angry with you.'

Watch Elizabeth. 'Of course it wasn't her.' I forced a laugh. 'I'm always spilling things. I must have done it myself, or maybe Dom did when he was bringing me some coffee.'

'You're right. Sorry. I didn't mean to …' She smiled apologetically. 'So, are you taking him to Mums Meet Up this morning?' She jiggled Finn, who was making a grab for her hair.

'Actually, I don't feel up to it.' Another wave of exhaustion crashed over me. 'I'm so tired, already.'

'Listen, why don't you go and have a lie-down and I'll take him?'

I looked at her, feeling as though I was standing on the opposite side of a glass wall. 'Won't it be weird, not taking Evie?'

'I'll just explain I'm working for you now,' she said with a shrug. 'They won't mind, and it'll be nice for Finn.'

I knew I should go too. Liv was on a month's trial and Dom wouldn't be happy I was letting her take Finn out without me, but wasn't that what nannies did? Wasn't the whole point of a nanny that they cared for children when the parents couldn't? And I was *so* sleepy. My eyelids were sagging. 'Well, if you're sure,' I managed, though another yawn.

'I'm positive.' She gave an encouraging nod. 'Go on up and we'll see you later.'

I gave a feeble wave and headed upstairs. Too tired to climb under the duvet, or even take off my jumper, I collapsed across the bed and dropped into a fathomless sleep.

Chapter 20

Liv

I grabbed the front door key, just in case Sophy was still asleep when I returned, and headed up the road pushing Finn in his pushchair, my eyes skittering over the oppressive houses in The Avenue, wondering if someone behind those elegant bay windows had called social services on Sophy, and if so, why? Did someone else bear her a grudge? Or what about Elizabeth? There was something a bit off with her, though Sophy couldn't seem to see it.

My mind flashed back to the day before. Seeing Sophy in such a state, visibly shaking when Tess what's-her-name appeared. The woman's words had given me so much pleasure. In fact, I'd wished I'd thought of ringing social services myself. I'd tried to follow them, couldn't wait to go inside the house and watch Sophy squirm. But then things changed. Sophy hadn't wanted my support. She'd placed her hand on Finn's buggy, as though claiming it – claiming him – letting me know Finn was her child. 'Go home, Liv,' she'd said, and I knew at that moment I had long way to go before she fully trusted me.

I hurried up The Avenue, past a pair of identically Lycra-clad women I didn't recognise, who stopped running when they saw me and watched with blank expressions as I shot past. I turned the corner and my phone buzzed in my pocket. *Ryan?* I'd left a couple of voicemails for him, desperate to know what he'd wanted to tell me about Sophy. Did he know more about her than I did? That she'd worked in London since university. That she'd met Dom at work and got married.

I pulled my phone from my pocket, and looked at the phone screen. It was an unknown number. 'Hello,' I said, pinning the phone to my ear, pushing the pushchair one-handed.

'Liv, it's Dom.'

'Hey, Dom.' Why the hell was he ringing me?

'Is Sophy with you?' He sounded anxious. 'She's not answering her mobile or the home phone.'

'No, she's in bed. I'm taking Finn to Mums Meet Up. Is everything OK?'

He was silent on the other end, and I remembered I'd promised to stay with Sophy for the first month. 'Dom?'

'Yeah, fine – no worries. I'm going to try to finish work early. To be honest, I'm worried about her.'

Christ. Was he confiding in me? My mind raced. This was my chance. 'I agree she doesn't seem herself.'

I expected him to bite back. Say I had no idea what Sophy's 'self' was. And he would have been right. I didn't know her at all.

'You're right,' he said. 'I keep turning to my mum to give Sophy support, but I'm not sure I'm doing the right thing.' He sounded desperate – as though he had no idea who to turn to.

'To be honest, I think Sophy needs to cope without your mother's help.' I smirked, couldn't help it. 'And I noticed Sophy was brighter when she'd been to London.'

'Yeah, Isaac's a good friend to her, always has been. He's a great bloke. Maybe I should invite him and his girlfriend round for a meal. I could cook.'

I felt my body sag. So Isaac was a friend. Nothing more. The photo and my trip to London had been a complete waste of time.

'Are you sure?' I found myself saying, quickly wishing I hadn't.

'Sophy wouldn't have an affair, if that's what you're asking.' His tone had hardened. Oh God, I had to bring this back.

'No, I mean are you sure about inviting Isaac and his girlfriend round? Sophy was only saying the other day that she'd hate any of her friends to see her in such a state.'

'Yes.' His voice softened once more. 'Maybe you're right. She never used to be like this. She was fun … happy.'

'If you ever need to talk, Dom, I'm always here.'

There was another brief silence. 'Listen, I've got to go, but as I say, I'll try to get away early.'

The line went dead. Had I overdone it?

'Olivia!' Kim was suddenly dashing towards me, Dougie perched on her hip. 'Are you going to Mums Meet Up?' She sounded out of breath, and I caught a slight whiff of body odour. Her eyes flicked about her, as if expecting to see someone else. 'No Sophy today?'

'No Sophy today,' I echoed, catching her eye, and morphing my face into what I hoped was a look of despondence. 'If I tell you something, Kim,' I went on as we fell into step, heading up the road towards Petra Rose's house. 'Do you promise it will go no further?'

She nodded several times, her cheeks flushing. 'Of course. Yes.'

'Well, Sophy had a visit from a social worker yesterday.'

'I knew it.' Her tone was triumphant. 'I was only thinking last night how Sophy is an accident waiting to happen. Elizabeth told me how she isn't coping at all.'

'There was a report of neglect.'

'Oh God, really?' Kim's attempt at a horrified tone didn't quite mask her glee.

'Mmm, and you know what I think—'

'No smoke without fire.' I'd fed her the words, and she looked positively joyous she'd finished my sentence.

I shook my head. 'What I was going to say was, those bloody

do-gooders should mind their own business.' I put on my sincerest smile, as though I really cared about Sophy. 'She's a good mum. I'm sure she doesn't mean to be—'

'Neglectful?'

'No.' I injected my voice with worry. 'I meant so tired all the time. She's asleep right now.' Going by the way Kim's eyes sparkled, like tiny marbles caught in the sun's rays, it wouldn't be long before gossip about Sophy being a neglectful mother spread throughout 'Mums Meet Up', and hopefully the surrounding neighbourhood. Whoever had called social services had made my job so much easier.

Kim keyed the code into the gate, and opened it, and he we headed down the path towards the annexe, where, through the window, I noticed Clare.

My heart sank, recalling how she was a good friend of Petra's, and most of the mothers in the neighbourhood.

I lifted Finn out of his pushchair, and followed Kim into the room that was alive with chatter, and the sound of children's squeals of laughter. It was easy for me to drift into the corner, as far away from Clare as I could get.

I lowered Finn onto the floor, and handed him a book, which he promptly put into his mouth, and found I couldn't tear my eyes away from little Evie. I missed her and hoped Clare was being a good mum to her.

Truth was, Clare seemed more animated than I'd ever seen her – interacting with Evie, making the little girl's face light up with pleasure. Maybe I'd done her a favour.

Suddenly she looked up, as though sensing my stare. She glared across the room at me, the smile she'd had for Evie vanishing. Would she cause a scene? Would she want everyone to know the reasons why I left my job?

Chapter 21

Liv

I lifted Finn from the floor, and onto my knee, and he grabbed at my hair, winding it round his little fingers. Clare looked as though she was about to rise, when Petra clapped her hands and initiated a sing-a-long, and I quickly found myself mouthing the words to 'The Wheels on the Bus'.

I was relieved when the meet-up ended without a confrontation with Clare, and couldn't get out of the building quick enough, hurrying down the hill, zigzagging the pushchair to and fro across the pavement, loving how Finn giggled and hiccoughed.

Back inside number seven, everything was quiet and still. 'Sophy?' I called, as I carried Finn through to the kitchen, and slipped him into his highchair, ready for his lunch. 'Sophy?' I strapped Finn in, and handed him his cup. 'Hold on there, little fella,' I whispered. 'I'm just going to find your crazy mummy.'

'Sophy?' I called, glancing into the lounge, before taking the stairs two at a time. The doors on the landing were closed.

I opened the door to her bedroom, and peered round. It was almost in darkness, just a sliver of light creeping between the heavy curtains.

'Sophy?'

I heard a small groan, and stepped in.

She was curled like a foetus on the far side of the king-sized bed. 'Sophy,' I whispered, and I was about to nudge her awake when I spotted an almost empty bottle of white wine, and a glass on its side, on the bedside cabinet.

I stepped back, as though scalded. Was Sophy a secret drinker? It would explain everything: the tiredness, the low moods, her inability to look after Finn properly. Did Dom know?

I grabbed the bottle and glass, intending to get rid of it, and was about to head downstairs, when I realised this opportunity was golden. I placed the glass and bottle back where I'd found them. Dom was coming home early. If I let Sophy sleep, he would see for himself. A smile stretched across my face. This was perfect.

I reached into my pocket, and pulled out her necklace. I'd been carrying it with me since I took it, waiting for the right opportunity – and this was it. I laid it next to the empty bottle.

I hope you're proud of me, Ben, I mused, as I left the room, and closed the door behind me, *because this is all for you, my darling brother.*

Later, after playing with Finn and giving him lunch, he fell asleep in my arms. I carried him upstairs and placed him in his cot, passing Sophy's closed door on my way back down. I was making my way into the lounge, intending to snoop, when I heard Dom's key turn in the lock. I raced into the kitchen, and was fake-filling the dishwasher when he appeared in the doorway, pushing his fingers through his hair, a troubled look on his face.

'Hey,' I said, looking up as he passed me. He was close to me as he grabbed a mug from the cupboard, and I recognised the smell of perfume. It was unmistakable. Eternity. I used to wear it. And I knew Sophy didn't.

'Where's Sophy?'

'Still asleep.'

He rubbed his hand across his chin, his eyes turning to meet mine. 'Listen, why not take off, Liv. I'm here now.'

'OK, if you're sure.'

'Yep. Positive. I need to talk to Sophy alone.'

'OK, well Finn's asleep in his room.' I pointed at the baby monitor next to the fridge. 'He'll let you know when he's awake, I'm sure.' I headed from the kitchen, raising my arm in a wave. 'I hope you guys sort things out.'

'Thanks,' he said, turning away from me.

Once in my car, I keyed Ryan's number into my phone. It went straight to voicemail.

'Hey,' I said. 'You left me hanging last night. Call me. Please.'

I leant back in the car seat and closed my eyes. I wasn't tired, but I needed to regroup my thoughts. Stop my head from spinning.

Who reported Sophy to social services?

What had Ryan meant last night when he said Sophy's not as she seems?

I started the engine, deciding I would pop round his house on my way home.

Ryan lived in an Edwardian detached house on a quiet road on the outskirts of Hatfield. It had once belonged to his father, who died of a stroke shortly after Ben's death. He left the place to Ryan.

I hadn't been there for ages, but there had been a time, when I was in my twenties, that Ryan and I had grown claustrophobically close. I was looking for answers, I supposed, and so was he – two broken reeds trying to hold each other up. We kissed once, I remembered, but it hadn't felt right. In fact we'd laughed at the awkwardness of it and then got steaming drunk.

We'd drifted apart around a year ago, me suggesting he needed help with his alcohol problem, that he should attend AA; him refusing, claiming he liked the feeling of oblivion alcohol created. I deliberately didn't call him after that, unable to watch him slowly kill himself. Well, until the other day.

Now, as I stood on his doorstep studying the grubby windows, the front garden over-run with weeds, I felt a pang of guilt. Perhaps I should have tried harder to be there for him.

I took a deep breath, and knocked on the door. No reply. I knocked again, and again, before crouching down, and opening the letterbox. 'Ryan,' I called through, feeling sure he was in there, ignoring me. 'It's Liv, open up. Please.'

As I made my way back down the path, I shuddered and turned quickly, my eyes scanning the windows. It was as though I was being watched.

I pulled up outside Mum's, my head still a tangle of thoughts.

Sophy Edwards' life was spiralling out of control, with little help from me, and I wrestled down a sudden feeling of doubt. Sophy didn't seem to be the wicked, evil witch I'd created in my mind following Ben's death. She was a sad, lonely creature.

I got out of the car, and walked up the short path. I didn't really want to talk to Mum and Freya. But as soon as I was in the house Mum called me. 'Come and see this, Liv.'

I took a deep breath, and entered the small conservatory, shoving the tips of my fingers into my jean pockets. Mum was sitting in her wheelchair at the computer screen, Freya next to her on a collapsible wooden chair that was normally propped in the corner.

'What's up?' I said, approaching, and they both turned. But before I could say a word, I saw they'd got a picture of Dom up on the screen. 'Why—?'

'Your mum was curious, Liv.' Freya gave a thin smile.

'Curious?'

'She wanted to know more about Sophy Pemberton – Edwards. You'd mentioned where she worked, and that her husband was still there, so ...'

'You're right about him being handsome, Liv.' Mum's voice broke, and tears shimmered in her eyes. 'Not as handsome as our Ben ...'

Oh God, I hadn't wanted this to happen, for Mum to get upset. That wasn't part of the plan.

'Well I'm not sure their marriage will last, quite honestly,' I said. 'As I've mentioned before Sophy's a complete mess. She even had a visit from social services. Reported by someone for neglecting Finn, apparently.'

'And is she?' Freya asked.

'Is she what?'

'Neglecting Finn.'

'I don't know. Maybe. Though not deliberately.'

'So what's going to happen now?' Freya's eyes were narrowed.

'Happen now?'

'With the social worker.'

'Oh. Nothing. They seemed satisfied she wasn't neglecting Finn. And she's got me, and Dom seems like a good dad when he's there.'

Freya shrugged. 'It isn't easy for social services. Making the choice to take a child from their parents, even if it's for their own good. But sometimes it has to be done.'

I glanced at the clock on the shelf, a miniature grandfather clock that Ben and I bought Mum when we were young. It was almost four o'clock. 'I'm going to my room for a bit,' I said. 'And, Mum?'

She looked up. 'Yes, love?'

'Maybe leave the Sophy research to me in future.' It was as much for Freya's ears as Mum's. 'We don't want you getting upset, do we?'

Chapter 22

Sophy

I was woken by a rough shake of my shoulder to see Dom standing over me, holding the neck of an empty wine bottle.

'What's going on, Sophy?' I looked blearily at his face as he sank on the edge of the bed, his expression cast in shadow by a grey wash of light through the window. 'You've been drinking.'

'Wha …?' I struggled upright, my arm numb where I'd lain on it, my head hot and heavy. 'Dom, I haven't been drinking,' I slurred. 'I've no idea how that bottle ended up in here.'

'So why do you reek of alcohol?'

'It's … it's *on* me, not inside me.' I tugged feebly at my jumper, my nose wrinkling at the sour smell wafting up from the duvet cover. My tongue felt thick and furry and I struggled to keep my eyes open, fighting to understand what was happening. A glass had tipped over on the bedside table, seeping liquid into my paperback. 'Dom, I swear I haven't been drinking.' I pushed trembling hands through my hair, feeling as if my head was about to explode. 'I was really tired so I came up for a sleep while Liv took Finn to the baby group—' I gave a jolt. 'Where are they, Dom? Where's Finn?'

'Oh, now you're worried about our son?'

'Dom, please …' I shuffled past him, swaying as I stood up. The room was spinning like a carousel and nausea gripped my stomach. 'Is he downstairs?'

'He's fine.' Dom grabbed me as I tilted. 'Mum's here.'

'What?' I wrenched my hand free and rubbed my wrist as I dropped beside him on the bed. 'Where's Liv?'

'Liv's gone home, and Mum knows.' Dom's voice was flat as he rose, moving across the room as if he needed to put some distance between us, the bottle still hanging loosely from his fingers.

'Knows what?'

'She bumped into someone called Kim from that baby group, who told her we'd had a visit from social services.'

'Oh, no.' I pressed my fingers to my temples. 'She must hate me,' I muttered.

'Sophy, of course she doesn't hate you.' Dom's voice was laced with frustration. 'Is this about the so-called note?'

'There *was* a note.' My voice rose in pitch. 'I wouldn't make up something like that,' I said. 'Does she know about that too?'

He shook his head, not looking at me. 'Mum's upset, of course she is, but only because she cares about Finn.'

My head jerked as though he'd slapped me. 'So do I.' It came out on a sob that hurt my throat and I clamped a hand to my mouth. 'How did Kim find out?' I said through my fingers. 'No one else knew, apart from Liv, and she wouldn't say anything.'

'I'm afraid she did.' Dom's tone held no room for argument.

'What?' *Why would Liv do that?* It would be round the whole neighbourhood now. 'I'll talk to her tomorrow.'

Dom was shaking his head. 'I don't want her here anymore.'

'No!' I was suddenly desperate to keep Liv; to not go back to only having his mother's support. 'Just let me talk to her, please,' I begged. 'There has to be another explanation.'

'If there is, I can't think what it is.' Dom's voice was cool. 'All I want is our son taken care of properly and to know he's safe.'

'That's what I want too.'

He looked at me a moment longer and the sadness in his eyes pierced my heart. He released a heavy sigh and waggled the wine bottle. 'We'll need to talk about this again, but I'm hungry and tired and need to be with my son.'

'Me too.' More than anything, I wanted Finn in my arms.

Dom dropped his chin to his chest. 'Not like this.'

Tears rose. 'Dom—'

'Drink some water, take a shower, then come down and have some dinner,' he said. 'If you're feeling better, you can put Finn to bed.'

'Your mum ...'

'I'll talk to her, don't worry. It'll be fine.'

He turned in the doorway. 'Oh, and Sophy.'

'Yes?' I waited, desperate for a kind word, knowing I didn't deserve one.

'She really does care, you know. We both do.'

He closed the door softly, leaving behind a trace of a floral scent I didn't recognise. It mingled unpleasantly with the alcohol fug from the bed, making my head swim.

I removed my jumper, wincing as the throb in my head intensified, then dragged the duvet cover off. I hadn't been drinking, I was certain of it, but how else could the wine have got up here? Maybe I'd sleepwalked downstairs and brought it up, tried to drink it and spilled it on the bed.

My eyes panned over the bedside table, where something glinted in the pool of wine on the surface. *My necklace.* I reached for it, heart racing. Had it been there all along, with the paperback I was convinced I'd lost? *What was happening to me?*

As I clutched the butterfly chain in my palm, my stomach rose and I dashed to the bathroom on shaky legs, making it just in time. I knelt over the toilet bowl, my body convulsing, wishing for a horrible moment that I hadn't woken up.

*

Dinner was a subdued affair, though I did my best to force down some of the fish pie Elizabeth had prepared. Thankfully, she'd gone by the time I turned up in the kitchen, showered and dressed, smelling of minty toothpaste. Dom said he'd explained the social worker's visit had been a mistake and wouldn't happen again.

'Mum's invited you to take Finn to see the horses tomorrow.' He was clearing our plates away, his movements stilted. 'I think you should go. It'll be good for you both.'

Elizabeth had never invited me to their home without Dom. 'But, Liv—'

'Just you and Finn,' he said firmly.

'So she can keep an eye on me?' *Watch Elizabeth.* Now she was the one watching me.

'Sophy, you can't really blame her.' Dom closed the dishwasher and set it going, turning to me with a look of exasperation. 'Finn's her grandson.'

'Maybe *she* reported me.' I was surprised by the conviction in my tone. 'Let's face it, Dom, she'd love to be able to look after Finn permanently.'

'I'm going to pretend I didn't hear that.' After a moment's hesitation, Dom came over and drew me tightly to him so that my forehead brushed his chin. I couldn't speak and felt power-less to let go. 'Whatever you believe, Mum loves you both, even if she doesn't always show it.'

I *did* want to believe it, so badly it hurt. I tried to remember a time I'd felt that Elizabeth wasn't just tolerating my presence in her son's life. It wasn't that she'd ever been hostile, or made me feel unwelcome – she always said and did the right things and could be charming – but she lacked a natural warmth and could be distant. Only with her beloved horses had I seen another side to her, relaxed and smiling, and now with Finn. No wonder Dom was happy to have her around as much as possible, basking in reflected glory after years of feeling disconnected from her. I knew I should be happy too, yet I envied Natasha, living at the opposite end of the country to her mother.

'I'm sorry,' I mumbled into his shoulder, breathing him in, wondering whether I'd imagined the smell of perfume, earlier. 'I didn't mean it.'

'She'd be so hurt if she knew what you'd just said.'

'Would she?'

'Sophy, don't.' Dom let go of me, exhaling a sigh, and I felt as if I'd lost a battle I hadn't known I was fighting. 'Have you taken your vitamin pill today?'

'For all the good they do.'

'You have to stick with it. Natasha said—'

'Fine, I'll take another, if that will make you happy.' Knowing it was childish, I crossed to the counter and snatched up the bottle.

'Sophy, stop it.'

I shoved two in my mouth and almost choked as I gulped them down dry. 'Satisfied?' I opened my mouth to show him it was empty, my eyes watering.

'For God's sake.' He turned away, but not before I'd seen that look again. The one that said he no longer knew who I was.

He hovered while I bathed Finn and read him a bedtime story, then insisted on sleeping in the nursery on cushions brought up from the sofa. 'So you can get some rest.'

The sorrow that came from feeling he no longer trusted me was overwhelming.

Half-expecting him to hang around to confront Liv the following morning, I was surprised when he said curtly that he had a meeting he couldn't get out of and left after extracting a promise I'd talk to Liv and would call if I needed anything.

I gave Finn his breakfast and settled him in his playpen with his toys while I got dressed and put the washing machine on, then waited for Liv to arrive. My nerves jangled like coins as I paced about, mentally rehearsing what to say, imagining her reaction. She'd probably storm out and not come back, but I couldn't let it

149

go. If she'd told Kim about the social worker's visit, it meant she was, at best, a gossip and at worst ... *what?* Unless my instincts were completely off, she was someone I'd thought I could trust. Someone who'd make a good friend, once I got past the guarded, spiky exterior she tried to hide.

She knocked on the door at nine. I checked Finn was engrossed in his favourite book and went to let her in. 'Hi.'

'Hey,' she said, taking her coat off, eyes darting to my neck. 'You found your necklace.'

My fingers went to the chain. I couldn't remember telling her I'd lost it but supposed I must have done. 'Yes, it was ...' I didn't need to tell her I'd found it in such an obvious place. 'Liv, I need to talk to you.'

She paused on her way to the living room, shoulders stiffening beneath her long grey sweater. 'What is it?' Her face was blank.

'You told Kim.' My heart thudded unevenly. I hated confrontation, but made myself hold her gaze. 'About the social worker coming to see me.'

'Oh, that.' She looked at the floor and I waited for her to deny it. 'I'm really sorry, Sophy.' When she raised her eyes, they were clear. 'It was just that she saw the whole thing as she was driving back to her house and I couldn't think on the spot, and when she said the woman looked like a social worker, I felt myself go red and she knew she'd guessed right.' Her words were rushed, her tone apologetic. 'I told her I didn't know the details and that I was sure it was a misunderstanding, but you've seen what she's like. She's such a nosy cow.' Her hands were wringing together. 'I made her promise not to say anything and I honestly don't think she will. She's a mother herself – she'll understand how awful it was for you.'

'How do you look like a social worker?' I said.

Liv gave a half-smile. 'I don't know. Maybe it's more than that. Maybe she knew her.'

She sounded so sincere my shoulders unclenched. Maybe my

instincts about her hadn't been wrong after all. 'The thing is—' I clasped my hands together to stop them trembling '—Kim went and told my mother-in-law and she came round here and Dom's upset and ...' Suddenly I was crying, great heaving sobs that made my shoulders shake. 'He thinks I've been drinking while he's at work, but I don't even remember it happening, and it's not the first time I haven't been able to remember something. I know Elizabeth thinks I'm a terrible mother and now Dom does too. I don't deserve to have a baby.'

As the last few words flew out on a series of hiccups, I felt Liv's hand on my elbow, steering me to the sofa and pressing me down. She disappeared and came back with a sheet of kitchen roll, which she thrust at me. 'Bloody Kim, I could kill her,' she muttered. 'I'm sorry, Sophy.'

I scrubbed at my face. 'Why didn't you wake me up when you got back yesterday?'

'I didn't want to disturb you.'

'Did you see the wine bottle?'

'No,' she said smoothly. 'I looked round the bedroom door, then came back down and waited for Dom to come home.' She paused. '*Do* you have a drink problem?'

My head whipped up. 'What? No!'

She held up her hands. 'Sorry, just checking.'

'I don't know what's going on, only that I feel terrible nearly all the time and I'm so worried about how it's affecting Finn.'

'He looks fine to me.' She sat beside me and we looked at him, banging a teething ring on his chubby thigh.

'How can I be certain he isn't absorbing everything?'

'Kids are resilient.' Sliding me a glance, she added, 'Is Dom being supportive?'

I glanced at her, my eyes feeling sore and swollen. 'He has been, but I think he's getting fed up that I'm not feeling better and yesterday was the last straw.' I looked at my fingers curled around the sodden kitchen roll. 'He probably wishes he'd never married me, in fact I'm sure he does. He's not here as much as I thought he'd be and sometimes he gets texts he doesn't want me to see.' I rubbed at my eyes once more. 'I worry he'll meet someone else.'

'Do you ever think he's really not the one for you?'

'What?' Liv's hand was on my knee. Although pale and slender it felt heavy, as if she could easily pin me there. 'Of course he is,' I said. 'I loved him almost from the moment we spoke. We just ... clicked.'

'So, no one special before that?'

Her gaze prodded like a finger, eyes wide and unflinching.

'Not really.' I sensed my answer was important in a way I didn't understand. 'A couple of boyfriends at university, one quite serious, and one relationship after, which fizzled out after a couple of years, then I met Dom.' I remembered Liv saying when we met that I could talk to her about anything. 'He got a photo the other day, of me and my friend Isaac having lunch in London.'

'Oh?' Liv's hand fell away from my knee. 'That's weird.'

'I know.' Finn gave a bird-like screech that made me jump. 'Someone's trying to make trouble for us and I know it sounds stupid but ...'

'Go on.' Liv stood and lifted Finn out of his playpen, taking him to the patio doors to look outside. I cursed myself for not recognising his screech had been a signal he wanted picking up. I couldn't even read my own son.

'I'm starting to think it might be Clare,' I said. 'She's the only person I can imagine having it in for me after ... you know.' I looked at her. 'Because you're working for me now.'

Liv turned, her face flushed pink. 'I don't know.' She grimaced. 'You really think she'd have followed you into London?'

'Oh, God, I don't know.' Doubt flooded me. 'Who else?'

'Elizabeth?' Liv raised her eyebrows. 'I know I keep saying it, but she's the one closest to you with a vested interest in Finn.' She swooped him high and he giggled. 'She obviously doesn't want me around, either.'

'Maybe you're right.' I pulled at my bottom lip. 'I got a note about her,' I confessed. 'It said *Watch Elizabeth.*'

'Really?' Liv's eyes widened. 'Where is it?'

'That's the thing,' I said, feeling foolish. 'I can't find it now.'

'Oh, right.' She lifted a hand to her forehead and smoothed her hair back. 'Did you throw it away?'

'I can't remember.' I sounded ridiculous. 'Look, it's probably nothing. A joke.'

'Have you told Dom?'

I shuddered, recalling the look of disbelief on his face. 'I did, but I wish I hadn't,' I admitted. 'When I couldn't find it, I could tell he didn't believe me. He thinks I've lost my mind. She can do no wrong in his eyes.'

'Maybe you should record her or something?'

I stared. 'Doing what?'

Liv's shoulders rose. 'Ignore me,' she said, as if tiring of the subject despite having raised it in the first place. 'Why don't we take Finn to the park?' she said. 'It's sunny out. I don't know about you, but I could do with some fresh air.'

I sagged. 'Elizabeth's invited me to her place with Finn, to see the horses.'

A flicker of frustration crossed Liv's face, then she turned to Finn with a smile. 'We'll enjoy that, won't we?'

'Just the two of us.' I felt a flash of guilt as I pushed myself off the sofa. 'I'm sorry, I know it sounds awful and you think she's got it in for me, but if we don't go, she'll mention it to Dom and it'll make things worse than they are.'

'Well, don't say you weren't warned.' Liv's smile was cool. She sniffed Finn's nappy. 'I'll change him if you like, then make myself scarce.'

'We'll go out tomorrow.' I wanted to make amends. 'Maybe

153

we could go to the swimming pool. Finn loves being bathed. I think he'd like the water.'

Her smile was tight. 'OK.'

As she headed upstairs to the nursery to change Finn's nappy, radiating a tension I didn't understand, I released a shaky sigh and headed to the kitchen to make some coffee. I needed more than a boost of caffeine and a vitamin pill before going out, but they would have to do.

Chapter 23

Sophy

Dom had left me the car and walked to the station, clearly not wanting to give me an excuse to get out of visiting Elizabeth. I was surprised he trusted me to drive, given the events of the day before, especially with Finn in the car. Maybe it wasn't so much an act of faith, as a plea for me to prove there was nothing wrong with me.

Tears were close by the time I'd checked Finn was safely strapped into his car seat, my hands shaky from the coffee I'd drunk in an effort to stay alert. Once Liv had slipped out with a quiet goodbye, I'd sent her a text, thanking her for listening to me pour out my troubles, hoping I hadn't offended her.

As I straightened, pushing my hair behind my ears, I was startled to see Kim at the end of the drive, Dougie staring out like royalty from his sling.

'Morning!' She waved a hand encased in a grey woollen glove. 'Everything OK?'

I felt I had no choice but to smile and nod as if I didn't know what she was alluding to. 'You?'

'Oh, we're fine.' She said it in a robust way that suggested they were always fine. In her full-length purple padded coat she looked somehow invincible, as though wearing armour. There wasn't much heat in the sun and I shivered in the belted cardigan I'd thrown on.

'I heard about your visitor,' Kim said, getting straight to the point. I guessed it was why she just happened to be passing the house and I wondered whether she'd planned to knock on the door.

'It was all a mix-up,' I said, walking round to the driver's side of the car after checking Finn was settled. 'But thank you for letting my mother-in-law know.'

If Kim detected my sarcasm, she chose to ignore it.

'She thinks the world of Finn.' She jiggled Dougie, holding him like a shield, clearly not quite brave enough to venture any closer. 'You're so lucky to have her to help out.'

'I know.'

'If I'm honest, I'm a bit surprised you've taken Olivia on when Finn's grandma is so keen to help out if you need it.' My hand froze around the car door handle. 'I don't have any relatives close by. My sister lives in Scotland, though she may be moving in with me for a bit,' Kim added, as if sensing my mounting annoyance. 'Not that we need anyone, do we, Dougie?' She tweaked Dougie's rosy cheek before meeting my gaze full-on. 'I do think Olivia was rather indiscreet, passing on gossip,' she said, with no sense of irony whatsoever. 'But I just wanted to say, if there's anything I can do to help, you must let me know.'

I wanted to tell her to mind her own business but Finn starting to fuss and whimper, straining against his straps. 'I have to go,' I said, glad to get into the safety of the car.

'See you next week at Petra's?'

I summoned a non-committal smile and slammed the door before she could say anything else, not caring that our exchange would now be at the top of her own gossip list.

So rude, I imagined her saying to her cronies at The Busy

Bean. *I feel sorry for that poor child.* Meeting Finn's teary gaze in the rear-view mirror, I felt sorry for him too.

'We're going to see Nana,' I said, in my children's-television-presenter voice as I started the car. 'And to look at the horses. You like the horses, don't you, little bear?'

He fell silent. I didn't know whether it was the mention of his grandmother or the horses, but either way, I was grateful. And at least I hadn't forgotten how to drive, though I wouldn't have minded getting lost for a while and delaying our visit, knowing I'd be under scrutiny from the moment we arrived.

I was startled when my phone rang. I'd forgotten Dom had synched it with the car radio system and the ringtone blared through the speakers. Careful to keep my eyes on the road, I pressed the answer button on the steering wheel, surprised to hear Isaac's voice.

'Hey, it's me. Thought I'd call as you don't always answer your messages,' he said. 'Just checking to see how you are after running out on me at the restaurant, and to say I'm sending over the stuff for the quiz show I was telling you about.'

I concentrated on slowing down and checking Finn in the mirror. He was gazing at the scenery flashing by as though finding it fascinating. My heart gave its customary squeeze. 'I'm sorry about rushing off,' I said. 'As you know, I don't get out much these days. I just felt a bit weird.'

'As long as you're OK,' he said. 'Come and visit Apex sometime, if you're up to it. Bring Finn. There are plenty of people here who'd love to see you both.'

'I will.' I doubted I would. My job at the TV station was a dusty memory I could barely recall, though days ago, I knew I'd talked about missing it. Could baby hormones still be affecting my mind? 'Actually, something strange happened. I don't know if Dom said anything to you.' It struck me that in the past, I wouldn't have needed to ask. Back when Dom and I didn't have secrets, when he wasn't consumed with work and worry, when I

157

wasn't too out of it most of the time to know what was happening in my own home.

'Strange?' I imagined Isaac's frown.

'Someone took a photo of us while we were eating.' My heart picked up speed as a lorry overtook me on a bend. 'Whoever it was wanted Dom to see it.'

'*What?*' Isaac was silent for a second. 'Well, he hasn't said anything, but our paths don't really cross much at work.' Another pause. 'It's funny, because now you mention it, I thought I saw someone hold up their phone at the restaurant window but didn't take much notice at the time.'

'Really?' Now my heart was racing. 'Did you see who it was?'

'I think it was a woman with a pushchair.' He paused as though thinking. 'Dark hair, maybe, I'm not sure.'

For some reason, Liv came into my mind. 'Was she wearing a dark coat?'

'Could have been, why?'

'Oh, nothing.' But the image of Liv wouldn't budge. Could she have followed me to the restaurant? Elizabeth had seen her going to the station after all, and Liv had definitely been on a train with Finn. But why would she photograph Isaac and me and give the picture to Dom, unless she was trying to make trouble? Maybe Isaac was wrong about the woman with a pushchair, but it seemed too much of a coincidence.

Oh God. I'd just unburdened myself to Liv, sent her a thank you text, and now I suspected her of spying on me. A woman I'd invited into my home, to look after my son. Something was going on here, I was sure of it. *Watch Elizabeth.* My breathing faltered. Could Liv have sent the note and them removed it? She'd been quick to point the finger at Elizabeth, accusing her of all sorts, maybe wanting her out of the way, and she had access to my house. Perhaps Liv was the one I should be suspicious of. 'Isaac, I'd better go. I'm on my way to my mother-in-law's with Finn.'

'Two trips out in a week, you're doing well.' He was joking, but there was an undercurrent of worry in his voice. 'Listen, call if you need to talk about anything, won't you?'

'I will.'

'And you'll look at the stuff I'm sending? It's right up your street.'

'I promise.' I pressed end-call and released a long breath, but there was no time to dwell on anything else as I'd arrived in Harpenden.

I pulled the car onto the circular drive in front of the house and adjoining stables and sat for a moment, gripping the steering wheel, looking at the impressive wood-and-brick exterior. The wisteria that had draped extravagantly across the front of the building earlier in the year was withered and brown now, the roots exposed and ugly.

I'd been wowed the first time Dom brought me here; by the house, the idyllic setting, the horse-riding and dinner-party life-style, which was the opposite of my ordinary upbringing with Mum in our modest end-of-terrace in Stevenage. I'd been so excited to get to know my future in-laws. Dom and I had been seeing each other for a couple of months and he'd already said he wanted to marry me. *I've never felt like this about anyone, Sophy. I want to be with you all the time.*

I'd understood because I felt the same, since our first date in The Dickens Inn, where we'd talked non-stop until closing time, and kissed in a shop doorway on the way back to his apartment like a couple in a romantic film.

I hadn't known then his family were what Mum called 'well-bred' and hadn't thought it mattered until I met Elizabeth, when I'd finally understood what Dom had meant when he told me she could initially come across as unapproachable.

As I unclicked my seatbelt with a heavy feeling in my chest, the wide oak door at the front of the house was flung open and Elizabeth strode out. She was wearing jodhpurs, shiny boots and her tweed jacket, no doubt fresh from a riding session. All that was missing was a whip. Or *crop*, as she'd once corrected me.

I tensed as I stepped onto the drive, noticing the toes of my boots were dusty, and braced myself for a barrage of questions about the social worker, about Liv, about my supposed drinking the day before, but to my surprise she was all smiles as she nodded a greeting before dipping into the back of the car to release Finn.

'You can carry him in his car seat,' I said, but she'd already plucked him out and was nuzzling his cheek with pursed lips, making kissy noises that delighted him.

'Come inside, it's freezing,' she instructed breezily as I spotted a familiar car parked next to Elizabeth's Land Rover.

'Natasha's popped over,' she said, seeing me looking. 'She was down this way, visiting a client, and thought she'd come and say hello. Isn't that lovely?'

'Natasha's here?' My spirits rose at the thought of seeing my sister-in-law.

'She's gone for a ride on Lady Madonna, hasn't been on a horse for ages.' Seeing Elizabeth's indulgent smile made me realise how ridiculous it had been to allow doubts about her to enter my mind because of Liv. I was certain now that she must have slipped the note through my door. She'd probably had her eye on a nannying job with me and wanted to discredit my mother-in-law. 'She'll be back soon,' Elizabeth went on. 'We'll have coffee first. I've got some lovely snacks for my little soldier.'

In the huge copper and slate kitchen, where double doors at one end opened onto the courtyard, she neatly divested Finn of his all-in-one polar-fleece, her smile slipping slightly when she saw the miniature grey jogging pants and matching hoodie underneath. I thought it was cute, but to Elizabeth, he probably looked like a young offender. She'd no doubt prefer him in a tuxedo, and trousers with a crease – the sort of outfit she liked

Robert in, despairing that my father-in-law was happiest at home in well-worn chinos and comfy jumpers.

After slotting Finn into the padded bouncer she'd bought specially, and offering him a sensory cube from the pile of toys she kept stacked in a basket, she moved across to the kettle on the marble worktop. *Was she humming?* I'd never heard her hum before and nearly giggled, but was ambushed by a yawn that made my jaw click.

'You look tired.' Turning, Elizabeth gave me a more familiar look as I pulled my cardigan closer and sank on a chair at the table where she hosted 'informal' lunches for her horsey friends. Behind her, tucked on a shelf at the end of a row of cookery books, was a silver-framed photo of Christopher, lying on a sheepskin rug, swaddled in a knitted blanket, wide eyes gazing at the camera; no sign of the heartbreak about to be wrought by his tiny, failing heart. There were several pictures of him in prominent positions around the house, so that visitors' eyes were drawn there first and not to the photos of Dom and Natasha at various ages. Several of them were on horseback, though Dom wasn't a fan of riding, preferring his feet on the ground. After having a go myself to humour Elizabeth not long after meeting, I'd understood why. I hadn't stayed in the saddle long, to Elizabeth's undisguised disdain.

'A coffee should wake you up,' she announced now, preparing two earthenware mugs, splashing in milk from a bottle. No supermarket cartons for her.

'Thanks,' I said through another yawn, which I covered with my hand. Pulling my gaze from the photo of Christopher, I looked at my mother-in-law, imagining grief still flickering inside her, like one of those candles that regenerates while it's burning.

She handed me one of the mugs and examined me coolly. I had the feeling she was going to bring up the wine episode from the day before but instead, she glanced at Finn, who was happily gnawing his cube and blowing raspberries, before returning to the worktop to stir her coffee.

'At least the sun's out,' she said, looking at the garden, as if the weather was the safest topic she could think of. It struck me in a distant way that our conversations never dipped below the surface. She'd rarely asked about my job when I was working, seeming happy to leave the small talk to Robert, who had a fascination for history, her gaze often suggesting she was somewhere else in her mind; galloping round a field on horseback, perhaps.

'It's chilly though. I should have worn a coat.' I yawned once more, willing the foggy, dragging sensation to go away. I hastily gulped half my coffee, welcoming the scalding sensation on my tongue. I needed to be on form, not fumbling towards sleep.

'Is Natasha staying for lunch?'

'Who knows?' There was a sudden brittleness to Elizabeth's tone. Her smile had vanished. 'She never stays long these days.'

It was true that Natasha rarely visited, but I knew how busy she was since relocating her family and interior design business to Cumbria. 'It'll be nice to see her.'

Elizabeth didn't respond, just carried on looking outside while nursing her mug, steam curling above her head. From the back, her hair looked like a helmet.

Silence fell.

I looked at Finn, waving his cube, a gummy smile on his face. There seemed to be two of him. Blinking, I finished my coffee and put my mug down. 'Hello, baby.' My words sounded garbled, as though I'd drunk too many cocktails.

Elizabeth turned, a frown marring her face, as though the sight of me defeated her. 'Why don't you walk Finn to the stables and show him Parsley, his favourite horse,' she said, amiably. 'I'll make some soup for lunch.'

When I hesitated, unsure whether I had the energy to stand up, she added, 'It's warm in there, he'll be fine,' as if my only concern was the temperature.

'Sure.' I rose with an effort, blinking to clear my vision. It was important I gave her the impression of being in control, despite feeling far from it. 'I'll just fetch …' I pitched forward and grabbed at the table. There was a rush of air, as though I was entering a tunnel, and everything went black.

Chapter 24

Sophy

When I opened my eyes, I was lying on the sofa in Elizabeth's lounge, Natasha sitting in front of me on a velvet, buttoned footstool. 'Hey, you.' Her worried expression cleared. 'You gave us a shock, fainting like that.'

'Hmmm?' I pushed off the woollen throw wrapped around me and struggled to sit up. My head felt like a block of concrete. 'I fainted?'

'More like collapsed in a deep sleep, according to Mum. She found you in the stables.'

'*What?*'

'It's OK.' Natasha's tone was soothing as I fell back on the cushions. 'I don't think you'd been out long.'

'What time is it?'

'Just after three.'

I'd been asleep for ages. *How had I got to the stables?* The last thing I remembered was being in the kitchen, standing up, then … *nothing.* 'Where's Finn?'

'He's fine, he's having a nap. Mum said she brought him in, then went back for you.'

'I took Finn out there with me?' This time, I sat up straight, despite the pain in my skull.

'Well … yes, I suppose so.' Natasha made a sympathetic face. 'I got back after the event, I'm afraid.'

'And your mum got me in here on her own?' *Why couldn't I remember?*

'She stronger than she looks,' Natasha said, wryly. 'And, let's face it, she looks pretty strong.' A smile warmed her face, which was like a female version of Dom's; strong-featured and open, blue eyes bright and inquisitive. 'I managed to get a little cuddle with my nephew before Mum whisked him away,' she said. 'I've missed him.'

'You're welcome to come and see us any time.' My words sounded slow and stupid as I tried to make sense of it all. 'I'm so sorry about this. I don't know what happened.'

Natasha shook her long dark fringe aside as she bent towards me. 'Has it happened before?'

I nodded, registering a twinge of surprise that Elizabeth hadn't told her about my appalling track record as a mother. 'A few times. Not this bad, though.'

'Poor you.' Natasha's face dropped its bright façade. 'What's going on, Sophy?'

Tears filled my eyes. 'I'm starting to think there's something seriously wrong with me.'

Reaching out, she took my hand. 'Have you seen a doctor?'

I nodded, which made everything spin and sent a cascade of tears down my face. 'I had some blood tests.' I sniffed. 'I'll give the surgery a ring tomorrow.'

'Have you been taking the vitamins I sent?'

'I have, but they don't seem to be making much difference.'

'It can take a couple of months. They've really transformed me,' she said, dropping her hand into her bag and pulling out a pack of tissues. She handed me one, reminding me of Liv doing the same thing with a sheet of kitchen roll, which had felt rough beneath my eyes. 'I remember after I had Toby my iron levels were on the floor. I couldn't keep my eyes open most of the day. Maybe it's the same for you.'

Slightly reassured, I wiped my eyes before swinging my legs to the floor. It felt like there were tiny hammers, banging inside my head. 'Did you get terrible headaches, and sometimes do things you couldn't remember doing?'

Natasha's eyebrows lifted. 'I did get headaches.' She gently touched my knee. 'I don't think I ever lost time, though. Mind you—' she gave a soft laugh '—those first few months with Toby are a bit of a blur. He had terrible colic for ages.'

'I remember you saying.' I was glad I could at least remember something. 'This feels more than that somehow.' Saying it aloud scared me. What if I was terminally ill? I couldn't bear for Finn to grow up without a mother.

'I'm sure you're going to be fine.' Natasha took both my hands and pulled me gently to my feet. She was taller than me, and much better put together in an expensive-looking ruffle-sleeved top and trousers, the only sign she'd been horse riding the rosy flush on her cheeks and a few strands of hair trailing from her bun. 'Better?'

I felt horribly sick but nodded, swallowing the rush of saliva that filled my mouth.

'I hope my brother is looking after you.'

I nodded again, not daring to speak in case I either vomited or cried – or both.

'I'm sorry I can't stay longer,' she said, reaching to the floor for her bag. 'I drove down to see an old client and thought it would be nice to take Lady Madonna out while I was here.'

'And to see your mother.' I managed a weak smile, feeling as wobbly as a newborn foal. 'She was happy you were here.'

'Not happy that I didn't have Toby with me.' Natasha's voice cooled slightly. 'Rory's picking him up from school but I want to get back in time to make them dinner,' she said. 'Old-fashioned,

I know, but I missed out a bit when Toby was a baby and I was setting up the business.'

It struck me, not for the first time, how unlike Elizabeth she was. In fact, both she and Dom were much more like their father. 'She misses you,' I said, making a huge effort to sound like my normal self – whatever that was. 'And Toby.'

Natasha didn't comment, but as we reached the front door – every step sending a throb of pain through my head and the room revolving – Natasha paused and glanced up the thickly carpeted stairs. 'Don't let her take over,' she said, so quietly I almost didn't hear. 'I know from experience she can be a bit much.' Her eyes flicked up again, as though expecting her mother to appear at any moment. 'Bye, Mum!' she called, her voice cheery. 'I'll ring when I get home. Love you!'

She gave me a close-lipped smile and squeezed my arm. 'Will you be OK to drive?'

I nodded, which seemed to be all I was capable of.

Natasha pressed soft lips to my cheek, filling my nostrils with her delicate scent. 'Take care, Sophy. Give Dom my love.'

'Come and visit soon, all of you,' Elizabeth called, hurrying downstairs, but by the time she reached the bottom the door had closed and Natasha was gone.

'Feeling better, are you?' Elizabeth's tone was neutral, her gaze bland when she looked at me.

'I'm so sorry. I honestly don't know what happened,' I said. 'Thank you for bringing me in and looking after us.'

'I'd better drive you home in case you have an accident.'

'There's no need.' My tongue felt stuck to the roof of my mouth. I was starving suddenly. I hadn't eaten since breakfast. 'I'll just go and get Finn.'

'You mustn't drive with a baby in the car.' She tensed her jaw so the tendons in her neck stood out. 'It's not worth the risk.'

I began to protest, but she was pushing something at me. Her phone; a photo.

'What's that?'

'This was how I found you,' she said. 'I thought you should know.'

As the image zoomed into focus, I saw with horror that it was me, sprawled in the stable, Finn propped awkwardly against a bale of hay in nothing but his little tracksuit, a big bay horse leaning over his stable door, the white flash on his face a contrast to his glossy black mane. It was obvious from the steam blowing out of his nostrils that it was freezing cold.

'I honestly don't remember going to the stables.' Sickness rose again. 'I was in the kitchen and then … that's the last thing I remember.'

'It's a good job I was here.' Elizabeth slipped her phone in her pocket and glanced at her watch. 'Now, I'll go and get Finn and take you home in your car.'

My breathing felt shallow. I couldn't seem to find the right words to tell her *no*. 'How will you get back here?'

'I won't need to.' Her chin rose as she turned back to the stairs. 'Dom won't mind me staying overnight.'

Chapter 25

Liv

I'd spent most of the morning holed up in my childhood bedroom, flopped on the single bed like a hung-over teenager, whilst going over the total cock-up I'd made earlier with Sophy. It hadn't occurred to me that Kim would tell Elizabeth about the social worker – and worse, that she would let Sophy know I'd spread gossip about her. *I'm such an idiot!*

But I was sure I'd wriggled out of it. Sophy wasn't in the right head-place to work things out, and seemed to be depending on me more and more; even spilled out her troubles, like I was her friend, convinced I would help her. She was beginning to trust me.

I sat on the edge of my bed, turning my phone over in my hand, wondering whether to attempt another call to Ryan. My eyes were fixed on the window, flagged by the same cheap chintzy curtains from my childhood. Outside, the day was as ugly and grey as my thoughts. Sophy had been so flippant about her university boyfriends; described her time with Ben as quite serious. *Quite serious!* Ben had loved her so desperately he took his own life, and yet to her he'd been simply *quite serious.*

'I won't give up, Ben,' I whispered, picking up a photo of us both on holiday at Butlin's, that stood on my bedside cabinet. 'I won't stop until the bitch has lost everything.' But my words seemed to lack my earlier conviction. Sophy wasn't a bitch, and her life was far from perfect.

I got up from the bed, and made my way onto the landing. I looked at the closed door to Ben's room, running my hand over the flaking paintwork. I rarely went in there – the shrine to my brother – but today I needed to feel close to him.

The door always got stuck on the carpet, as though allowing a moment to think before going in. I gave it a shove, thoughts of Ben bombarding my senses. Inside, everything was as it had been that awful day I found him – even the mug with Thor on, he'd used hours before his death, still sat on his desk. He'd loved Harry Potter, Marvel, DC, Star Wars, and his shelves were full of models, the walls covered with posters. Books he would never look at again were crammed onto bookshelves. One lay open, butterflied on his bedside table. I dashed away a tear. Mum hadn't changed a thing.

Why am I in here, putting myself through this?

Attached to the mirror, which was propped against the wall on an old chest of drawers, were photos of Ben with his friends. Groups of lads, arms round each other, cheering at the camera, beer bottles raised – happiness radiating from their young faces. There were no photos of Sophy, but the remains in an ashtray of photos Ben burnt the day he died were still there, and I'd always believed they were of her.

I touched the glass ashtray with my fingertips. I'd hated that he'd smoked in his room, but now I would have given anything to find him flopped on his bed puffing away, headphones on, tapping his foot to his heavy metal music.

I lowered myself onto the bed, and began moving the charred pieces of photographs around. I picked up a fragment – a nose, perhaps – a red-checked shirt maybe.

'Liv!' It was Freya, calling from the bottom of the stairs. 'Liv, have you got a minute, please?'

I wiped away a tear, and placed the burnt offering back in the ashtray. I rose and looked once more around my brother's room. *What a tragic waste of a beautiful life.*

Downstairs, Freya was waiting for me. 'Couple of things,' she began, smiling. 'Shall we go into the kitchen?'

I followed her through, and she pulled out a chair at the tiny table that seated two. Once we'd sat down, she opened her spiral-bound notepad, licked her finger, and flicked through the pages. 'First off,' she said, with a bouncy tone, 'I'm heading to my lodge in Southwold, so Shari will be filling in for me. She's new, but I've worked with her before, and she's lovely. Your mum's aware, and more than happy.' She put a huge tick next to what she'd written in her notebook.

'I hope the weather cheers up for you.' I glanced towards the window, my mind drifting to Dom, the smell of Eternity on his clothes. Maybe this was how I would bring Sophy to her knees. She was dependent on him for everything. If he was having an affair it would ruin her.

'Well, I'm not that bothered about the weather, truth be told,' Freya was saying. 'I'll spend the time reading and walking – my idea of heaven.'

I stood up, my mind not fully on Freya's holiday plans, an idea forming in my head, and causing a surge of excitement. 'Is that all you wanted me for? Because I need to do something.'

She put down her pen and took hold of my hand. 'I do care about your mum, Liv,' she said. 'I wouldn't be going away if I didn't need a break. I am entitled to time off.'

'Yes, of course, I know that.' I furrowed my forehead. 'You don't have to explain it to me, Freya.' I looked towards the open kitchen door, pulling my hand free. 'Where is Mum, by the way?'

'She dropped off to sleep in front of Miss Marple.' Freya rose too. 'I'm going to make her a nice cup of tea and a slice of cake.

I've made a lemon drizzle. What about you? Would you like a cuppa?'

I shook my head. 'Not right now.' I left the kitchen, and grabbed my jacket from the hook near the door. 'I've got to be somewhere.'

The train stood at Finsbury Park Station when Ryan called me.

'Thank God,' I said, on answering. 'I've been worried sick about you.'

'Why?' He sounded like a little boy, trying to act innocent.

'You know why, Ryan. You leave some bizarre message about Sophy.' My voice was rising, and a man opposite peered at me over his *Financial Times*. 'You were pissed when I rang,' I continued, reducing my voice to a whisper. 'You weren't at home when I called round.'

'So I'm supposed to stay in in case you drop in on me for the first time in a year?'

His words stung. 'That's not what I'm saying.' I bit down on my anger, as the train pulled away. 'You said Sophy wasn't who she seemed.'

'Did I?' He was making a bad job of pretending to sound puzzled. 'I was pissed, Liv. I didn't know what I was saying.'

'You must have an idea, surely. It's important. I want to know all I can about the woman.' Silence. 'Ryan? Ryan?' *Damn*, I'd lost the signal.

Situated near London Bridge, Apex TV emerged in its enormity as I stepped out of the railway concourse, into a bright afternoon. The ugly grey sky had been replaced with pale shades of blue and fluffy white clouds, though it was bitterly cold.

It was almost 5 p.m. and office workers, in their flat shoes, carrying laptops, surged towards me, heading homeward. I stepped to one side, my eyes skittering around the area. I was there to catch Dom out, but in cold reality, how likely would it be that I would see him at all, let alone catch him with his other

172

woman? And the affair was only an assumption anyway. Based on what? Unfamiliar perfume on his clothes? The fact his wife was falling down a rabbit hole of depression and possibly alcohol abuse, driving him away?

People streamed from the tall building. My hopes rose as I stepped out of sight behind a bus shelter, and rummaged in my bag for my phone. If he did appear – with *her* – I needed a photograph.

Following a stream of workers, I saw him, making his way through the revolving glass doors in narrow black trousers, and a calf-length black coat, the collar up.

I dived from behind the bus shelter, my heart pounding, and followed him. He moved fast, heading away from the station. I had to trot to keep up, my phone camera at the ready, feeling like a private detective. He went into a chemist, and I hung about outside, peering in through the window as he queued, keeping his distance from other shoppers.

It was as he stepped back out onto the wide pavement, dragging his fingers through his dark hair, and looking into his bag, that I saw her. Tall with long blonde hair, and high cheekbones, dressed in a navy coat belted at the waist, a pink scarf in the neck. She linked her arm through his elbow, and, as he looked up and into her face, a surprised expression on his, she moved in closer. As she touched his cheek, he grabbed her hand, said something, her name perhaps? I was too far away to hear. I fumbled with my phone, bringing up the camera app, but when I looked up, they'd gone.

I spun on the spot, before heading down the road. The London street had got busier, and my heart raced as I rounded the corner, and searched the throng of people for Dom. A black taxi hooted as I stepped into the road without thinking. But I still couldn't see them.

I turned and headed back to the station, my heartbeat slowing as I realised it didn't matter. I didn't need a photo. I'd seen him, and that was enough. All I had to do now was suggest Dom *was* having an affair, cast doubts in Sophy's mind, and I felt sure she would begin to believe it. Then I would reveal how I'd seen him with another woman.

Chapter 26

Liv

'Livy? Is that you?' Mum called. It was six-thirty, and I felt like crap, my head pounding. How people travelled to and from London in rush hour every day was beyond me.

'Yes, it's me. The prodigal daughter has returned.' I shuffled free from my jacket, and peered round the lounge door. 'What are you two up to?' I said, although it was obvious. Freya and Mum were sitting close together, their heads almost touching, as they worked on a jigsaw puzzle of a village scene.

'We're pretty sure Sparky's eaten a few pieces.' Mum smiled as she stroked the dog, curled up on her lap asleep.

'There's definitely a corner missing,' Freya, said, slotting a piece in place. 'And we're sure the church spire is working its way through the dog's digestive tract as we speak, aren't we, Sparky?'

The dog looked up at the mention of his name, chocolate-brown eyes curious.

'We probably won't be able to use the pieces when they appear again,' Mum said with a laugh. 'Where have you been, love?'

I sat down on one of the dining chairs, which creaked with

age, flopped my head backwards, and closed my eyes, my mood a million miles from theirs. 'London.'

'You've not been with Sophy Edwards today, then?'

'I went first thing, but she was taking Finn to his grandmother's house.' I opened my eyes, my thoughts roaming from Elizabeth to Dom. 'Something's not right in that house.'

'Such a shame, especially as there's a little boy in the mix,' Mum said. 'He'll be the one who suffers in the long run.'

'Indeed he will.' Freya slotted a piece of jigsaw in place. 'The child will end up in care, if things don't improve.'

The words reached deep into my conscience. I thought how Sophy desperately wanted to be a better mother, how unwell she seemed. But then Finn did nothing but cry in her presence. He'd be better off without her, *wouldn't he?* He'd still have Dom, *and Elizabeth.*

'Are you OK, Liv?' Mum said.

'I'm fine,' I muttered, rising to my feet, and heading for the door. 'I just need to go out for a bit.'

I pulled up outside number seven and killed the car engine. I wasn't sure what I was going to say to Sophy – my head seemed to be a mass of tangled thoughts. I climbed out of the Mini.

Dom's car was on the drive, and my heart galloped. Was he home? What if he'd seen me in London, spying on him? No, I was being ridiculous. Of course he hadn't seen me.

I headed up the steps and pressed the doorbell, and waited. The Avenue was dark and silent; the houses brooding and watchful. Another blast of the bell, and the door opened – my heart sank. 'Elizabeth?'

'Liv.' She eyed me up and down, making my skin prickle with unease. 'Whatever are you doing here at this hour?'

I could ask you the same question. 'Is Sophy here?' I said, keeping my voice even.

'She is, yes, but she's having a lie-down. Actually ...' She looked back over her shoulder and into the house, and lowering her voice, added, 'She did say she won't need you anymore. I'm staying for a while to help out.'

'Really?'

'It couldn't have escaped your notice that Sophy is suffering with mental health problems. It's a family issue.'

'But I'm her friend, I can help too—'

'She needs professional help, and I will make sure she gets it.'

A child's cry from inside the house sent Elizabeth scurrying down the hallway, and a failed attempt to slam the door on me gave me a chance to follow her in.

I reached the kitchen where Elizabeth was now holding Finn, singing to him, rocking him to and fro. There was no sign of Sophy.

'You can't just walk into someone's house uninvited,' Elizabeth said, lowering Finn into his playpen.

'But it's not your house, is it?' I spoke with more confidence than I felt. 'Where's Sophy?'

Elizabeth's face relaxed into a smile. 'Perhaps we've got off on the wrong foot,' she said. She reached for the kettle. 'Let me make you a coffee, and perhaps we can have a little talk.'

I stared, as she grabbed mugs and took a jar of coffee from the cupboard, spooned in granules. 'Sugar?'

I shook my head. Wanted to say I preferred tea. But it didn't seem important.

Once we were sitting one each side of the breakfast bar, I looked deep into the woman's eyes, searching for who she really was.

'I've got two grandsons,' she said, as I sipped my coffee. 'And I like to think I'm a good grandmother. I do my best. Natasha always says that.'

'Natasha?'

'My daughter. Dom's sister. I don't get to see her much, and rarely get to see Toby. That's why it's so good to help Sophy out. Be here for little Finn.' She threw him a fond glance.

'Liv?' I looked up to see Sophy standing in the kitchen doorway. She looked so pale, her red hair falling about her face in a tangled mess.

I jumped to my feet. 'Is everything OK?'

She looked at Elizabeth, then back at me.

'Sophy's not too well, are you, dear?' Elizabeth's words were firm.

'What's the time?' Sophy glanced at her wrist, though she wasn't wearing a watch. 'I seem to have lost track again.'

Within moments the front door opened, and Dom's heavy footsteps sounded oddly menacing as they carried him down the hallway. 'What's going on?' he said as he entered the kitchen, looking at each of us in turn.

'I'm going to stay for bit, darling,' Elizabeth said, putting her mug of coffee down. She nodded to a small case propped against the wall. 'Sophy isn't at all well.'

'What's wrong?' Dom looked over at his wife, a crease between his eyebrows.

'I'm tired, that's all. I'm always tired.'

'I found Sophy asleep in the stables,' Elizabeth said. 'Finn left unattended.'

Dom stepped towards Sophy, his face full of anguish. 'Is this true?'

I urged Sophy to speak up. Order Elizabeth out of her house. But she looked vacant, her eyes too big, her face sallow.

Elizabeth opened her handbag and took out her phone, tapped the screen and showed it to Dom. 'Here,' she said. 'I felt awful taking it, but thought you should see for yourself how bad things are.'

He took the phone from her, his hand shaking, his eyes watering as he stared at the screen. 'Sophy?'

A deafening silence fell, as though time had stopped, and Sophy covered her face with her hands.

Eventually Dom looked at his mother. 'I'll call Dad to fetch you, Mum,' he said, handing her phone back. 'Whatever Sophy and I are going through, we need to sort it out ... just the two of us.'

'Oh. OK. Right, no worries,' I said, realising that meant I should leave too. My eyes met Sophy's, as her hands dropped back to her sides. 'If you're sure you're OK, Soph.'

'She's fine,' Dom said, pressing his phone screen with his index finger. Elizabeth's lips formed a thin line.

'Well, I'll be back in the morning, Sophy,' I said. 'You have my number if you need me.'

'I said, she's fine.' Dom gave me a hard look, before turning his back. 'Dad, it's me,' he said into the phone, and I headed for the front door, and out into the start of a downpour.

I sat for some moments in my car, watching raindrops wiggle their way down the glass, morphing into different shapes on the windscreen, my head still pounding from earlier. I felt a sudden, all-consuming, exhaustion. Maybe it was the trip into London, or the emotional roller coaster of today. Whatever it was I needed an early night.

Chapter 27

Sophy

Once Robert had picked up an unusually subdued Elizabeth and led her away, I tried to explain that the photo she'd shown him didn't mean I was neglecting Finn, but even I had to agree the picture was damning. 'I can't even remember going to the stables,' I said, hearing the desperation in my voice. 'You have to believe me, Dom.'

'For God's sake, Sophy, what am I supposed to think?' Dom's eyes were hard and tension rippled his jaw. 'Something could be wrong with you that's putting our son's life at risk.' His words landed like punches. 'What would have happened if Mum hadn't been there?' I didn't bother to argue or mount a defence. How could I? 'Seeing that photo … it's really brought home how bad things are.'

We didn't say much after that, but Dom's tormented silence was recrimination enough as he attended to Finn, suggesting I go to bed early as though *I* was the child, though he told me it was because I looked 'wrung-out'.

I didn't mention my worries about the photo at the restaurant and whether Liv might have taken it, as well as sending me the note about his mother – the one he didn't believe existed. I did tell him that Kim had seen the social worker, which Liv had confirmed – that she wasn't gossiping – and promised I would call the doctor's the following morning, but it didn't do much to banish the by-now familiar tightness in his expression.

'The results aren't back yet,' I told Dom, once I'd hung up the phone to the surgery. 'They said to try again tomorrow.' Making an attempt to put on a normal front, I gritted my teeth against the thudding of my head while I showered and dressed, and sang nursery rhymes to Finn as I helped him eat breakfast, gratified he didn't seem to mind. I loaded the dishwasher while Dom circled around, looking grey with tiredness, my stomach churning like a tumble dryer. I couldn't face coffee, so made some mint tea and toast, which Dom ate standing up, his phone in his hand. He kept glancing at it with a harried expression. It had been pinging with texts since he got up and just as the sound of the doorbell pealed through the house, he said reluctantly, 'I'm sorry, but I have to go to the office and deal with this.' He let Liv in, eyeing her warily as he asked her to keep an eye on me, adding sternly, 'I've asked Mum to come over too. She'll be here at ten-thirty.' He squatted to kiss Finn and stroke his hair. 'She wants to make sure he's OK,' he said, catching my expression, daring me to argue. 'She won't stay long.'

Once he'd left, spinning the car out of the drive like a formula one racer, Liv looked at me with raised eyebrows. 'Do you think he's having an affair?'

'What?' Shocked, I looked at her as she picked up Finn and squashed a kiss on his cheek. 'Why do you ask?'

She looked at me over Finn's curly head of hair. 'Just …' She paused, as if unsure of her response, yet I had a strong sense she knew exactly what she wanted to say. 'The way he is with you. How he goes rushing off, even though he's supposedly worried about you.'

181

'I know I told you I was worried he'd meet someone else, but …' I thought of the text messages I wasn't privy to, and how Dom had just left as though he couldn't wait to escape from me. 'But I don't really believe it.' *Do I?* 'He's got a lot on at work and needs his job so he can support us. It's important to him.'

'I'm sure your mother-in-law would be more than happy to help out on the money front.'

Even as I registered the truth in Liv's words, I wondered why she thought she had the right to talk the way she did. I took a deep breath. 'Did you follow me into London the other day and take a photo of Isaac and me at the restaurant and give it to Dom?'

The little colour in Liv's cheeks faded to white. 'I don't know what you're talking about.'

'So, you *didn't* take a picture, print it out and give it to my husband?' My voice sounded hard but calm.

'Why would you think it was me?'

'I don't know, Liv.' I watched her place Finn in his playpen, trying to read her body language. Forcing mine to relax, I unfolded my arms. 'It just seems odd that it happened right after you started coming here, and you were on a train the same day I went to meet Isaac.' I willed her to deny it, aware she'd shown no surprise when I mentioned a photograph, almost as though she'd expected me to. 'You tell me who would do something like that.'

Liv bit her lower lip as she faced me. 'Someone your husband is having an affair with, to make him think you're cheating too, so he won't feel bad.' Her voice crept up in pitch. '*If* he feels bad. How do you even know he's dealing with work stuff right now?'

I put a hand to my chest and felt my heart beating fast. 'Why are you so sure Dom's cheating on me?' Her face worked briefly. As the moment stretched, I had the weird feeling she held my future in her hands. 'Liv?'

'I just …' She gave her hair a restless swipe. 'I'm worried about you, that's all.'

I was certain it wasn't what she'd meant to say, but felt a swoop of relief all the same. For a horrible second, it had struck me that *she* could be the one Dom was seeing behind my back and had wangled her way into our lives deliberately. I reminded myself that Dom had promised to love me forever and had never given me any reason not to trust him. *Until now.*

'My husband isn't like that,' I insisted. An image of Alicia Bainbridge flicked into my mind. 'He can't stand people who have affairs – it's one of his things.'

Liv's eyes narrowed, her mouth a twist of disbelief, but she merely shrugged and bent over the playpen and picked up one of Finn's books. He slapped his thighs and gave a shriek and a gummy grin. Surely he wouldn't be so happy to see Liv, to be in her company, if she wasn't a good person? I thought of the note about Elizabeth and how it had vanished. Liv could have taken it while I was in London. She could have sent it. But, for some reason, I couldn't bring myself to ask. Instead, I watched her with Finn and wished I could drop down beside her and talk to my son with the same ease that she showed as she flipped through the book, making cute animal sounds. I stayed glued to the spot, feeling redundant and slightly sick.

'Are you feeling better today?' She looked at me over her shoulder. 'You seemed really out of it when I came round last night.'

I started. I'd forgotten Liv had called while Elizabeth was there. She must have seen and heard everything. 'Why did you come round?'

'I wondered how you'd got on at your mother-in-law's, yesterday.' She turned back to Finn. 'It sounds like it didn't go well.'

Pain pulsed behind my eyes, reminding me that a headache was never far away. 'I don't know what happened, but I do feel better today.' It was true, I realised. In spite of my woolly-headedness and dry mouth, the world felt slightly more stable, colours in higher definition, as if a veil had been drawn back.

'Actually, I didn't feel that great when I got home.' A frown crossed Liv's brow. 'I don't even remember driving there and getting into bed. It was more like passing out than sleeping,' she said. 'Maybe there's something going round.'

Her comment was oddly cheering. 'Maybe.'

'Hey, why don't we go into London, see if Dom's really at work?'

'What?'

'Put your mind at rest.'

Was she really suggesting following my husband, spying on him? 'Liv, I'm not doing that.' My breathing felt shallow. 'Why would you—?'

'I just thought … It doesn't matter.' She shook her head, her hair falling across her face so I couldn't see her expression. 'How about we go swimming, like you suggested yesterday?' She rose, clutching one of Finn's toys – a felt dinosaur Mum had sent over – and when she looked at me, her gaze was keen. 'It would be nice to get out. I've got my swimming stuff in the car.'

'I can't.' I tried to shrug off her first suggestion. 'I'm worried I might pass out again.' I wrapped my arms around my waist, a shiver rippling through me. 'Until I have my blood test results back, I need to be careful.'

Disappointment – or maybe it was irritation – flared in Liv's eyes. 'OK.' She looked at Finn. 'Would you like me to take him out while you have a sleep, or I can just play with him down here? Maybe do a bit of housework.' Her gaze flicked over the surfaces, which thanks to Elizabeth's efforts weren't too dusty, to the clothes trailing from the washing machine in the kitchen, where Dom must have pulled out a shirt last night to dry. 'Or, we could try the soft-play centre on Granville Road. I took Evie there a couple of times and she loved it.'

'Isn't Finn a bit young?'

'There's an area specially for babies. He'll be fine.'

'Sure, why not.' I was suddenly desperate to be out of the house, somewhere with life and people, where I could behave like any other mother with a baby – and a nanny. 'I should be OK as long as I have somebody with me.'

'Someone who's not your mother-in-law.'

'Exactly.' Maybe she didn't want me relying on Elizabeth, but it wasn't exactly a crime. Grasping the olive branch, I smiled, feeling a stab of guilt as a memory pushed though, of Dom saying he would deal with the picture of Isaac and me, as if he knew who'd sent it. I'd completely forgotten and hadn't had a chance to ask him about it. 'Listen, Liv, I'm sorry I accused you just now, of taking that photo.'

She waved a dismissive hand, before bending to pick up Finn. 'It's fine, only natural you'd ask. It's a pretty horrible thing to do.'

'It's just, with social services coming round, and then the photo, and the note warning me to watch Elizabeth—' I kept my eyes on her face, but there wasn't so much as a ripple '—it really does feel as if someone's out to get me.'

Liv looked at Finn cuddled against her. 'We should get ready to go,' she said, as if I hadn't spoken.

'I'll go and get changed.' I was aware of my shapeless jumper and baggy mum-jeans, and the kink in my hair where I'd slept on it. 'I'm not fit to be seen in public.'

Once upstairs, I tried calling Elizabeth to let her know I was going out, but the line was engaged. I left a voicemail, knowing she'd pick it up as soon as she finished her call. On impulse, I checked my emails for the attachment from Isaac, containing details of the new quiz show, but there was nothing in my inbox, or the spam folder. Perhaps he hadn't got round to sending it. He was busy, I reminded myself, squashing a pang of disappointment. I'd check again later.

It was a fifteen-minute walk to Granville Road, the October sun warm on our backs. I was hot and bothered by the time we arrived after trotting to keep up with Liv, who didn't seem inclined to talk as she marched along pushing Finn in his buggy. Already, I was wishing I'd gone for a sleep instead – anything

185

to stop the stream of questions circling my mind, demanding answers I didn't have.

When I entered the overheated building and spotted Kim with Dougie, my heart dropped, until I realised she was putting their coats on, ready to leave. I didn't fancy another gossipy encounter.

'I was going to suggest we keep our heads down, but looks like they're going,' Liv said, as I busied myself taking a twenty-pound note from my purse. 'You take him through, I'll pay.' She took the note and thrust Finn's pushchair at me. 'You can leave it over there.' She nodded to an area crowded with buggies, before pulling up her coat collar and hurrying to the reception. She obviously didn't want to bump into Kim either.

'Hey, Sophy, good to see you!'

I inwardly cringed at Kim's greeting, busying myself with parking Finn's pushchair while he drummed his legs and started to cry. 'Hi,' I mumbled, noting how calm Dougie was in his sling, his round face placid. 'Is it very busy?'

'Not too bad at this time of morning.' Kim's smile was tinged with faux-sympathy as she watched Finn flex like a fish. 'I tend to leave before the hordes get here.'

'Right.' Turning from her too-bright gaze, I bent to unstrap Finn.

'Ooh, I've just seen your gorgeous husband.'

My hands stilled. 'Sorry?'

'Is he joining you here?'

I straightened, attempting to keep a neutral expression in spite of my racing heart. 'He's working, actually.'

'Ah, so that's why he was in that funny little café,' she said. 'I suppose if you have a laptop you can work anywhere these days. My hubby spends a lot of time on the golf course, closing deals.' She gave a trilling laugh.

'Café?' Why was Dom in a café? Unless Kim was mistaken and she'd seen someone who looked like him, as I had the other day.

186

'That awful greasy spoon on Victoria Street,' she said, seeming not to notice I sounded baffled. 'I don't normally walk that way, but we were early this morning and took the long route here.' She pulled on her woolly gloves. 'He stood out like a sore thumb, I must say, but I suppose he won't be bothered by anyone he knows in there. I certainly wouldn't set foot inside.' Another laugh, less certain this time. 'Nice to see you out and about. I do hope you'll make it to Mums Meet Up next week.' Her greedy gaze scanned towards the exit. 'No Olivia today?'

Still struggling to understand why Dom wasn't in London, I turned. There was no sign of Liv. 'She must be in the ladies' room.'

'Probably the cold weather.' Kim gave an exaggerated shiver. 'I can't wait to get out to our place in Spain again. We're thinking of spending New Year there.' Her eyes moved to Finn. 'Exciting that this year will be his first Christmas,' she babbled on. 'Not that they remember anything about it, but it's nice for the grown-ups. I've already ordered a tree.'

Christmas seemed aeons away. Mum had mentioned coming over for a week. I hoped she would. I felt a longing to see her in person. 'It will be nice.'

Sensing she wasn't going to get a conversation out of me, Kim finally stepped past. 'Right, we'd better get home for elevenses.'

'Bye,' I said weakly, watching her retreating back, Dougie's legs bouncing either side of her waist.

'Thank God she's gone.' Liv reappeared, her face pale, hands in her coat pockets. 'What did she say?'

'It's Dom,' I said in a daze, jigging Finn's pushchair. He'd stopped crying and was looking around with watery eyes. 'She said he's in a café on Victoria Street.'

'Alone?' Liv seemed oddly unsurprised. 'She's sure it was him?' I nodded.

She looked at me for a moment, eyes searching my face. 'Go on then.'

'What?'

'Go and talk to him,' she said. 'I'll look after Finn – don't worry.'

Once again, I found myself hurrying away from a concerned expression, and Liv *did* look concerned, more than I'd seen before.

It didn't take long to find the café. It wasn't quite the greasy spoon that Kim had described, but not the sort of place to meet her exacting standards with its steamed-up windows, laminated tables and English breakfast-style menu chalked on a board outside.

I hadn't rehearsed what to say, simply focused on finding the place. Poking my head inside, I was glad I hadn't bothered. There was no sign of Dom, just a table surrounded by tradesmen in overalls with mugs and empty plates in front of them, and a woman sitting alone in the corner. Kim had seen someone who resembled my husband; that was all.

Stepping back on the pavement, I glanced at my watch, my breath coming fast. If Kim had passed on her way to the soft-play centre, Dom could have been and gone by now.

As I dug around in my bag for my phone to call him, the woman emerged from the café, tucking a pink scarf into the neck of a navy coat. My heart seized.

'Alicia?' She had the sort of looks you couldn't forget; a sheet of blonde hair spilling from under a black fedora, skin pulled taut over aristocratic cheekbones and intense, almond-shaped eyes. 'What are you doing here?'

She'd frozen in the act of tying her coat belt around her tiny waist. 'Sophy!' Her voice was deeper than I remembered; husky, as though she'd been crying, though her irises were clear as she took me in. 'I suppose you're looking for Dom,' she said casually. It was so unexpected, all I could do was stare, wondering whether I'd passed out again and was experiencing a nightmare. 'I don't know how you found out about us, but it's probably better that you have.' She pulled the strap of her soft, black tote bag onto her shoulder. 'If I were you, I'd let him go without a fight. You can't want to be with someone who doesn't want to be with you.'

'We have a baby.' The words came out as a whisper, my body trembling as though I had a fever.

'He knows I'll be a good stepmother.'

Blood roared in my ears. 'Leave him alone, Alicia.'

Her eyes blazed with sudden passion. 'We're in love.'

'I don't believe you.'

'He's realised he should have married me, but he feels sorry for you.'

'Sophy?' I turned to see Liv approaching, coat flapping as she thrust Finn's pushchair along the narrow pavement. 'What's going on?'

I spun round to see Alicia striding away, head down as she turned the corner out of sight. 'You were right.' I looked back at Liv through a haze of tears. 'Dom's been cheating on me.'

Chapter 28

Liv

'Who is she? Do you know her?' I turned back to Sophy, whose teary eyes were fixed on the corner where the woman I'd seen with Dom in London had been moments earlier. 'Sophy?' I touched her arm, a small part of me wanting to comfort her.

She looked round at me, and moved away so my arm fell away. 'I don't know why I'm surprised,' she said with a sniff. 'It all makes sense doesn't it?' She grabbed the pushchair from me and gripped the handle. Without it I felt oddly exposed, as though she could see right through me. 'I need to get back to the house,' she said. 'Wait for Dom.'

With that she took off, racing along the pavement, wiping her wet cheeks with her sleeve every few moments. I hurried along beside her, struggling to keep up.

'Do you think she called social services?' she said. 'Sent the notes?'

'Sophy, please, slow down a bit.' I tried to catch my breath.

'I mean what would she gain from that?'

'Sophy, who is she? Do you know her?' I said again, once we'd reached the house, and she'd stopped by the gate.

'Alicia Bainbridge.' She said the name like an insult. 'She worked …' She bit down on her lip as she looked up at the house, casting her eyes over the black Range Rover parked outside the house next to Dom's car. 'Oh God, I should have known she'd turn up,' she whispered.

'Elizabeth?'

She nodded as she moved her eyes to the silhouette of her mother-in-law in the window, a fleeting shadow of Dom appearing behind her for a moment.

'It'll be OK, Sophy. He's bound to have an explanation.'

She turned to look at me. 'He told me once Alicia had a bit of a thing for him, but it was a while ago,' she continued. 'He said it was nothing, that she would get over it. But now …' She covered her mouth as though stifling a sob. 'I don't know what to say to him. I feel so angry, so stupid—'

'Maybe there's an explanation. Maybe it's not what it looks like.' I wasn't sure I believed my words, but I knew I didn't want it to be true, though I couldn't explain why. Surely this was what I'd wanted all along, and yet … 'Give him a chance to explain.'

She nodded. 'I need to talk to him alone, find out what's been going on.'

I took the hint. 'OK. Fine. But as soon as you get inside tell that awful mother-in-law of yours to take a hike.'

A small smile flickered and died on her lips.

'Are you sure you don't want some moral support?'

She shook her head. 'I need to do this by myself, but thanks, Liv.'

'Of course, no worries.' I moved forward, tempted to give her a hug, but changed my mind. 'You know where I am if you need me, right?'

She nodded, took a deep breath, and pushed Finn up the path towards the front door. 'And, Liv,' she called without looking back, 'please don't say anything to anyone.'

As the door closed, Elizabeth moved away from the window, and I headed towards my Mini parked on the street. A couple in their sixties, wearing matching blue jackets, appeared with a white Labrador from a house opposite, and headed up The Avenue with uniform strides. I looked back at number seven, trying to imagine what was going on inside, and my curiosity got the better of me. I pulled up my hood, and hurried down the path that ran alongside the house. There was a gap in the wall where the gate didn't latch properly. I pushed the gate open.

'Can I help you?' The female voice, high-pitched and aristocratic, came from an upstairs window of the house next door. Without looking up, I hurried away, back onto the street, bumping headlong into Kim.

'Olivia,' she said, as though I was exactly the person she wanted to see. 'No Finn today?'

I glanced up at number seven. 'Not today,' I said, trying to manoeuvre past her, but she'd trapped me at the end of the pathway.

'I don't suppose you fancy a cup of tea at Indigo Cottage.'

'Indigo Cottage?'

She laughed. 'Sorry. I mean, do you fancy coming round to mine? I have nothing on and it would be nice to have the company.'

I wondered if she was lonely, or perhaps she wanted to show off her house; either way, I didn't have anything else to do, and was curious where this woman lived. I smiled at a sleeping Dougie in his sling. Head pressed against Kim's chest, dribble running down his chin, 'Why not?' I said with a shrug.

Chapter 29

Sophy

I hadn't been surprised to see Elizabeth's car parked outside the house. Deep down, I knew she would ignore my message and turn up anyway, because she wouldn't miss an opportunity to see Finn. She must have been upset with Dom the night before, for asking his dad to take her home, and would no doubt be cleaning and tidying, perhaps even cooking, keen to insert herself at the centre of our lives once more.

My heart thumped and my breathing was jerky as I parked Finn's pushchair in the hall, wishing I'd thought to ask Liv to take him to the park. I didn't want him absorbing a difficult atmosphere, but I couldn't let my encounter with Alicia go unmentioned.

'You're back.' Dom emerged from the living room wild-eyed, his hair rumpled, shirt half-untucked. I imagined him with Alicia, their lips locked, the pair of them wishing I'd disappear. He reached for Finn, visibly relaxing. 'Where did you go?'

'Where did *you* go?' I half-turned so he couldn't reach his son. His eyebrows flicked together. 'What?'

'You heard me.' Finn was sucking his finger, his eyes swooping from me to his father and I suddenly couldn't bear to do this in front of him. Catching sight of Elizabeth hovering by the living room door, I marched towards her.

'Would you mind giving Finn his lunch?

Finn lunged for his grandmother, hands clutching at the gold chain resting against her soft wool sweater. Unable to resist, she took him from me, her eyes straying to my face. 'You still don't look well.' Her voice was sweet, but her eyes were hard, no doubt recalling me slumped in her stable the day before, my son freezing nearby. 'Shall I make some coffee?'

I didn't need caffeine; my blood was humming with the adrenaline that had fuelled my dash home from the café. 'No thanks.' I kept my voice sunny, mindful of that awful image of me on her phone. 'I need a few minutes to talk to Dom in private.' I stroked a reassuring hand over Finn's soft curls, avoiding Elizabeth's narrowed gaze. 'We'll be outside.'

'Outside?' She glanced at the window, where grey clouds hung low over the garden. 'In this weather?'

'It's not that cold.' There was a sheen of sweat on my upper lip, heat in my armpits. I felt as if I was unravelling, my hair tumbling out of its clip, my face flushed. 'If you'll excuse us.'

Before she could protest, I turned to Dom in the hallway, watching me with an unreadable expression. 'Now,' I said in a tone I couldn't remember using with him before.

He moved to the front door, not bothering with a coat. 'What's going on?'

'Not here.'

I led the way around the side of the house, where the only window belonged to the downstairs toilet. I checked it was closed, in case Elizabeth decided to eavesdrop.

'Has something happened?' Dom was rubbing his arms in their shirt sleeves, the chill more biting than I'd realised. 'Where did you go this morning?'

'I took Finn to the soft-play centre and bumped into Kim,

who said she saw you in a café on Victoria Street.' I rounded on him, fury burning through me. 'I went to look for you and guess who I bumped into?'

Dom's face paled as understanding dawned. 'Sophy, I—'

'How long has it been going on?'

'It's not what you think.' He looked as if he was going to be sick. 'You have to believe me, Sophy.'

'You're not denying you were with Alicia Bainbridge, then?'

'No, but …' He pressed his fingers to his mouth then let them drop. 'Sophy, whatever she told you, we're not having an affair.'

I made a sound of disbelief, recalling the light in her eyes as she said, *We're in love*. 'You would say that, wouldn't you?'

'Because it's true.'

I couldn't believe this was happening; that we were saying words like 'affair'. A year ago, on my birthday, Dom had taken the day off and spent it pampering me. I was six months pregnant, still suffering bouts of sickness and hadn't felt like going out, so he'd made me breakfast in bed, run a bath for me to soak in, massaged my feet while we watched back-to-back episodes of *Outlander*, and after my favourite dinner of cheesy mashed potatoes, he'd read aloud from my Philippa Gregory novel, putting on a silly voice for Edmund Tudor that had made me weak with laughter. All the while, he'd kept a hand on the curve of my belly and I'd imagined our baby listening to our voices. I'd felt cherished; certain of our future. Now, we were huddled outside our house, being buffeted by the wind, discussing his affair while his mother was inside, feeding our son.

I brushed aside strands of hair blowing over my face, the echo of Alicia's words trailing a path of acid to my stomach. 'Are you in love with her?' I hadn't been a good wife lately, had struggled to connect with my feelings for Dom, but they were still there, trapped beneath the surface. 'Tell me the truth.'

He tipped his face to the darkening sky and shook his head.

'Sophy, I swear on Finn's life, I'm not having an affair with that woman.'

That brought me up short. Dom wouldn't swear on our son's life if it wasn't true. It was an unspoken rule, somehow wrong – tempting fate. Only someone without a conscience would swear on their child's life and not mean it.

'She said you told her she'd make a good stepmother to Finn.'

'Jesus Christ!' He pushed his knuckles against his forehead before digging his phone from his trouser pocket. 'She's more delusional than I thought,' he muttered, swiping the screen. 'Look.' He thrust his phone at me, just as his mother had done with hers the night before, pushing it under his nose so he could see me sprawled in her stables like a drunk. 'Alicia's been messaging me,' he said. 'It's been going on for a while. I thought I could deal with it, without having to worry you on top of everything else.'

Tearing my eyes from his face, I looked at the string of messages. Words leapt out: *I love you Dom, I know you feel the same x We both know you married the wrong woman x We can make it work, but you have to tell her x I'll be the best stepmother. I won't try to come between him and Sophy x* I shuddered, seeing my name. *I need to see you, let's talk this through. I can come to St Albans again x*

'You haven't replied,' I said, starting to shiver.

'Of course I haven't.' His face seemed pulled out of shape. 'I didn't want to encourage her.'

'How does she have your number?'

'She's still in touch with a couple of colleagues at work, said I promised to give her a reference for a new job she'd applied for. I called her back and we met a couple of times in London because it seemed innocent, then.'

'You knew she liked you.'

'Not that much.' He sounded bitter. 'Something had happened since she left Apex, she was … different. Less together, somehow. She seemed convinced we'd had something special, that we were meant for each other.'

'But you still went to see her.' Something struck me. 'I saw you once before, when I was in that café with Liv. Alicia too.' I thought back to the flash of silky blonde hair. 'I thought I was imagining things.'

'She wanted to meet,' Dom said, sound chastened. 'I thought if we could sit down face to face and talk like adults for ten minutes, I could make her understand there was no future for us, that if I handled it carefully, she'd get the message and leave me alone.'

'But she didn't.'

His lips twisted into a humourless smile. 'She thinks I'm staying with you out of some weird sense of loyalty.' He said it as if he couldn't believe it. 'That all she has to do is wait and I'll come to my senses and somehow we'll be together.'

Alarm fluttered in my chest. 'Dom, if this is true, you should go to the police.'

He shook his head. 'She's not dangerous, just ... troubled.'

I dug my fingernails into my palms, willing myself to stay strong. 'Why are you protecting her?'

'I'm not.' He took hold of my hands, unfurling my fingers. 'I was trying to reason with her, Sophy.' There were rings of exhaustion under his eyes. 'I didn't want to involve the police and risk escalating things.'

His words provoked a fresh shiver. I thought of the social worker. Was that Alicia's doing? 'Why didn't you tell me?' But the answer was obvious, even before he said it.

'You've not been well.' His hands were gentle, sliding up my arms. 'I didn't want you to worry when you've not been yourself.' He rested his forehead on mine. 'I'm so sorry you had to find out like this.'

I looked into his eyes, so close I could see the tiny black flecks around his pupils – the eyes that had looked into mine on our wedding day as he recited his vows, adding a few words of his own to make me smile – and wondered how I could have doubted him. 'I'm sorry too.' Guilt flooded in. Dom had been dealing with this alone while I'd been too tired, too engulfed in whatever was happening to me to notice, thinking his preoccupation was about work, that he was regretting marrying me. I shut my eyes, tears squeezing out.

'Hey, don't cry, please don't cry.' Dom stroked away my tears with his thumb. 'I'm glad you know, if I'm honest. It's been hard, keeping it from you.'

'Do you think she took that photo of Isaac and me?'

He took a deep breath and nodded, letting me go as he pushed his phone back in his pocket. 'She swears she didn't, but I'm sure she thought if I saw you like that, with him, I'd leave you.'

'That's what Liv said.'

His shoulders tensed. 'Liv knows?'

I nodded, wiping my face with the heels of my hands. 'I needed someone to talk to, Dom, stuck here, feeling so awful all the time.'

'You can talk to me …' His words trailed off. 'I suppose I haven't been around much, but Mum—'

'Please don't say it.' I held both hands up, warding off what I knew was coming. 'I can't confide in your mother, I'm sorry. We don't have that kind of relationship.'

His expression changed into neutral. 'You could, if you tried a bit harder.'

I shook my head. 'I know you don't believe me about the note—'

'Sophy, please stop.' He pointed towards the house. 'She's in there, taking care of our son.'

'Yes, I'm aware of that,' I said tightly. Biting back the urge to say more, I forced a calming breath. 'What are you going to do now?' I said. 'About Alicia?'

He exhaled heavily. 'I honestly don't know. Ignore her, I suppose.'

'And if she doesn't go away?'

'Then I'll go to the police and see about getting a restraining order.'

'Maybe you should tell her that.'

His phone started ringing and he swore under his breath. 'It's work,' he said, reluctantly pulling it out and showing me the screen. 'I know it's not the right time, Sophy, but I have to deal with this. I've been letting things slide a bit, what with … everything.'

'It's fine,' I said tightly. 'I'll go and get Finn.'

I grabbed at the doorframe as I went indoors, my knees buckling. I felt sick, suddenly, my stomach rising. The walls zoomed towards me as I doubled over and sweat prickled down my spine.

'Sophy?'

Gasping, I looked up to see Elizabeth looming over me, her gold chain swinging in front of my eyes. 'Where's Finn?' I managed.

'You know, there are women who'd give anything to have what you have and you don't appreciate any of it.' She sounded close to crying, and even as I battled the nausea surging through me, I thought of Christopher, the baby she'd lost, and felt a wave of pity – until she leant closer and whispered, 'You don't deserve to be a mother.'

'Sophy?' Dom had come in and his hand was on my back. 'What's wrong?'

'Did you hear what she just said?'

'What?' Dom's hand dropped away.

'I think she's having a panic attack.' Elizabeth's voice was laced with concern and I wondered whether I'd imagined her cruel words. 'Sophy, why don't you go and sit down and I'll make some coffee?'

I shook my head as my stomach spasmed once more. 'I'm going upstairs.' I pushed the words through gritted teeth. 'I'll be fine.'

As I ran up to the bathroom, the last thing I heard was Elizabeth saying kindly, 'Go and do what you have to, Dom. Sophy and Finn will be safe with me.'

Chapter 30

Liv

We'd walked to Indigo Cottage, a large Victorian House at the far end of a cobbled drive, the entrance flagged by pillars, a Mercedes parked on the drive. Kim looked at me for what felt like a reaction, as we made our way into the house. I never gave one.

From a spacious hallway, she led the way into a dark-wood kitchen that smelt vaguely of baking. 'Give me a hand,' she said, as she heaved Dougie from the sling, and I leapt forward to pull it away from her hefty body. Once he was free, his chubby legs kicking, she propped him on her hip as she filled the kettle and flicked it on, and he watched her every move with bright eyes.

We carried our over-milky tea through to the lounge, which looked out over a long stretch of garden, and I perched on one of the three expensive-looking sofas, cradling my mug. Toys were scattered everywhere, and Kim finally let go of her grip on Dougie, and placed him amongst them. He grabbed a drumstick and banged it on a toy xylophone.

'So how are you enjoying working for Sophy, so far? Is she any better?'

'She's getting there,' I said, making a resolve not to discuss

Sophy anymore. She'd got enough on her plate without Kim gossiping about her.

'Funnily enough, I saw Clare earlier. She didn't seem herself at all. Very quiet.'

'Really? Is Evie OK?'

'Oh yes, bright as a button.'

'That's good,' I said with relief. My eyes drifted around the room, landing on the many photos of Kim with a balding man I assumed was her husband. There were photos of Dougie too – mainly professional – and a picture of Kim hugging another woman – their resemblance uncanny, and I wondered if it was the sister she'd spoken about, the one in Spain trying to work out things with her husband.

'How is your sister?' I said, for something to say, the sound of Dougie clanking on the mini xylophone grating on my nerves.

She nodded. Took a long sip of her tea. 'Fine,' she said, leaning forward to take the drumstick from Dougie, replacing it with a stacking cup, and I guessed the state of her sister's marriage wasn't up for discussion today.

What followed was Kim's attempt to brag about her life, and I realised, not for the first time, that I had nothing in common with the woman. She painted a picture of her happy family, her wonderful husband – how they planned to renovate Indigo Cottage, travel. My life was an empty canvas by comparison. I didn't envy her exactly. There was something sad about Kim I couldn't quite put my finger on, but at thirty-two I'd achieved nothing. My whole life, since I was sixteen, had been a grieving-fest for my brother.

I gulped back my tea, looked at my watch, and rose. 'I need to get home,' I said. I didn't offer a reason, and she didn't ask.

She lifted Dougie from the floor and perched him on her hip. 'I'll show you out,' she said.

*

Mum was in the kitchen baking when I got home. The aroma reminded me of my childhood, when I would stand on a chair, wearing an apron, and lick the icing bowl after we'd made cakes together. I poked my head round the door to see her reversing her chair, and sliding a red velvet cake into the oven. 'Hello, love.'

I raised my hand in a wave. 'I'll want a slice of that later,' I said with a smile. 'Or maybe two.'

'Of course.' She smiled back as she closed the oven door.

I headed up the stairs, towards the sound of a vacuum cleaner, and fluttered my fingers at Freya who was whizzing the vacuum around Mum and Dad's old room. She tended to clean upstairs once every six weeks or so, as, other than the times I stayed, the rooms were no longer used. The dining room had been transformed into Mum's bedroom after her accident, and she always used the downstairs shower room. In some ways it was good that she couldn't come upstairs and lose herself in Ben's old room, where she'd spent hours in the months after his death, lying on his bed, holding one of his T-shirts to her face, or weeping into his pillow, while Dad sat alone downstairs, blaming himself for not seeing how unhappy his son was, when he should have been blaming Sophy.

'You're home early,' Freya called above the noise, pushing her hair from her face. 'How's Finn?'

'Fine. Sophy and Dom just need some time alone to sort things out.'

Her eyes widened as though she wanted to hear the latest saga of the Pemberton household, but I didn't want to talk about it, and before she could say anything else, I stepped into my bedroom, and closed the door.

I lay on my bed, my head full of Sophy. How had she ended up with a husband who cheated on her, and a mother-in-law who, from what I could tell, seemed set on being in Finn's life full-time? A huge part of me needed to know more about Sophy. The woman she was before she married Dom. Had he made her into the crumbling wreck she seemed to be? Had Elizabeth? Was she suffering with what my mum called the baby blues? Or was there more to it? I remembered what she'd said about a quite serious relationship at university. Had what happened to Ben affected her in some way? Had she buried it in her subconscious, and it was revealing itself now? Could I get her to talk about it?

We'd known so little about Sophy when Ben fell in love with her. Just that he'd found someone special, and he would introduce us soon. Mum and Dad were excited. Ben hadn't had any serious relationships before Sophy. Far too bookish and studious, Mum always said. She had been thrilled Ben was so happy, quickly joking about one day being a grandma, and saying she couldn't wait to pick out a big hat with feathers for the wedding.

'I'm in love,' he'd told me once in a call from university, and I could hear it in his voice that he was. 'It's like nothing I've ever felt before.'

The drone of the vacuum cleaner was making me weary, and, not wanting to sleep, I pulled myself upright, and grabbed my phone.

I dialled Ryan's number, relieved when he picked up.

'Hey, Liv,' he said, his voice a monotone.

'You OK?'

'Aha.'

'Listen, you said Sophy—'

'Not this again, Liv – it was nothing. I was pissed. Talking crap.'

'Yeah, I get that, but I need to know more about her, Ryan. What was she like at uni? What were Ben and Sophy like together? Did she seem as much in love with him as he was her?'

'Christ, Liv, we went through all this at the time. It was years ago.'

'So you're telling me you've forgotten Ben?' I sounded bitter. Ryan hadn't forgotten Ben any more than I had. 'Sorry, that came out wrong. Sorry.'

'It's fine. No worries.' He pauses for a moment, before adding,

'But, like I said back then, I didn't really know Sophy. Ben wasn't with her long, Liv. It was all a bit of a whirlwind, you know that.'

'Yeah, I remember. But she obviously meant a lot to him.' I bit down on my lip, trying to hold in my annoyance. 'She clearly made a big impression. There must have been something special about her.'

He sighed. 'Well, as you probably know already, she was pretty. She had a confidence about her, was clever – popular, but that's all I've got.' He paused. 'You need to let this whole obsession with Sophy go, Liv. People make mistakes, especially when they're young. Maybe she didn't mean to hurt him. Maybe something stood between them – something she could do nothing about.'

'I get all of that, Ryan. But she barely seems to remember him. How can she forget someone who was so deeply in love with her?'

The sound of the vacuum cleaner rhythmically banging against the door was irritating. I was about to get up and ask Freya to stop for a few minutes, when the noise ended, and a plug was pulled from the wall.

There was a knock on my door. 'Hang on,' I said into the phone, and walked across the room and opened up to a smiling Freya, who was winding the wire around the cleaner.

'I'm about to make a few sandwiches for your mum,' she said. 'Would you like some?'

'Sounds lovely.' I realised I was hungry. 'Give me a minute and I'll come down and give you a hand.'

'That's very kind,' she said, lifting the vacuum cleaner and heading away.

I closed the door once more. 'So when can I see you?' I asked Ryan, feeling calmer.

'Any time you like,' he said, but I wasn't sure he meant it.

'Great. I'll text you.'

'OK. But please, in the meantime, stop this thing with Sophy.'

'To be honest, I'm beginning to feel a bit sorry for her,' I admitted. 'Her life's a mess. Her husband is cheating on her, and her mother-in-law took a photograph of her yesterday passed out in the stables. It was quite damning, made it look as though she was neglecting her little boy. I'm really not sure what's going on in that house.'

'All the more reason to let things go.'

'I can't help the way I feel, Ryan.' My stomach twisted as I realised there was still a smouldering of anger there, even if the flames weren't as raging as they once were. Even so, I didn't want to fight with Ryan. 'Listen, I'd better go and give Freya a hand with lunch. Talk soon.' I ended the call and made my way down the stairs to where Freya was grabbing a loaf from the bread bin. Mum had gone, but the cake smelt delicious.

Freya glanced round at me. 'Cheese and pickle?'

I nodded, and took cheese from the fridge. 'Are you looking forward to getting away tomorrow?'

'Very much so.' Freya laid out six slices of bread, and grabbed the cheese grater. 'I'm hoping to do a bit of walking, and I've downloaded three novels to my Kindle.'

'I'll miss you.' It was Mum, heading into the kitchen.

'You'll be fine with Shari, Martha.' Freya smiled. 'She's lovely.'

'So you keep telling me,' Mum said, but I was worried. I normally cared for Mum when Freya went away. This was the first time she'd been with anyone new.

I opened the door to Shari, and had an instant good feeling about her. She was around the same age as Freya, but unlike Freya, Shari gave off an open, what-you-see-is-what-you-get kind of vibe. She was wearing a uniform, a white dress with the company's emblem, a wide belt around her plump midriff, and a short black corduroy jacket. Her curly, black hair was scooped away from her round face and tied into a small, frizzy ponytail.

'You must be Liv,' she said, her tone upbeat, her smile wide. 'Freya's told me all about you.'

'All good, I hope.'

'Of course.' She slipped off her jacket as she stepped in. 'So how's Mum today?'

'Good. Cheerful.' I dropped my tone to a whisper. 'Though if I'm honest, she's in a bit of a panic about Freya not being here.'

'Understandable.' Shari nodded her head as she hung her jacket on the hook near the door. 'It's not always easy having a stranger in the house, and I know she's close with Freya.'

I nodded. 'A bit too dependent at times.'

'I worked with Freya several years back, when she was a social worker, and I couldn't believe it when I saw her name on the rota. It's lovely to see her doing so well after ...' She stopped abruptly, as though she'd said too much. 'Anyway, she's told me everything I need to know about your mum, and I'm sure we'll get along just fine.'

Half an hour later, Shari had tempted Mum to a boiled egg, and they were doing a crossword puzzle together.

I pulled on my coat. 'You have my number if you need me,' I said.

'We're fine, aren't we, Martha?' Shari gave me another one of her broad smiles.

Mum glanced up at me, and my stomach knotted. Sometimes she looked so lost, and I wondered at that moment, if she really had come to terms with Ben's death, and if, without her Freya security blanket, she would be OK.

'See you later,' I said, raising my hand.

And stepping out into the cool morning air, I closed the door behind me.

'Hey,' I said, when Sophy answered the front door, a grizzling, red-cheeked, Finn in her arms, which seemed pretty much the norm.

'Hey,' she mirrored, and turned and made her way into the house, dragging her feet as she headed down the hall. She'd been crying – that much was obvious.

'How did things go yesterday?' I asked, as I followed her into the kitchen. She put Finn in his playpen, and handed him his teddy. 'With Dom, I mean.'

'I know what you mean, Liv.' Her voice was dull and lifeless. 'But I haven't got the energy to talk about it right now.' She rubbed her neck with both hands and sighed. 'I've had Elizabeth round already this morning, and feel pretty dreadful.' She turned, headed for the kitchen door. 'Can you keep an eye on Finn? We can talk later. I'm going back to bed.'

I bit down on my frustration, as I listened to her footfalls on the stairs, slow and heavy, as though her feet weighed too much. I wanted to know everything that had happened the day before – whether her marriage was over – if Dom had let her down. 'No worries,' I called after her. There was nothing else I could say.

I turned to Finn. 'Right, sweetie.' I lifted him from the playpen, and held him to me, kissing his head, breathing in his baby smell. 'Let's have a bit of quality time just me and you, shall we?'

I walked into the lounge, Finn propped on my hip, enjoying the feel of his little fingers touching my cheek, before putting him down on the floor, next to the sofa. I handed him his favourite book, which he immediately stuffed into his mouth.

'Right let's get some light on the subject, shall we, little man?' I padded towards the patio doors, and pulled back the curtains. The air was still and heavy in the room, the only life the flashing light of a message waiting to be heard on the home phone. I threw open the doors to let some fresh air in, my shoulders sagging with the heavy sadness here. I looked at Finn, caught up in the middle of it all, tangled in the web of unhappiness that was Sophy and Dom. He deserved better than this, and I knew Ryan was right. I had to let my anger go.

I played with Finn until his eyelids grew heavy, then took him upstairs, changed his nappy, and popped him down for a sleep in his cot. I walked over to the window and looked out for some moments. Finn's bedroom faced The Avenue, and outside was still and quiet, only two cars parked along the road – a maroon Volvo Estate, and a white saloon – and there wasn't a soul about. I closed the panda curtains, smiled at Finn now fast asleep, and headed back downstairs.

I was about to fill the dishwasher, when my phone rang.

'Liv. Liv, it's Shari.'

'Shari? Is everything OK?' I used to worry about my mum all the time years ago, but when Freya started caring for her, I'd allowed myself to relax. Now those old emotions and fears rushed to the surface.

'It's your mum, Liv.' Her voice was raspy. Gone was the confident upbeat tone of earlier.

'Is she OK?'

'The ambulance is on its way.'

'Ambulance?' My heart thudded in my ears. 'What's happened?'

'She had pains in her chest. Can you come here, please.'

'Of course, I'm on my way.'

I ended the call, grabbed the baby monitor, and raced up the stairs, suddenly angry that Sophy was asleep again. I threw open her bedroom door and raced in, my head throbbing as I dragged back the curtains. I turned to see her huddled under her duvet. 'Sophy,' I said. 'Sophy, you need to wake up. I've got to go.'

She groaned, but didn't move.

'For Christ's sake, Sophy.' I nudged her. 'I've got to go, and you need to get up and look after Finn.' I dragged back the quilt, my heart thumping. 'Sophy!'

'What?' She pulled the cover back over her, seeming almost afraid of me. 'What's wrong?'

'It's my mum. She's …' I could hear the tears in my voice. 'I have to go.' I headed for the door. 'Finn is asleep in his cot, but you need to get up. Make sure you're not asleep when he wakes. OK?' I placed the baby monitor beside her.

'OK. Yes.'

'Just promise me you won't go back to sleep.'

'I promise,' she said, as I turned and left the room.

Chapter 31

Sophy

I rose from the depths of sleep once more, a sweep of goose-flesh alerting me to a presence that shouldn't be there. Fighting through layers of tiredness I tried to sit up, but was pulled back into blackness.

What felt like hours later, a sound inserted itself into my brain; the insistent ringing of my phone. I groped blindly at the bedside table, eyes refusing to open.

''Lo,' I croaked, pressing the phone to my ear. My voice was thick and slurred, my tongue dry. I tried to swallow but seemed to have run out of saliva. 'Hello?'

No one replied, but I was sure I could hear shallow breathing. With an effort, I hoisted myself up on one elbow, squinting as light from the window assaulted my eyeballs. 'Who is this?'

The line went dead. Flopping onto my back I blinked at the screen with sticky, heavy eyes. I didn't recognise the number. Couldn't be important.

My stomach churned and I rolled over with a groan. How long had I been sleeping? Shoving my hair off my face, I peered at my phone again: *2.30 p.m.* I'd been in bed for ages.

The silence in the house felt solid. Finn was sleeping too, I remembered. Liv had said so. She told me to listen out for him. I glanced at the baby monitor on Dom's side of the bed, checked the green light was on. Finn always slept soundly after lunch but if he wasn't awake by three, he wouldn't sleep tonight.

Hadn't Liv said something about her mum? An image rose of her standing over me, shaking me awake, her presence knotting with a nightmare where I was fighting for air, arms pushing upwards to hold open the lid of a coffin.

I should call Liv and find out what had happened but the effort felt too great.

As my stomach rolled and settled, my mind cycled back to last night and I let out another groan as I recalled being violently sick before falling into bed, stomach rising and falling as though I was at sea, and crying myself to sleep.

Dom had brought me a mug of coffee first thing, perching on the side of the bed and apologising again for not telling me sooner about Alicia.

'Does your mum know?' I'd felt relief when he gave a tight-lipped shake of his head. Part of me had wanted to go over it again, for Dom to reassure me that Alicia wasn't going to become an even bigger problem. I kept recalling her fine-boned face, her certainty that she and Dom were in a relationship, and even while I acknowledged that she was – to use Dom's term – delusional, I couldn't help worrying that she wasn't going to give up easily. But he'd looked worn out, troughs of tiredness beneath his eyes after another night spent in the nursery with Finn, and guilt had threatened to swallow me whole. Instead, I'd squeezed his hand and promised him I was feeling better, which was true. Even so, he'd asked his mother to call round as he had to go to the office and Liv had phoned to say she'd be late in. 'Please let Mum help,' he'd said stiffly, sensing my resistance. 'For Finn's sake.'

I thought of Elizabeth the day before, telling me I didn't deserve to be a mother. I hadn't repeated her words to Dom, and he hadn't asked me to elaborate. Perhaps in my nauseous state, I'd misunderstood. To her credit, she hadn't referred to yesterday's events – perhaps Dom had warned her not to – but after glancing at my presumably waxy face and my crumpled pyjamas had announced that I needed to line my stomach and ordered me to sit down. She'd insisted on cooking a heap of buttery mushrooms, piling them on two thick slices of toast, and I'd forced it down beneath her eagle gaze, following it with another mug of coffee. I even summoned a smile as she danced round the kitchen with Finn in her arms as though I wasn't there. I'd wished it was me he was smiling for, wide eyes fixed on my face instead of hers, dimpled hands reaching for me and not his grandmother. But he'd looked so happy and the sight of his beaming face had sent a warm glow through my core.

After I'd showered and dressed, as weak as if I was recovering from a bout of the flu, Elizabeth had left, remembering she'd called the vet out to look at one of the horses and that Robert was 'out somewhere'. Almost as soon as she'd gone, the tiredness that had started to lift rolled over me in thick waves, so by the time Liv arrived, all I wanted to do was drop back into bed, pull the duvet over my head and shut out the world. Finn hadn't settled until Liv took over, as if sensing the scale of my incompetence. I'd felt like wailing with him but my eyes were dry, the effort of holding them open almost too much to bear.

Sympathy had burned brightly in Liv's expression, but I'd glimpsed something else as I handed Finn over – scorn, perhaps, that I was so weak, unable to look after my son on my own. She was probably starting to think Dom *would* be better off with someone else, that Finn could do with a nice new mother, one who wasn't too exhausted, or ill, to care for him. I knew she wanted to talk about the day before, find out what had happened with Dom, but I couldn't explain until I'd had a sleep. Pausing at the top of the stairs, I'd wondered whether I should call the doctor again, but instead, held on to Natasha's words, about how she could barely remember the first few months of Toby's life, telling myself I'd be fine after a nap.

Now, as sleep began another descent, I forced myself upright, yawning widely and rubbing my eyes. I reached for the glass of water by the bed and drank it in swift gulps. It was tepid, but at least my tongue felt less furry when I'd finished. As I put the glass down, my eyes grazed a photo on the dressing table, of me with Finn just after he was born, the only one of us taken in hospital because I'd been in no fit state for the first week after giving birth. I was smiling softly at Finn in my arms, a little numb from the painkillers, certain that once I was home everything would fall into place, and the maternal instinct I knew was trapped like water under ice would gush out in a steady flow.

How wrong I'd been.

Tears screened my eyes as I hauled myself out of bed. It wasn't too late to try. Maybe I'd call Mum and stop pretending I was OK; ask whether she'd suffered anything like this when I was born. Maybe it was hereditary, though surely she'd have said something if that was the case – warned me, even.

As I dropped back on the bed, I noticed I'd had a few missed calls: one from Elizabeth, a couple from Dom and a text from Mum. Surprised, I opened it and read, *We're coming over for Christmas, hope that's all right. I can't stay away any longer!! Speak soon, hope you're OK, love Mum xxx*

It was as if she'd read my mind and knew I needed her. *Can't wait, it'll be so good to see you in person xxx.* I realised I was smiling and crying at the same time and wiped the back of my hand across my nose.

As I stood up again, my phone started ringing and I answered, expecting it to be Dom, injecting some vitality into my voice. 'It's OK, I'm fine, I'm awake.' *Only just.*

''S that Sophy Edwards?' It was a man's voice I didn't recognise, slightly blurry, as though he'd been drinking.

'Edwards?' He'd used my maiden name. 'Who is this?'

213

'You probably won't remember me.' He paused, as though weighing up what to say next. 'We went to the same university.'

'Oh?' The bedroom felt small and airless, weak sun glinting off the dressing table mirror. I felt a strong urge to check on Finn and moved to the door. 'How did you get my number?'

'S'Liv,' he said.

Every cell in my body seemed to freeze. 'You know Liv?'

'Not who you think she is.' He hiccupped and swore softly. 'She's messed up, Sophy. You gotta be careful.'

'What?'

Downstairs, the front door slammed, making me jump. 'Look, I don't know who you are, or what you're talking about.' I walked onto the landing on unsteady legs and gripped the banister rail. 'Who did you say you were?' But he'd gone.

'Sophy?'

Dom was back, taking the stairs two at a time, one hand clutching his tie. His face was taut with tension.

'You're home early.'

He stood in front of me, out of breath. 'Mum phoned to say she had to go and see the vet and couldn't get away. She tried ringing to see if you were OK and got no reply. I had a meeting I couldn't get out of, then you didn't answer my calls …' He came to a stop, running both hands through his hair. 'Why didn't you answer your phone?'

'Dom, it's fine. I was tired. I needed a nap. Finn's in his cot. I haven't been asleep that long,' I lied, feeling a need to soothe him, to ease the lines of worry from his face.

'Where's Liv?' He looked around, as if she might be hiding somewhere.

'She had to leave early.' I tugged the cuffs of my jumper over my hands. It was cold on the landing, a draught coming from somewhere downstairs, winding around my bare feet. 'There was a problem with her mother.' I thought of the call I'd just had, but couldn't process it now. 'I was on my way to get Finn.'

214

Dom glanced at my crumpled clothes, at the open bedroom door behind me. He took in the heaped-up duvet hanging off the bed and looked at my hair. 'You've just woken up, haven't you?'

Before I could protest, he was striding to the nursery, flinging the door wide. I followed close behind, suddenly desperate to hold Finn, to feel his warm sweet breath against my neck. 'I was just about to wake him. I—'

'Where is he?'

My stomach vaulted with fright. 'What do you mean?'

'He's not here.' Dom spun round, eyes raking past me to the stairs as though Finn could have walked down them on his own. 'Where the hell is he?'

'Of course he's there.' I pushed past Dom and ran to the cot in the middle of the room. Grabbing the side, I peered over, a whimpering sound escaping from my throat. 'Finn?' I whispered, staring at the empty space where he should have been, at the Finn-shaped dent in the mattress, at the tiny strands of russet hair clinging to the sheet. It was inconceivable that he wasn't where he was supposed to be, that he could be somewhere else. A thought pushed its way through the panic. Liv must have returned and taken him to the park. 'Wait,' I said to Dom. 'I think I know where he is.'

I rushed to get my phone, stumbling a little, heart racing as I waited for Liv to answer. 'Is Finn with you?'

'Sophy, hi.' She sounded annoyed, or maybe stressed.

'Have you got Finn?'

'What? No, of course not. I'm at the hospital with my mum,' she said. 'I told you I was leaving, I tried to wake you up.' She took a breath as though forcing herself to be calm. 'What's going on?'

'Oh, nothing.' Another thought had occurred. 'Elizabeth must have him.'

'Are you sure everything's OK?'

I hung up. 'He must be with your mum,' I said to Dom, who

215

was standing right behind me in the bedroom. 'Call her.' I felt dangerously out of control and knew I wouldn't be able to hold back if I spoke to her myself, if she'd taken him out without telling me.

Dom was shaking his head in a way that made me want to scream. 'No, she's helping organise a horse-riding event in Berkshire this afternoon, she mentioned it when she rang to tell me she couldn't get hold of you.'

'What?' My breath blocked my throat. 'So, where is he, where's Finn?'

I heard Dom's feet thundering down the stairs, his voice, shouting out our son's name, as if he could answer, *Here I am!*

I found myself back in the nursery, palm pressed to the mattress in the cot. It was still warm. There was no sign of Jiggles, which Liv would have put there with him.

'Why are the patio doors open?' Dom was heading back up the stairs.

I couldn't drag my eyes from the cot, willing Finn to reappear, to form beneath my hand, living and breathing; to open his big blue eyes and smile at me. 'Sophy!' Dom's hands dragged me away, spinning me to face him, his eyes pools of torment in the whiteness of his face. 'Did you leave the doors open?'

'What?' I was shivering in convulsive bursts. 'I ... no, I ... I don't know, I don't think so, no.' Terror leaked in. The thought of how vulnerable Finn was made me retch. Dom let me go and I dropped to my hands and knees on the floor. 'Oh my God, where is he?' I choked the words out, tears falling and catching on the backs of my hands. 'Call the police.'

Dom was breathing hard. He pulled out his phone, dropped it, fumbled to pick it up. As I lifted my head and watched him press the screen, a thought hit me like a juggernaut.

'Alicia.' Infused with a sudden, terrifying rage, I staggered to my feet, grabbing at Dom's arm. 'It's her,' I said. 'It must be her, Dom. She's taken Finn to get to you.' My voice rose higher, words spitting out of me. 'It's got to be her, she has motive. You have to talk to her, Dom. He could be in danger. You have to talk to her, *now.*' Finn was in danger. My baby was in danger. I doubled over, trying to breathe, Dom's echoing expression of horror etched on my brain.

'Come on, pick up,' I heard him mutter through clenched teeth. I couldn't seem to pick myself off the floor as I imagined Alicia driving Finn to some unknown destination, punishing Dom for not choosing her, refusing to give up our son unless Dom agreed to leave me. He would do it. He would do anything to get Finn back. *I hoped he would.* 'Agree to whatever she wants,' I cried, my throat raw. 'Find out where she is, keep her talking. I'll call the police.'

Fear took hold once more, paralysing my limbs. Something unspeakable could be happening to Finn. I wanted to scream, yell, claw my nails down Alicia's perfect face. *I was his mother. I should have been taking care of him.*

'Alicia, it's Dom. What have you done with my son?'

He'd put her on speakerphone. I heard the split second of silence before she said, 'I've no idea what you're talking about.'

'My son is missing.' His voice sounded like cracked glass. 'Did you come into my house this afternoon and take him?'

I pressed a shaking hand to my mouth and closed my eyes. This couldn't be happening.

'What? Of *course* I didn't. Why would I do that?' Alicia's voice was sharp with fright. 'Dom, what's going on?'

'Where are you right now?'

'I'm having lunch with my sister.'

'Put her on.'

Another voice, with a blade-like edge. 'I don't know what you've said to my sister, but I'd advise you to leave her alone,' the woman said. 'You've strung her along for long enough, promising you'll marry her.'

'I've promised her nothing,' Dom roared. 'Has she got my son?'

217

'My sister's just driven down to Cornwall to stay with me for a few days, so I'm guessing no.'

Dom ended the call. 'She hasn't got him.' His tone sent a fresh flood of fright crashing through me. 'I believe her, Sophy.'

'Call the police.'

While he spoke to the emergency services, I sprang into action, flinging myself around the house as though Finn might have magically appeared. I was racked with sobs when I saw his high-chair in the kitchen, his playpen in the living room, his scattered toys – no sign of Jiggles – and a gaping hole at the centre of it all, where he should be.

There was a cold draught coming from the patio doors. The sun had gone in and rain pattered against the glass. The thought that this had happened because of me – that I'd left the doors open – made me want to howl. Someone had simply let them-selves in and walked out with my baby.

I staggered, clutching at the arm of the sofa. I had to do something, had to find him. Maybe Liv could help … *Liv.* Time seemed to slow. I remembered the phone call, moments before Dom came home. What was it the man had said?

Not who you think she is. She's messed up. Be careful.

What if Liv wasn't really at the hospital?

I was stumbling back upstairs as Dom ran down.

'The police are on their way,' he said, meeting me halfway. He looked powerless, tears rolling down his face. 'What is it?'

Chapter 32

Liv

'A panic attack,' the doctor had told me. 'Possibly brought on by anxiety. She says there's nothing worrying her, but I wondered …'

'She's had a change of carer,' I'd said. 'She's not keen on change.' But I'd known it was more than that. My obsession with Sophy had opened up old wounds, caused her stress.

When Ben died, Dad and I witnessed only half the person she'd been before. The doctors said it was grief and severe depression that made her hang up on life. The trauma of her accident and losing her ability to walk realigned her thinking. Things improved, as she focused on her recovery, determined, she'd said, to be there for me, saying she should have been there from the start, helping me through the turmoil I'd felt at not only losing my brother, but finding him too.

But now I'd raked it all up again, and prayed I hadn't done any lasting damage.

'Are you OK to keep an eye on Mum for a bit?' I asked Shari. She was sitting in the lounge with Sparky on her lap, as Mum dozed in the armchair, exhausted from her trip to the hospital. 'I just need a breath of fresh air.'

'Of course,' she said, with a nod. She'd been so good coming to the hospital. I liked Shari.

It was raining as I made my way through the wooden gates of Weston Road Cemetery, and parked up. I walked down the path towards the graves, and knelt down by his stone, the dampness of the grass seeping into my jeans, painful tears behind my eyes. 'I miss you so much,' I said, running my fingers across his name. 'I've made such a bloody mess of everything, Ben. I'm so sorry.'

My phone vibrated in my pocket, jolting me from my sadness. I pulled it out and looked at the screen. Sophy.

'Where is he?' she yelled down the phone, as I put it to my ear. I barely recognised her voice. 'What the hell have you done with him?'

'What? Slow down.' I rose to my feet. 'What's going on?'

'It's Finn. It's my baby. He's gone.' Sophy's voice broke off. She sounded terrified. 'What have you done with him, Liv? Why would you take him?'

'Hang on, Sophy.' My heart thudded against my chest. 'What do you mean Finn's gone? I thought Elizabeth had him.'

'Liv.' It was Dom. 'Can you come round, please?' His voice was calmer than Sophy's but I could hear a tremor. 'We've called the police. It would be good if you could be here.'

'OK. But I don't know what Sophy's talking about. Finn was in his cot—'

'Just come round, Liv. Please. The police will need to talk to you.'

I ended the call without a response, my heart galloping as I stared down at my phone. Somebody had taken Finn, and panic shot through me, as his little face came into my mind. My head spun. I should have made sure Sophy was out of bed. God, I'd left the patio doors open. Had the intruder come in that way? Was this my fault? Would the police think I took him? I closed my eyes, imagining how devastated Sophy must be feeling right now. Whatever she'd done to Ben, she didn't deserve this.

After calling Shari to say I wouldn't be home straight away, insisting she ring me if Mum needed me, I climbed into my car and started the engine, my mind reeling.

As I pulled out of the cemetery, the loud beep of a car horn made me jump, and I braked hard. The woman in the Fiat glared as she swerved round me, and I could feel tears rising, my hands trembling on the steering wheel. 'Sorry,' I mouthed.

Once at Sophy's I pulled up behind a silver Audi, noticing a couple of police cars parked along the road. I climbed out of my car, and headed up the path, preparing myself for more accusations.

A slim woman in her forties, with sleek black hair pulled back in a ponytail and a heavy fringe resting above brown eyes, opened the door. 'Liv Granger?' she said, and I nodded. 'I'm Detective Sergeant Jo Lane.' She stepped aside. 'Come in.'

I followed her into the lounge, where Dom – head in his hands – and Sophy sat on the sofa. Sophy was twisting a tissue, tiny pieces falling from it like snow onto her creased trousers. A man in his fifties looked up from where he was sitting in an armchair.

'What have you done with him, Liv?' Sophy's voice was weak, trembling, the anger she'd shown on the phone muted by grief. My eyes skittered around the scattered toys Finn and I had been playing with earlier, and a lump rose in my throat.

'I haven't done anything, Sophy, I promise.' I moved towards her, but stopped, sensing her tense. 'Finn was in his cot when I left. I'm so sorry—'

'Not who you think she is.' Her stare was cold.

'What?'

'That's what he said about you, Liv.'

'Who?'

'He said I should be careful. That you are messed up.'

'I don't know what you're talking about—'

'Sophy had a phone call just before I got home,' Dom said, looking up at me.

'He said he knew me from university.' Sophy's eyes were fixed on mine, and my whole body stiffened. Words wouldn't form. *Ryan?*

The man moved forward in his chair, and the DS sat down. I felt on show in the middle of the room, my arms folded, being weighed up by curious eyes.

'I'm Detective Inspector John Barker,' the man said. 'I understand you were the last person to see Finn.' His question was aimed at me.

'Yes, but that was hours ago. What are you doing to find him?'

'We're searching the immediate area, Ms Granger – doing a house-to-house. Leave that to us. We just need to ask you a few questions.'

I nodded, rubbing the back of my neck. 'Fine. But I'm not sure what I can tell you. 'I had to go in a hurry. My mum was taken into hospital. I woke Sophy, who'd been asleep for some time, and told her I had to go.'

'And did anyone see you leave?' the DI asked.

'Yes, Sophy.' I looked towards her, but her gaze didn't meet mine.

'Sophy saw you leave the house?' He glanced her way, and back at me.

'No, but she knew I was leaving.'

'And what did you do during the time you've been away?'

'I've been at the hospital with my mum. You can call her and check if you don't believe me. Call the hospital too, if you like.'

The officer nodded. 'We will.'

'If you ask me, you need to ask Dom about Alicia.'

'Alicia?' the DI looked at Dom.

'She's in Cornwall with her sister,' Sophy cut in, her head down. 'Dom called her. She hasn't got Finn.'

'We'll need her details,' the DI went on, and Dom nodded.

'What about Elizabeth, have you spoken to her?' I said.

Dom shot me a look. 'Mum? She's in Berkshire. This has nothing to do with her.'

'Are you sure about that?' I looked at Sophy. 'Have you told him about the note?' I was aware I'd sent the note myself, but it couldn't hurt to divert their attention from me. And, if I told the truth, I didn't trust Elizabeth.

'You told *her* about the note?' Dom turned to the DI. 'I never saw it,' he said. 'It apparently disappeared.'

Sophy flashed me a frosty glare. 'Someone put a note through the door.' She wiped what was left of the tissue across her nose. 'It said, *Watch Elizabeth.*' She looked at Dom. 'I know you don't believe me, but it's true.'

'So, where did it go?' Dom stared at us all in turn. 'How could it just vanish?'

'I don't know.' Sophy lowered her head. Twisted the tissue.

Dom rubbed his face in disbelief.

DS Lane looked up from jotting something down. 'So, Elizabeth is your mother?' she said to Dom. 'We'll need to speak with her.'

'Of course, yes, but she has nothing to do with this. She's been like a second mum to Finn. Helping Sophy. She wouldn't … I mean why would she take Finn? She can see him whenever she likes. She loves him. She would never want to worry us like this.'

The DI stared at Sophy. 'What do you think?'

Sophy shook her head, tears falling. 'I don't know anymore,' she said in an almost whisper, rising from the sofa, still twisting the tissue. 'But sitting here talking about it, isn't going to bring my baby back.'

I pulled up outside Mum's house, desperate to head straight to my room. After being questioned by the police, practically accused by Sophy, and told I would need to give a statement, and the police would need to talk to me again, I felt drained and emotional. It had been such a long day.

'Hello, love,' Mum called out, when I opened the front door. Her voice came from the lounge, and sounded bright, and I was relieved.

'Hi, Mum,' I called back, as Shari appeared in the hallway, smiling, Sparky trotting beside her.

'Your mum seems really well, considering her ordeal,' she said, grabbing her jacket. 'I didn't want to leave her though, not until you got back.'

'Thanks so much,' I said.

'You're welcome.' She poked her head round the lounge door, 'I'm off now, Martha. See you tomorrow.'

I made my way into the lounge. 'How are you feeling?' I asked Mum, as I tickled Sparky's ears, and sat down beside her on the sofa.

'I'm OK. Just got myself into a bit of a panic all round.'

'It was my fault, wasn't it?' I took hold of her hand and squeezed. 'I shouldn't have gone on about Sophy. But it's in the past now, Mum. I promise to leave well alone.' I meant it. Sophy was going through enough.

Mum nodded. 'That's good. Ben wouldn't want you to still feel so angry.'

'No. You're right.'

She smiled. 'Good. Time to move on.'

I gulped back thoughts of Finn. Mum didn't need to know. 'Shari seems nice,' I said.

'Yes, she's lovely. I was surprised how well we got on. It was good to have a change of carer really. I'd got a bit dependent on Freya, I suppose.'

Once Mum had dozed off in front of the TV, I made my way up the stairs, and headed into Ben's room. I sat on the edge of his bed, my head spinning. Someone had called Sophy and I knew it was Ryan.

I looked again at the photos Blu-Tacked to the mirror, and pulled off the one of a group of lads, beer bottles raised, my eyes picking out Ben in his green polo and combats, Ryan in a red checked shirt and jeans, standing next to Ben.

I got his number up on my phone. First he'd warned me that

Sophy wasn't who I thought she was, next he warned Sophy about me. What was he playing at?

But perhaps I was wrong. How would he have got Sophy's number anyway?

I pressed call.

'Hey, Liv.'

My mind whirred. 'You called Sophy, didn't you?'

There was a small silence, before he said, 'I can explain.'

'I'm listening.'

He was silent for a moment, and I wondered if he was choosing his words with care. 'Come round,' he said finally. 'I can't do this over the phone.'

'Fine.' I ended the call, and raced from the room.

Downstairs, Mum had woken up, and was now glued to the TV. 'Will you be OK if I go out for a bit?' I said.

She looked up and smiled. 'I'm fine, Liv. Honestly. The hospital were pleased with me. Said my heart is sound as a bell.'

'But you'll call me if you need me?'

'Of course, now just go.'

Chapter 33

Sophy

As soon as Liv had rushed in, eyes wide with fright and worry, my certainty had wavered.

The urge to fly at her, shake her, demand that she return my son had fallen away. Why would she have come, if she'd taken Finn? Unless she'd given him to someone. That man who called. Maybe they were in it together; he was her partner and knew Liv was going to take my baby and decided to warn me. She hadn't explained what that call was about. I didn't even know the man's name, hadn't thought to ask as she'd protested her innocence and told the detectives she'd been at the hospital with her mum.

Why had I let her into our lives, Finn's life, knowing next to nothing about her?

The police probably thought the same thing as I wept on the sofa – a seemingly endless river of tears – as Liv had been allowed to leave. I'd seen the looks exchanged when she told them I'd been asleep, the look Dom gave me. Everyone thought this was my fault, my punishment for being a bad mother. And why had she told them about the note? She knew it was a sore point with

Dom, that we'd argued about it. But the note had existed. I knew I hadn't imagined it.

You don't deserve to be a mother. Maybe I hadn't imagined Elizabeth's words either. Should I bring it up? Then my mind circled back to the phone call, the slurred voice telling me Liv wasn't who I thought she was, and something clicked into place.

Standing so fast my head swam, I grabbed the female detective's arm. 'You have to talk to Liv again.' DS Lane and her colleague had brought an air of calm authority into the house, while officers had searched inside and out before leaving to talk to the neighbours, looking for witnesses and checking for CCTV. The activity had been reassuring to start with, but not even the softly spoken officers could quieten the chaos raging in my head. 'That call, the man, you should ask Liv about that—'

'We have,' DI Barker said gently but firmly. 'We'll be talking to him, and Alicia Bainbridge. Officers from Devon and Cornwall police are on their way to her sister's house. We're doing everything we can, Mrs Pemberton.'

Mrs Pemberton. It made me think of Elizabeth again.

Dom was showing the female inspector another photo on his phone, of Finn in his cot, a square of sunlight creating a golden glow that burnished his curls, his blue eyes mini replicas of Dom's. Why hadn't I got photos like that on my phone? The last one I'd taken was weeks ago, Finn asleep on his blanket in his playpen after a crying jag, his face turned away, his red curls squashed. He could have been anyone's baby.

'Elizabeth,' I blurted, pushing the word past the knot of grief in my throat. 'You really should talk to my mother-in-law, check she is where she's supposed to be.'

'Sophy.' Dom's voice was laden with pain, but the warning underneath was clear. 'Please … don't start this again.'

'Go on.' Jo Lane, that was the detective's name, gave me a nod of encouragement, her gaze steady beneath her heavy fringe. Maybe she had children. She was wearing a plain gold band on her wedding finger. Perhaps she could imagine all too easily the bone-melting terror of having your baby go missing, of him not being where he should be, of how the thought of him needing me – his mother – made it hard to breathe, as if the air was water and I was drowning.

'She has a key to our house and is always coming in, taking Finn from me, taking him out. She makes me feel useless and I know I have been, but if she wasn't around so much, I ...' I was struggling for air, words piled up in my chest, as if they'd been waiting to tumble out. 'She's so determined to be better than me – she has been from the start. It's as if she's his mother, not me. As if she doesn't want me to get better because then I wouldn't need her.' I looked at Dom, willing him to understand. 'She makes me feel worse.'

'Look, she's protective of Finn, of course she is. She loves him; she's his grandmother.' Dom massaged his brow with shaking fingers. 'She's been a godsend while you've not been well.'

'I wish we'd never moved out of London.' My words were oiled with a sudden fury. 'You were so desperate for us to move out here for a better standard of living, yet you can't wait to get back there every day, regardless of whether or not I'm "ill".' I made quote marks with my fingers, bits of balled-up tissue falling to the floor. I sounded mad, but didn't care. 'At least there I knew people and didn't have to rely on your mother. She's been waiting for something like this to happen and now it has.'

'Sophy, don't.' Dom looked older, the lines around his mouth more deeply etched. 'You've got her all wrong.'

'And why do you think Elizabeth might have taken Finn somewhere?'

My head snapped round at the sound of the female voice. I'd almost forgotten we weren't alone. 'She's done it before, a couple of times.' I wrapped my arms around my middle. My whole body ached, as if I'd been in a fight. 'Not like this, but long enough for me to worry.'

'When?' Alarm sharpened Dom's voice.

'I told you before, she took him to the park and didn't come back for ages, or she'll go to the stables without telling me and then not answer her phone.'

Dom's expression emptied out. 'I got the impression she'd told you but you didn't remember because you were tired,' he said, and because I couldn't be certain, I didn't argue. 'And I'm only not home as often as I should be because as soon as we moved here, things got complicated at work and I can't risk losing my job by not going in, and there was all that stuff with Alicia to deal with.' His eyes implored me. 'Do you think I wouldn't rather be here with my family? You and Finn are everything to me. I've been worried sick about you.'

I began to cry again, feeling helpless. 'I just want Finn back.'

'Oh, Sophy, so do I. That's all I want, but it doesn't make sense that Mum would have him and not tell us.' He sounded close to tears, but I couldn't look at him. 'Whoever it was came in through the patio doors. Like you said, Mum has a key for the front door. Why would she come round the back of the house and sneak inside?'

'We don't know for certain they came in that way,' I said.

'We'll be looking for footprints.' Jo Lane was calm, her voice steady. 'And if it's OK, we'd still like to talk to Elizabeth.'

With a shaky inhalation, Dom took out his phone.

'She's not picking up,' he said after a moment of tension. Before anyone could speak, he pressed the screen again and waited. 'Natasha, have you spoken to Mum today?'

I heard the tinny sound of his sister's voice at the end of the line. Dom was shaking his head. 'Finn's missing.' When his voice cracked the horror of it all hit me again. 'No ... I can't get hold of her, I just ... we wondered whether Mum might have taken him out and forgotten to let us know.' I felt a flash of gratitude that he'd said 'we'.

Dom began to pace to the window and back, hand rubbing the

back of his head. 'No, of course I don't.' I strained to hear, aware of the detectives listening too, as motionless as statues. There was a pause as Dom seemed to wait for Natasha to respond. I could smell Jo's perfume, something sweet like geraniums, and my stomach turned over. 'OK, thanks for looking.' Dom came to a halt and closed his eyes. 'Look, I don't need this, Tash. Just let me know if you hear from her, OK?'

He ended the call and looked at the officers, a defeated slope to his shoulders. 'My sister hasn't heard from her, but when she visited the other day, Mum mentioned the horse-riding event in Berkshire this afternoon, so I don't think she's lying about that.' He put his phone on the table. 'Tash just looked the event up online and it's definitely happening.'

'But your mum always answers her phone when you call.' I shivered as a hazy recollection broke through, of Natasha telling me to take care, to not let Elizabeth 'take over'. For the first time, I wondered whether Elizabeth had behaved the same way after Natasha had Toby, and that was why the family had moved to Cumbria – not so much to be closer to Rory's family, but to get away from Elizabeth. 'What else did Natasha say?'

'Something about Mum being possessive with babies because …' He swallowed, his Adam's apple sliding up and down. 'Because our older brother Christopher died when he was a baby.' He hesitated, as if something unpalatable was taking shape in his mind. 'But she'd hardly go to these lengths when she has access to Finn whenever she wants,' he said quickly. 'And it's not as if we're planning to move away like Natasha did.'

'I don't blame her.' I wanted to be cruel. 'I can completely understand her wanting to escape your mother.'

A nerve twitched in Dom's jaw. I sensed the effort he was making to not argue and wished he would so I could shout, rant; make something happen.

As DS Lane cleared her throat, breaking the silence, reality slammed into me once more. 'Please,' I said, wanting to fall to my knees in front of her. 'Please, please find our baby.'

'What can we do?' Dom's voice rose. 'There must be *something* we can do.'

'The best thing is to wait here.' DI Barker was standing now. He looked at me with such fatherly concern that, for a second, I wanted to press myself against his chest and sob all over his suit jacket. 'You've been assigned a family liaison officer, Laura Deacon,' he said. 'She'll look after you and keep you updated of our progress, and you can ask her anything.' He nodded to a woman in the living room doorway.

'I'll put the kettle on,' she said briskly. I had no idea how long she'd been there. She looked too young, too inexperienced to understand what we were going through.

As the detectives made to leave, there was a kerfuffle at the front door and my mother-in-law burst into the living room.

'What's going on? What's happened?' Her eyes were wide and unfocused as she looked around her, her hair blown sideways by the wind. 'Where is he? What have you done?' She lunged at me and Dom pulled her back, gripping her by the arms.

'For God's sake, Mum. Sophy hasn't done anything.'

She collapsed against him, looking up into his face. 'Your sister called while I was in the car. I didn't realise you'd been ringing me, didn't know what had happened.' Her skin was mottled crimson. 'Please tell me it isn't true, that my baby hasn't gone.'

Dom looked grimly at DI Barker over her head. 'I think it's clear my mother knew nothing about this.'

'Oh, Sophy.' As Dom let her go, Elizabeth pressed a trembling hand to her mouth, shaking her head wildly from side to side. 'I'm so, so sorry.'

'Sorry for what?' My voice sounded frozen. 'Please, tell the truth, Elizabeth. We just want Finn back.' I felt capable of killing her with my bare hands, could almost feel her throat yielding beneath my fingers.

'I would never … *never*, I promise.' Her voice rasped as she clutched at my sleeve. 'I would never harm a hair on that little boy's head. I love him, Sophy, with all my heart. I don't know where he is, I swear. I'm just, so … I'm so very, very sorry.' She began crying, great gulping sobs that made her mouth gape and her shoulders shake. Dom looked frightened, cradling her to him like a child.

I felt sick, but it wasn't the nausea I'd felt before. 'I'm going out.' My voice rang with anger. 'Someone must know something.'

'Sophy, wait,' Dom began, but I was already pushing past, ignoring DS Lane's plea to wait. I ran down the drive, a sob catching in my throat, and almost cannoned into Kim.

'Sophy, I heard what's happened.' She was clutching the handle of a pram, panting as though she'd been running, and smelt of stale sweat. 'Petra called me. She's had the police round.'

'Oh, Kim, do you know anything?' It was cold, the wind biting through my clothes, but my cheeks felt hot. 'Please tell me.'

'I saw a car.' She took one of my hands, her fingers icy. Darkness had fallen and everything looked nightmarish, no street lights to dispel the blackness. As clouds pulled away from the moon, Kim's face looked ghostly. 'I thought it was odd because it wasn't the sort of car you'd normally see on this street.' She was blinking too fast. 'I only noticed because I was taking Dougie for a walk, trying to get him to sleep.'

My heart hammered. 'Did you see the driver?'

'It was a woman, I think, but she was wearing a hood.' She nodded firmly, as if trying to convince herself as much as me. 'Maybe the police can check to see if anyone has CCTV that might have picked up the car. It was a maroon Volvo Estate. My father used to have the same model.' She hesitated. 'You don't … you don't think Olivia had anything to do with this, do you?'

'What?' I pulled my hand from hers, still processing the information about the car. 'Why would you think that?'

Kim's eyes glittered, and part of me registered that she was enjoying the drama. 'It's just that Clare told me Olivia tried to seduce her husband and although I like Olivia, I did think she was rather indiscreet, as I said before, gossiping about your social worker.' She hesitated. 'It made me wonder whether she was behind it all, had made the call herself.'

I remembered the anonymous man on the phone, telling me Liv was messed up. 'Actually, Kim, Clare's husband was the one trying to sleep with Liv and got nasty when she refused.' I wasn't sure why I was defending her, when I no longer trusted her myself. 'Liv drives a Mini, anyway,' I added. 'She told you the social worker's visit was a misunderstanding and you promised you wouldn't tell anybody.'

'I didn't.' Kim bristled. 'Liv seemed delighted about it. I got the impression she wouldn't mind me passing it on. I told Elizabeth because I was concerned.' She gave a dramatic gasp. 'Oh, my goodness, you don't think ... Could that social worker have taken Finn?' She immediately shook her head, as if realising it was a ludicrous thought, then reached for my hand again. 'Look, if anything happened to my Dougie—' she glanced anxiously at the pram '—I don't know what I'd do.' Her eyes were wet with tears. 'I'm just saying, there's more to Olivia than meets the eye, that's all.'

Kim was the second person to have said it.

'Well, the police are talking to everyone, so if she's involved, they'll soon find out.'

'Good.' Kim squeezed my hand and let go. 'Tell them about the car,' she said. 'I hope you get your baby back soon.' Her voice wavered. 'If I can do anything at all, come and get me.' She wasn't wearing a coat and had started shivering. Maybe she *was* just trying to help, but I was desperate for her to leave.

'Thank you,' I managed.

She nodded, biting her lip before turning the pram and hurrying away, swallowed by the darkness at the end of the drive.

I stood for a moment, welcoming the cold air on my face, letting it sharpen my brain, half-aware of voices in the house behind me as my phone began ringing in my trouser pocket.

I pulled it out, saw Isaac's number and answered on autopilot.

'Hey, you,' he said, and I was struck by a wave of rage that the world was normal, things carrying on when my life had been upended, my baby out there somewhere without me. 'Why haven't you replied to that attachment I sent. I thought you were keen on having some work to do.'

'I didn't get it.' My words jerked out through chattering teeth.

'Weird,' he said. 'I definitely sent it.'

'Finn's missing.'

There was a beat of silence. 'What?'

'I have to go, Isaac.'

I cut off his exclamation and hurried back inside for the car keys. The answerphone light flashed on the landline phone on the hall table, though I couldn't recall moving it there. Dry-mouthed, I picked it up. Had we missed a ransom demand? Would kidnappers leave a message? It seemed absurd, but I picked up the phone and pressed play. Looking through the living room door I saw Dom's mouth moving, and the liaison officer's brows pinch together, but all I could focus on was the call.

'Hello, Sophy, it's Doctor Crawford. I left a message on your mobile, I hope you got it OK. I've made an appointment for you to come in and see me tomorrow at 9.30. Let me know if you can't make it.' The message had been left yesterday.

I slammed the phone down and grabbed the car keys lying next to it.

'Sophy, where are you going?' Dom's voice was hoarse from talking and crying.

'I have to go out. I can't sit here doing nothing,' I snapped. 'I just spoke to Kim and she saw a maroon Volvo Estate, hanging around a while ago. The police need to look into that.'

'Sophy, you mustn't drive.' Elizabeth had shot out of the living room, looking as if she was unravelling, her face swollen and blotchy with tears. It seemed obvious now, seeing the state she was in that she couldn't – wouldn't – have taken Finn.

'I have to,' I said.

'Not in this state, it's not safe.'

'You heard the police, Sophy. We're better off staying here.' Dom glanced from the liaison officer to the detectives in mute appeal. DI Barker was making a note in his pad.

'The woman you spoke to,' he said. 'What's her name?'

'Kim Harrison. She lives at …' I tried to remember. 'Indigo Cottage.'

'Why didn't she come in and speak to us?'

I felt as if I there was a gale-force wind in my head, tossing my thoughts about. 'She was about to when I bumped into her.'

'It would be better if you waited here now.' DS Lane's voice was firm but kind. 'Everything is being done to find your baby.'

I thought about Liv telling Kim I'd had a visit from social services and how she'd sounded delighted, had wanted Kim to pass it on. Why had Liv lied? And that man on the phone, telling me to be careful, that Liv couldn't be trusted. *Who was Olivia Granger?* I felt as if I didn't know her at all.

'I'm sorry, but I can't stay here.' I felt plugged in, blood pulsing hotly through my veins. 'I think Liv knows more than she's letting on,' I said to Dom. 'I'm going to find out.'

Chapter 34

Liv

I'd driven to Ryan's house in a heightened state of anxiety, thoughts leaping to Finn. I even became convinced Ryan had taken him. Imagined him drunk, creeping into Sophy's house and snatching Finn out of some twisted revenge of his own. After all, Ben had meant everything to him too.

But now, as I pulled on the handbrake and looked up at his house, those thoughts seemed ridiculous. Ryan wasn't capable of stealing a child.

He answered the door within seconds, his dark hair in disarray. 'Hey, Liv.' He rubbed his red-rimmed eyes, and moved to one side. 'You'd better come in.'

Despite feeling sure Finn wasn't in the house, I found myself searching for signs of a baby, as I followed Ryan to the lounge, but as far as I could tell, there were none.

There was a hum of alcohol in the air, and I noticed a glass half full of a clear liquid on the smeared, cluttered coffee table, and knew it wasn't water. The curtains at the window had been there since before his dad died – expensive once, but now dated and faded. The same went for the three-piece suite.

The TV was on, some sci-fi thing – muted. Ryan sat down on the sofa.

'Finn's been taken,' I said.

'Finn?' His forehead furrowed as he leant forward and picked up the drink. Took a gulp. 'Lemonade,' he said, as though I was judging. *I was.*

'Sophy's son. She was asleep when …' I gulped back a lump in my throat. 'He was taken from his cot. Someone walked into their house and just took him away.'

'Jesus.' He put down the glass, rubbed a hand over his stubbled chin. 'Shit,' he went on, voice breaking. 'Her little lad – that's awful. Who the hell would do that?'

I sat down next to him. 'It wasn't you?'

'What?' His eyes widened as though he couldn't believe what I'd said, that I would even consider it.

'So why did you call her, Ryan?' I held up a hand. 'No wait, how the hell did you even know her phone number?'

'I found it on your phone, the day we met up.'

'What?'

'I looked it up when you went to change the baby, and copied it into my phone.' He massaged his temples with his fingers. 'I wanted to warn her.'

'About me?'

'Yes, about you, Liv.' He picked up his glass and put it down again. 'I'm sorry, but I felt sorry for her. I'd hoped you'd stop the whole revenge thing.' He stared into my eyes. 'But you didn't did you?'

I looked at him for a long moment, trying to take in what he was saying. 'What did you think I was going to do, Ryan?'

'I don't know. What *were* you going to do?' He looked at me hard, anguish in his face. 'Christ, you didn't take the kid, did you, Liv?'

'No!' I rose. Began pacing the room, before stopping and stuffing my hands in my pockets. 'She was the reason Ben died.'

My emotions were all over the place. Finn had gone missing. Sophy's beautiful child had vanished. Tears filled my eyes. 'But, I don't know, it's like … I want to hate her, but I can't.' I brushed away tears. 'I feel sorry for her. Sometimes I think I'm ready to forgive her for what she did.'

'She doesn't need your forgiveness, Liv.'

'What? What are you talking about?'

He closed his eyes for a moment, tears resting on his lashes. 'Are you OK?'

He opened his eyes and took a long deep breath. 'Sophy wasn't to blame for Ben's death.'

I froze. 'What? Of course she was.'

'No!' he yelled. 'I lied to you, Liv.' Tears fell from his eyes, rolling down his face. 'Ben died because of me.'

'What are you talking about?'

'I was weak.' He dropped his head into his hands.

'Ryan?'

He looked up at me. 'I should have had more courage.'

'Hey.' I sat down once more, and placed my hand on his arm. 'What are you trying to tell me, Ryan?' But through the silence that followed, the pieces fell into place. The burnt photos in the ashtray – the singed pictures – Ryan's red-checked shirt. They hadn't been photos of Ben and Sophy. They were of Ben and Ryan.

'We were in love,' he said through his tears 'But Dad was a total prick. He would never have understood.'

'But it wasn't the 1950s, Ryan.'

'Dad thought it was. You met him, Liv. You knew what he was like.'

I had met him. Just the once, after Ben died, and shortly before his own death. He was a complete arse of a man, who seemed to have control over Ryan, criticising him at every turn, ignoring him when he spoke.

'I couldn't hack it,' Ryan continued. 'The thought of Dad making our lives hell.' Tears rolled down his cheeks. 'I had to

238

choose – Dad or Ben – and I've hated myself every day since for making the wrong choice. I've never got over Ben. I loved him so much, Liv.' He gasped. 'God it feels better to say that.'

My body stiffened, but I kept my hand on his arm. 'He loved you too,' I said through a sob of clarity.

He nodded, his eyes straight ahead of him, face damp with tears. 'He was going to introduce me to you guys as his partner, but I wimped out. Couldn't face my father knowing I was gay. I ended it, and I've never regretted something so much in my life. I'm so sorry, Liv.' He turned to look at me, and my heart cried out in pain. 'I hate myself every single day.'

'But why pretend?' I pulled a tissue from my pocket and swiped it across my nose. All this time I'd blamed Sophy. 'Why pretend it was Sophy who broke his heart?'

'As a family, you needed to know who he was in love with, and I was afraid you'd realise it was me – blame me for his death.'

'We never would have,' I said.

He tilted his head. 'Are you sure?

I wanted to believe I never would have, but the truth was we'd needed someone to blame for Ben's death, to take away the guilt we all felt.

'I thought about Sophy,' Ryan said. 'I knew she'd already left university, and with a name like Edwards, I felt sure you would never find her. She was even in the photo of the skiing trip, although she didn't go in the end. She seemed perfect.'

My emotions were all over the place. Sophy hadn't let my brother down. She wasn't the reason he killed himself. Ryan was.

'I need to go,' I said, rising. 'I need to think this through.'

'Please.' He tried to grab me, but I moved away. 'Forgive me, Liv.'

I stared at him for a long moment, but I wasn't seeing him. I was thinking about Ben. There had been signs. He'd dropped out of university. Withdrawn into his room, refusing to see anyone, his appearance shabby and unkempt. He'd fallen into a depression we couldn't pick him up from. My parents had thought it would pass, naïve about mental health. But when he died they'd blamed themselves for not spotting how desperate he was – for not doing something. And I'd ignored him on that awful night, desperate to see my mates, barely giving him a second thought, and that guilt had gnawed away at me for years.

I rubbed my eyes, pushing back tears. 'I don't need to forgive you, Ryan,' I said, reaching down and touching his cheek, realising the two of us had a lot in common – we'd tried to cope with the part we thought we'd played in Ben's death for sixteen years. 'You're not to blame,' I said. 'None of us are.'

As I left the room, his relief that it was out there now was tangible, and I wondered, for a moment, if I'd finally forgiven myself too.

Outside in the car, I leant over the steering wheel and sobbed, tears dripping onto the vinyl. Everything I had thought for years about my brother's death had been founded on a lie. Sophy hadn't even known Ben, and yet I'd set out to ruin her life. I was so desperate to shift blame away from the fact I'd walked out on him when he needed me most, I'd ended up targeting a stranger who was going through hell already. I would never forgive myself if anything happened to Finn.

'Oh, Ben, what a bloody mess,' I cried, as though he could hear me.

I attempted to dry my eyes on my sleeves, and checked my phone for messages – there were none. I desperately wanted to call Sophy, ask if there was any news on Finn – if there was anything I could do – but I knew she wouldn't want to talk to me.

I started the engine. I would go home. Wait to hear. There was nothing else I could do.

As I came through the front door I heard Mum talking. I hung up my jacket, and made my way to the lounge. Mum had Freya on speakerphone, her voice sounding far away.

'I'm glad you're OK, Martha,' Freya was saying.

'And I'm glad you've arrived safely,' Mum said. 'You really didn't seem yourself when you left. I was worried about you.'

'No, well hopefully a bit of sea air will make things right. Escaping here usually sorts my head out.' There was a noise in the background – a cry of a seagull perhaps. Though it sounded bizarrely like a baby's cry. 'They've added hot tubs since I was here last.'

'Will you use them?'

'I doubt it. Not really my thing.'

I entered the room, and sat down on the sofa, and Mum smiled at me from her chair. I was still reeling from Ryan's revelation, unsure if I should tell Mum.

'I wouldn't mind sharing one with Tom Jones,' Mum was saying, and Freya burst out laughing.

'You are naughty, Martha,' she said. 'Anyway, I'd better go and finish unpacking.'

'Are you OK, love?' Mum said once she'd hung up. That was the thing about my mum: she could still pick up if I wasn't myself, even though I tried hard to hide it.

'I'm fine,' I said. 'Is Freya OK? I heard you say she wasn't herself when she left.'

'She was getting herself in a pickle about Finn, that's all.'

'Finn? Why?' I leant forward, met Mum's eyes. She looked so well, considering her earlier ordeal.

'She was just worried about him.' She bit down on her lip. 'If I tell you something, you have to promise not to be cross with Freya. She only did it because she was worried.'

'Did what?'

'She called social services.'

'That was Freya?' My heart pounded. 'Why would she do that?'

'She made a wrong decision once, a long time ago. She was a social worker. A child died.'

'Oh my God, that's awful.'

'There had been reports from neighbours about the little boy being neglected by his mother. She was always asleep, and the husband worked long hours. Freya visited the mother a couple of times, and was convinced by her. She'd told Freya the neighbourhood had it in for her. A week later the woman smothered her child, and took her own life.'

I covered my mouth in shock.

'Freya blamed herself. Gave up her job after that. Said she couldn't cope with the responsibility, and didn't want to be put in that position ever again.' Mum shook her head. 'That's why she reported Sophy. It had all the tell-tale signs of the case she'd worked on.'

'I suppose I do sort of get it, but Sophy is nothing like the woman who killed her son. She would never hurt Finn.' My mind drifted to Freya's reaction, when I told her about the social worker descending on Sophy. '*It isn't easy for social services. Making the choice to take a child from their parents, even if it's for their own good. But sometimes it has to be done.*'

I'd seen a maroon Volvo Estate outside Sophy's house the day Finn disappeared – Freya owned a maroon Volvo Estate. Oh God, she'd been worried about Finn – would she have taken him? Had the sound I'd heard on the phone line been a baby's cry after all?

My pulse raced. 'What's the site called? The one where Freya is staying?'

Mum shrugged. 'Hearts and Roses, I think.'

I dived to my feet. 'I have to go,' I said. 'I may be late. Will you be OK?'

'Of course, I will. Where are you going?'

'Just out.' If Freya had taken Finn I would get him back, and make everything right.

Chapter 35

Sophy

I drove on autopilot, half expecting to be chased by a police car as I headed into Stevenage, passing through the old town where I grew up, past the little house that belonged to someone else now. I'd cried when it was sold, helping Mum pack our belongings, our memories, into cardboard boxes. I hoped the owners were as happy as I'd been, back when things were simple, my future a fuzzy daydream.

My eyes strained at road signs through the darkness as the streets grew unfamiliar, in parts of the town I'd never been to before, until I reached Chells Way, a seemingly endless road of near-identical, two-storey houses with lit-up windows, their curtains pulled across. I didn't know which house belonged to Liv's mum, but was prepared to hammer on every door until I found her.

Halfway down, a familiar figure hurtled out of a short driveway onto the pavement and I slowed the car, my heart catapulting into my throat. It was Liv, yanking at the door of her Mini, her coat flapping in the wind. In the sodium glow of the street lamp her face was drawn, lips parted as though in shock. *Was she going to him? To Finn?*

I wanted to leap out and shake the truth from her, rattle her until her eyes rolled back in her head, but knew as I pulled up to the kerb a couple of cars behind, I had to be careful not to scare her off. I didn't know Liv's agenda and my instincts screamed that to find my baby, I needed her.

On the dashboard, my phone lit up with another call from Dom. He'd been ringing since I left the house, but I'd ignored it, as well as the raft of messages he'd sent. Hopefully, he'd call his father. Kind, dependable Robert, who would comfort his wife, reassure Dom that Finn would be found, that I would be fine, that everything would be OK.

If only I believed that.

I forced myself to focus on the car's tail-lights as Liv reached the end of the street and turned left, taking care to hold back in case she spotted me. I was grateful for the darkness that swallowed us up as we left the lights of the town behind. It was unlikely she'd recognise the car, even if she suspected she was being followed.

I fleetingly thought about calling the police, but if Liv knew they were onto her, she could change her mind, decide not to reveal where Finn was. The thought made my stomach flip. I couldn't risk it.

As we reached the A1 motorway, fear flooded my veins. *Where was she going?*

My shoulders were rigid with tension as I gripped the steering wheel. Tears scalded my cheeks and my breath came in bursts when I looked in the rear-view mirror and saw Finn's baby seat in the back, his blue blanket strewn across it.

Hold on, baby boy, I'm coming to get you.

Maybe Liv thought Finn would have a better life with her and her mystery man than with a mother who slept her life away, hardly present even when she was awake, too frightened to take proper care of her own child.

The strange thing was, I didn't feel tired anymore. The cotton-wool feeling that had blanketed my senses for so long had peeled away, leaving my nerves exposed. I could feel everything; the blood pulsing hot and thick in my temples, my limbs fizzing with pent-up energy, my heart beating a rapid tattoo in my chest. *Find Finn, find Finn, find Finn.*

I started to bargain with a God I didn't believe in. Let Finn be safe and I'd never take my eyes off him again. I would get to the bottom of whatever was wrong with me and be a better mother, take more interest in our lovely house. I'd be a better wife to Dom, apologise for accusing his mother of stealing our son. I would even forgive Liv for whatever her part in this was. She was clearly troubled, had wormed her way into my life for a reason. *I'll do anything, God, just let my baby be safe.*

My eyes were tight and sore with tears and from keeping Liv's car in view as she darted from one lane to another, breaking the speed limit. My foot ached on the accelerator from resisting the impulse to catch up, to let her know I was there.

I tried to read the road signs as we shot past, but there were so many place names it was impossible to pin down where Liv was heading. *Cambridge? Bury St Edmunds?* Somewhere remote, I was betting. Imagining Finn with a sinister stranger in a run-down cottage in the woods made me want to howl, to bang my head on the steering wheel, to rip my hair out. I tried to slow my breathing and clamped my jaw to stop a scream escaping.

As we diverted onto the A505, my phone rang again, the sound like a scratch in my brain. I hit answer on the speaker system, more to stop the noise than anything else.

'Dom, I—'

'Sophy, it's Mum.' I swerved the car and the lorry driver behind me blasted his horn before overtaking. 'Where are you?'

'Oh, Mum.' It came out sounding strangled. 'Finn's been kidnapped.' The words sounded as though they belonged in a film, not my life. 'He's missing.'

'Dom told me.' Her voice was thick with tears and dread. 'He said you've taken off and they don't know where you are.'

'I'm going to find my baby.' It seemed obvious. She, of all people, would understand. Mum had fought so hard for me, to give me the best childhood she possibly could. She'd have done anything for me.

'He said you've not been well.'

I gave a dull laugh. 'I'm fine, Mum,' I said, brushing tears from my cheek with my wrist. 'I have to bring him home.'

'Sophy ...' Her voice grew muffled, as though she'd pressed a tissue to her face. 'Why didn't you tell me what was going on? I could have come over—'

'It doesn't matter,' I said. 'I just need to find Finn.'

'That poor baby.' More smothered weeping then her voice came back, stronger this time. 'Do you know where he is?'

'No, but I think I know someone who does.' My resolve tightened, a hard ball in my chest. 'I'm following her now.'

Mum gave a whimper of fear. 'Sophy, you should let the police deal with this.' Her words were a plea. 'It's not safe; *you're* not safe.'

You're my baby, she was saying. Her worst nightmare would be something happening to her child, just as mine was something happening to Finn. 'I have to go.' My throat was tight. 'I'll let you know when I've found him.' I ended the call, knowing she could at least tell Dom I was alive.

Liv was several cars ahead now. Panic sliced through me as I put my foot down, the glare of headlights on the other side of the motorway making my head pound. What if, after all this, she was simply taking a break, getting away from me? There could be a suitcase in the boot of her car. *My baby could be in her car.*

Oh God, why had the police been so quick to let her go?

I thought how quick Liv had been to deflect suspicion from herself by accusing Elizabeth, and wondered whether that was part of her plan.

Time had taken on a nightmare feel, speeding up and slowing down. It seemed as if we'd been driving for hours when Liv took the slip road onto the A14. Nausea rolled in my stomach. I was thirsty, my eyes like burnt coals in my throbbing head, but my thoughts took on a pin-sharp quality as I realised she'd been following signs to Suffolk and sensed we were almost there.

It started raining, splattering the roof of the car and bouncing off the tarmac. The windscreen wipers swayed hypnotically as I peered harder at the Mini in front. I could make out the shape of Liv's head, unmoving above the car seat. What was she thinking? She'd seemed so fond of Finn. Surely she wouldn't hurt him or let him come to harm.

Please God, don't let her hurt my baby.

As the roads grew narrower, more rural, my heartbeat accelerated. There was less traffic. It would be more obvious Liv was being tailed. I had to hope she was so intent on her destination she wasn't checking the car behind her. Even so, I veered into a lay-by and let a car overtake before pulling out again.

When she stopped and indicated, I hung back. As she turned the car into what looked like the entrance to a field, I drove past slowly and saw a sign, spot-lit from above. *Hearts and Roses Holiday Lodges* was painted in dark, cursive script.

It was a holiday site; the sort of place Mum and I had stayed sometimes when I was growing up, but with lodges instead of caravans. Had Liv booked one in advance, knowing all along this was where Finn would be brought? Was this where her accomplice was staying?

It seemed so unlikely, but maybe that was the point. The police had already alerted the airports and docks, so where better to hide a baby than a holiday site in Suffolk, seemingly designed for pensioners, and parents with young children?

I swerved the car down the next turning and doubled back to the site, my nerves raw. This was the place, I was certain of it.

The rain eased as I entered the site, bumping the car over a cattle grid. I braked hard when I saw Liv had pulled up ahead and was leaning out of her window, talking to someone housed in a brightly lit hut. Sweat prickled my scalp. It must be one of those places you couldn't drive into without a booking and proof of identity.

Liv's head ducked back into her car and she pulled away.

Without thinking, I drove to the hut and lowered my window. 'I'm with her,' I said to the woman inside. She looked like someone's grandmother with thick white wavy hair, round glasses and smiling eyes, her shirt depicting the hearts-and-roses logo in pink and green thread. 'Liv Granger, she's my sister,' I added. My heart banged as though trying to break through my ribs. I pinned on a smile, hoping I didn't look as terrible as I would in broad daylight. 'I don't have any …' I struggled for something convincing. 'I can show you my driver's licence, if you like.' I waved my hand in the direction of the Mini, slowly disappearing up a winding road lined with hedges. 'I'm not staying, I just need a word with—'

'It's fine. She explained about your aunt.' *Aunt?* The woman smiled, lines fanning around her eyes. 'Good luck!'

'Thank you.'

Almost panting with relief, I drove slowly after Liv, tyres swishing through puddles. I supposed an aunt was a good cover story, but it meant Liv couldn't have booked a lodge herself. The 'aunt' could be the man who'd called me, tried to warn me about Liv. But it didn't make sense. Why warn me to be careful and then collude with Liv to kidnap Finn? Maybe she had some sort of hold over him. Unless it wasn't the man and she was working with someone else.

Or maybe I'd just wasted two hours on a wild goose chase.

The site was well lit with solar lamps studded along the borders, the lodges big and well-spaced, with raised verandas and hot tubs. Several were in darkness, unoccupied at this time of year. Liv drove at a snail's pace, her head turning as if searching for the right place. Each wooden building had a name on a post outside, easy to read as long as you looked carefully.

I hoped Liv was too busy concentrating to spot me behind her.

A cold breeze flowed through the open car window, bringing a salty tang. I realised we must be close to the sea. Dom and I had talked about taking Finn to the seaside, back when it was possible to think about the future; before we moved to The Avenue and everything went wrong.

Pain pulsed behind my eyes. My palms were damp, my knuckles white on the steering wheel. Time seemed to slow. My phone rang on the passenger seat and Dom's name flashed up. Reaching across, I picked it up.

'Sophy, where the hell—?'

'Have they found Finn?'

'No, but the police are still trying to find Alicia's sister, so—'

'I don't think she's there, Dom, I'm sorry. I don't trust Alicia, but I don't think she has Finn.'

'Just come home, Sophy, please.' His words tore at my heart. 'Let the police do their job.'

'I'm sorry, Dom.' I swallowed a sob. 'I have to do this.'

I rang off as Liv parked at the top of an incline, the outline of a lodge etched against the sky, partially screened by tall trees. Lights were on inside but it was impossible to see anything else from where I was.

I switched off the engine and headlights, fear swelling like fog as I watched Liv get out of her car and gently close the door.

Her head whipped round. For a second, I thought she'd seen me and ducked, but when I peered over the dashboard she was walking towards the lodge. She looked furtive, almost creeping up to the door, her movements slower than I'd have expected. Maybe whoever was in there was volatile – capable of violence – and Liv was wary of upsetting them.

Please don't hurt my baby.

I stepped out of the car, feeling jerky and brittle, as if my bones were wood that could easily splinter. A seagull shrieked and I jumped, clamping a hand to my mouth to stop a cry escaping.

I grabbed Finn's blanket from the back seat and darted up the slope, past a wooden sign that read *Starfish Lodge*. My breathing stuttered when I noticed a dark-coloured Volvo Estate parked outside and remembered the car Kim had seen.

An icy sea wind flayed my skin and squeezed my lungs, making it hard to breathe. I wasn't wearing a coat and my trainers were soaked as I splashed through puddles, but nothing mattered except getting into that lodge.

A sob punched out of my chest as I slipped and almost fell, before dipping behind a tree as I realised Liv was still outside, peering through one of the windows.

What was she doing?

She moved into the shadows. There was a pause before a sliver of light broke into the darkness in front of the lodge. She'd opened the door without knocking. Her outline slid inside and the slice of light disappeared.

Clutching Finn's blanket like a talisman, I ran up the path and pressed my hand against the door. I pressed my ear to the frame. It was silent inside.

The wind rustled through the trees and the plaintive cry of seagulls sent icy fingers down my spine. There was a sour taste of bile in my mouth.

I moved to where Liv had been standing, leaning to peer through the window. She was there, immobile, looking around the small, open-plan living space. There were barely any signs of life, other than a cardigan draped over the back of a chair.

As if making up her mind, Liv spoke, but I couldn't make out what she'd said until she repeated it, much louder this time, the word reaching through the cold glass.

'Freya?'

I didn't recognise the name.

'Freya!' Louder this time, Liv's tone was urgent as she moved through an adjacent door.

Who was Freya?

Heart thumping, I ran to the front of the lodge and turned the door handle.

Chapter 36

Liv

'Freya!' I called, hearing the front door open. There was no sign of Finn, but it didn't mean she hadn't taken him. The drive had definitely compounded my theory that she must have. She'd called social services. She'd been worried Finn was in danger, just like the child who'd died in her care. I almost felt sorry for her, though I knew if she had Finn I needed to handle her with care.

But as I dashed from the bedroom, I gasped. It wasn't Freya.

Shaking, anger burning in her red and swollen eyes, her face waxy, her fist clenched around Finn's blanket, Sophy glared at me as though she wanted to kill me.

'What have you done with him?' she cried. 'Where's my baby?'

'Finn's not here, Sophy, I've looked. There's no sign of him.'

'You took him, didn't you? You and that man who called me.' She looked about her, eyes zigzagging across the lounge. With a jolt, she ran across to the door to the bedroom; where I'd just come from, throwing it open. 'What have you done with him, Liv?' she sobbed.

I followed her into the bedroom, my heart thudding. 'Sophy,

Finn isn't here. There's no sign of him. But I think—'

She swung round, her eyes meeting mine. 'You think what?'

'I think Freya may have him.'

'Freya?'

'This is her lodge.'

'So, what? You planned it together?' She was opening cupboards now, as though Finn might be inside. Slamming them shut. 'Who is she? Who's Freya?'

'I didn't plan anything, Sophy. You've got it all wrong. I'm here looking for Finn.'

'I don't believe you.' She swung to face me. 'I think you and this Freya took him from me. You conned your way into my house so you could steal him.' She was distraught, tears rolling down her face.

'OK, yes, you're right.' It was time to throw all my cards on the table. 'I did con my way into your house.'

'I knew it' She took a step closer.

'But I would never take Finn.'

'Then why?' She stopped and stared at me. 'Why did you pretend to be my friend?'

Guilt surged through me. 'Because of Ben.'

'Ben?'

'My brother.'

'What's your brother got to do with anything?'

I went to take her arm, but she snatched it away. 'I thought you broke his heart. I thought you were the reason he died. But I was wrong.' I was crying now – for Ben, for Finn, for the mess I'd caused. 'I thought you didn't care that he'd killed himself – that you'd just got on with your life.' I dropped down onto a chair, scrubbed my face with my hands, before calmly adding, 'but I was wrong. I was *so* fucking wrong.'

She stared at me through watery eyes. 'I don't know what you're talking about. How could I have broken your brother's heart?'

'I can explain—'

'It doesn't matter. I don't care. I'm sorry he died, but all I want is Finn back.'

I stood up. 'I didn't take him, I promise.'

She looked around wildly, clutching Finn's blanket. 'You think this Freya woman took him?'

'Maybe. She's my mum's carer.' But however much everything pointed to Freya, I was beginning to doubt she was capable. She'd always been so kind to my mum. 'She's on holiday here. She was the one who reported you.'

There was a moment's pause while Sophy took it in. 'But why report me? She doesn't even know me.'

I lowered my head, fiddled with my hands. 'I told her about you, the way you kept falling asleep—'

The door swung open. *Freya.* She stepped in and pulled the hood of her anorak down, so her mass of frizzy curls sprang free. Her eyes fell on me, wide with shock. 'Liv?'

'Freya, I—'

Sophy flew at her. 'What the hell have you done with Finn?' she cried.

'What?' Freya's eyes widened further, as I pulled Sophy back. 'What are you talking about?' She put down her bag. Stood statue still.

'What have you done with my son?' Sophy screamed, trying to pull away from me. 'It was you, wasn't it? You reported me. Where's Finn?'

'Finn's gone?' Freya looked genuinely shocked.

'You know he's gone.' Sophy was shaking, crying. 'You've taken him, haven't you?'

'Was it you, Freya?' I said.

Freya shook her head, hurt in her eyes. 'I haven't got Finn. How could you even think I would take a child, Liv?'

'I …' Had I got it wrong?

Freya made her way into the kitchen area, grabbed a bottle

of gin and sloshed some into a glass, before knocking it back.

'Mum said you were worried about Finn, that you reported Sophy.'

She nodded. 'That's true. I was worried about him. It's not a safe world out there for children.' She glared at Sophy, who was bent over, sobbing. 'Have you thought he might be better off without you?' Freya said, igniting more tears. 'That whoever has him will take better care of him than you can?'

'Freya, please,' I said. 'Sophy's devastated – can't you see that?'

She took another gulp of her drink. 'I haven't got your baby, Sophy. I came to terms with what happened to me a long time ago. The way I missed vital signs that could have saved a child's life.' A pause. 'I have low times, but I come here and reset.'

'But you called social services about me?'

She stared at Sophy. 'From what Liv told us, you were neglecting your child. I was right to make that call.'

Sophy turned to me, more tears spilling over. 'You told her I was neglecting my baby?'

'It wasn't like that, Sophy,' I said, but the words felt meaningless.

Sophy turned back to Freya. 'You drive a Volvo. You were outside my house, weren't you? Sitting in your car. My neighbour saw you.'

Freya's face twitched.

'Well?' I said. 'Were you?'

'Yes. I was on my way here.' She poured more gin, her hand trembling. 'I wanted to be sure Finn was OK before I left. I parked outside for about ten minutes, that's all.'

'And then you took him,' Sophy yelled. 'You took my baby.'

'No.' Freya's tone was hard. 'I saw Liv's Mini parked outside, and convinced myself Finn was OK with her. But he wasn't, was he?'

I looked about me. There were no signs of Finn ever being there. There would be something, *surely* – something that pointed to Freya having him.

'Where were you when we arrived?' It sounded accusing.

'Out walking along the beach.' She paused, meeting my eye. 'Liv, I haven't got Finn, I swear.'

Sophy's sobs were out of control now, as she buried her head in her hands, calling Finn's name.

'You need to go back, Liv,' Freya said. She turned to Sophy, tried to hand her a packet of tissues, but Sophy bashed her hand away, and they fell to the floor. 'Go home,' Freya continued. 'You'll be needed there.' She paused, her eyes fixed on her fingers. She pushed her left thumb across the palm of her right hand. 'You won't find your son here.'

I realised as we stepped out of the lodge and into the darkness, that Sophy was incapable of driving. She shook, and sobs and gasps burst intermittently from her crumpled body. I looped my arm around her shoulder, and when she didn't object, guided her to my car.

'I'll get you home,' I said, opening the passenger door, and she folded her body into the passenger seat, and put on the seatbelt. 'We can collect your car once you've found Finn.'

She looked up at me, the sadness in her eyes thick and deep. 'I will find him won't I?' she said, her voice helpless.

'Of course.' I closed the door.

But if Freya hadn't taken him, who had? What if a random stranger had him?

As I made my way to the driver's side, I glanced back at the lodge to see Freya standing in the window, staring out at me. She raised her hand in a wave, but I couldn't bring myself to wave back. The act felt trivial, something you do when you are happy, when you're greeting someone, or saying goodbye to a friend after a catch-up. And I was still so angry with her for calling social services. I looked away and climbed into the car.

We were silent for some time as I drove. Eventually, I looked across at this woman who had once been my enemy, someone

I had hated with every fibre of me, but now desperately wanted to help.

As though sensing my stare, she said, 'Freya was watching me, my house.'

I nodded, eyes back on the road. 'It seems that way.'

'That's so weird, don't you think?' I felt her eyes boring into me. 'Although no wonder she was worried, if you've been telling people I'm a terrible mother.'

'I'm so sorry, Sophy. My head was in a different place back then. I thought—'

'I know what you thought. It's not an excuse.'

'No. No you're right.' I paused for a moment. 'For what it's worth, I don't believe Freya has Finn, but you still need to tell the police about her when you get home. They'll need to question her, check we haven't missed anything.'

'It was Kim who saw her Volvo. I saw her earlier with Dougie in his pram.' Her voice broke, and she fumbled in her pocket for a tissue. 'I thought when I saw the Volvo outside the lodge that everything was going to be OK. That we would find him.'

'We will find him, Sophy.' My mind swam once more with thoughts of how awful I'd been to her. Had my terrible actions somehow led to Finn's disappearance? I would never forgive myself if they had.

'Shouldn't you answer that?' I said, when Sophy's phone rung for the third time.

'It's Dom,' she said. 'I can't face talking to him.'

'But he might have news about Finn.'

She shook her head. 'He's texted too. He just wants to know I'm OK.'

I looked across at her. She was low in the seat, almost childlike, as she clenched Finn's blanket to her cheek. 'He'll be worried.'

In response, she grabbed her phone from her pocket, and pressed the screen.

'There. I've let him know I'm on my way home.' She laid the phone on her lap. 'That I haven't found Finn.' She began to weep again, covering her eyes. 'Dom probably thinks it's my fault.

No, it's my fault.

She looked up suddenly. 'Alicia must have him.'

'What? I thought—'

'Dom said he believed her when he called, and I did too, but what if we're wrong and she was lying all along?'

'When did he call her?'

'Just before we rung the police, about three o'clock.' She paused, took a breath. 'He spoke to Alicia's sister, who said Alicia was with her and that Finn wasn't there – but what if ...'

'What if?'

'What if it wasn't Alicia's sister?' I tried to keep up with what she was trying to say, but she was talking too fast, dragging herself up in her seat. 'What if Dom was actually talking to Alicia when he thought it was her sister? I mean, how would he know? And the police haven't been able to get hold of her sister. Has she even got a sister?'

'Then call him,' I said. 'Call Dom now, tell him your concerns.'

She picked up her phone, pressed the screen.

'Dom.' A pause. 'I'm OK, I just ...' Another pause as she listened. 'I'll be back in about half an hour, but you have to listen. Get the police to make Alicia a priority. She has Finn. She has him, I know it.'

There was a long pause, and I could just make out the tinny sound of Dom talking on the other end of the line.

'No,' Sophy cried. 'No, it has to be her. It has to be. Tell them to speak to Alicia's sister again, search her house. Her sister must be protecting her.' Sophy was yelling now. 'No I won't calm down, Dom. I can't – my baby is missing. *Our* baby. We have to find him.' She ended the call – threw the phone into the well beneath her feet, and burst into tears.

Finn had been gone for eight hours. And I couldn't help worrying, as I pushed down on the throttle heading for St Albans, that time was running out.

Chapter 37

Sophy

Time was running out. The thought solidified as Liv pulled into The Avenue. I'd seen enough crime shows to know that timing was critical when searching for a missing person, a baby. The longer they were gone, the less likely they were to be found. I was terrified that Finn could be absolutely anywhere.

I twisted his blanket in my hands as Liv braked outside number seven, the engine ticking loudly. The house was lit up, despite it being almost 11 p.m. Normally, I'd be either passed out in bed, or desperately trying to stay awake to tend to Finn while Dom snatched some sleep. I couldn't imagine ever sleeping again.

'Shall I come in?'

Liv's voice scattered my thoughts and I shook my head. We'd barely spoken for the last half hour, speeding through the darkness while I stared out of the window, alternately dry-eyed and weeping. What was there to say? Liv hadn't taken Finn and neither had Freya. The woman Liv had told I was a terrible mother, who'd been so concerned she'd alerted social services. Shame burned, deep in my belly.

'Maybe Freya's right and Finn's better off with whoever's taken him.'

'Don't say that.' Liv's hand circled my wrist, her fingers cold. 'You're ill and I should never have said the things I did to her, or anyone else.' I heard her swallow while I stared at her knuckles. 'I'm sorry, Sophy. I don't expect you to forgive me. I can't forgive myself.' She sounded wretched, but I didn't have space in my head for her guilt as well as my own.

A sob escaped. 'What if he's never found?'

'He will be.' Her grip tightened. 'You have to try and stay strong.'

'I don't know if I can.' I squeezed my eyes shut, fresh tears swelling. 'I think there's something wrong with me that can't be fixed.'

'You saw the GP.' Liv rubbed my back as I sank my head in my hands. 'If there was anything seriously wrong, she'd have got back to you by now.'

'She left a message.' Tears dripped through my fingers. 'I'm supposed to go in and see her but I can't face being told I'm dying, not now.' Grief lanced through me. 'I have to get Finn back first.'

'I'll do anything I can to help.' Liv sounded on the verge of tears herself. 'Go inside, be with Dom,' she urged. 'I have to get back to my mum, but I'm not giving up. There's something we're missing and I'm going to work out what it is.'

I suddenly remembered what she'd said at the lodge. Something about me breaking her brother's heart, that she thought he'd killed himself because of me.

'Don't bother.' Anger burned away my tears. 'You used Finn to hurt me and I don't even know why.'

'Sophy, I'm sorry.' Her face was pale in the darkness. 'For years I thought *you* were the reason my brother killed himself, that you broke his heart and didn't care.'

'So you said, but I never even met your brother.' I didn't want to listen, but she carried on talking.

'You were at the same university,' she said, her voice low.

I remembered the voice on the phone. 'I didn't know anyone called Ben.'

'I know, it was … I found out today that Ben was actually in love with his best friend, Ryan, the man who called you.' Her eyes shimmered with tears. 'It was Ryan who ended things because … it's a long story. He panicked after Ben died, when we started asking questions. Ben had left a suicide note, you see. He couldn't find a reason to carry on living without the one he loved.'

'I can't listen to this now.' As I reached for the door handle, Liv grabbed my arm.

'Please, Sophy, let me explain.'

I froze as she kept pushing words out. 'We wanted to know who she was, this girl we thought had broken Ben's heart.'

'And Ryan said it was me?'

Liv nodded. 'He showed us a photo. You were in it, about to go on a trip to France. There was a group and you were in it.'

I frowned, remembering the proposed trip which I'd saved up for; how excited I'd been to learn to ski. 'I didn't go in the end.' I touched my necklace. 'My grandmother died.'

'Well … Ryan picked you out, said *you* were the one Ben was in love with and he couldn't cope when you dumped him. I don't think he realised the impact, that I couldn't forget your face or what you'd … what I *thought* you'd done.'

'So, all these years, you thought Ben died because of me?'

'I thought you had this perfect life you didn't deserve and I wanted to destroy it. I sent you the note about Elizabeth, stole your necklace—'

'Oh my God, that was *you?*' Fury flared once more. 'I thought I was losing my mind when things kept going missing.'

'It was just the necklace.' She shook her head, as if she couldn't believe it either. 'I took the photo of you and Isaac too and sent it to Dom,' she rushed on. 'If I'd known—'

'What?' A ball of emotion filled my chest. 'If you'd known I was a mess and that someone was going to steal my baby, you'd have been nicer to me?' I choked back a sob. 'What was the end result going to be? *Murder?* You could have just asked me about your brother.'

'I wasn't thinking straight.' Tears glimmered on her cheeks. 'I don't blame you for hating me, but I really am sorry and I really do want to help. Please, Sophy. Let me make it up to you.'

'No thanks.'

I climbed out of the car, holding Finn's blanket, feeling as if I'd aged a hundred years. My limbs were stiff, my head spinning and my stomach felt as if it had been scooped out.

'Go round the side.' Liv's voice was desperate as she leant over the passenger seat. 'There's a press van further down.'

Ignoring her, I stormed down the access lane at the side of the house, avoiding the large van sat in the road, a TV logo on the side, satellite dish on top. I imagined the neighbours being interviewed, their houses practically hidden from the outside world. It was impossible anyone could have seen or heard anything; a miracle Kim had been out with Dougie and seen the Volvo, but even her 'lead' had come to nothing now we'd confronted Freya. *We.* Liv and I weren't a 'we'. I never wanted to see her again.

The kitchen door was unlocked and I let myself in, aware of holding my breath, ears pricked for the familiar sound of Finn crying. *Nothing.* Just the chatter of low voices in the living room.

'Sophy!' Dom leapt up as I entered, relief temporarily smoothing his face. 'Where did you go?' he cried, reaching for me. 'I've been worried out of my mind.'

The curtains had been drawn against the darkness outside and the overhead light was too bright. 'I thought Liv knew something.' I blinked at him, stiffening as he tried to take me in his arms, clutching Finn's blanket to my chest. 'I followed her to Suffolk.'

He reeled back, eyes roaming my face, which felt tight and swollen. 'You've been to Suffolk?'

'It's a long story.'

'What happened?'

'Liv thought her mum's carer Freya had taken Finn, because it turns out she was the one who called social services. She thought I was neglecting him.' Seeing Dom's confused expression, I added, 'She used to be a social worker, a baby died under her care, so she's … I don't know, she's got some issues, but we searched the lodge she's staying at and there was no sign of a baby, and Liv doesn't believe she took Finn, even though she was parked outside the house.'

'Did she see anything?' It was Laura, the liaison officer, rising from the dining table where she'd been listening to our exchange.

'I didn't think to ask, but I don't think so.' Sickness rose. 'She said she saw Liv's car and thought Finn must be OK so she drove off.'

'I'll call it in,' Laura said quietly. I gave her the address of the holiday site and she slipped out of the room.

Dom was shaking his head, a hand over his mouth. Breaking the weighty silence, he eventually said, 'You left the car in Suffolk?'

Exhaustion crashed over me. 'It's the least of our worries, Dom.'

'I know, of course. I was just so scared.'

I didn't have the strength to respond, to reassure him I was fine. I wasn't and we both knew it.

A strangled sound made me turn. Elizabeth had been there all along, sunk into the armchair, holding a throw cushion to her chest. She looked older and appeared to have shrunk. The sight was unsettling, like seeing her without make-up, or drunk. 'Where is he?' she said. 'Where's Christopher?'

'Mum's devastated,' Dom said quickly. 'You mean, Finn, don't you, Mum?' His face was sheened with sweat. He looked as sick as I felt.

'What are the police doing?' I said, too loudly. 'Do they have any leads at all?'

Dom closed his eyes and shook his head again. 'Not yet.' His words snagged. 'I heard them talking about a media appeal, us appearing on TV.'

264

Fear whipped my spine. 'But that might scare off whoever has Finn, make them more likely to run, or hold on to him.' I scrabbled at his sleeve. 'I think it's a bad idea.'

'It might jog someone's memory.' Dom took hold of my fingers. 'Whoever it is, they can't hide forever. Someone might know something.' I heard a threat in his voice and knew he was holding it together by the slimmest of threads. 'The police know what they're doing Sophy; we have to trust them.'

'I've made some tea.'

We sprang apart as Robert came in carrying a tray, which he placed on the coffee table; five steaming mugs of dark liquid, a jug of milk, a bowl of sugar. 'I'm so glad you're safe, Sophy.' His voice held a tremor. His normally clean-shaven jaw was layered with silver stubble and his forehead was lined with worry. 'I'm so sorry this has happened.' His grey eyes filled with empathy and I had to look away as I nodded an acknowledgement. 'Natasha messaged to say she's just stopped for petrol,' he added, moving to rest a hand on Dom's shoulder. 'She should be here soon.'

Why? I wanted to cry. *What can your sister do?*

'Your mum's coming too,' Dom said to me, hands hanging helplessly by his sides. 'She got the first flight out after speaking to you.'

I took a step back, a hand clamped to my mouth. Mum coming meant this was real. This was the process when the unthinkable happened. Family rallied round, ashen-faced and disbelieving, wanting to help in some small way, offer their support. I'd never imagined it happening to us.

'Have you been out looking for him?' I rounded on Dom, tears flying from the corners of my eyes. 'Have you been here all this time, doing *nothing?*' Anger was like a fire raging through me. 'How can you sit there, drinking tea, while our son is … is … when he's out there somewhere, *needing* us? *How?*' I wanted to punch him, hit something, tear down the walls, but my energy drained. I sagged against the back of the sofa, while Dom sank his head to his chest and covered his eyes with his palms.

'I did go out.' He sounded tormented. 'I knocked on doors, but most of the neighbours didn't even answer and the press were gathering, trying to take pictures and asking questions, so I came back.'

'You must try to get some rest.' The liaison officer was back, guiding me with gentle hands. 'As soon as we hear anything, we'll let you know,' she said. 'Why don't you try to get some sleep.'

'Sleep,' I scoffed. 'Has your baby ever gone missing?'

She remained silent, her eyes soft and understanding.

As if from a distance, I heard muffled sobbing from the armchair. *Elizabeth.* Robert said some soothing, meaningless words that only made her cry harder. I couldn't look at her, couldn't stand to witness her suffering. I felt an anger out of all proportion that she was in my home, claiming the grief as hers, doing nothing remotely useful. In that moment, I hated everyone. The feeling galvanised me towards the hallway, holding tight to Finn's blanket as I threw off Laura's hand and stumbled up to the nursery. I slammed the door and sank to my knees on the rug by Finn's cot. Pressing the blanket to my belly, I folded forwards and rested my head on the floor. *Finn. Where are you?*

I felt close to him in here; imagined I could hear him gurgling as he watched his mobile spin, casting rainbow colours across the wall. I shut my eyes tight and saw him staring at his starfished hand, as if it was the most fascinating thing in the world; I inhaled, and smelt the milky, sweet scent at the back his neck, better than any perfume.

Maybe if I'd loved him properly, not been so scared after he was born, this wouldn't have happened. Whichever way I looked at it, this was on me and all the ways I'd failed him.

I had to get him back, because no one else would. The police had nothing to go on, no CCTV, no sightings, no witness statements. Nobody knew anything.

I wondered what the neighbours were thinking, Petra and the other mums; whether Clare and Gary had heard my baby had been stolen. They'd be thrilled by the drama in their midst, glad it hadn't happened to them. They would blame me, the mother, and why not? Liv told Kim about the social worker's visit, so gossip would have spread in kitchens up and down The Avenue and further. There was no reason Kim wouldn't have believed Liv's version of my life. It was the truth.

I stretched out on the floor, Finn's blanket at my nose as I tried to breathe in his fragrance, but all I could smell was my own sour breath, the interior of Liv's car and a trace of gone-off milk.

My eyelids drooped shut and I snatched them open. I'd wasted enough of the last few months asleep when I should have been wide awake, taking care of my baby.

Someone knocked gently on the door. Not the urgent knock that heralded good news. Someone checking up on me.

'Sophy, Dom needs you.'

Elizabeth. 'Go away.' My throat was dry, my tongue thick.

There was silence for a few moments, then footsteps retreated down the stairs.

Below me, voices rose and dipped.

Blackness swirled around and I felt the walls looming in, closing around me like a tomb. My body felt broken, as though I'd been hit by a lorry.

I cried for a while, pointless, stupid tears as loneliness circled, then I got up and stumbled to the bathroom.

After using the toilet, I splashed my face with cold water at the sink, then caught some water in my palms and drank, feeling the icy trickle reach my empty stomach. I drank some more, felt my brain sharpen.

Someone had to know something.

Think.

Gripping the edge of the sink, I stared at my reflection in the mirror above. Moonlight slanted through the window. My hair was a coppery smudge around a ghost-white face, my eyes sunken and wild with a gleam of determination.

I would talk to the neighbours myself. Never mind what they thought of me and my parenting skills, or whether they thought I deserved what had happened. I'd shame them into recalling the tiniest detail that could lead me to my son.

I dried my face, smoothed my hair and pulled on a hooded top before hurrying downstairs, careful not to make a sound. In the kitchen, the dishwasher whirred as I slipped through the back door and ran to the gap in the wall at the side of the house, then jogged down the lane to the street where Liv had dropped me an hour ago.

The moon lit my path and my breath misted the air in front of my face. I jumped when a fox shrieked in the distance, my heart speeding up. No one was around, the windows of the houses dark, like shut eyes. Even the TV van had gone. People were sleeping soundly, without a care in the world, but not for much longer.

I'd scream the whole street awake if I had to.

Chapter 38

Liv

I'd been parked outside number seven for almost an hour worrying about Finn, about Sophy. I'd called to check on Mum. She was in bed reading and told me not to worry about her. She seemed OK, her ordeal behind her.

I don't know why I hadn't gone straight home. Maybe I thought if I sat there long enough I would recall something vital that would lead to finding Finn. But despite thoughts of Freya, Ryan, Alicia and even Elizabeth bouncing around my head, I'd come up with zilch. Nothing.

I straightened up and rubbed my tired eyes, and was about to start the engine, when I saw Sophy heading up The Avenue, hugging the shadows. I climbed from my car, and opened my mouth, about to call out, but there was something in her determined strides as she turned the corner that made me change my mind. I didn't want another confrontation.

I locked the car, and ran up the silent avenue, trainers smacking the pavement sounding too loud in the darkness, the cold air slapping me awake. I glanced back before reaching the corner. The only house lit up was number seven. I imagined Dom inside pacing, praying for his son's safe return, and a lump rose in my throat.

I turned the corner to see Sophy hurrying across the wide empty road, looking both ways, before disappearing through an open double gate that led into a private lane. She was heading for Kim's house.

I continued to follow at a distance, my heart hammering as I entered the lane.

Sophy was up ahead, her phone torch lighting her way. Indigo Cottage came into view, lit by a porch security light. The white pillars looked eerie in the darkness, the heavy bay window frames giving the place an oppressive feel.

The only other light came from an arched bedroom window. I held back, and stepped behind a tree as Sophy approached the front door, and rang the bell. She stood for some time, waiting, turning on the spot, before thudding on the door with her fist three times. Finally the door opened.

I stepped out of the darkness – moving closer, trying to hear what she was saying. Kim emerged, dressed in checked trousers, and a knitted jumper. Her eyes narrowed as she looked towards me. 'Olivia? Olivia is that you?'

Crap.

Sophy spun round. 'What are you doing here?' Her tone was hostile.

I folded my arms across my chest. 'I could ask you the same question.' It sounded dumb, and she looked bewildered. 'I was trying to catch you up,' I continued. 'I saw you come out of your house, but you were too far ahead—'

'Listen it's very late,' Kim interrupted, 'and I really don't think I can help you any more than I already have, Sophy.'

I moved closer.

'I was just asking Kim if she remembered anything else from this afternoon.' Sophy's voice was cold.

Kim stroked her hand down Sophy's arm. 'I wish I could

270

help. But I honestly can't recall seeing anything more than I've already told you.' She looked down at her fingers, turned a small plastic object over in her hands. 'The car – the Volvo – well as I said before it looked suspicious.' Her eyes were back on us. 'The driver was huddled in the front seat with their hood up ... but you say the owner didn't take Finn.' She shrugged. 'I've told you all I know, and I really haven't anything to add. I'm so sorry.'

Sophy shook her head. 'I'm desperate to find him.'

'Of course you are. Have you considered Elizabeth?'

'Elizabeth?'

'Now don't get me wrong, I like her very much,' Kim said. 'But she's quite obsessive about Finn – you must see that.'

Sophy looked at her with wide watery eyes. 'I know, but—' She paused, seemed to be considering something.

'She can be a bit possessive,' I said.

'And she felt her nose was being pushed out, that's what she told me,' Kim said.

'She said that?' Sophy's tone sharpened.

'I didn't take it seriously, but who knows what she might do if she's desperate. I feel awful pointing the finger at his grandmother, but she told me many times how much she'd love to have Finn full-time. It would never surprise me.'

'But she's devastated,' Sophy said.

I shrugged. 'And you think she's genuine?'

Sophy's gaze briefly met mine. 'I just don't know anymore,' she said.

'Go check on her.' Kim turned to head back into the house.

Tears fell from Sophy's eyes. 'She wouldn't hurt him, I know she wouldn't.'

'We should get back.' I took hold of Sophy's arm, but she shook me off. 'We need to go. Now.' I strode across the drive, as Kim closed the door.

I fumbled in my pocket for my phone, and turned on the torch to light our way.

'I don't know what I was thinking going to see Kim at this hour,' Sophy said when we'd almost reached the gate, her tears drying on her cheeks. 'What if she's right about Elizabeth?' She seemed to be almost talking to herself. 'But where would she have taken him? It doesn't make sense.'

It was as we turned into The Avenue something struck me. I stopped, out of breath. 'Hang on! Wait up.'

'What?' Sophy stopped too, and looked over her shoulder, her voice wary.

'You said when you saw Kim. When she told you about Freya's car, that she was walking Dougie in his pram.'

Sophy nodded. 'And?'

'Kim made a big deal about Dougie hating his pram, that he won't go in it. She always has him in that sling thing.'

I sensed her thinking. 'He was definitely asleep when I saw him. Snuggled right down. Maybe he was a bit off colour.' She headed off again, disappearing into the darkness.

I caught up with her. 'I don't trust Kim,' I said. 'Did you see how edgy she was? The way she pointed the blame at Elizabeth. The way she twisted that dummy over and over in her hands.'

Sophy stopped. Spun round. Her eyes widened with shock. 'Oh my God,' she cried. 'I need to get back there.' She began running in the opposite direction, as though her life depended on it.

I jogged after her. 'What? What is it?'

'The dummy.' She was breathless. 'It's got to be Finn's.'

'All dummies are the same, aren't they?'

'She disapproves of them, made me feel like a failure that day at Mums Meet Up, with her views on pacifiers.'

As we headed up the lane towards Indigo Cottage, Kim was stuffing a suitcase into the boot of her car.

'Kim,' I called, as we ran. 'Kim, wait!'

She flashed us a startled look. 'Why are you two back?' she cried, but she didn't wait for an answer. She got into the driving seat, and started the engine.

272

'Stop her!' Sophy cried, as the car came towards us.

As Kim swung the car to face the lane, headlights blinding, I caught sight of a baby carrier in the back seat. I could barely see the child, and tried to tell myself it was Dougie. But the odd way Kim was behaving filled me with doubt. Why was she heading off so late? Why wouldn't she stop?

As she passed, I launched myself at the side of the car. Tried to grab the door handle. She swerved and I was knocked backwards, thrown to the ground. I tried to get back to my feet, but it was never going to happen, my head was spinning, and I dropped back down. The sight of Kim's car heading away caused a sob to rise in my throat. 'You have to stop her, Sophy,' I cried. 'I think she's got Finn.'

Chapter 39

Sophy

Liv lay unmoving just beyond the pool of the security light. As I took a step towards her, she lifted her head. 'Sophy, stop her!'

The car's rear lights glowed red as Kim sped towards the end of the lane. I sprinted after it, feeling as if my lungs would burst. Had she got Finn? Why else hadn't she stopped?

The car braked, giving me time to catch up. I ran in front of it, barely aware of what I was doing, only that I had to stop Kim disappearing. I threw myself on the bonnet as the car began to move forward, but wasn't prepared for the slam of pain that winded me, or how hard it would be to hold on to the wide, slippery surface.

Kim spun the steering wheel, her face a mask of shock. Her eyes met mine through the windscreen, glazed with panic and fear. Behind her, in the back, was a car seat containing a blanket-shrouded bump, the head barely visible. Dougie … *or Finn*?

'Kim, let's talk.' I was breathless, my voice small and useless. 'Please, don't leave.' The wind whipped my words away. 'I just want to ask you some questions.' *The dummy.* It had to have been Finn's. She'd been so adamant Dougie wouldn't have one, unless …

274

The thought hit like a brick. Maybe she'd been saving face, too embarrassed to admit she'd caved in; that she wasn't quite the perfect mother she made out. She was revving the engine, her face expressionless now, as if she'd made a decision.

'Kim, *no!*'

A vision of Liv streaked across my vision, hauling herself onto all fours at the top of the lane. The car shot forward then stopped and I flew off the bonnet. I barely registered the agony as I thudded heavily onto my back. I pulled myself up and wrenched at the door handle, desperate to get inside the car, but it was locked.

My heart stalled as I peered inside. The baby was so still, head slumped to one side of the seat, lips pursed. A familiar swirl of red curls, damp on his forehead, was visible beneath a knitted hat. 'Finn!' I slapped the window, pulling hard on the handle. 'Kim! Open it, *now! Please*, I'm begging you.'

In the driver's seat, Kim was motionless, hands on the wheel, staring straight ahead. I rattled the handle again, yanking hard, sobs hurting my throat. Why wasn't Finn waking up? He never slept this deeply, even in the car, especially when it wasn't moving.

I daren't let go of the handle, knowing Kim could take off again. She was going to have to drag me with her.

'Kim!' I choked the word out as I slammed my palm against the window once more. There was a dull *thunk* as the internal locking system was activated. The door finally opened, sending me reeling back. Then I was clambering into the car, reaching for Finn, my cold, shaking fingers fumbling with the straps on the seat. 'It's OK, I'm here, Mummy's here, it's going to be fine, I love you so much.' The words poured out as I freed my son and clasped him to me, breathing him in as though I'd been starved of oxygen. Tears of relief and love streamed down my face as I pulled off the hat and stroked the curve of his cheek, kissed him over and over and whispered, 'I love you so much, little bear.' I placed my cheek to his nose, felt the puff of warm air on my skin and slumped with relief. 'Why isn't he waking up?'

'I gave him Calpol.' Kim's voice was toneless.

'Calpol doesn't make him sleep.'

'I mixed it with brandy. Not much, just enough to make him tired.'

I began to cry softly as I stared at Finn's peaceful face, lit by the moon slanting through the rear window. 'How could you?' I wept, then Liv was climbing into the back of the car, the side of her head clotted with blood. Her eyes widened when she saw I was holding Finn. 'Oh, thank God,' she cried, putting an arm around my shuddering shoulders. 'Is he OK?'

I nodded, turning from her to press my face into Finn's hair. 'She gave him brandy to make him sleep,' I said. 'He's too warm.' Laying him on my lap, I stripped him to his vest and nappy then held him close once more, the feel of his sturdy body like everything wonderful I'd ever experienced magnified by a thousand. 'Why?' I spoke to the back of Kim's head. 'Why did you *do* this?'

'Bloody good question.' Liv's voice quivered with fury. 'I've called the police – they're on their way.'

Kim hadn't moved; made no effort to get out of the car, or even look at us. She sat there in her padded coat, hair gleaming like dull metal. She remained perfectly still, even as the night sky lit up with flashing blue lights and the wail of police sirens sliced through the silence.

Something struck me and I looked around, searching for signs of her son; another baby seat, his blue cup, his toys – but there was nothing. 'Kim.' She didn't reply. 'Kim, where's Dougie?' Perhaps he was with his father. Apart from a mention of him closing deals on the golf course, I had no idea what her husband did or where he was. There'd been no sign of him at the house. 'Where's Dougie?' I repeated, fear sharpening my tone.

'There is no Dougie.'

'*What?*' Liv's shocked tone echoed mine and for a split second, our eyes met in mutual disbelief.

'He's not my son.' Still that expressionless voice, as though her life-force had been sucked out of her. 'He's my nephew, my sister's boy. I was looking after him for her, but she worked things out with her husband and wanted Dougie back.' She made a noise in her throat, a mix of grief and anger. 'I couldn't stand it.' She bent her head and covered her face with her palms. 'I couldn't bear that my little boy was gone.'

I was struggling to process her words and could tell that Liv was too. I remembered how confident she'd been at the baby group, how she'd seemed like the textbook mum, so much better than the rest of us. 'So, you just decided you'd take mine?'

'I couldn't get pregnant again after I lost my baby boy. It's why my husband left me.'

'Your husband left you?' Liv and I exchanged looks, her confusion mirroring mine. 'He's got twins now, and I ...' She half-turned, as if registering the police car that had pulled up, the officers getting out and walking towards us. 'You don't know how lucky you are.' Her voice was loaded with bitterness now, feelings returning like blood to a deadened limb. 'Elizabeth was right about you.' She looked at me then, her eyes small and mean. 'You're not good enough for that little boy. I'd have given him everything.'

I hadn't misheard or imagined it. Elizabeth really had said it, to me as well as Kim. Had her cruel words fired something in Kim, given her the nudge to take my baby like a jealous child helping herself to another's favourite toy?

'How did you even think you'd get away with it?' I shook with the intensity of my feelings.

'You must have known you'd get caught,' Liv said.

'I wouldn't have.' Kim gave a mirthless laugh. 'It's easier than you think. If you two hadn't turned up, I'd have been on my way to the airport now and no one would have been any the wiser.'

'Finn doesn't have a passport,' I said.

'I still have Dougie's.' She spoke so matter-of-factly. 'My sister had it with her when she returned from Spain to collect Dougie. She had no idea I'd hidden it.'

'How would you explain to your family you suddenly having a baby?'

'Our parents are dead,' she said baldly. 'I'd have come back from Spain in a year or so, told her I'd become pregnant out there.' It was chilling how clearly she'd thought it through. 'It was perfect, really.'

'Shit,' Liv said. 'She really could have got away with it.'

The driver's door was pulled open, sending a draught of cold air through the car. In my arms, Finn stirred and sighed. I held him tighter.

'Kim Harrison?' an officer said. 'Would you please step out of the vehicle?'

'I can't believe this,' Liv whispered, watching as Kim was helped out of the car and read her rights.

'Me neither,' I muttered. 'I keep thinking I'm going to wake up in a minute.'

'We'll need to check the baby over.' A kind-faced paramedic peered in. 'You too,' he added to me, no doubt shocked by my appearance. 'Just as a precaution.'

'And me, if you don't mind,' Liv said. 'My head hurts like hell.'

Chapter 40

Sophy

Back home, Dom couldn't take his eyes off Finn. Our baby was awake now, but quiet and calm in my arms. I was glad in a way he was sleepy, not absorbing what had happened. At least, I hoped – prayed – he wasn't. Prayed, too, that there wouldn't be any after effects of Kim dosing him with brandy. If I thought about that too hard, about her wanting to keep Finn quiet so she could disappear with him, my insides bubbled like molten lava and I felt capable of murder. I forced myself to breathe, because Finn needed me. He needed me to be tranquil, and Kim would get her comeuppance. The thought of her going to prison was some kind of solace, knowing how much she would hate it; hate the story coming out and all the neighbours knowing. It was still less than she deserved.

Dom looked like a man who'd been given a reprieve from Death Row, his emotions raw, flowing out in a torrent of endearments, words of love that encompassed me too as he pulled us close. After an initial cuddle with his dad, I'd wanted Finn back with me. I wanted to hold him forever. Dom had to make do with encircling us in a tight embrace, blinking back tears as he murmured, 'I thought you were both dead.'

We'd returned after being checked over in the ambulance, while Kim was driven away in the back of the police car, her face averted. The door of her house was open and officers had moved inside where they'd retrieved Finn's blue and white cat. She hadn't even bothered to pack it for him, had obviously been in a hurry to leave after Liv and I turned up unexpectedly. Though maybe she'd intended to leave his toy behind. She wouldn't have wanted to take anything that might identify Finn.

I still couldn't get my head around what she'd done. How she'd crept into our home and brazenly taken Finn from his cot, no doubt kept abreast of how easy it would be to steal him by my mother-in-law, who – it seemed – had been discussing my state of mind with her.

Elizabeth had leapt to her feet as soon as I entered the house flanked by Liv – who refused to go to hospital once she'd been told her head wound was superficial – and DI Lane, her body language protective as she ushered us inside.

'Oh, thank God!' Elizabeth had cried, rushing forward to greet us. I instinctively turned to avoid her outstretched arms, moving to Dom, whose face was streaked with tears as he realised his son was safe.

Now, she stood awkwardly to one side, knotting her hands together, her face creased with emotion while Robert hovered at Dom's shoulder, clearly overcome and speechless with relief. The police had left, along with the liaison officer, her expression bright with satisfaction that there was a happy ending – 'It doesn't always turn out like this,' I'd heard her say to Robert – just as Natasha arrived, bringing a fresh burst of thankful exclamations, tears and hugs.

'I can only imagine how you must have felt,' she said, gazing in wonder at Finn, her expression so like Dom's I nearly laughed. Lightness moved through me with each passing moment until I thought I might float off, even with the weight of Finn cradled against me.

Exhaustion mingled with a feeling of liberation. It was as if nothing could trouble me again, now Finn was back. Soon, I would say sorry to Dom for treating his mother badly, forgive him for appearing to take her side when he'd been right to defend her; apologise to Elizabeth for my attitude towards her.

I tuned out of the chatter around me as Liv introduced herself to Natasha and obeyed an instruction to fill her in on what had happened. My anger at Liv ebbed and flowed. She'd driven all the way to Suffolk because she thought Freya had taken Finn, and she'd been the one to suspect Kim, but it didn't make up for all the things she'd done. She'd lied to me, made my life worse for a while, but I was trying to understand she'd had her reasons.

In the meantime, I would make an appointment with the doctor. Whatever the news was, I'd handle it. I just prayed I wasn't dying. Now I had Finn back, I wanted to be there for him, be properly present in his life, savouring every moment being the mother I should have been from the start. It felt possible – everything felt possible now. I knew Dom felt it too, feelings crackling between us like electricity as we caught each other's eye, his hand still on my waist: Alicia, his problems at work, my health, our disagreements about his mother … everything fell away, back to how it had been at the start, when all that mattered was that we had each other and our son.

As I looked from Dom to Finn, whose big blue eyes were fastened on mine, his fingers unfurling to touch my face, all my uncertainty tumbled into joy. It was going to be OK.

'I'm shattered,' Natasha said, finally shedding her coat and dropping onto the sofa. She hadn't said much to Elizabeth, I noticed – had barely looked at her mother. 'I need a hug with my nephew.'

I reluctantly handed Finn over, knowing Natasha would be thinking of her own son, safely tucked up in bed at home, and saw a look of torment cross Elizabeth's face.

'Maybe Mum could have a cuddle next?' Dom's face was so

full of happiness, I didn't have the heart to protest, to tell him the things that Kim had said, that his mother had told me I wasn't fit to be a mother. I doubted she'd dare set a foot out of line again. By the look of her, she'd been almost as distraught as me and was still pale and barely speaking.

Liv came over, looking tired but calm. 'How crazy has tonight been?'

'On a scale of one to a hundred, I'd say a hundred.'

We exchanged wary smiles. She didn't smile much, I realised, but maybe she hadn't had much reason to, with her mum and the grief of losing her brother. 'Listen, thanks for being there,' I said. 'If you hadn't tried to slow the car down, she might have got away.'

Liv shrugged, then winced. I guessed she'd hurt her arm when she fell and didn't want to say so. 'I'm just glad Finn's OK and that no one I knew had taken him.' She raised her hands and pushed her fingers through her hair. 'I don't think I could have lived with myself if I'd brought someone capable of that into your life.'

'I'm going to be looking after Finn myself from now on, I hope you understand.'

She nodded, her eyes filling with tears. I remembered how optimistic I'd felt about making a new friend, just a short time ago. 'We could stay in touch,' I said on impulse. 'Finn obviously loves you.'

'I'd like that.' She blinked away her tears. 'Thank you.'

'You're welcome,' Dom said. He was by my side once more, dragging his eyes from his son, being bounced gently on Natasha's lap while Robert looked on with an indulgent smile and Elizabeth stared into space, her gaze oddly vacant. 'I really appreciate you being there for Sophy … and Finn,' he said to Liv, with the generosity of someone who'd narrowly escaped a tragedy and didn't know the full story. 'I'm sorry you were injured.'

'Oh, it's nothing.' Liv's fingers moved to the side of her head in a self-conscious gesture. 'I only wish I'd got my hands on Kim. I want to punch her bloody lights out.'

282

Dom's lips tightened. 'She'll get what's coming to her.'

Elizabeth had a hand pressed to her mouth and seemed to be struggling to contain herself. As if sensing her distress, Natasha gave a dazzling smile and said, 'Well, I don't know about you lot, but I need coffee and lots of it.'

'Good idea.' Robert spoke in a hearty way that said he appreciated his daughter's efforts to divert attention away from Elizabeth, who'd lapsed into an almost catatonic state. I guessed Finn being taken had brought back traumatic memories of Christopher. Despite everything, I felt sorry for her.

'I'd love some coffee,' I said to Robert, though what I really wanted was for everyone to leave so Dom and I could be alone with Finn. 'Just the instant stuff for me.'

'I'll go and put the kettle on,' he said, heading for the door. 'Elizabeth?' He looked at his wife, who was staring at him as though he had two heads. 'Coffee?'

'No.' The word seemed forced out of her. 'No … thank you.'

Robert looked momentarily puzzled. Elizabeth loved her coffee and never turned down an offer. 'Tea?'

'We should all have tea,' she said, seeming to come back from wherever she'd been, passing around a bland smile that didn't reach her eyes. 'Coffee's too stimulating at this time of night.'

'Just what I need.' Natasha rose and gently delivered Finn back to my waiting arms. 'I didn't stop on the drive down and would love a mug of strong black coffee. I don't care whether it's instant or not.'

'Just as well,' Dom said, smiling as Finn's head dropped against my shoulder. 'That's all we've got.'

'I'll have one too, please.' Liv glanced at me as if seeking permission. When I nodded, she smiled and said, 'I'll come and help.'

As she made to follow Robert into the kitchen, Elizabeth's hand shot out and grabbed her arm. 'No!'

'Sorry?' Liv wrenched out of her grasp, paling as she rubbed her upper arm.

The rest of us stared at Elizabeth. She was breathing hard. Her eyes looked baggy with panic, her mouth a frustrated twist in her scarlet face. 'No coffee.' She shoved a strand of hair behind her ear. 'We should go, it's late.'

Suddenly, the light in the room seemed too bright, the air solid with tension. Something was pulling at the edge of my memory, but before I could bring it into focus, Liv let out a gasp.

'It was you.' Her voice was loud in the silence that had followed Elizabeth's outburst. 'Oh my God.' She turned to me, her eyes brimming with horror. 'It's all her fault,' she said. 'Sophy, don't you get it?'

'What?' I looked at the confused expressions around me, but even as I spoke, something was taking shape in my mind. My constant sleepiness, especially after Elizabeth had been round, or when I'd visited her house; the crashing exhaustion I couldn't fight that meant I lived in a permanent twilight world, struggling to bond with my son, to take care of him properly while Elizabeth worked on Dom, trying to persuade him I needed more help with Finn. How even my morning coffee didn't give me the burst of adrenaline I needed. If anything, it made me feel worse. *Much worse.*

'You drugged me.' My voice was wondering, the words exploratory, because they couldn't be true. It couldn't be real. My mother-in-law couldn't really want me sedated, in a permanent stupor, so she could get to her grandson.

But Liv was nodding, pointing, her eyes flashing with the anger I knew I should be feeling, *would* be feeling, once the numbness of disbelief had worn off. 'I knew something was off,' she was saying. 'I had a coffee here the other day. I don't normally drink it and left half, but felt weird afterwards. I can hardly remember driving home and I slept like the dead that night.' Her cheeks were flushed, eyebrows drawn down. 'You put something in the coffee to keep Sophy asleep, didn't you? What was it? Something you give your bloody horses when they need calming down?'

284

At this, the room seemed to erupt. Robert held up his hand and told Liv to slow down, to hang on, that he had no idea what she was talking about, while Dom looked at his mother, white-faced, and said, 'Please tell me it isn't true,' his voice a horrified rasp. Even as he spoke, I could see in his eyes, and Robert's ashen face, that understanding was dawning; the terrible realisation that the mother, the wife, they loved so much and believed in was, in fact, someone they barely knew.

'Mum?' Dom stared at Elizabeth, his tone a plea for denial. 'Please tell me you didn't try to hurt Sophy.'

'Hurt her?' She looked at him, provoked at last into responding, her face crowded with hurt. 'Of course I didn't want to hurt her. It's absolute nonsense—'

'Why didn't you want us to have coffee, Mum?' Natasha turned to face her mother. Her face was parchment pale in contrast to Elizabeth's florid cheeks. 'It actually doesn't surprise me,' she went on, before her mother could reply. 'You were weird with me for ages when Toby was born, like you thought you knew better than I did, putting me down all the time. Not in front of anyone,' she said to her dad when Robert tried to interject, his face ashen with shock. 'She was subtle about it, but it was clear she wanted him to herself, would have done or said anything to look after him full-time. Why do you think we moved away?'

'Tash, you never told me.' Devastation crept over Dom's features, blotting out the happiness from just moments ago. I hated Elizabeth even more for that. 'I can't … I just can't believe this.'

'You would never have seen it, Dom.' Natasha's eyes swam with tears. 'You were too busy trying to fill Christopher's shoes, we both were, but especially you. We wanted Mum to love us as much as she'd loved him. We never stopped trying to please her, but neither of us quite managed to fill the gap.'

'You're talking rubbish,' Elizabeth snapped, taking a step towards Dom, one hand held out. 'I love you both very much. Finn is my world.'

285

He moved away from her, his eyes not leaving her face, as though he was superimposing this new version of his mother over the old one. 'But you don't love Sophy.'

I reached for him as Finn shifted and sank back into sleep. 'I was right all along,' I said. 'She told me I didn't deserve to be a mother.'

He looked from me to Elizabeth. 'How could you?' His voice was almost a growl. 'Sophy's been unwell.' He closed his eyes as if the full horror was too much. 'Unwell, because of you.' He turned to face me, a naked expression of torment on his face. 'I should have believed you,' he said. 'I'm so, so sorry.'

I shook my head, tears filling my eyes. 'Who would want to believe their mother was capable of ... of *that*?' I was still having trouble believing it myself. 'She's the one who should be sorry.'

'Enough.' Robert moved to put an arm around his wife and looked stricken when she stiffened and shifted away. 'Finn is safe and that's all that matters.'

'Hang on.' Liv held up a hand. 'Do you think it's okay for Elizabeth to have drugged her daughter-in-law to get her hands on Finn? To make out Sophy's a terrible mother, all because she lost her own baby?' She sounded furious. 'Elizabeth could have *killed* her, for Christ's sake, don't you get that? It's a criminal offence, what she's done, and I bet that's not all. Sophy told me about things going missing, then turning up again, the house being left in a mess when she thought she'd tidied up—'

'The photo in the stables.' My voice sounded faint. 'She must have set that up. And the doctor said she'd tried to get hold of me. She left a message I didn't receive, and Isaac emailed me a document that went missing ...' I trailed off as the awful truth sank in.

'Must be easy to delete messages, or shift things about, tip wine in the bed when your daughter-in-law's out cold, to make it look like she's losing her mind,' Liv stormed. 'You do know that Sophy's convinced she's dying?' She moved closer to Elizabeth, who seemed rooted to the spot, her mouth opening and closing like a fish. 'I wonder what the blood tests will show? No wonder you don't want Sophy speaking to the doctor.' She cocked her head. 'Anything to say?' When Elizabeth didn't reply, Liv looked at me. 'We should call the police back. Have her arrested.'

'No.' Robert's voice was firm, belied by the desperation on his face. 'Please, just … just let us go, Sophy.' He held out a hand to his wife and she took it, obedient as a child all of a sudden. 'I promise she'll leave you alone if you let it go.'

'Mum …' Dom was staring at her as if he'd never seen her before. 'Aren't you going to deny any of this?'

'What's the point?' The look she flashed me was pure venom, her mask of civility stripped away. 'She's clearly made up her mind about me.'

'We'll have the coffee tested, shall we?' Liv folded her arms, matching Elizabeth's expression. 'Wouldn't be hard to prove what's in it.'

'I can't … I *cannot* believe you'd do this to Sophy, to *us*,' Dom said, tears standing in his eyes. Natasha took his arm and buried her face against his shoulder.

'I'm so sorry I didn't say anything sooner, when Toby was born, but I convinced myself that things would be better with me out of the way,' she said. 'I even thought I'd imagined the way she could be, that I was being oversensitive.'

'Look, we're leaving now.' Robert was leading Elizabeth to the hallway. She didn't try to resist and let him drape her jacket around her rigid shoulders. 'I'm so, so sorry,' he said, to no one in particular. I realised that, for all his niceness, Robert was weak. He would never stand up to Elizabeth, and while I understood they'd lived through the unbearable tragedy of losing a son, in that moment, I despised him too.

I moved closer to Dom and his arm wrapped around my waist.

'Just go, Dad.' His voice was barely recognisable. 'Get her out of here.'

287

None of us moved until the front door was suddenly thrust open and somebody burst inside and dropped a brightly coloured holdall at the foot of the stairs.

'I'm sorry it's so late, the flight was delayed and I had to wait for a taxi. Please, please, somebody tell me my grandson is safe. I've been trying to call and no one's picking up their phones. I've been going out of my mind.'

As a familiar figure came into view, I burst into tears. 'He's OK, Mum.'

'Oh, sweetheart!' Mum hurried over to take me in her arms, her familiar fragrance filling my senses 'Thank heavens. What happened? I don't understand. Who took him? Where was he? Oh, darling girl, please don't cry. I'm here now, your baby's safe and everything's going to be fine.'

She pulled back and kissed Finn's hair, stroking and murmuring before looking around at the stunned faces as the front door quietly closed behind Elizabeth and Robert.

'I'll put the kettle on, shall I?' She was laughing and crying at the same time. 'I could murder a coffee.'

Chapter 41

Three months later

Since Finn was found, I'd realised three things:

One – never slam your body against a moving car, because it bloody hurts.

Two – I cared about Sophy and her family more than I thought.

Three – It wasn't my fault that Ben died.

I'd blamed myself for so long, believing that if I hadn't gone out that night, he would still be alive. And I'd dealt with that guilt by blaming Sophy. But the truth was, Ben was suffering with severe depression, his mental health in tatters. I couldn't have known how close he was to the edge.

'Hey!'

I turned from filling the dishwasher to see Ryan framed in the kitchen doorway, his eyes no longer shadowed, his skin less pallid. He'd been chatting with Mum in the lounge for the past half hour, and I knew she was helping him come to terms with everything. It was the third time he'd visited. The first time he came he told Mum about his relationship with Ben, his voice slurred as he sat on the sofa. I'd heard him cry as Mum took him in her arms. 'You can't blame yourself, Ryan,' she'd said. 'I did that for years. Certain I should have spotted the signs – and maybe I should have. But I forgave myself. I'd thought he would be OK, you see. That a broken heart is a rite of passage.' She'd taken hold of his hand and squeezed, insisted she didn't blame him for Ben's suicide. Made him promise to think of the happy times he'd shared with Ben.

'Your mum sent me out on a custard cream hunt,' he said now, no slur in his voice today, and I hoped he had given himself permission to live again. He smiled, and stepped into the kitchen. 'Or bourbons.'

'Well, she's out of luck. We only have chocolate digestives.' I reached into the cupboard for the biscuits, handed him the pack.

'Is there any news about Kim?' he asked.

I shook my head. Kim had been charged with child abduction, but there'd been no date for the trial yet.

We now knew it was when her sister returned from Spain and told Kim she wouldn't be moving in with her with Dougie, that Kim decided if she couldn't have Dougie, she would take Finn. She took him the day Mum went to hospital. I have moments where I regret leaving Sophy, knowing she wasn't fully awake, and leaving the patio doors open. I'd been such an idiot.

I leant against the worktop. 'I still keep thinking if Kim had got to the airport, got on that plane, Sophy may never have seen Finn again. It breaks my heart to think about it.'

'But she didn't get on that plane, because of what you and Sophy did. You did good, Liv.'

'Ryan, where's those biscuits?' Mum called from the lounge.

'You've been summoned.' I laughed, and he raised the biscuits like a baton in a relay, and hurried away.

I turned back to the dishwasher, popped in a tablet, and set it going.

Freya hadn't returned to Mum after our showdown in Suffolk, deciding to move there permanently. She'd called to tell Mum, and I had thought it would upset her, but Mum seemed to like Shari, and had wished Freya well.

I was now working in a nursery in Stevenage Old Town, and enjoying it. Sophy was managing well now her awful mother-in-law wasn't drugging her. It turned out Elizabeth had swapped the vitamin tablets Dom's sister sent for sleeping tablets, as well as tampering with Sophy's coffee.

I still think Elizabeth should have been reported to the police, but it hadn't been my call to make. I was surprised Sophy told me the details, but I'd called to see how she was and she'd blurted it out. Maybe she wanted to tell someone who'd been there, who knew what had been going on. Funny how I'd told her to watch Elizabeth. I like to think I'd had a sixth sense about her, but admit it was nothing of the kind.

Sophy and Dom were doing OK now. Dom had been a wreck following the revelations, struggling to comprehend what his mother had done. Punishing himself for not seeing what she was capable of, and not protecting his wife. In fact, the roles at number seven The Avenue had reversed for a while. Sophy transforming – strong without drugs being pumped into her – determined not to let Elizabeth destroy her family.

Elizabeth was not allowed anywhere near Finn. It was a condition of them not telling the police what she'd done.

My mobile vibrated across the worktop. *Sophy.*

'Hi there,' I said into the phone.

'I'm on my way to London,' she said, her voice bright. She couldn't face leaving Finn with a stranger to return to work, but had been doing some stuff at home for a history show, and meeting Isaac regularly to discuss another project. 'And you'll never believe who I just saw?'

'Go on.'

'Clare.'

'As in Clare and Gary, Clare?' I hadn't thought about them for ages – preferred not to.

'Yep. And you'll never guess what? She's thrown him out.'

'Gary?'

'Apparently he harassed their babysitter, and she recorded the sleaze-ball on her phone.'

I laughed. It was so good to hear Sophy sounding happy – normal – gossiping even. 'Everyone gets their comeuppance in the end,' I said, though I wasn't sure they did.

Once I'd ended the call, I put the phone on the worktop, and closed my eyes. The sound of Mum and Ryan laughing in the lounge was comforting. I would never get over losing my brother, but like my mum, I was learning to live with losing him, happy memories of him keeping me going. And by a strange twist of fate, Sophy and I were on the way to becoming friends.

For the first time in a long time, I looked forward to the future.

Epilogue

Elizabeth

Three years later

It's quiet up here in the field, just me and the horses. They trot over as soon as they see me, nuzzle my pockets for the carrots they know I'll be carrying. They don't judge me.

I still miss my darling Finn. The way his face brightened when he saw me, and how his chubby fingers gripped his bottle as he fed in my arms, blue eyes fixed on mine. He loved my horses too. I'm sure, one day, he would have been a good little rider – just like my Christopher would have, if he hadn't been cruelly taken from me.

After what happened, I was barred from seeing my grandsons, wasn't permitted to be anywhere near either of them. I can't forget the look in Dom's eyes when he told me, as if he had a gun to his head. Of course, *she* was behind it. I knew when he met her that Sophy was a terrible choice of wife, just like Rory was the wrong man for my daughter, whisking her miles away, making excuses whenever I enquired about visiting. All because I wanted to be involved in the lives of my grandsons when I could see they weren't being looked after properly. Sophy and Natasha weren't natural mothers – not like me, who never got the chance to see her first-born child grow up.

Finn was the spitting image of my lost little boy. As soon as I held him, it was as if time had rolled back and I'd been given a second chance. This time, my baby would achieve everything he deserved. For a while, I even forgave Dom for marrying that drab little woman he met at work when he could have done so much better.

When Toby was born, Natasha was overprotective from the start, didn't like me touching her baby – no doubt influenced by that Northern oaf she married – but it was clear from the second Sophy handed Finn to me in hospital, while she slumped about looking pasty and sweaty – as if she was the first mother to ever have a Caesarean – that she needed my help. Naturally, I was only too happy to give it. I was hooked. It was like falling in love. When Dom persuaded Sophy they should move out of London to be nearer me, I was ecstatic. Robert was happy too, because I was happy. My husband's moods had always depended on mine, back then.

I was horrified when Sophy didn't manage to pull herself together, but secretly pleased it meant I had Finn to myself. I knew then that I wanted more, that I'd never be able to let go. And that little boy adored me, I was the light of his life. He turned to me, not his mother. He was probably still missing me terribly. I wondered what they would tell him about me, whether they would mention me at all.

I hadn't intended Sophy to die, at least not to begin with. Grinding pills down to mix with that revolting instant coffee she drank by the gallon had been absolutely perfect, and when I did it once and got away with it … well, let's just say it got easier, almost addictive, and swapping those useless vitamin tablets my daughter sent her with sleeping pills was a bonus. They didn't look like vitamin tablets, but she hadn't even noticed. It had come to me gradually that Sophy might suffer an 'accidental' overdose. I had a separate bottle of pills all ready to spill over the bed, alongside a bottle of wine, and a story for Dom about how his wife had called me and begged me to look after her son and how worried I'd been that she was suicidal. Once she was gone, Dom would have seen the sense in me caring for Finn full-time. Who better, than his loving grandmother? But now it's all too late.

The blood test results weren't proof of anything. At the time, I'd thanked heaven for that. There was an anomaly, a trace of the strong sedative I'd persuaded my old doctor to keep prescribing for me to help me through a 'rough patch' that Sophy would deny taking voluntarily, but I would have argued with – said she'd asked me for something to help her sleep, which I'd reluctantly agreed to.

I'd prayed the doctor would give up once I deleted her messages from my daughter-in-law's mobile phone – so easy to unlock with her fingerprint, once she was passed out – along with an emailed document from some colleague at the television company she worked for, where she'd met my son. I didn't read the email. It was fun making it disappear, just like it was to move things around the house to places they shouldn't be, to fool her.

If only that awful woman Liv hadn't come along, getting Sophy out of the house, making her think she could be like other mothers, poking her nose into things. I could still be there now with my grandson and my son, not living at the opposite end of the country with no close neighbours and only my horses for company. Robert decided he couldn't live with me after all. He demanded a divorce and said he'd tell our friends and neighbours what a supposedly terrible person I was if I didn't agree. Once I realised he was serious, he sold our beautiful house and moved up to Cumbria to be near Natasha, who hasn't been in touch with me once since that night. I don't miss Robert as much as I thought I would. He never really understood how I felt about losing Christopher, once he was past the grieving stage. After Natasha came along, and then Dom, he threw himself into spoiling them rotten, as if our first-born had never existed.

I bought this little farmhouse and tried to reinvent myself, giving riding lessons to local schoolchildren and growing vegetables in the garden and reading in the evenings. I got rid of the television after switching it on last year and seeing Sophy fronting a programme on the history channel about the wives of Henry VIII, very obviously pregnant. I tried calling Dom, willing to forgive his silence, but he must have changed his number. When I phoned their house, I was told by a stranger that the previous owners had moved to London, and when I rang the TV company, Dom refused to take my call.

Nights are the worst. If I think too hard about my life now compared with before, I feel a physical pain in my chest and wonder whether I'm going to have a heart attack. Only being with the horses calms me down.

All that's about to change, though.

Kim got in touch. We kept in contact after the trial, where – after a mental health assessment – she was sentenced to eighteen months in prison. I went to visit her because I felt sorry for her. I'd been furious at first, absolutely heartbroken that she'd tried to steal my grandson, but then I forgave her. She'd lost her firstborn too. I understood. Desperate women do desperate things. Of course, if her plan had succeeded, I'd have left no stone unturned in trying to get Finn back, but ... well, that didn't happen. I'm not allowed to see him ever again, anyway. And Kim had no idea about the circumstances of my falling-out with my family and my treatment of Sophy. She seemed pathetically glad to see me.

Her sister hadn't been to visit, she told me, and the chances of ever seeing her nephew again were as likely as me seeing Finn. I was all she had. We'd always got on well. She knew how much I'd cared about Finn, how I'd do anything for him. At first, I felt bad that I'd been the one to inadvertently inspire her to steal my grandson, by telling her how terribly tired Sophy was all the time, sleeping most of the day, leaving that poor baby to his own devices – until Liv came along, but she was just as bad, leaving the garden doors open so goodness knows who could walk into the house. I wasn't sure how Kim had known they'd be open, but I figured she'd have found a way into the house somehow. She had apologised so many times, even confessed she'd planned to invite me to Spain, once the dust had settled, so I could see my grandson. I hadn't believed her, of course, but appreciated her saying it.

Anyway, it's the most wonderful news. After her release, Kim decided to relocate permanently to Spain. There was nothing for her in St Albans and she'd been in the press a lot, so everyone knew who she was. The residents of The Avenue must have had a field day, finding out one of their own had turned out to be a baby snatcher.

It seems, once she was out in Spain, she had a one-night stand – making up for lost time, I suppose – and surprise, surprise, fell pregnant! After years of thinking she couldn't have another child, following the loss of her son, it happened just like that! Incredible really. The trouble was, it wasn't an easy birth and she's struggling. She's lonely over there, keeps herself to herself, not wanting to risk anyone finding out she's the St Albans' kidnapper.

She knows I'm divorced now, that I live alone too, and wondered whether I'd like to go out and stay with her, help with the baby. She remembers how wonderful I was with Finn, could do with some advice, some familiar company.

I have to say, her phone call made my day – my year, actually. She had a little boy and, in a twist that made tears fly to my eyes, has called him Christopher! Well, wild horses won't keep me away. Not even my own horses. I've sold them, along with the farmhouse and, tomorrow, I'll be on my way.

No one here will miss me and I'm glad. It will make it so much easier to settle into a new life, in a nice part of Spain, in the small townhouse Kim bought with money from the sale of Indigo Cottage, the one piece of property her husband left her in the divorce settlement. I literally can't wait to get there and hold little Christopher in my arms.

I say a final goodbye to the horses, who've been my faithful companions, and make my way back to the house where my bags are packed, ready to go.

One more thing to check. I feel around the inside pocket of my holdall for the little bottle of pills I've hidden there. Just as an insurance policy, in case Kim finds she still can't cope and needs something to help her sleep.

Acknowledgements

There's a brilliant team behind every book, and we're lucky to have such a great one.

We would like to thank our editor Belinda Toor and our agent Kate Nash. Thanks too must go to Helena Newton for their copy-edit, Loma Halden for their proof-read, Anna Sikorska for a brilliant cover design, Audrey Linton for all her help, and everyone at HQ who helped bring our book to publication. It's been a wonderful journey.

Enormous thanks to the readers, bloggers and reviewers who continue to support us, and of course to our families and friends for their unwavering belief and support.

Special thanks to our husbands, Tim and Kev – we couldn't do it without you!

Keep reading for an excerpt from
The Secret Sister …

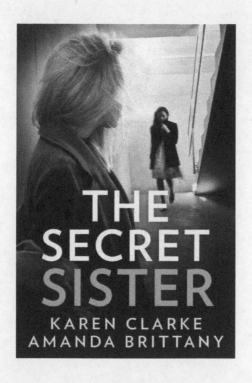

Prologue

Ella

When you've led a charmed life, I suppose it's inevitable that it'll fall apart at some point.

It happened to me after my mother died, though her death was the catalyst, not the cause.

Mum had been ill for a while and had come to terms with dying. She'd lived to see me happily married, and to meet her precious granddaughter. I thought we'd had time to say all the things that mattered.

When the end came it was peaceful, with her family gathered around, and I was holding her hand.

It was much later, while clearing out her bedroom, that I realised I hadn't known my mother as well as I thought I had.

The one thing that *really* mattered had been left unsaid.

Chapter 1

Colleen

Saturday

The sun woke me, slanting through the half-open curtains, hurting my eyes. I rolled out of bed, pulled my hoodie on over my pants, and padded to the window.

My brain pulsed against my skull. I felt sick and fragile. It had been years since I'd suffered a hangover, but I'd never forgotten the feeling.

The view from the ground-floor window of the guesthouse was nothing special – an area for cars, a scruffy garden with plastic furniture and faded umbrellas – but there was something soothing about the silence. Apart from the occasional cry of a seagull it was a respite from my shite-awful life.

I squinted up at the sky as the sun grew bigger and rounder – a shiny ball of hope. It would disappear within hours, if the puffy grey clouds approaching were anything to go by. Hope never stayed around long.

A solitary magpie landed on the window ledge with a thud and a flap of wings, and I jumped. I'd been on hyper-alert since leaving my husband, nerves jangling at the slightest thing. I prayed

Celia wouldn't tell Jake where to find me – not that she cared. The woman I'd called mother for thirty-three years had long since lost interest in me.

I turned and scanned the room, trying to work out how I got so pissed the night before that I now barely remembered arriving.

A folder on the bedside table informed me the guesthouse was close to the Atlantic Ocean, near Rosses Point, and a forty-minute walk to Sligo.

I turned to look at Gabriel, sprawled face down on the crumpled bed, taking in his narrow shoulders, his flop of lank blond hair. Hopefully, he would be out for hours.

A flashback of me talking too much, and later my words slurring into an incomprehensible blur filled my head.

What had I said to him?

I eyed his open wallet on the floor, stuffed with a wad of euros. A table by the door was littered with rolling tobacco, two empty bottles of wine and half a line of cocaine. I etched a finger round my nostrils, praying I hadn't taken any. I'd been clean since meeting my husband, Jake, fifteen years ago.

How had I let this happen?

My heart pounded as I tried to recall the night before. But, despite raking around my head for clues, I could barely remember a thing, just tiny bursts of memory that floated in and out in disjointed flashes. 'But I don't drink,' I could hear myself saying in a silly flirtatious voice that didn't suit me, laughing as a large glass of wine was pushed in front of me. 'Not anymore.'

I heaved with self-disgust as my eyes skittered around, looking for my rucksack, noticing a row of cheap-looking seascapes, fixed to the wall with nails in case some loser tried to take off with them.

Had Gabriel booked us into this horrible dump?

I couldn't remember.

There was a laptop on the dressing table, its charge light flashing, and a rubber plant in a plastic pot on the floor, starved of everything it needed, but somehow surviving.

I finally spotted my rucksack, lying on the floor beneath a pillow. I grabbed it and headed into an adjoining bathroom that looked as if it hadn't been updated since the Seventies. I closed the door quietly, filled a tumbler with water and gulped it down as I stared at my pallid, blotchy reflection in the mirror above the sink. Already, I didn't look like me. I hadn't worn a hoodie before, for a start. Jake would never have approved.

I retrieved the black hair dye and scissors I'd bought the day before, and taking a length of my hair between my fingers, snipped it off. Another clump followed, and another. I daren't look at the honey-coloured strands of hair in the sink in case I cried.

My eyes stung as I mixed the dye and pulled on the plastic gloves. Once I'd massaged the lotion into my hair, I thought I might puke and hung over the toilet, but after retching several times, nothing happened. I rose and sat on the edge of the bath, waiting, striving to make sense of everything, trying to work out how I got here. I pummelled my temples. *Still nothing.* Gabriel certainly hadn't forced me to drink wine. I could see myself, willingly knocking it back. Perhaps Jake had been right. Perhaps he was the only person who could stop me from self-destructing. I'd proved him right within a day of leaving.

Twenty minutes later, I rinsed off the dye and studied myself again. My hair was so dark my skin looked like Snow White's, my freckles more distinctive.

Jake won't recognise me now.

I threw the remnants of the dye in the wicker bin then took a lukewarm shower. Afterwards, I pulled on black skinny jeans and a black T-shirt. I didn't bother with a bra.

Jake would call me a tramp. He knew I'd gone. He'd already cancelled the credit cards, and texted me.

Where the hell are you?

I returned to the bedroom, opened Gabriel's wallet and took out the wad of notes. There must have been over a thousand euros. It would help me get by until I found my father. What little money I'd withdrawn from a cashpoint before Jake cottoned on wouldn't go far.

Gabriel was snoring into his pillow, his spine rising and falling. Had we had sex? Surely I'd have remembered that.

He suddenly swung his arm above his head and it landed with a thud on the pillow, making me jump. A flash of memory of his arm tightly round me, him whispering, 'I love you, Colleen.' Had that happened?

I shoved the money back in his wallet and left it on the table.

After pulling my hoodie back on, I pushed my feet into my trainers, grabbed my rucksack, and left without looking back.

Thick clouds gathered as I walked towards Sligo, and heavy spots of rain began to fall. A bus drew up at a shelter, and I ran and jumped on it. It was empty, apart from an old lady talking to herself.

As the bus revved a man leapt on, tall and slim with dark hair slicked to his head. My heart began to hammer against my ribs. I dragged up my hood, and slid down in my seat, but the man wasn't Jake. Apart from his build and hair colour, he looked nothing like him. My heartbeat slowed as he sat in front of me and took out his phone.

Before I walked out yesterday, I'd felt sure Jake had been following me for months. 'Are you having an affair?' he'd asked more than once, as though something had happened to raise his suspicions.

I'd wanted to say, 'When? When the hell do you ever let me out of your sight long enough to meet anyone?'

My phone vibrated in my pocket, making me jump. I pulled it out and saw Gabriel's name flash up. Christ, I'd given him my number. I declined the call and within seconds a text came through:

Hey gorgeous. Shall we meet in the same bar tonight in Sligo? xx

'Not a chance in hell,' I whispered, typing a reply.

It was a mistake, Gabriel. I'm sorry.

I deleted his contact details, just in case.

My head pounded as the bus rocked and jolted on its way, and I prayed I wouldn't throw up. I hadn't even got a bag to be sick in, just the hood of my jacket, which would be all kinds of messy. I breathed deeply, fighting nausea, watching the sea through the window, spreading endlessly.

Rain speckled the window like tears, blurring the view. I gripped the necklace – a letter 'B' – that I always wore, and rested my head on the glass. I closed my eyes, but the sound of the man in front watching videos on YouTube on his phone and shifting in his seat prevented me from dozing.

As the bus stopped in Sligo its exhaust backfired, jolting me alert. It had been dark when I arrived the evening before and I hadn't appreciated the colourful buildings curving around the banks of the River Garavogue. A smile tugged at my mouth. This was the town where everything would change.

I jumped from the bus, bought a local paper from a stand, and searched the pages for somewhere to stay.

The cheapest place I could find was a bedsit, near the town centre.

'It's yours if you want it,' said the man who answered the phone, with very little charm. 'You can rent on a day-to-day basis.'

It was obviously basic, probably terrible, but it didn't matter. I was in Sligo, where I needed to be. This was where I would find Reagan, my father. Everything would be better then. I'd have someone on my side, to look out for me, protect me – maybe convince Jake I didn't want to be with him anymore.

'Leave her alone, you controlling bastard,' I imagined my father saying.

Words I could never quite say myself.

As I headed towards the bedsit address, the rain eased off and my thoughts drifted to Celia. I couldn't call her my mother anymore. Not after what she'd told me two weeks ago, during one of my rare visits.

'It's time you knew the truth, Colleen.' That's how she'd started the conversation, out of the blue.

We'd become estranged over the years, but I made the effort to see her now and then. We would sit in her dark kitchen – it was always dark, even with the lights on – and she would make tea, a mug for me, and always a cup and saucer for her. We'd sit at the old pine table, barely saying a word, until it was time for me to leave.

But it had been different this time.

'I'm not your real mother,' she'd said, fiddling with her spoon, not looking at me. There was no preamble. No preparation. The words sounded surreal, as though she was trying them out to see what they sounded like. As if it was a game. But Celia never played games.

'What are you on about?' I said, with a laugh that didn't sound like mine – not that I laughed often.

She put down her spoon. 'She died six months ago,' she said. 'Your real mother.'

Just like that.

I'd stared at her for what felt like an hour. She kept biting her lower lip with her small teeth, her eyes looking anywhere but at me.

'And you tell me this now?' My brain couldn't form a coherent thought. 'Now I'm thirty-three?' I paused. 'When my real mother is *dead*? Christ, Mam.'

'Don't blaspheme, Colleen.'

Seconds passed. I rose and began pacing, questions flooding my mind. *Who was my father? Why did my mother leave me with Celia? Was Bryony adopted too?* But I knew better than to mention my sister.

'I only found out myself because her death was reported in a magazine.' Celia's voice cut through my frantic thoughts, and I stopped pacing. 'She, Anna, is … was … a successful artist.'

I sank back down in the chair. 'Go on.'

'I should have told you a long time ago, I know that,' she said, her fingers twisting together. 'I should have given you a chance to find her.'

'Too right, you should have.' My heart was beating so hard I was surprised she couldn't hear it.

'I'm sorry.' Her eyes shimmered with tears, but this was nothing new. Celia spent nearly every moment on the edge of a nervous breakdown. And the truth was, now her words were sinking in, finding out Celia wasn't my biological mother wasn't such a shock, not really. It explained so much.

'I wouldn't have wanted to find her,' I said, anger bubbling up. 'Any mother who could give up a child—'

'But you don't know why, Colleen,' Celia cut in. Her voice was soft, and her green eyes – eyes I'd thought were like mine – darted around the kitchen as if looking for a quick escape. She rose from the table, smoothed her apron, and went to look out at the garden. It had grown wild since her second husband walked out, years ago, but she had recently cultivated a little vegetable patch. It had made me wonder if she was improving, if her depression of so many years was finally lifting. 'I want to tell you who your da is too,' she said, not turning. 'It's time you knew everything.'

'Jesus, you're full of news today,' I said, my mind reeling. I'd always believed Celia's first husband – the man we'd lived with in Cork until I was five – had been that man: my father. But Celia was about to destroy that belief too.

She crossed to a kitchen drawer, opened it, and took out a photo. 'His name is Reagan Brody.'

'Wasn't Brody your maiden name?'

She nodded and sat back down. 'Reagan's my brother,' she said. 'He lived abroad for a long time, but he's back now. He's living in Sligo.'

'Your brother?' I cried, covering my mouth.

She nodded, her straight grey hair hanging limply on either side of her face.

'So, I'd have called him Uncle and Da, had I ever met him?' My voice was rising. 'What a bloody mess. Jesus Christ.'

'Please don't take the Lord's name in vain, Colleen.'

'So he – my father – knew where to find me all along?' I snatched the photo, hands shaking. It was too much to take in. I stared at his face, trying to convince myself there'd been a terrible mistake. Unable to take in that he was part of the family, and yet he'd never bothered to contact me.

'We thought it was for the best,' said Celia, her voice calm.

As I stared at his image, something tugged at my memory. His tanned face, that fair unruly hair, his cheery smile. He looked familiar. Or maybe it was just that I'd inherited *his* green eyes, not Celia's.

I felt so many things, all blended together so they were indistinguishable, my mind buzzing with thoughts. But Celia closed off after her confession, as she so often did; never quite living in the real world.

Yesterday, after I walked out on Jake, I went round to see her to say goodbye and let her know where I was heading. She'd slipped a piece of paper into my hand.

'I've never used it,' she said, as I read the email address she'd written down. 'It's Reagan's. He sent it to me a couple of years back, in case I needed to get hold of him.'

She clammed up again after that. I wasn't even sure she'd heard me tell her where I was going.

Now, after settling into the bedsit, which was as grubby as I'd feared, I pulled out a bottle of vodka I'd picked up at a nearby off-licence. It wasn't a good idea, but I still had a throbbing hangover from the night before. I would only have the one little drink, something to smooth the jagged edges, while I thought about finding my father.

Dear Reader,

We hope you enjoyed reading this book. If you did, we'd be so appreciative if you left a review. It really helps us and the author to bring more books like this to you.

Here at HQ Digital we are dedicated to publishing fiction that will keep you turning the pages into the early hours. Don't want to miss a thing? To find out more about our books, promotions, discover exclusive content and enter competitions you can keep in touch in the following ways:

JOIN OUR COMMUNITY:
Sign up to our new email newsletter: hyperurl.co/hqnewsletter
Read our new blog www.hqstories.co.uk
🐦 : https://twitter.com/HQDigitalUK
📘 : www.facebook.com/HQStories

BUDDING WRITER?
We're also looking for authors to join the HQ Digital family!
Find out more here:
https://www.hqstories.co.uk/want-to-write-for-us/
Thanks for reading, from the HQ Digital team

ONE PLACE. MANY STORIES

ONE PLACE. MANY STORIES

If you enjoyed *The Perfect Nanny,* then why not try another utterly heart-racing read from HQ Digital?